PERIL

Also by
OLIVIA MATTHEWS

Mayhem & Mass

Alibis & Angels
(coming March 2019)

A Sister Lou Mystery

OLIVIA
MATTHEWS

KENSINGTON PUBLISHING CORP.
www.kensingtonbooks.com

KENSINGTON BOOKS are published by

Kensington Publishing Corp.
119 West 40th Street
New York, NY 10018

All Kensington titles, imprints, and distributed lines are available at special quantity discounts for bulk purchases for sales promotions, premiums, fund-raising, educational, or institutional use. Special book excerpts or customized printings can also be created to fit specific needs. For details, write or phone the office of the Kensington sales manager: Kensington Publishing Corp., 119 West 40th Street, New York, NY 10018, attn: Sales Department; phone 1-800-221-2647.

ISBN-13: 978-1-4967-0940-0
ISBN-10: 1-4967-0940-3

First printing: July 2018

10 9 8 7 6 5 4 3 2 1

Printed in the United States of America

First electronic edition: July 2018

ISBN-13: 978-1-4967-0941-7
ISBN-10: 1-4967-0941-1

TO MY DREAM TEAM:

- MY SISTER, BERNADETTE, FOR GIVING ME THE DREAM.
- MY HUSBAND, MICHAEL, FOR SUPPORTING THE DREAM.
- MY BROTHER RICHARD, FOR BELIEVING THE DREAM.
- MY BROTHER GIDEON, FOR ENCOURAGING THE DREAM.

♥ AND TO MOM AND DAD, ALWAYS, WITH LOVE. ♥

THIS SERIES IS ALSO DEDICATED WITH RESPECT AND AFFECTION TO THE CONGREGATION OF DOMINICAN SISTERS OF PEACE FOR INSPIRING ME WITH THEIR GREAT COURAGE, STRENGTH, DETERMINATION, AND JOY.

Chapter 1

"Can we all calm down?" The second the words left her lips, Sister Louise "Lou" LaSalle knew she'd poured accelerant on a campfire.

"I. *Am.* Calm." Sister Marianna Tuller's gray gaze could freeze a volcanic eruption. She sat beside Sister Lou in the Briar Coast Cabin Resort owner's office.

"So am I, Sister." Despite Autumn Tassler's assurances, the resort owner's periwinkle blue eyes snapped with irritation.

It is going to be a long Thursday morning.

Sister Lou counseled herself to relax against the scarlet-cushioned guest chair in front of Autumn's large walnut desk. She and Sister Marianna were here to finalize details of their congregation's annual Advent retreat. The Advent season begins every year on the fourth Sunday before Christmas. During that four-week period, the faithful prepare for the coming anniversary of Jesus Christ's birth.

Traditionally, the Congregation of the Sisters of St. Hermione of Ephesus's annual weeklong retreat started on the first Advent Sunday. That was a little more than four weeks away. The clock was ticking, but they wouldn't make progress on the event planning today, not with Sister Marianna's and Autumn's hostility coming to a boil.

Autumn's spacious walnut wood office created a rustic cabin feel that should have been soothing. It even smelled of cedarwood and pine. The vivid abstract throw rug that lay across the hardwood floor kept the room from seeming stern. The walnut wood–framed paintings mounted to the walls celebrated stunning scenes from nature: soaring mountains, mighty trees, rushing rivers, majestic animals.

"Let's review our roles." Sister Marianna was at her pedantic best. "*I'm* in charge of my congregation's retreat. *You're* the vendor working for *us* to provide the location and meals. To be clear: the meals that *we* choose."

There was a pause as though Autumn was weighing the value of the congregation's contract against Sister Marianna's officiousness.

Lord, please, let the congregation's contract win. Amen.

"Sister, you and I both want your retreat to be a success." Autumn sat behind tidy stacks of paper. Her mail was neatly collected in her in-box. "I believe the entrées I'm suggesting would be more enjoyable than a plate of chopped vegetables and bottles of water."

I agree wholeheartedly. Sister Marianna's health-conscious selections were punitive compared to Autumn's recommendations.

"This retreat isn't a vacation." Sister Marianna spoke with a precision in keeping with her tidy brick red skirt suit. "It's a time of reflection and preparation for our minds, spirits, and bodies. Rich pastas and starchy, fatty foods aren't conducive to that."

Everything in moderation, Marianna.

How could she convince the other woman to meet them halfway?

Sister Marianna fussed with her teal silk scarf, causing the garment to hang loosely around her neck. Sister Katharine "Kathy" Wen had organized a group of sisters to handcraft and sell the one-of-a-kind silk scarves. All of the proceeds benefited an orphanage on the Caribbean island nation of Haiti. They were very popular with the congregation's sisters, associates, and donors, who'd purchased several scarves each. Unfortunately, Sister Marianna couldn't seem to keep one on for an entire day.

Autumn straightened on her chair as though Sister Marianna's slurs against her menu suggestions mortally offended her. Her sudden flush almost matched her ruby red sweater. "The meals I'm proposing aren't rich, starchy, or fatty. Our chef uses fresh and healthy ingredients."

"I read your menu proposals, Ms. Tassler." Sister Marianna's gray gaze remained cool in her thin face. "You can't mean to compare the meals I selected to yours."

Autumn's expression tightened. "I'm not comparing

your beets and broiled fish to the vegetable lasagna and tossed green salad I offered as an alternative."

"I don't need advice on planning the congregation's retreat." Sister Marianna smoothed her cap of snow-white hair and readjusted her scarf. "This isn't my first event."

"It's not mine, either." Autumn paused, running her long, pale fingers through her chestnut hair. "I'm offering you at no extra charge my event planning expertise to help ensure that everyone has a great time."

For all of Autumn's patient reasoning, she was coming into contact with the immovable force that was Sister Marianna.

This was the congregation's first experience with the Briar Coast Cabin Resort. Sister Marianna had opened the retreat to competitive bids for room, board, and meeting spaces with the goal of reducing the event's budget. She had reported to the congregation's leadership team, of which she and Sister Lou were members, that the resort was much more affordable than the hotel Sister Lou had used in the past.

But was this conflict worth the cost savings?

Sister Lou jumped back into the fray. "There's a simple solution to this impasse."

"I'm listening." Autumn looked hopeful.

"What is it?" Sister Marianna stripped the silk scarf from her neck with impatience. It floated onto her lap.

"We should ask the congregation to vote on the menu." Sister Lou shifted uncomfortably on the seat.

There wasn't much padding. At her age, she really appreciated padding. "We could send an online survey to get their ideas on several aspects of the retreat, including the meals."

"That's a wonderful idea." Autumn spoke on a sigh of relief.

"A survey is a perfectly unnecessary project and I don't have time to coordinate it." Sister Marianna's curt dismissal overlapped the resort owner's response.

"As your able assistant, I'd be happy to organize it for you." Sister Lou tried a persuasive smile.

"All right," Sister Marianna acquiesced with dampening reluctance.

She stood, indicating she was done with this meeting, and yanked the strap of her black bag farther up her narrow shoulder. Her movements were jerky. Her jaw was set. It would be a long drive back to the congregational offices.

Sister Lou rescued a pile of silk from the floor as she rose. "Marianna, you're forgetting your scarf." *It isn't the first time.*

"Thank you." Sister Marianna had the same startled look she wore every time someone retrieved her scarf for her.

"When do you think you'll have the results?" Autumn's question was a subtle reminder that they were falling behind schedule.

She escorted Sister Lou and Sister Marianna down a wide hallway to the lobby. Their surroundings continued the rustic cabin theme from Autumn's office.

Sister Lou waited a beat for Sister Marianna to

respond. When the other woman ignored them, she answered the question herself. "We'll make it a priority. I'm estimating one week."

"Thank you." Autumn seemed relieved.

Beneath a strained veneer of geniality, Sister Lou sensed the thinning thread of patience between Sister Marianna and Autumn. It was worrying. Their relationship had been fraying since its start. *Will they still be speaking to each other by the Advent retreat?*

A couple conversing in the lobby broke off conversation when they spotted Autumn. The woman appeared to be in her early forties, like the resort owner. The man was perhaps a decade older. The temperature in the room dropped markedly when Autumn noticed them.

She gave the pair a brittle smile. "Hello, Rita. I'm surprised to see you before noon. Mr. Crane, you're here so often perhaps you should rent a room."

"Montgomery just wants a few minutes of our time, Autumn." The pretty blonde's large brown eyes were defiant. "We'll wait in your office."

Autumn stepped to block their way. "No, you won't." She locked eyes with the tall, attractive older gentleman who stood beside Rita. "I don't have time for the eighty-ninth rendition of your sales pitch. I wasn't persuaded the first eighty-eight times. I won't be persuaded today."

Sister Lou had had enough drama for the morning, as the students of the College of St. Hermione of Ephesus would say. "Autumn, we'll get back together once we've tallied the retreat survey responses."

"Since Autumn won't introduce us, I'll do the honors myself." Rita offered her hand first to Sister Lou, then to Sister Marianna. Her figure-hugging sage green jersey dress under her honey brown light-weight coat complemented her shoulder-length curls and peaches-and-cream complexion. Her brown eyes twinkled in her triangular face. "I'm Rita Morris. I co-own the resort. And this is our business associate Montgomery Crane of Crane Enterprises."

"I'm Sister Lou LaSalle." Sister Lou released Rita's soft, narrow palm to accept Montgomery's large, callused hand.

"It's a pleasure to meet you." Montgomery's tall, slender form and regal bearing complemented his dark suit. He had a smooth cocoa complexion.

"Sister Marianna Tuller." The introduction was almost insulting in its brevity. "We have to go."

Sister Lou hoped her parting smile took the edge off Sister Marianna's rudeness. Without a doubt, the journey ahead would be taxing.

Autumn watched the nuns leave. No, not nuns, sisters. Sister Marianna had made that very clear when she'd corrected Autumn during their initial project meeting. Nuns were cloistered. Sisters were in the community.

"Did I sense tension between you and your clients?" Rita sounded genuinely surprised.

"Creative differences. We'll sort them out." Autumn crossed her arms over her chest.

"I'm sure you will. You always find a way to keep our customers happy." Rita's smile was faked. The other woman didn't think Autumn could tell, but she could.

And what did she mean by *our* customers? Autumn planned the marketing campaigns and drew up the contracts. What was Rita's contribution?

What possessed me to take on Rita Morris as a business partner?

Autumn had asked herself that question several times a year for the past three years. She still didn't have an answer.

"Give it a rest, Rita." She considered her partner and the business rival who wanted to take her company from her.

Over my dead body.

Autumn could use some of Sister Lou's diplomacy right now. Otherwise, there was a good chance she'd say something she'd regret, if not in this life, then in the afterlife.

Montgomery Crane was a handsome, charming, and interesting man. Under different circumstances, Autumn would want to be his friend. But as things stood between them now, she didn't want him here—and Rita knew that.

"We're not having this conversation again." Autumn gave herself high marks for restraint as she spun on her black heels and strode back to her office.

"Montgomery has increased his offer. *Again.*" Rita's voice was far too loud and much too close.

Hot temper seared Autumn. She whipped back toward Rita. "Keep your voice down." Her gaze darted around the reception area. "If our employees hear you, you'll start a panic. I'm trying to run a business. Do you think I want to deal with mass hysteria— *alone*—while you're out doing God knows what?"

"Fine, then, we'll discuss it in your office." Rita started around Autumn.

Autumn once again moved to block the other woman. "There's nothing to discuss. My answer is no, just as it's been all of the other times you've asked me."

"Autumn." Montgomery's warm, deep voice was like a neck massage. "We've never discussed my offer. I suggest an amount. You decline it, and that's the end. I'd like to have a conversation with you this time."

He sounded so reasonable. To decline his request would be unreasonable. Without a word, she led them to her office and took a seat behind her desk. She watched her unwanted guests settle onto the chairs in front of her.

Autumn leaned into her desk and braced her folded arms on its smooth, cool surface. "I'm not selling my resort. I'll never sell my resort, so, in fact, we have nothing to discuss. Any questions?"

"Just one: Why not?" Montgomery relaxed onto one of the guest chairs as though he had all the time in the world. His slate gray suit, crisp white shirt, crimson power tie, and black Italian shoes probably cost as much as three nights at her resort.

Autumn tried to imitate his casual confidence. It wasn't easy. "First, tell me why you keep raising your offer. Have you discovered oil in my backyard?"

"No, I haven't." Montgomery smiled. "Your resort has great potential. It's in a prime location and offers high-demand features."

Autumn struggled to mask her pleasure at his words. "I know that my property's valuable. What makes you think I'd sell it?"

"For the money." Rita was the source of all the tension in the room. "Montgomery's offer is too good to refuse."

Autumn leveled a look at her far-from-silent partner. "You've said that about every offer he's made."

Urgency emanated from Rita like cheap perfume. "This time, I mean it."

She'd also "meant it" all the other times, too. "If you want out of the resort, I'll buy your share." Autumn was running low on patience. "It's not like you're doing much to keep the business going, anyway. I won't even notice your absence."

Rita scowled. "That's harsh, Autumn."

Autumn arched an eyebrow. "So is the fact that the only time you come into the office is to tell me when Montgomery has an offer for the resort."

"You only offered my share of the market value for this place." Rita gestured toward Montgomery. "He's offering us a lot more. *That's* the money I want."

Autumn briefly squeezed her eyes shut. She was so tired of repeating herself. "Rita, our contract only requires that I offer you the fair market value for your share."

Montgomery's smooth voice cut through their tense exchange. "Why are you opposed to selling your resort?"

Autumn turned back to her business rival. "You purchase independent operations to add to your chain of hotels and resorts."

"That's right." Montgomery was using his reasonable voice again. He didn't seem to understand Autumn's concern.

Autumn found comfort in the familiar scents of cedarwood and pine that filled her office. She shouldn't have to have this conversation. Her "no" should be explanation enough.

"Owning and operating this resort has been my goal ever since I was forced to accept the inevitability of my divorce." Autumn spread her arms to encompass the resort as a whole. "I need to make this a success for myself. I don't want to be someone's employee. I don't want to be part of a chain. I want my own vision."

The question in Montgomery's dark brown eyes resolved itself into understanding. He pushed himself to his feet and extended his right hand. "Autumn, thank you for taking the time to explain your decision to me. Under the circumstances, I won't bother you with my buyout offers any longer. Instead, I'll wish you success and happiness with your vision."

Autumn rose to accept his gesture. His hand was

rough in hers. A workingman's hands at odds with his power broker image.

She gave him a real smile. "Thank you, Montgomery. I wish you continued success with your empire."

Rita stood with them. Her startled pale brown gaze swung from Autumn and settled on Montgomery. "What about me?"

Montgomery shrugged into his coat. "This was an all-or-nothing proposition, Rita. Autumn's unwilling to sell her share of the business. I'm going to respect her wishes."

"The only way I'd sell is over my dead body." Autumn moved to escort Montgomery from her office. She paused at the expression in Rita's normally bright brown eyes. Her fixated stare was dark with anger. "I'm willing to buy you out, Rita."

"It's not enough." The other woman's voice was barely audible, but Autumn caught what she'd said—and what she'd left unsaid.

A chill chased down her spine. In that moment, Autumn knew Rita wouldn't be opposed to her dropping dead.

Chapter 2

Sister Lou reversed her orange compact sedan out of its space in the Briar Coast Cabin Resort's parking lot. The main cabin, which she and Sister Marianna had just left, was reflected in her rearview mirror as she drove away.

"There's a lot of tension between Autumn, her business partner, and their associate." She hadn't meant to make the observation out loud.

There was a rustling sound as Sister Marianna shifted on the passenger seat to face her. "Will it affect our planning for the Advent retreat?"

"I don't think so." Sister Lou navigated out of the lot and onto the main road.

"Then it's none of our business." The rustling sound returned as Sister Marianna shifted on her seat again, this time away from Sister Lou. "And can you possibly slow down, Louise?"

"Of course." Sister Lou eased up on the accelerator.

She hadn't imagined the tension. It was as real as the conflict between Sister Marianna and Autumn, but Sister Marianna was right. They shouldn't let it distract them from their retreat planning.

The resort was impressive. Autumn had given Sister Lou and Sister Marianna an extensive tour during their first in-person meeting. The walking trails were picturesque and lush. With the late-fall colors, the property looked like a Thanksgiving invitation. She could only imagine that the scenery would resemble a Christmas card in the winter.

"Today's meeting wasn't as productive as it could have been." Sister Lou pointed her little car south, back to the offices of the Congregation of the Sisters of St. Hermione of Ephesus. "We spent more time on the menu plan than I thought we would."

"We wouldn't have if that account manager hadn't tried to tell us how to run our own retreat." The snap in Sister Marianna's voice reverberated around the car's interior.

Sister Lou glanced at Sister Marianna before returning her attention to the sparse midmorning traffic on this final Thursday in October. "Autumn isn't the resort's account manager. She's the owner, and she was trying to be helpful."

Referring to Autumn as an account manager was the kind of strategic tactic Sister Marianna sometimes used to minimize her adversary's position.

"Well, she failed." Sister Marianna sniffed as she adjusted her teal scarf around her neck. "If she was trying to be helpful, she would have accepted my decision when I declined her advice, then we would have made it through every item on our meeting agenda. Instead, it's her fault that our project has been delayed."

"It'll be helpful to get feedback on the menu from the rest of the congregation. We should've thought of that earlier." *Feedback* and *menu*. Sister Lou enjoyed her pun. Sadly, her efforts were lost on Sister Marianna. The other woman had no discernable sense of humor.

"You mean *I* should have thought of that sooner." Sister Marianna's tone sharpened at the implied insult.

My dearest Marianna, why must every word out of everyone else's mouth elicit a combative response from you? Surely, in a previous life, you were a champion pugilist.

Sister Lou smiled at the image of Sister Marianna as a mixed martial arts fighter. "That's not what I meant."

"Of course you did. I'd been planning this retreat by myself for weeks before Barbara insisted you work with me. If you weren't referring to me, then to whom were you referring?"

Sister Lou had no idea why the congregation's prioress, Sister Barbara Yates, had asked her to assist Sister Marianna with the retreat. She and Sister Marianna weren't exactly on favorable terms. But when the prioress had sought her help with the project, it had seemed ungracious to say no.

And it had seemed like such a reasonable request . . .

Sister Lou turned left onto Town Street. "I literally meant *we*. We're working on this project together."

"There you go again, playing the role of peacemaker, first at the resort and now here."

"Blessed are the peacemakers, Marianna. They shall be called the children of God." Sister Lou took pleasure in paraphrasing one of the beatitudes from the Gospel of St. Matthew.

Sister Marianna sighed. "You can't always run from confrontations under the guise of being a peacemaker. Sometimes you have to take a stand. You know what they say: if you don't stand for something, you'll fall for everything."

"I may not chase after confrontations." *The way you do.* "But I do stand for what I believe in."

"Like what?"

"I took a stand when I investigated Maurice's murder." Sister Lou grew somber at the memory of her friend's tragic death barely a month ago. In the distance, she could see the roof of the Sleep Ease Inn Hotel. Dr. Maurice Jordan had been a guest at that hotel when he'd been killed.

Silence settled over the car's interior like a prickly blanket. Was Sister Marianna remembering how hard she'd argued to stop Sister Lou's investigation? She'd even brought her objections to the congregation's leadership team. Despite her many dogged efforts, Sister Marianna had failed to end Sister Lou's sleuthing precisely because Sister Lou had stood firm for what she'd believed in: justice for her friend.

"I'm sorry." Sister Marianna was much more subdued.

An apology? From Marianna? I'm going to note this date on my calendar for an annual remembrance. "You, Autumn, and I are on the same team. We all want the retreat to be a success, but we're running out of time to plan it. The retreat starts in a little more than four weeks."

Sister Marianna shifted to face Sister Lou again. "What would you suggest?"

Sister Lou tensed as she drove past the Sleep Ease Inn Hotel. *Rest in peace, dear friend.*

She turned onto Main Street. "I'll coordinate the online survey. We'll need a quick turnaround, then you and I will meet to discuss the results."

"That would be fine. However, when the congregation chooses *my* healthier menu items, Autumn had better accept the results."

Sister Lou had been with the congregation for seven years. She was fairly confident that the majority of the sisters wouldn't choose lima beans and tofu over dill potatoes and rotisserie chicken. "One step at a time, Marianna."

As uncomfortable as this morning's meeting had been, it would pale in comparison to the next one, when the survey results weren't in Sister Marianna's favor.

"Give me a hint. What am I supposed to be looking for in the mayor's office?" Not for the first time, Sharelle "Shari" Henson, investigative reporter with *The Briar Coast Telegraph*, wondered what her editor in chief expected her to uncover when he assigned her to snoop around the mayor's office and town hall.

She considered Diego DeVarona as he stopped by her cubicle late Thursday morning. He'd been the

Telegraph's editor for a month. In that short period of time, he'd given the staff a renewed sense of purpose and pride. He'd reintroduced real journalism, pushing reporters, copy editors, editors, and photographers, challenging them to be more critical of their news coverage and holding everyone to a higher standard. Shari pinched herself every morning before coming to work.

"I can't tell you what you're looking for." Diego propped his right shoulder against the threshold of Shari's cubicle and sipped his coffee. The Texas transplant's porcelain mug was emblazoned with the Toronto Raptors National Basketball Association black and red franchise logo. She still didn't believe his story that he'd had to buy the mug after losing a bet.

The newspaper's overhead lights sparkled on the few silver strands hiding among the thick waves of his mahogany hair. His tall, lean form was outfitted in a cerulean blue shirt, navy tie, and coffee brown slacks. He must have left his suit jacket hanging in his office.

Shari regarded her boss with suspicion. "If you can't tell me what I'm looking for, how do you know there's anything to find?"

"Instinct." He was doing his sphinx impersonation again.

Shari stared at him. "You assigned me to dig into the background of an elected official, her administration, and every member of the five-member Briar

Coast Town Council on 'instinct'? Are you pranking me, Diego?"

"No."

"How can I meet your expectations if I don't know what they are?" Shari cradled the porcelain mug he'd gifted her with when she'd returned to the newspaper. The front bore the screened question CAN I QUOTE YOU?

Diego shook his head. "Don't worry about my expectations. You're good at what you do. That's why I asked you to take this project."

Shari blinked. "Okay. Thanks." His praise had rattled every one of her brain cells. She scrambled to remember the other matter she'd wanted to discuss with him. "I think the sheriff's office's still sulking over my helping Sister Lou with her investigation into Dr. Jordan's murder."

"It's been almost four weeks."

"I know, but they're pretty tight-lipped when I call for news updates."

Diego sipped his coffee. "Your article did expose the deputies' inability to solve the case. You, Sister Lou, and her nephew, Chris, did that."

Shari took a moment of silence to bask in the joint achievement. "How do you think I should handle this?"

"Make an extra effort to be professional and nice to Deputies Cole and Tate. We can't file crime stories without a quote from the sheriff's office." Diego saluted her with his coffee mug before disappearing in the direction of his office.

Shari turned back to her desk, muttering under her breath. "I'll need a miracle to get the deputies to work with me. Ever. Again."

"Amen." Christian "Chris" LaSalle lifted his head once his aunt, Sister Lou, finished saying grace over the dinner he was sharing with her and Shari at the Congregation of the Sisters of St. Hermione of Ephesus's motherhouse Thursday evening. He made the sign of the cross, touching the first two fingers of his right hand to his forehead, chest, and left and right shoulders.

He sat across from his aunt at their square, blond wood table, which cozied up to a window framed by bright flower-patterned curtains.

Shari examined one of the boiled broccoli spears on the end of her fork. "Is it my imagination or are the meals being prepared a little differently lately?"

"I was wondering the same thing." Chris looked askance at his aunt.

Even the seasonings that scented the air in the dining room had changed. They used to tempt the taste buds even before the first bite. Now they left the decision up to the diner. Were they going to consume just enough to satisfy their hunger or were they going to clean their dinner plates?

Sister Lou took off her brown blazer. Her expression was wry. "Marianna's on a health kick."

"It's. Different." Shari had the disposition of someone who'd experienced worse. She popped the broccoli into her mouth, then chewed tentatively.

"I agree." Sister Lou's words were dry. She adjusted her pale pink blouse before cutting into the broiled chicken breast. "But not everyone likes change, especially when it affects their food."

"I can understand." The previous cooking style had spoiled Chris. He turned from the broccoli for now and added salt to the chicken.

"Marianna wants to spread her new health awareness to the retreat menu." Sister Lou accepted the salt shaker from Chris. "Based on the sisters' reactions here, I don't believe that's going to go over well."

His aunt might be right. At a glance, the sisters' response to the new meal preparation ranged from dismay to disgust. The salt and pepper shakers at each table were getting extra attention. The change had even affected the mood of the dining room. The usual animated conversations and merry laughter were noticeably absent.

"How's your apartment hunting going?" Sister Lou directed the question and the salt shaker to Shari.

Shari added the seasoning to her chicken. "I've looked at a few places. They've all been nice, but nothing has jumped out at me."

"When are you hoping to move?" Chris coated his chicken and broccoli with pepper before offering the shaker to Sister Lou.

"Before Christmas." Shari's eyes sparkled with anticipation.

His brain took a moment to catch up with his vocal cords. "You've been in your current place less than three months. Didn't you sign a one-year lease?"

"Do you always play by the rules, Slick?" Shari's eyes flashed a challenge. In her warm orange blazer and cream shell blouse, she looked as bright as a new day. "I have a month-to-month lease. I didn't know whether this Briar Coast experiment would work out."

Sister Lou offered Shari the pepper shaker. "What do you think now?"

Shari sprinkled pepper liberally over her meal before returning the shaker to the center of the table. "I like it. I have a great job and good friends. I'd call it a success."

Sister Lou seemed pleased. "So would I."

"I would, too." Chris returned his glass of lemonade to the table. It could use more sugar. "But why did you ask for a month-to-month lease? Can you really tell whether you'll like a place in just one month?"

"Probably not." Shari tilted her head. Lustrous raven curls framed her heart-shaped face. "That's why I was going to give the paper and the town six months before moving on."

Well, six months is better than one, although not by much.

"You've moved around quite a bit over the years." Sister Lou cut into her broiled chicken. "I'm glad that you're willing to give Briar Coast a chance."

Chris was still hounded by curiosity. "Why do you move around so much? What are you looking for?"

Shari's smile seemed strained. "You missed your calling. You would've made a great reporter."

"I'm just curious." He tried a nonchalant shrug.

"Why should I stay where I'm not happy?" Shari glanced at Sister Lou as though seeking validation.

Why is she answering my questions with questions?
"That's a good point."

"Indeed it is." Sister Lou eyed her dessert of angel food cake and vanilla ice cream with an air of defeat. "If you aren't making the situation better for yourself or the people around you, then you should leave, if you can. Find a place where you can make a positive impact for yourself and your community."

Shari looked at Sister Lou with admiration. "That's what I want to do, make a positive impact."

There was more to it than that. Shari was comfortable asking questions, but she didn't like being on the receiving end. Why was she so secretive? And why did her secrecy make him even more curious about her?

If she didn't know what she was looking for—or even that she was looking—how could he be sure that she was here to stay?

Chapter 3

It was just past six o'clock on the last Friday morning in October. Each day, the sun took longer to rise. Sister Lou didn't mind, though. Neither did her jogging partner, Sister Carmen Vega. Over the past seven years, their almost daily five-mile jogs had become a habit, like a reflex.

As they drew closer to the campus of the College of St. Hermione of Ephesus, Sister Lou's gaze was drawn to the base of one of the mission-style, wrought-iron lampposts that lit the parking lot between the congregation and the college. The sleek, furry form of a familiar cat stretched out with regal nonchalance on the asphalt lot.

Haven't I seen that cat gliding around the student dormitories? Probably. She recognized the calico's gold-and-brown markings against the snow-white furry background.

As though sensing Sister Lou's thoughts, the cat stirred herself to turn her head in Sister Lou's direction. Her pale green eyes held the sister's gaze until she came abreast of the calico. Then the cat condescended to greet Sister Lou with a brief and casual lift of her chin. It was a humanlike How-Ya-Doin' gesture that made Sister Lou grin. She nodded in return.

Sister Lou gestured toward the cat to call Sister Carmen's attention to her. "That cat is moving closer to the motherhouse and away from the dorms."

Sister Carmen blew a breath. "Do you blame her? She probably still needs a break from all the midterm tension two weeks ago."

"Good point." Sister Lou turned her thoughts away from the cocky calico. "Several companies and nonprofit agencies already have agreed to partner with us on the outreach mission." With each deep breath, Sister Lou drew in the sharp, sweet scents of the season. The crisp autumn air was perfect for their aerobic workout. Birdsong added harmony to the rhythmic beats of their footfalls.

"Wonderful." Sister Carmen was a bright glow in her lemon yellow wicking jersey and grass green runner's pants. Beside her, Sister Lou felt lacking in creativity with her gray jersey and black pants. "I'm really happy about the success you're having. But what I really want to know is how was the meeting with the resort owner and Marianna?"

Memories of that traumatic session took some of the spring from Sister Lou's steps. "It was about what you'd imagine."

Sister Carmen grimaced. "That bad?"

Sister Lou didn't need to elaborate. Everyone knew how confrontational Sister Marianna could be.

Some people loved chocolate. Others enjoyed pasta. Sister Marianna lived to argue.

Sister Lou and Sister Carmen finished their first loop around the residence halls, then turned toward the college's oval. Federal-style, redbrick academic buildings and stately old trees flanked the well-manicured lawns and pedestrian pathways in the heart of the almost 160-acre campus. A handful of joggers and a few walkers—mostly students, but some faculty and staff—also braved the predawn chill to exercise.

Sister Lou wiped the sweat from her upper lip with the back of her wrist. "She disagreed with the resort owner's suggestion to include a few popular menu choices with the healthy meals she'd ordered."

Sister Carmen grunted. "If her grocery list for the retreat is like the meals she's been ordering for the motherhouse, the event will not go over well."

"I know." Sister Lou sighed. "IT's helping me put together an online survey for the congregation to select their meal preferences."

"Good idea." Sister Carmen nodded. "You may not want to show Marianna the final results, though. Her feelings could be hurt."

"It's no secret that Marianna and I don't see eye to eye." Sister Lou waved at familiar faces along their path. She'd heard that the college community referred to her and Sister Carmen as the Running Sisters. Students in particular always seemed excited to see them. "I don't understand why Barbara's so adamant that I help Marianna with the retreat planning."

"I do." Sister Carmen smiled and waved at the joggers and walkers she recognized. She had the air of a rock star.

"Care to share your insight?"

"You're the only one who challenges Marianna."

Sister Lou almost stumbled in surprise at Sister Carmen's pronouncement. Her jogging partner caught her arm to steady her. "No, I'm not. Marianna argues with *some*one. Every day."

"You're wrong." Sister Carmen's two favorite words. Scratch that; her two favorite words were *I'm right.* "Most people give in to Marianna. Some people, like me, ignore her. But you stand up to her."

"It's not only me. Most of the sisters openly supported Maurice's invitation to be our keynote speaker for the Saint Hermione presentation." Sister Lou recalled the most recent—and most devastating—example of people disagreeing with Sister Marianna.

Sister Lou had invited her longtime friend, the noted theologian Dr. Maurice Jordan, to be the congregation's guest speaker for its St. Hermione of Ephesus Feast Day presentation this past August. Sister Marianna's objections had been immediate, persistent, and loud. She'd considered Maurice's perspectives too controversial. For that reason, she hadn't wanted the congregation to associate with the theologian.

Much to Sister Marianna's consternation, the overwhelming majority of congregation members had supported Sister Lou's recommendation to invite Maurice. Tragically, her friend had been murdered the morning of his presentation. Sister Lou had found his body.

Sister Carmen was quiet as though she also was remembering that sad event. "We were all happy to help with the event, leaving you in Marianna's crosshairs."

"Perhaps I should have listened to Marianna. Perhaps if I had, Mo would be alive today."

"Stop it." Sister Carmen was firm if a bit breathless. "The person who murdered Maurice is responsible for his death. Your invitation had nothing to do with it."

Maybe not, but Sister Lou still hadn't come to terms with the regrettable connection. She returned to her more immediate dilemma as a distraction. "Marianna's penchant for arguing is going to be a problem with this retreat. She doesn't believe in compromise, and she thinks I compromise too much."

"Everyone knows Marianna's difficult to work with. She's stubborn. If there's a way to make working with her easier, no one's figured it out yet."

The sun continued to rise as they finished their third lap around the oval. Sister Lou jogged beside Sister Carmen as they followed other runners and walkers onto the path that led to the center of town. Their destination was the path's two-mile marker. At that point, they'd return to the college and retrace their steps. The scents of earth and foliage surrounded them on the trail. The towering trees were dazzling with autumn colors. Tangles of ground cover grew along the well-worn path, shadowing the silver lampposts the town council had installed.

Sister Lou interrupted their companionable silence. "How am I supposed to work with her?" *Does anyone on earth have an answer to that question?*

"You can handle her. You came up with the survey idea."

"I wanted to end the arguing." Sister Lou shook her head. "She treats everything like a conflict. How do I help her to see that it's not?"

"I don't think Barb meant for you to change Marianna's style. That would take a Christmas miracle. Maybe you can work on that for Lent."

Sister Lou laughed as Sister Carmen obviously meant for her to. "All right. I'll pace myself with her."

Sister Carmen chuckled. "Barb's going to owe you a pretty spectacular Christmas gift."

Sister Lou shook her head with a smile. "Working with Marianna is ruining my Christmas spirit."

One of them could use more sleep. Autumn glanced at her pearl gray cell phone lying beside her forearm on her desk. It wasn't yet eight a.m., but she and her director of finance, Gary Hargreaves, had been discussing the resort's month-end financial report for more than ten minutes. Either she wasn't asking the right question, he wasn't making any sense—or they both needed more sleep.

"My numbers are correct." Gary was starting to repeat himself. He sat on one of the scarlet and wood chairs on the other side of Autumn's desk. "They're the same numbers I sent you."

The accountant was a clothes horse. Today's double-breasted smoke gray suit looked tailor-made for his tall, lean figure. How could he afford his wardrobe on the modest salary she was paying him? His golden blond hair was expertly cut in the latest style. He hadn't gone to a neighborhood barber.

Autumn searched his bright green eyes. "Gary, are you keeping two sets of books?"

The accountant looked stunned. "Absolutely not."

She hadn't thought so. She trusted Gary, but she still had to ask.

Autumn tapped the thick, detailed report on her desk with her right index finger. "If the report I have and the one you're showing me are the same October month-end reports, why are the numbers so different?"

According to the financial file Autumn had received, the Briar Coast Cabin Resort was realizing very comfortable profits in keeping with the events and guests Autumn had worked very hard to contract. However, the company's bank balances didn't reflect that success. She'd asked Gary to meet with her to explain the discrepancy between his report and the resort's bank balances. Where was their money?

"I think someone's hacked your computer." Gary's voice was heavy with tension.

Autumn was speechless. Gary had just given voice to her growing fear. Of all the business challenges she'd imagined before opening the resort—low sales, lawsuits, incompetent vendors—it had never before occurred to her that someone would hack her computer and steal from her. "You think someone's hacking into my e-mail system and altering the financial reports you're sending me? Who would do that?"

A flush darkened his soft, pale features. "I don't know how else to explain it."

Autumn sat back on her brown faux leather executive chair. Her attention was on her open office door. She couldn't ignore the signs anymore. "That's a hefty charge. Whoever's doing this must've known they'd get caught."

Gary ran his well-manicured hand through his perfect hair. "It's the only explanation that makes sense. I swear that I'm not stealing from you."

She believed him or at least she wanted to. But could she? He looked nervous. Was that because he was guilty or because he wasn't? "Do you think it's another member of the staff?"

"I don't know. It could be one of our vendors."

"How do we get to the bottom of this?"

A knock on her door interrupted their conversation. Autumn saw the resort's head chef, Urban Rodgers, standing in her threshold. He was dressed in his usual black pants and shirt; today it was a collarless jersey.

"Morning, Autumn. Gary." Urban's smooth brown features were expressionless. The middle-aged chef was handsome despite the long, angry scar on the left side of his face. "Autumn, do you have the congregation's retreat menu?"

Her mind nimbly switched gears. "The sisters are still working out the details. We should have their meal selections by the end of next week."

In the almost ten months that Urban had worked for her, Autumn had never had any conflict or cause for concern with him. He was a hard worker, a talented cook, and a responsible employee. But did that mean she could trust him? Was he the one stealing from her?

Urban allowed a flicker of concern before again masking his expression. "Our schedule is getting tight. I'll need time to evaluate the budget and purchase the ingredients."

"I know." Autumn glanced at Gary, who was following her exchange with Urban. Was he also wondering whether the chef was behind the hacks? She returned her attention to Urban. "They know that we're behind schedule, but we should be all right with the timing. They're not looking for anything fancy." An understatement, considering Sister Marianna's preference for boring, tasteless entrées.

Urban nodded as he turned to leave. "I'll check back next week."

"Thank you, Urban," Autumn called after him.

"I should get to work." Gary stood, checking his silver Movado wristwatch. Where did he get the money for it? "I'll do some research on tracing computer hacks."

"Thanks, Gary." Autumn mentally shook her head. Would she start looking at all of her employees differently now? Three months ago, she'd thought she could trust them. She thought they were a team. Now a seed of suspicion had been planted in her mind. She had to get to the bottom of this before more of her money was stolen and additional damage was done to her company.

Chapter 4

"That's a risky proposal." Lorna Alexander, the vice president for finance at the College of St. Hermione of Ephesus, spoke with the finality of a person who thought her position was much higher than it was.

Chris sat on the pale blue–cushioned chair next to hers. The proposal to freeze the college's tuition for four years and increase the number and value of the scholarships awarded was commendable. Did the idea have risks? Yes. But Chris was willing to listen to Sister Valerie Shaw's proposal. First, because it was an intriguing idea that was at least worth exploring. Second, because the older woman who had called the meeting and who was seated on the blue cloth executive chair on the other side of the desk wasn't faking power. As president of the college, she had it.

The president's office smelled pleasantly of hazelnut coffee. Like his aunt, Sister Valerie was an early riser. The rumor was that she never slept. It was just after ten o'clock on the last Friday morning of October, but she'd probably already invested four or five hours of the day toward her beloved college, which her congregation had founded in 1871, 146 years ago.

Sister Valerie was a 1972 alumna of the college. After taking her vows, she'd earned her doctorate in education, then returned to teach at her alma mater. She'd climbed the ladder from faculty member to division chair to provost, and now led the college as its ninth president, a position she'd held for almost eight years.

"I understand that this proposal presents some challenges." Sister Valerie's blue, gold, and white Hermionean cross was pinned to the right lapel of her cool green suit jacket. "That's the reason I invited the two of you to my office to discuss it. I'm not going to announce that the college will freeze tuition effective tomorrow. Considering the estimated cost of this decision, I realize we need to identify how and when to make it feasible."

Translation: Sister Valerie wasn't an idiot. This was a monumental task—but she was determined to make it work.

Lorna wasn't as attuned to Sister Valerie's subtext. "Well, let's start with the money." She gestured with her right hand. Her long, bloodred nails seemed to drip from her thin, honey brown hand. "The figures available now are based on a prior year's budget. I'll need to crunch numbers based on projected costs of future markets. Those will be very rough estimates. In fact, they could be completely wrong."

Sister Valerie folded her small, pale hands on the mahogany surface of her desk. Her wavy chestnut hair was liberally threaded with strands of gray that winked beneath her office's fluorescent lights. "I have faith in your expertise, Lorna. I'm confident that you'll be able to approximate a realistic estimate of future years' expenses."

Chris's brain sorted through options and ideas. "We'll have to grow our pool of donors to help get us to our goal."

"That's right." Lorna seized on his words. She crossed her long legs, on display beneath the midthigh length of her red skirt suit, an exact match to her nail polish. "You're talking about a lot of money, Sister. We're already pressuring donors for money for other budgetary needs: capital improvements, programs, and services. We can't go back to them to ask for even more money."

Lorna's persistent negativity was like kryptonite, the mineral that drained Superman of his superhuman strength. She never said an encouraging word, or made one positive observation about others' plans and proposals to enhance the institution. She never offered ideas, either. If the college's management had been left to her, it would still be operating from its original building with four classrooms on the ground floor and a community bedroom above.

"I realize that this is the greatest amount of money we've ever considered raising for our school." Sister Valerie turned to Chris. "As vice president for college advancement, fund-raising is your purview. What are your thoughts?"

"I was going to say that my team has been cultivating new donors for some time. We can invite our new donors to make a gift first, then return to our long-term supporters after the New Year."

The look in Lorna's almond-shaped midnight eyes was skeptical. "You've only been vice president for advancement for a month. Do you really think you've had enough time to work those new relationships?"

"You're right, Lorna." Sister Valerie interrupted their exchange. "Chris has only been vice president for one month. Before that, he was interim for almost five months. All told, he has ten years of experience as an advancement professional. Just as I have faith in the expertise you hold in your field, I also have faith in his."

Lorna shrugged her thin shoulders. "I'm glad fund-raising isn't my responsibility."

Lorna was trying to use the Jedi mind trick that the *Star Wars* character Obi-Wan "Ben" Kenobi used to plant suggestions in his enemies' heads. Chris wasn't falling for her efforts to make him second-guess himself.

Sister Valerie gave Lorna a chastening look. "I've always said that fund-raising, just as student recruitment, is everyone's responsibility."

"Sister, we're not a huge university." Lorna swung her right foot, shod in a snow-white three-inch stiletto. The action was irritating. "We're a small, private college. It's hard enough getting media coverage, much less money. The last time we were in the papers, someone had to die."

Sister Valerie's sharp intake of breath ushered silence into her office.

Chris broke that silence. "Dr. Maurice Jordan was a good friend to my aunt."

Sister Valerie pressed a hand to her chest. "The congregation's still grieving the loss of Dr. Jordan. He was taken from us far too soon."

"I apologize." Lorna looked from Chris to Sister Valerie. "I didn't mean to make light of the tragedy. I just meant to show how hard this fund-raising proposal will be."

Sister Valerie's warm brown gaze scanned her surroundings as though seeking something. On her office walls, framed black-and-white and color photos of events at the congregation joined images of college events. She'd once told Chris that she wanted to remain in that office until the walls were covered—floor to ceiling—with commencement photos. Like him, she was driven to serve the needs of their students.

"The cost of obtaining a degree from an institution of higher learning has grown out of control." Sister Valerie spoke with measured words and quiet passion. "This country is in a crisis that I no longer want our school to be any part of. Instead, I want us to lead the way toward bridging the education gap and giving students who are our future a fighting chance to succeed. Will you help me?"

"Yes, of course." After the president's inspiring

words, Chris would have found a way to change lightbulbs on the moon, if that's what she'd wanted.

Lorna still hesitated. "We're going to look like fools if we go around asking for money to freeze tuition but then don't raise the money to keep our word."

Chris considered his associate. Her negativity was driving him to madness. "And what will we look like if we don't even try?"

"Sister Lou, it's good to see you again." Autumn Tassler glanced toward her office door as she circled her desk. "Is Sister Marianna joining us?"

"I'm afraid not." Sister Lou shook Autumn's hand. "Marianna and I discussed the preliminary equipment list for the retreat sessions so that I could review them with you this morning."

Was that relief in the resort owner's eyes?

Autumn closed her office door, then turned back to her desk. "That should help us get back on schedule, since we weren't able to review the lists yesterday."

Sister Lou settled onto the thinly cushioned guest chair, smoothing the skirt of her pale peach suit beneath her. "Marianna's fine with us going over the list as long as it's understood that this is a *preliminary* list."

"As long as it's understood that the estimate I give you today will be a *preliminary* estimate." Autumn grinned as she returned to her chair.

"Of course." Sister Lou inclined her head. "Most

of the presentations will have audiovisual needs. For the weeklong retreat, we'll have—"

The office door slammed open, the sound a sharp explosion. Sister Lou sprang to her feet and spun around. Vengeance faced her from the doorway.

Autumn's administrative assistant rushed in behind the tall, angry woman who'd crossed into the room. Kelsey Bennett's yellow blond corkscrew curls shook nervously around her chubby features as she jostled for position with the female force of nature. "Autumn, I'm so sorry."

Sister Lou watched Autumn rise to her feet. Her movements were wary, bordering on defensive.

"You stupid slut," the tall woman raged over Kelsey's words. She bore an uncanny resemblance to the resort owner, with her thin features, dark blue eyes, and light brown hair.

"Ms. Potts pushed her way past me. I'm so sorry." Kelsey raised her voice to be heard over the antagonist.

"I know you're sleeping with my husband!" the woman screeched even louder.

"What?" Autumn couldn't have looked more surprised if an alien spaceship had landed in her office and its crew had invited her to tea.

"You heard me." Amazingly, the screaming woman's volume increased again.

Sister Lou feared her ears would bleed. Dogs all over Briar Coast County must have been on their way to the resort.

Autumn pulled her gaze from her accuser and shifted her attention to her assistant. "Kelsey, there's nothing to apologize for. I'll take care of this. Thank you."

Kelsey didn't wait to be told twice. Her curls hopped frantically as she turned and hurried from the room, bouncing on her toes. Sister Lou stood to follow her.

"I'll wait outside." According to her crimson Timex wristwatch, it was just after ten o'clock on the last Friday morning of October. Hopefully, this interruption wouldn't last long.

Autumn raised her hand, palm out. "That won't be necessary. My cousin's leaving."

Cousin? That explained the resemblance. How do they explain the hostility? Reluctantly, Sister Lou sat.

The other woman stood, arms akimbo. Her figure-hugging bronze dress skimmed past her full hips to end midthigh. "The *hell* I'm leaving. Not until I *damned well* have my say."

"January!" Autumn sounded scandalized. She gestured toward Sister Lou. "This is—"

Sister Lou understood that Autumn felt uncomfortable with her cousin's use of coarse language in front of a member of a religious order. But one of the reasons she and other sisters chose not to wear traditional habits was to allow them to move freely among the community they served. After Vatican II, many orders chose not to wear habits because it made them seem less approachable. Besides, it wasn't the language that concerned her as much as the emotion behind it. What was the cause of it?

January's cap of light brown hair swung forward as she leaned toward Autumn. "I don't give a *damn* who that is. Did you think I wouldn't find out that you were *screwing my husband*? Do you think I'm an *idiot*?"

Sister Lou's eyes widened. She didn't want to believe that of Autumn. She turned to the resort owner.

A furious blush stained Autumn's sharp cheekbones. "You're interrupting a business meeting. Leave now. I'll call you later so we can straighten this out."

"Your *damn* meeting can wait, you traitorous *skank*. I'm not going to let you ruin my marriage."

Sister Lou flinched at January's ugly, angry language. "Ms. Potts, Autumn makes a good point. Neither of you is in a position to clear up this misunderstanding right now."

January swung her glare to Sister Lou. "Mind your own *damn* business."

That order was laughable, considering January was the one who interrupted a private meeting. Sister Lou spread her arms to indicate Autumn's office. "By charging in here, you made it my business. This isn't the time or the place for this argument."

Autumn sent Sister Lou an apologetic look before returning to her cousin's wrath. "January, listen carefully. I don't know what makes you think I'm sleeping with Sherrod. I'm not. I've *never* slept with him. I *never* would sleep with him. He is and always has been all yours."

"Bull—"

"*January!*"

"You're a *damned* liar!" January marched back to the door and yanked it open. She glared at Autumn once more from over her shoulder. "You've already destroyed *your* marriage. I will *kill you* before I let you ruin mine!"

January slammed the door hard enough for the walls to shake. Sister Lou flinched. The exchange had been tense and uncomfortable for her. She could imagine how upset Autumn felt. "How are you?"

"I'm sorry for the interruption." Autumn reclaimed her seat. Her face was flushed and her eyes were downcast.

Sister Lou empathized with the younger woman's discomfort. "You don't need to apologize. Take a moment to collect yourself."

"I'm fine." Autumn's stilted response contradicted her words. She seemed to brace herself before meeting Sister Lou's eyes. "I'm not having an affair with my cousin's husband."

"Why does she think that you are?" Their discussion of the congregation's audiovisual needs for the retreat could wait. In any event, Autumn didn't seem in a condition to return to their meeting's original purpose.

Autumn expelled a breath. "Sherrod, January's husband, is very handsome and successful, and January's . . . insane."

The resort owner's eyes were dark with sorrow rather than anger. The cousins must have loved each other very much once, or at least Autumn had loved January. What had happened to end that bond? Had it involved Sherrod? Or was it something else entirely? Old hurts long forgotten perhaps but not quite forgiven.

"Is she dangerous?"

The confusion in Autumn's expression cleared. "Oh, you mean her death threat? I'm not worried. January's high-strung. She thrives on creating drama. She always has."

"Are you sure?"

"I'm sure. Besides, if she were serious, she'd have to stand in line. I'm at the top of quite a few people's hit lists for one reason or another." Fact or fiction, the idea seemed to weigh on Autumn.

"I hope you and your cousin are able to work this out." Sister Lou drew a deep breath. The cedarwood and pine scents that lingered in the office soothed Sister Lou. Hopefully, they would have a similar effect on Autumn.

"The only way I could imagine reconciling with January is if she apologized. I can't believe she thinks I'd sleep with her husband." Autumn's voice trembled. The accusation must have hurt deeply.

"Why is she so insecure about him?" The old Sister Lou would never have dreamed of asking such an impertinent question—out loud. Shari's influence was connecting her with her outer voice.

Autumn's gaze circled her office as though searching for something among the wood-framed artwork in the spacious wood-paneled room. "Sherrod is the full package: looks, money, and he's really very nice. Much better husband material than my ex turned out to be."

"Your cousin must love him very much." Sister Lou hoped the two women would reconcile. Family was so very important.

You don't even realize how important until you lose them.

"I'm afraid our relationship has other problems, Sister." Autumn drew her writing tablet closer to her, then picked up a pen. Her smile seemed forced. "But you're not here to talk about my dysfunctional family. Let's go over the audiovisual needs for your event."

Sister Lou managed to refocus on the retreat, but Autumn wasn't as successful. She was tense and distracted. Even from the other side of the desk, Sister Lou could sense the younger woman's agitation. Sister Lou's heart was heavy. For Autumn's sake, she hoped the situation didn't deteriorate further.

Chapter 5

"Can you tell me anything more about Val's idea or did she swear you to secrecy?" Sister Lou lowered her glass of ice water to their lunch table in the Briar Coast Café.

Coming from anyone else, Chris would think the person was fishing for information. But he knew his aunt's question was genuine. "Sister Valerie didn't swear me to secrecy, but I think she wants a complete plan before she presents her proposal to the college's board of directors."

In addition to being a member of the leadership team for the Congregation of the Sisters of St. Hermione of Ephesus, his aunt was on the college's board of directors. How had she found time to solve her friend's murder last month?

Chris bit into his roast beef and provolone on toasted whole grain sandwich. The homemade bread was the perfect consistency—not too soft, not too hard. The spicy, tender roast beef had his taste buds dancing to James Brown.

He'd taken his aunt to the Briar Coast Café for a late lunch Friday afternoon. The café was close to the congregational offices and the college, which made it a convenient destination when they wanted to get away.

The café was bursting with the aromas of warm breads, fresh vegetables, and well-seasoned meats. With Halloween only four days away, the scent of pumpkin spice also teased diners. A handful of other late-lunch customers lingered around the pale wood tables.

"Val's wise to keep the project silent until she has a full proposal." Sister Lou scooped her spoon into her bowl of chicken vegetable soup. "The directors are a tough crowd, too many naysayers."

"Sister Valerie seems to encounter a lot of those." An image of Lorna Alexander came to mind.

"She does have a lot of experience dealing with pessimists."

Chris silently agreed. "I hope I can meet her expectations."

"Concentrate on satisfying *your* expectations and you'll do better than fine." Sister Lou gave him a proud smile.

"But I don't—"

Sister Lou held up her small hand, palm out. "Chris, Val made you vice president for advancement because you hold yourself to a much higher standard than anyone else could. If you approach this project with the same commitment you give every project, you won't fail."

Chris smiled. "Thanks for the pep talk, Aunt Lou."

"You're welcome." She picked up her soup spoon again. "And don't worry. I'll keep Val's secret."

Chris finished his sandwich. He poured vinaigrette dressing over his small house salad. "Speaking of secrets, I think Shari's keeping secrets about her past."

"What makes you think that?" There was a note of caution in his aunt's voice. Perhaps Shari was keeping secrets only from him.

"She never talks about her family or the friends she had before she came here. It's as though she's running from something."

"Or perhaps she values her privacy."

His aunt knew something. "Why would she get an apartment that offered a month-to-month lease?"

Sister Lou's movements were very deliberate as she moved aside her now-empty bowl of soup and replaced it with a small bowl of salad. Chris sensed her measuring her words and weighing her response. "I'm sure Shari will tell us all about her past when she's ready."

But will he live that long? "Do you know why she won't talk about it now?"

Sister Lou's eyes twinkled with good humor. "Do you know anyone who, within days of meeting people, will pull up a chair and tell them his or her life story? Would you do that?"

"We've been friends with Shari for almost two

months. I don't know any more about her today than I did the first day we met. Whenever I ask her something, she changes the subject."

"Give her time, Chris. She'll tell you everything you need to know—when you need to know it."

"We've proven that she can trust us. Why won't she confide in us now?"

"I can't answer that."

Can't—or won't? "How do we know she's not in some kind of trouble?"

"If she was and she wanted us to know, she'd tell us."

Now Chris was sure of it; his aunt was withholding information. It was in the way she avoided his eyes. The too-casual gestures she made with her hands. "What do you know, Aunt Lou?"

"Chris, it's not my place to share Shari's personal information any more than it was my place to tell Shari all about you when she asked me." Sister Lou gave him a shaming look. It didn't work.

"She asked about me?"

"That's not the point." Sister Lou's tone was midway between amusement and exasperation.

He tried to identify his reaction to learning that Shari was curious enough about him to have questioned his aunt. "I think I'm flattered."

Sister Lou gave him a reluctant smile. "If you want to know something about Shari, ask her. Or better yet, listen. She'll tell you everything you need to know."

Chris swallowed a groan of frustration. "Aunt Lou, I can't do that Vulcan mind meld with people the way you do." His reference to the *Star Trek* mythology made his aunt chuckle.

"Then either try harder—or be patient."

"I'll try harder." Patience wasn't his greatest gift. It was in even shorter supply when it came to learning about Shari.

"Excuse me, Autumn? Isabella Fortney is here." Kelsey made the announcement from the doorway of Autumn's office Friday afternoon. "She doesn't have an appointment, but do you have time to see her?"

"Of course, she'll see me." Isabella shoved Kelsey out of the way and took her position in the doorway.

A surge of fury propelled Autumn from her chair. She slammed the bowl of salad she was eating for lunch onto her walnut wood desk and confronted her ex-husband's trophy wife.

"Don't you ever touch any member of my staff. Ever. Again." She was shaking with anger. "Kelsey, are you all right?"

"I'm fine. I'm fine." Kelsey could be heard but not seen behind Isabella.

Autumn wasn't satisfied. She pinned Isabella with a look meant to shrivel her from the inside out. "Apologize."

Isabella's jaw dropped. "I will not." In her irritation, her fake British accent was more pronounced. Isabella was born and raised in Ann Arbor, Michigan.

Autumn settled her fists on her hips above her

pale gray pants. "You will if you don't want me to throw you out. Literally."

Isabella crossed her arms. She glared in the direction of Kelsey's voice. "I apologize."

Kelsey's round features, framed by swinging corkscrew blond curls, made a brief reappearance in Autumn's doorway. Her dark blue eyes were warm with gratitude. "I'll be at my desk, Autumn."

"Thank you." Slightly mollified, Autumn returned her attention to Isabella. "What do you want, Izzy?" As though she needed to ask.

"Don't call me that." The former aspiring catalog model and current drama queen stomped farther into the office. She wore a red spring cape that pulled the pink accents from the abstract pattern of her multicolored wraparound dress. The clingy garment showed off her every curve. How much had that dress cost? "Autumn, you simply have to end these alimony payments. They're destroying us. Roy can't continue with them."

What on earth had she done to deserve this much drama in one day?

Autumn glanced down at the advertising proofs she'd been reviewing during her working lunch. Both the proofs and her homemade grilled chicken salad would have to wait. Autumn snapped the lid back onto the plastic salad bowl.

"Why can't he continue the payments?" Autumn returned to her cushioned executive chair. It took everything she had to remain calm while confronting the woman her husband had left her for five years ago.

Isabella sank onto one of Autumn's guest chairs with a dancer's grace. "Our business has not been making as much money. The alimony is taking far more of our profits."

Our profits? Autumn's eyes stretched with disbelief. She'd worked two jobs to support herself and her husband while Roy had established his accounting firm. She'd even helped manage his company— for free. That's how much she'd believed in the man she'd married and the dreams he'd had. But once the snake had grown his firm and was bringing in profits, he'd divorced her to marry Isabella. The profit they were enjoying now was *hers, not* Isabella's.

"You and Roy are enjoying the lifestyle that my sacrifices have made possible for you. You're welcome." She gave a mock salute with her bottle of diet soda. "Izzy, the fact is that a judge awarded me a monthly alimony that recognizes my contributions to the creature comforts of your life." She gulped the soda to help dislodge the boulder-sized lump in her throat.

"But we simply can't afford to keep paying you." Isabella crossed her long, shapely legs, drawing attention to her dagger-toed red stilettos.

"According to the terms of my divorce decree, only my marriage to another man could end my well-deserved alimony payments." Autumn shrugged coyly. "Unfortunately for you, I haven't found my soul mate. I've been spending all of my free time with my resort."

"Autumn, you can't keep asking for these alimony payments." The British accent Isabella had appropriated was slipping with her growing desperation. "Roy and I are pregnant. We're going to have a baby."

Someone had thrown a bucket of ice in Autumn's face. She couldn't breathe. She couldn't move. She could barely speak. "Baby?"

"Yes." Isabella's smile revealed the joy of an expectant mother.

The announcement was another knife to Autumn's gut. While they'd been married, Roy had insisted that they didn't have enough money to raise a child. They should wait until the business was stronger, more established, successful, he'd said. But once that happened, he'd had her served with divorce papers, then submitted the announcement of his engagement to *The Briar Coast Telegraph*. Yes, that's how she'd found out her husband had been having an affair with a wannabe catalog model.

She hadn't read the *Telegraph* since.

Autumn found her voice. "Your pregnancy doesn't have any effect on the amount or schedule of the alimony payments."

Isabella's contented smile disappeared. "This is ridiculous. Why do you even need that money?"

"Because I *earned* it." Autumn clenched her teeth.

How dare the other woman question her right to alimony payments after all she'd sacrificed to ensure *Roy's* happiness? Who was going to ensure *her* happiness? For that, she was on her own.

"What are you doing with the money?" Isabella spread her arms, looking around the office. Her voice was a sneer. Her pretend accent gone. "Are you dumping it into this place? What a waste."

It felt as though Autumn were grinding centimeters from her teeth. A pulse drilled in her temple. "This is *my* place, and that's *my* money. I'll spend it any way I choose."

"Stop wasting your time—and my husband's money." Isabella crossed her arms over her ample chest. "Sell this place. It's not worth your time."

"Neither are you. Get out." Autumn jerked her chin toward her door.

"Sell your business." Isabella rose, placing both palms on the surface of Autumn's desk. "You've already received a generous offer for it. Much more than this dump is even worth. You'd be doing yourself a favor by selling it."

Autumn unclenched her jaw. She rose, leaning in toward Isabella and forcing the other woman to take a step back. "Did Rita tell you about the offer we received from Crane Enterprises?"

Isabella's expression said it all. Yes, Rita had told her—and probably Roy—about Crane Enterprises' interest in her resort. Sadly, Autumn wasn't surprised by this betrayal. Since Rita wasn't a fool, Autumn surmised that she'd told Isabella not to let Autumn know that she was aware of the business offer. It's too bad that Isabella didn't have the wits to follow that simple instruction. Autumn would have a talk with her business partner later.

She stood. "Tell Rita and Roy, and anyone else who'll listen, that I will never, ever sell this resort while I still have breath. Please also remind Roy that my alimony check is due at the end of the month. You can check the divorce decree if you want to verify the due dates. I'm sure Roy has a copy that he can share with you."

"Why can't you understand that we need that money for our child?"

"You need more money? Get a job." Autumn viewed Isabella through a red haze of anger. "While I was married to Roy, I had two, and I still found time to help him build the company that's now supporting you. Who knows? Maybe some direct-mail catalog will finally hire you. You can model maternity clothes."

Isabella clenched her fists. Her face reddened with fury. "You'll regret your words. I won't allow you to threaten my child's security."

"And *I* won't allow *you* to rip me off. Roy will pay every cent of the alimony he owes me for the rest of my life. And on time."

"I hate you! I wish you'd drop dead!"

"Get in line!"

Isabella whirled and stormed across the room. She threw the office door open, allowing it to slam against the inside wall. That probably left a dent.

Autumn collapsed onto her chair. With luck, that was the last of the drama for the week.

Chapter 6

"You may've been right." Shari strode into Diego's office at the *Telegraph* the afternoon of the last Friday in October.

"Of course." Diego hit a couple of keys on his board before spinning his chair to face her. He planted his large hands on his beige modular desk. "What about?"

It was a pleasure to enter the editor's office now that it had a new—or relatively new—occupant. Shari no longer felt under attack by piles of . . . stuff. Diego had cleaned out the filth and confusion his predecessor had sheltered. Diego must have worked mornings, nights, and weekends to transform that chaos into a spotless organizational hub so quickly. He'd even gotten rid of the stench of burnt coffee and old newsprint and reintroduced the concept of fresh air.

His faded gray–cushioned desk chair no longer squealed with its every move. Weeks-old copies of newspapers from nearby community and metropolitan areas no longer grew along the beige walls in stacks almost as high as the conference desk. Now each publication was reviewed that morning. Relevant articles were distributed to the section editors with requests to look into Briar Coast connections. Instead of being swollen with press releases and news clippings, the black metal in-box on the corner of his walnut wood desk was empty. For now.

"That the town council and the mayor's office may be covering up a potential scandal." Shari stood behind the two faded gray chairs in front of Diego's desk.

Her editor seemed disappointed to have been right. "What's the scandal?"

"I persuaded a source to speak off the record. According to my source, the Briar Coast town council president's planning to challenge Mayor Stanley in the next election." This information would be important to her readers. Those who supported Mayor Stanley's policies would have to make sure to vote. Those who wanted a change would have a choice.

Judging by the concern in Diego's eyes, he could be a Mayor Stanley supporter. "Ian Greer wants to run against the mayor? They're in the same party."

"I know. If Ian Greer chooses to run, he'd force a primary."

"How well do you know this source?"

"Not well." Shari was impatient to build solid relationships with quality sources but she'd need more time. That was one of the reasons she was so cautious with her research. "We've only known each other about a month, but this information gives me a direction to do more digging."

Diego's coffee brown eyes remained troubled. "If the information's correct, we'll need to understand Greer's motivation, the effect his decision will have on the party, and the impact of this primary election on the town's budget."

"Right." Shari glanced at the notes she'd scribbled onto her notepad during her lunchtime meeting with her confidential informant. "My source doesn't know whether the mayor intends to run for office again or whether the mayor knows that Greer's considering challenging her in the election."

"Heather definitely has plans to run for reelection. I'm sure of it."

Heather? "How well do you know the mayor?"

Diego seemed distracted. "Good work on digging up this information, Shari."

"Thank you, but you were the one who clued me in to a scandal in the mayor's office. How did you know?"

"Just a hunch." Diego shrugged his broad shoulders. His lavender shirt and black tie warmed his café mocha complexion. "There's always a scandal brewing in a mayor's office."

"I don't buy that." Shari gave him a skeptical look. She channeled her inner Sister Lou, calling on the Catholic sister's impressive insight to try to glean Diego's secrets. "You were anxious for me to investigate Mayor Stanley's office and the council. Did you see something—or hear something—that tipped you off?"

Diego leaned back on his seat and linked his fingers over his flat stomach. "When you've been in this business as long as I have, you start to smell where the bodies could be buried."

"Fine, keep your secrets. For now." Shari checked the time on her black cellular phone. "I'll try to get a meeting with Mayor Stanley to ask her about her plans for reelection."

"Don't question her directly. She'll just dodge you. Get her on record with something about the successes and challenges her administration has had so far. Try to get a sense of how she thinks her administration is working with the town council and whether she's feeling any pressure or frustration."

"Good advice." Shari called over her shoulder. She was already leaving his office. "I'll keep you posted."

She'd also look into Diego's past.

What isn't he telling me? And why?

"The congregation has selected *your* menu recommendations, according to the survey responses." Sister Marianna spoke as though she were delivering the medical results of a malignant contagion rather than the retreat meal selections.

It was the first Friday morning of November. Sister Lou, Sister Marianna, and Autumn were meeting in the resort owner's office more than a week after their last meeting. Sister Marianna had tallied the survey responses several times, each time getting the same results. She'd eventually accepted the survey's validity, although not graciously. Judging by the waves of displeasure Sister Lou sensed from Sister Marianna, who was seated beside her, she hadn't come to terms with what the results meant.

"Thank you for letting me know. We'll move forward with our preparations." Autumn wore a simple black scoop-necked jersey.

She didn't display any reaction to the meal decision. Still, the cedar-and-pine-scented air in Autumn's spacious office crackled with tension as always. Sister Lou took in the walnut wood walls and abstract-patterned area rug. Would changing their meeting venue make a difference? Probably not.

"The sisters should have chosen the healthy meals." Sister Marianna was firm in her judgment. "Good nutrition is a vital ingredient for a healthy body. Obviously, the survey results—if they're even accurate— reflect very poor decision-making on the other sisters' part." She gave Sister Lou a pointed look.

It had been difficult admitting to her retreat planning partner that she'd been one of the sisters who'd voted for more appealing meals.

Autumn broke the awkward silence. "I'm sure you double-checked the results."

"Yes, we did." *Quadruple-checked.* Sister Lou avoided Sister Marianna's accusatory eyes.

Autumn spread her hands. "Then I'm sure your

results are correct and the sisters know what they want."

"Apparently, they don't." Sister Marianna tugged the black, gray, and red silk scarf from her neck.

Sister Lou didn't bat an eyelash at Sister Marianna's assertion. She was used to the other woman's stubbornness. Autumn wasn't.

The resort owner uttered a short, sharp laugh of disbelief. Her eyes shifted from Sister Lou to Sister Marianna. "These are mature, responsible women, just like you. They know what they want just as well as you do."

Sister Marianna worried the scarf in her hands. "I want the healthy food choices for the retreat."

Autumn began shaking her head even before the final words had left Sister Marianna's mouth. "No, a deal's a deal. We agreed to conduct a survey. You did that. Now we have to abide by the results."

"Then we'll do another survey. And this time, *I'll* coordinate it." Sister Marianna's grip tightened on her scarf.

Autumn sighed. "We don't have time for another survey. Your retreat is in three weeks. Frankly, we should have decided the meals before today."

Sister Lou raised a hand to step in. "Ladies—"

Sister Marianna interrupted her. "I'm the client."

"Yes, you are." Autumn gave a jerky nod as though she was exerting restraint on her muscles and her temper. "And you told me that you wanted the congregation to take a vote on the menu items. So you did."

Sister Lou tried again to be heard. "I have—"

This time, Autumn talked over her. "Now that the results aren't what you expected—or what you wanted—you're trying to change the rules."

Sister Marianna tugged on the scarf between her hands. "I want this event to be perfect."

"So do I." Autumn's voice was tightly constrained.

Sister Lou raised her voice and both hands. "Everyone, take a breath."

Shocked silence descended on the office. Sister Marianna and Autumn turned to Sister Lou with almost identical wide-eyed, openmouthed expressions.

"Louise!" Sister Marianna recovered first. "What on earth has gotten into you?"

Sister Lou frowned. "I've been trying to get a word in, but the two of you are more interested in arguing with each other than working on a solution to something that really shouldn't even be a problem."

"It *is* a problem." Sister Marianna's scowl was darker than anything Sister Lou could attempt. "I want to do what's right. Autumn wants to do what's popular."

"We agreed to abide by the survey results." Autumn waved a hand between Sister Lou and Sister Marianna. "The survey wasn't even my idea. It was yours."

"Listen to me." Sister Lou lifted her voice again. This time, neither Autumn nor Sister Marianna was surprised. "There's another solution."

"Tell me," Sister Marianna demanded.

"What is it?" Autumn spoke at the same time.

"The menu could be popular recipes that are still

healthy." Sister Lou turned to Autumn. "Your chef could make the menu items the congregation chose, but cook them in a healthier way. Cut back on the salt. Reduce the fat. Substitute chicken or turkey for beef."

"That's an acceptable compromise." Sister Marianna turned to Autumn.

Autumn nodded. "We'll do that."

Sister Lou allowed herself a brief sigh of relief, but she kept her wits at the ready. They'd resolved this dispute, which allowed them to move on with the retreat planning. But with Sister Marianna's penchant for arguing and Autumn's tendency to respond with equal and opposing enthusiasm, this wouldn't be the only conflict she'd have to mediate. She didn't think the event was out of the woods yet. *Pun intended.*

"How's your apartment search going?" Sister Lou's question carried back to Shari as she followed the older woman to an empty table near a window toward the center of the Briar Coast Café Friday afternoon. Her lunch companion's multi-fabric skirt suit was a calming tan that matched her sedate cream flats.

"I haven't found anything that I can see myself staying in for a whole year." Shari took a deep breath of the intoxicating aromas that were a part of the café: fresh bread, confectioners' sugar, and strong coffee.

They settled at a recently vacated pale wood table.

Shari bowed her head and waited for Sister Lou to say the grace over their meal. Before meeting the Catholic sister a little more than two months ago, Shari had never said grace over her food, not even when she'd lived with the religious fanatic foster mother. Now, she couldn't imagine eating a meal without giving thanks.

Sister Lou sprinkled the serving of vinaigrette dressing over her house salad. "It'll take some time. You've only been looking for a few weeks."

Shari nodded as she considered her friend seated across the table from her. Sister Lou's black eyebrows arched above calm, almond-shaped onyx eyes. With her smooth, gently rounded cinnamon cheeks, delicate chin, petite nose, and full pink lips, she appeared at least a decade younger than her sixty-three years. Must be all that chai tea and her regular morning jogs with Sister Carmen.

Shari's gaze dipped to her lunch tray: house salad, chicken and wild rice soup, and fresh lemonade. She was eating healthier meals now, too. Her new friend was a powerful—if subtle—role model. Shari also started on the salad first, pouring a generous amount of honey mustard dressing over the bowl of vegetables. "I'm not sure what I'm looking for."

"Did you make a list of the features you want?" Sister Lou asked between forkfuls of salad.

"Yes, I've even watched some of those house-hunting shows." Shari shrugged a shoulder. "I just don't know what I want."

She glanced out the window beside their table. It was a bright autumn day. The sky was a cool blue liberally dotted with fat clouds. A few red, orange, and yellow leaves clung determinedly to the trees that edged the sidewalk. Despite the day's cheery appearance, her spirits were flagging.

Shari ate a forkful of her salad. She couldn't see her sage green car in the parking lot. She'd pulled into a space too far away. But she spotted Sister Lou's sedan. She considered the vivid orange compact before shifting her attention to her friend's tan skirt suit and the crimson Timex watch on her wrist. Her friend had a lot of hidden depth.

"You were right when you suggested I spend time learning more about myself." Shari stabbed her fork into her salad bowl, picking up more lettuce, carrots, cucumbers, and celery.

"What have you discovered?" Sister Lou started on her chicken and vegetable soup.

"I can play well with others, at least when I try. That was a surprise." A reluctant smile curved her lips.

The lights in Sister Lou's onyx eyes danced with amusement. "What else?"

Shari glanced around the café as she considered her answer. As usual, the establishment was packed with customers either dining in or collecting takeout. Small groups gathered around the pale wood tables lined up across the café's white-tiled flooring. Their animated conversations and boisterous laughter filled the room. A few solo customers were reading the *Telegraph* or working on their computer tablets.

She split her attention between Sister Lou and her bowl of soup. "I'm finding out what I want and what

I don't want for my future. Where I am and where I want to go."

"Good for you." A glint of admiration lit Sister Lou's eyes. "But before you start planning too far into the future, you should come to terms with your past. Take time to appreciate who you are and how you got here."

Shari felt the weight of her friend's advice. "This is all new territory for me. I have a lot of questions."

"I might be able to help with some. What are they?"

Shari's attention dipped to the blue, gold, and white Hermionean cross pinned to Sister Lou's suit jacket lapel. "How do I know whether the *Telegraph*'s where I'm supposed to be?"

The pause that followed her question was several seconds longer than Shari had expected.

Finally, Sister Lou responded. "How does your job make you feel? Is it fulfilling? Are you making a positive impact on your community? You have to decide what's important to you, and only you can answer that. Remember, the *Telegraph* may be right for you now, but things change. You may want other challenges in the future."

Shari nodded. "I know that I like it here. I've lived in a lot of big cities. I'm surprised that I'm so comfortable in a small town."

"I know what you mean." Sister Lou flashed her warm smile. "Briar Coast is very different from Los Angeles. It's cold, but I love it here."

"I like my friendship with you and Chris. I've never

had real friends before. I'm not even sure I'm any good at being one." A hot blush rose in Shari's neck.

Sister Lou reached across the table to give Shari's forearm a comforting squeeze. "You're doing just fine. We enjoy your friendship, too."

"How will I know when I've attained this exalted level of self-awareness?" Shari had never felt so frustrated. She didn't know what she didn't know and she couldn't find the questions to get her answers.

"At the risk of sounding very Zen-like, self-awareness isn't a destination. It's a journey." Sister Lou sat back on her chair across the table. "Shari, you're not the same person you were last year or even six months ago. And six months from now, you'll be someone else again. And so will I."

"Mind. Blown." Shari tapped her temples with her fingertips. "What does that mean?"

"If we're not learning, we're not living." Sister Lou spread her hands, her soup apparently forgotten. "Every day, we learn something new about ourselves. As we add to our self-awareness, we adjust to what we've learned. It changes us, and that's a good thing."

"This is a lot to absorb." Shari sighed. "I may not have the patience for it."

Sister Lou's eyes glittered with suppressed humor. "Baby steps, Shari. Let's just start with today."

"May I have a moment, Lou?" Sister Barbara Yates paused in the threshold of Sister Lou's office.

"Of course." Sister Lou glanced at her wristwatch. It was after five o'clock on Friday afternoon. How did it get to be so late?

She closed the electronic file she'd been updating on her computer, then turned to face Sister Barbara.

The congregation's prioress strode to one of the well-cushioned powder blue and honey wood guest chairs in front of Sister Lou's desk. In her moss green blazer, white blouse, and black slacks, she looked as fresh and crisp at the end of the day as she'd appeared when Sister Lou had seen her earlier this morning.

"You looked so focused on what you were doing, I hated to interrupt you." Sister Barbara winked at Sister Lou as she settled onto the chair closest to the wall. Her hazel green eyes were warm behind her silver-rimmed glasses. Her graying chestnut hair framed her round face.

"I don't mind the interruption." Sister Lou braced herself for what she suspected would be a delicate conversation. "What can I do for you, Barb?"

Sister Barbara crossed her legs and settled more comfortably on her chair. "How would you assess the progress on the retreat planning?"

Sister Lou had anticipated this question. Why else would the prioress seek her out at the end of the workweek? Sister Barbara's eyes were kind and her voice was gentle, but Sister Lou sensed a trap. "Have you had a chance to speak with Marianna? She's the project lead."

"Yes, I spoke with Marianna earlier today. She

assured me that the retreat's on schedule." Sister Barbara's sharp eyes kept a close watch on Sister Lou's expression. "Is it?"

She needed to buy time while she considered her answer. Sister Lou took a drink of chai tea from her half-full white porcelain mug. She grimaced. It had grown cold.

"As of today, we're a little behind schedule." Her stomach muscles knotted at contradicting Sister Marianna, but she wouldn't lie to Sister Barbara. "I believe, however, that we can make up the time. Also, we're well under budget."

"That's good news about the budget." Sister Barbara looked pleased. "Why are we behind schedule?"

Sister Lou felt like a schoolgirl being pressured to be a tattletale against a classmate. She wished Sister Marianna had had this conversation with Sister Barbara. But since she hadn't, Sister Lou forced herself to sit still and maintain eye contact with the prioress. "There was a disagreement about the retreat menu. It's been resolved, but we're a couple of days—less than a week—behind. We'll make up the time, though."

Sister Barbara's eyes were dark with concern. Was it caused by the project delay—or was she troubled that Sister Marianna hadn't mentioned it herself?

"What are your impressions of Marianna's event management style?"

Oh boy. The questions weren't getting any easier, were they? "Marianna's very well organized and detail oriented. She's decisive—"

"You know that's not what I meant, Lou. Marianna was quite upset about the survey results for the menu. Did her disappointment cause a problem during your meeting with the resort owner?"

That's an understatement. Sister Lou struggled to control her expression under Sister Barbara's scrutiny. "We came up with a compromise."

"We?" Sister Barbara sighed. "Lou, everyone knows that Marianna's temper can be a problem. That's one of the reasons I asked you to partner with her on this project. I knew I could count on your diplomacy to keep things moving forward."

"What was the other reason?"

"Marianna needed a project partner that she couldn't push around. You're the only member of the congregation who won't hesitate to challenge her."

Sister Carmen was right about the reason Sister Barbara had asked her to work with Sister Marianna. Her friend wouldn't let her forget it. "Marianna's doing a good job with the retreat."

"I'd hoped some of your diplomacy would rub off on her." Sister Barbara lowered her gaze. Her attention seemed far away. "Marianna's temper not only reflects poorly on her, but it could hurt the congregation's image. I've asked her to remember that when she's interacting with the community."

"We're past the decision-making part of the retreat planning. We shouldn't have any further disagreements."

Sister Barbara looked askance at Sister Lou. "What are the chances of that with Marianna's involvement?"

Good point. "Perhaps we're not putting Marianna's strengths to their best use. Not everyone's a diplomat."

Sister Barbara's expression brightened. "You have an excellent point. Do you have any suggestions?"

An image of Sister Marianna wearing boxing gloves came to mind. That particular talent wouldn't be appropriate for the congregation, though. "Let me think on it."

Chapter 7

Where is Autumn?

Sister Lou stood on the other side of Autumn's closed office door Monday morning. She knocked for a third time, then leaned forward, listening for sounds beyond the door. According to her watch, it was a few minutes before nine a.m., their agreed-upon meeting time, but Autumn had assured her that she routinely started work hours earlier than that.

Sister Lou glanced up and down the empty, walnut wood hallway. *What should I do now?*

She'd come to the resort alone again. She'd intended only to give Autumn the draft of the retreat presentation schedule. She and Sister Marianna were even more anxious to get the event back on schedule after Sister Barbara's feedback Friday. Sister Lou also wanted to collect Sister Marianna's scarf, which the other woman had left in Autumn's office Friday.

Two doors down the hall, Sister Lou noted light spilling from an open office. She walked past two closed doors and a supply room before coming to a stop in front of a spacious office.

She recognized Rita Morris, Autumn's business partner, seated behind the desk. She knocked briefly against the door. "Good morning, Ms. Morris. I don't know if you remember me. I'm Sister Lou LaSalle. I have a nine o'clock appointment with Autumn. Do you know where she might be?"

Rita rose and walked to Sister Lou, right hand outstretched. Her navy A-line dress ended just above her knees and was coupled with a pale silver blazer. "Sister Lou, of course I remember you. How are the plans progressing for your congregation's retreat?"

Sister Lou temporarily dampened her concern over Autumn's absence and accepted Rita's hand. "Everything's progressing very well. I have a copy of the event schedule to share with Autumn."

"I'm surprised Autumn's not in her office." Rita checked the time on her cell phone, then walked past Sister Lou and down the hall.

Sister Lou followed her to Autumn's office and waited while this time the business partner knocked.

"Autumn, are you there?" Rita pressed her ear to the door.

Nothing.

Rita waited several seconds before knocking again, this time harder. She raised her voice. "Autumn, Sister Lou LaSalle is here for your meeting."

Again nothing.

Rita seemed uneasy as she turned back to Sister Lou. "This is so odd. It's not like her at all. She must still be in her cabin."

"*Her* cabin?" Sister Lou walked with Rita down the hall to the reception area.

"She has her own cabin on the premises. This resort really is her life. She breathes, eats, and sleeps it." Rita stopped beside the registration desk and glanced at Kelsey. "Have you seen Autumn this morning?"

Kelsey looked up, startled. "No, I haven't. I thought she was in her office. Is something wrong?"

Rita turned away from Kelsey and drummed her long, black-polished nails against the chest-high walnut wood desk. Her manner was dismissive. It was clear that Rita didn't have the warm relationship with Kelsey that Autumn had.

Sister Lou responded to the administrative assistant. "I had a nine a.m. meeting with Autumn but she's not here. Perhaps she's running late."

"But Autumn's never late." Kelsey's voice was thin. Her blue eyes darkened with concern.

"Could you try reaching her on her personal phone?" Sister Lou looked from Kelsey to Rita.

The business partner pulled her cell phone from her blazer pocket. She pushed two buttons, then held the device to her ear. Rita's blond hair was stylishly piled on top of her head. Wispy strands framed her triangular face.

Standing between the two women, Sister Lou sensed Rita's impatience as she waited for Autumn to answer. Kelsey's anxiety was like a physical presence moving among them. Sister Lou's own concern weighed on her.

Within seconds, Rita disconnected the call. "It went into her voice mail." Her gusty sigh revealed confusion and frustration. "Wait here. I'm getting my car keys."

"Where are you going?" Kelsey was startled.

"Sister Lou and I are going to her cabin." Rita walked past her and back toward her office.

We are?

Sister Lou was surprised but grateful to be invited along. She didn't want to leave without knowing whether Autumn was all right. Her watch read almost a quarter after the nine o'clock hour. The resort owner had never been late for their meetings. A long list of tasks waited for Sister Lou in her office, but she wouldn't be able to concentrate on any of them.

"I'm really worried about Autumn." Kelsey's quiet admission touched Sister Lou.

"Perhaps she slept in because she's not feeling well."

"She would've called." Kelsey turned her anxious eyes to Sister Lou. "She's been under a lot of stress. Rita's really pressuring her to sell the resort."

That's not a good sign. "Is the resort not doing well?"

Kelsey gave a quick shrug. "I really think Rita just wants the money. She's usually not here before noon. I was really surprised to see her here so early this morning. But Autumn really loves this place. She really wants to keep it, and I really want to keep my job."

"Hopefully, Autumn was exhausted and just

overslept." Sister Lou couldn't think of anything else to say.

"I really hope so." Kelsey continued in a low voice, "I really like working for Autumn. She's so nice. Rita's hardly ever here but when she is, she acts like I really don't matter."

Sister Lou was still searching for a response when Rita's voice sounded behind her.

"Let's go." She strode past Sister Lou toward the front door without even a glance in Kelsey's direction.

Sister Lou pressed Kelsey's hand where it lay on the registration desk. "Everything will work out."

She followed Rita to a torch red Chevrolet Corvette. "That's your car?"

"Yes." Rita seemed distracted as she deactivated the car alarm and pulled open the driver's door.

Sister Lou touched the hood of the Corvette. It was cold, reflecting the brisk late-autumn weather. Its sleek, aerodynamic lines promised a thrilling, powerful ride. Its wide, sculpted headlights hinted at danger. The jet-black leather bucket seats invited her to share the adventure. Sister Lou settled onto the passenger seat and resisted the temptation to ask Rita if she could drive.

Rita shifted the automatic engine into gear. It purred like a satisfied cat. "It's not a long walk, but it's a quicker drive. Besides, it's too cold to walk."

"I don't mind the ride." Sister Lou tried to mask her excitement over her first ride in an expensive sports car. The vehicle looked and smelled new.

Rita zipped backward out of the parking space. With a quick tap of the brake and a jerk of the transmission, they took off over the asphalt surface. The road from the main cabin to the private lodgings was wide enough for only two cars and a very few courageous pedestrians. Rita was a confident, commanding driver. She made quick work of the trip. A slight smile curved Sister Lou's lips. She wondered if Rita would let her drive them back to the main cabin.

Rita jumped the asphalt path and drove up a graveled driveway. In front of them, a single-story log cabin with a gable roof stood about three football fields from the main cabin. With the walnut wood cottage-style structure nestled against a backdrop of stately old trees, the scene looked as though it had been teleported from a Walt Disney animated feature film. Sister Lou looked around for the magical beings and talking animals.

Rita turned off the engine, then climbed from the car. Sister Lou did the same. Her anxiety returned as she wondered again why Autumn hadn't been in her office. The air was light and brisk, and swollen with the scents of moist earth and aging leaves.

Sister Lou followed Rita across the lawn. A row of miniature barberry bushes grew on either side of the front of the cabin. Two steps lifted them to the porch, which stretched the width of the cabin. To the right was a dark walnut–stained porch swing. In addition, there were six matching rocking chairs, three on either end. That was a lot of seating. How much entertaining did Autumn do?

Five large pots of coleus plants congregated on the left side of the porch: red, rose, pink, maroon, and yellow. Wasn't it late in the season for coleus? But the plants seemed to be thriving.

Rita didn't look toward the chairs, the swing, or the coleus pots. She walked directly to the door. Then froze.

The first stirrings of unease tousled the hair at the nape of Sister Lou's neck. "What is it?"

Rita turned toward her. Her brown eyes were wide with dismay. "The door's open."

Chapter 8

Sister Lou's heart sprang into her throat and stayed there. Rita was frozen in Autumn's doorway. Sister Lou stood just behind her. But the scene in front of them pulled her back to the Sleep Ease Inn Hotel, back to the room in which Maurice had been murdered. She fought to stay in the present. Autumn needed her. Rita needed her. She couldn't give in to the echoes of her grief. No, not yet.

Autumn's cabin looked like the Tasmanian Devil had thrown a tantrum all over it. Furniture in the front room had been upended. Dark, patterned cushions were ripped from the sofa, ripped from the armchairs, and tossed to the hardwood floor.

She exchanged a panicked look with Rita.

"Autumn?" Rita shouted as she rushed into the cabin.

Sister Lou followed her. Together, they hurried through the dwelling, shouting Autumn's name. With each step, Sister Lou's heart beat faster. Images of Maurice clung to her mind.

Please. Don't let this be a repeat of that day. Please.

The scene from the front room had been replayed in both bedrooms, bathrooms, the dining room, and kitchen. Drawers jerked open, their contents tossed to the floor. Closets ransacked. Mattresses stripped and flipped. Sister Lou and Rita raced to the Corvette and sped back to the main cabin.

"Where could she be?" Panic lifted Rita's voice several octaves.

"Why would someone toss her home?" Sister Lou's mind spun.

Who had broken into Autumn's home?

When did this happen?

What were they looking for—and had they found it?

Rita didn't return to her parking space. She jerked to a stop in front of the main cabin and threw herself from the car. She jogged to the entrance. Sister Lou followed close behind.

Rita shoved the door open and rushed to the registration desk. Her actions drew the attention of several guests. "Someone broke into Autumn's cabin."

Kelsey's hand flew to cover her mouth. The color leached from her face. "Oh no."

"Autumn wasn't there." Sister Lou strained to sound reassuring, but her words shook. "Can you let us into her office?"

Kelsey fumbled in one of the drawers before retrieving a thick set of keys. She passed the set to Sister Lou, leading with the key that would unlock Autumn's office.

"Shouldn't we call the sheriff's office?" Rita sounded frazzled as she followed Sister Lou down the hall.

"Unless she had another appointment—and I don't believe she did—there are only two places Autumn would be at this time of day, her office or her home." Sister Lou shoved the key into the lock and turned it. "She's not in her home."

She took a moment to square her shoulders and brace herself. *Please let Autumn be all right.* Then she threw open the door.

God answers all prayers. But sometimes, His answer is no.

Autumn was sprawled on her brown faux leather executive chair behind her desk. Her skin was pale. Her expression was frozen. Her mouth hung open as though she were still gasping for breath. But it was Autumn's periwinkle blue eyes that traced a cold chill down Sister Lou's spine. They were wide and sightless, staring past the ceiling as though asking God, "Why?"

Later Monday morning, Sheriff's Deputy Ted Tate entered the resort's conference room, where Sister Lou waited with Kelsey and Rita. "Sister Louise LaSalle, two murders in Briar Coast in three months—and you're on-site for both of them."

"It's an unhappy coincidence, Deputy." Sister Lou's gaze moved to Ted's partner, Sheriff's Deputy Fran Cole, who stood in silent disapproval beside him. Other deputies were processing the crime scene.

The law enforcement officers carried their brown felt campaign hats. Fran looked sharp in her uniform of brown winter jacket, tan shirt, black tie, and spruce green gabardine pants. Ted looked like he'd slept in his.

He folded his arms over his burly chest. "No such thing as coincidences."

Kelsey's gasp of surprise cut across the abrupt silence. She'd reacted as though the statement had been meant for her.

Ted's pale gray eyes zeroed in on the hapless administrative assistant before returning his attention to Sister Lou. "So what happened? You weren't able to solve this one so you thought you'd tap us in?"

Sister Lou chose not to respond to the taunt. Why encourage Ted or the wrestling references that he obviously didn't expect her to understand? Instead, she observed the other women seated around the dark wood table on matching scarlet velvet-padded seats. She'd arrived almost an hour ago to give Autumn documents for the congregation's retreat— and to retrieve Sister Marianna's scarf. Instead, she'd found herself in the middle of a homicide investigation. Another one. Sister Lou didn't know Autumn well, but she grieved for her tragic death.

She sipped the coffee Kelsey had offered her. Its warmth helped to steady her nerves. At least her hands weren't shaking as much. The scents of cedarwood and fresh pine needles that filled the resort also helped.

"Are comments like those even necessary?" Rita spoke in a tone laden with disgust.

"You must not have heard of Sister Lou. She's a famous crime fighter." Ted's hard gray stare bored into Sister Lou. The deputy could hold a grudge. It had been a month since her friend's murder had been solved. Wasn't it time for Ted to let go of his resentment over her role in the investigation?

"Why don't you show some respect?" Rita's cool tone could frost a margarita glass. "My business partner's lying dead in a room down the hall and you're in here playing games with us."

"She's right, Ted. Give it a rest." Fran rested a hand on one of her partner's thick shoulders, before addressing the room. Her touch seemed to pull him back from the edge. "I'm Deputy Fran Cole and this is Deputy Ted Tate. We're sorry for your loss. We just have a couple of questions for you about your boss and what happened here."

"She wasn't my boss." Rita took a deep breath as though trying to calm down. "As I said, we were business partners."

"You're Ms. Morris, right?" Fran waited for Rita's nod of confirmation. "Then we'll start with you. How long were you and Ms. Tassler partners?"

"Autumn and I started our resort about three years ago. I had the connections. She had the business degrees. We both had the money."

Fran's eyes were glued to her notepad as she scribbled across the page. "When last did you see her?"

"We spoke on Thursday." Rita gave a restless shrug. "It was about five o'clock."

Kelsey sent Rita, seated beside her, a quick, curious look before lowering her gaze to her lap. Had she noticed as Sister Lou had that Rita didn't say she'd *seen* Autumn, only that they'd spoken? Did that mean she hadn't gone to the resort on Friday?

"You didn't see her at all on Friday?" Sister Lou hadn't meant to ask the question aloud. Was this another example of Shari rubbing off on her?

"Sister, we'll ask the questions." Fran's interjection barely covered Ted's snort of disgust. "Ms. Morris, did you see Ms. Tassler at all on Friday?"

Rita shook her head. "I don't usually come into the office on Fridays."

"So you haven't seen her in at least three days." Fran slid a glance in Sister Lou's direction as she continued to take notes. "What did you talk about?"

"Just business." Rita's sigh was equal parts frustration and impatience.

What about the business? Did Rita and Autumn have another disagreement about selling the resort? Sister Lou's thoughts came to a halt. She wouldn't ask the question. The deputies had already chastised her for her previous interference. Hopefully, Fran would get Rita to elaborate on her response.

But she didn't. The deputy let Rita's ambiguity stand unquestioned.

Fran continued questioning Rita. "How did Ms. Tassler seem during your conversation?"

Rita shrugged a shoulder. "She seemed like her normal self."

Tension in the room was rising. Was it coming from Rita or Kelsey—or both?

Fran directed her next questions to Kelsey. "Who're you and what's your role here?"

Kelsey seemed surprised by the deputies' attention. "I'm . . . Kelsey Bennett. I'm . . . I was . . .

Autumn's administrative . . . well, her assistant, really. At the desk. Really at the front desk."

"For how long?" Fran's eyebrows knitted. She appeared impatient with the other woman's hesitations.

Rita sighed and straightened on her chair. "Why do you care about our jobs? What do these questions have to do with *anything*, much less finding whoever killed Autumn? Isn't that what you're *supposed* to be trying to do?"

Ted tore his gaze from Sister Lou long enough to answer Rita's question. "We need this background information to help with our investigation. Is that all right with you or do you have someplace else to be?"

Rita growled back, "No, it's not all right with me, but do I have a choice?"

Was Rita hoping to return to her office before telling the deputies that she'd wanted to sell the resort? Why would she withhold that information—unless she thought her candor would take her to the top of the deputies' suspects list?

Kelsey interrupted the tense exchange. "I worked for Autumn for really like almost a year." Her voice rose on the last word as though she was asking Fran a question rather than answering one. "Her last admin got another job, but really I'm sure it wasn't because of Autumn. She's a really great boss. Or she *was* . . . really . . . great. She treated everyone with respect." Again her voice lifted as though she was asking rather than answering.

There was something Kelsey wasn't telling them. It was there in her speech, which was even less confident than usual. It was in her unsteady gaze, which followed a continuous flight path from her lap to Sister Lou to the wall and back again, never landing on either of the deputies. Was Autumn's confrontation with her cousin, January Potts, weighing on the administrative assistant's mind? It was weighing on Sister Lou's.

Fran turned the page on her notepad. "When was the last time *you* saw her?"

"Friday?" Kelsey nodded as though emphasizing her certainty. "Autumn worked really long hours. She was always the first to arrive and the last to leave. I really tried to get in when she did or to stay as late as she did, but I really couldn't do it. Those were really long days."

"How did she seem on Friday?" Fran crossed her arms as though admitting defeat to Kelsey's nervous chatter.

Kelsey took a moment to consider the question. "She seemed the way she normally seemed: really busy but also really focused. But she really seemed her usual self. I really think she ate, drank, and slept business." She sounded as though she admired that about Autumn.

There was that phrase again, *her usual self.* What did it mean? Was Autumn happy, sad, anxious, relaxed, focused, distracted? Why wasn't anyone else curious about what her state of mind could tell them about her murder?

"Thank you, Kelsey. Really." Fran turned another page in her notepad. Sister Lou wondered whether she was the only one who caught the subtle insult of Kelsey's speech pattern. "Sister Lou—"

Ted cut Fran off. "Why are you here?"

The question came at her like a bullet. Was the deputy still trying to unsettle her? It wouldn't work. Sister Lou met Ted's still, stern gaze. "I had a nine a.m. meeting with Autumn. Her resort has contracted with the congregation to host our retreat."

"You in charge of the retreat?" Ted continued his rapid-fire delivery.

Sister Lou would not be intimidated. She sipped her coffee and took her time answering. "Marianna and I are working on it together."

"When did you make this appointment?" Ted sounded as though he didn't believe there had been a scheduled meeting.

"I called Autumn about it on Friday." Sister Lou held up one hand, palm out. "And before you ask, she sounded a bit distracted but otherwise she seemed her *usual self.*" She emphasized those two words, which Rita and Kelsey also had used. The reference was lost on her audience.

Ted studied Sister Lou for several long minutes. Was he expecting her to crack under his silent intimidation? Sister Lou sipped more coffee and maintained eye contact.

Finally, Ted inclined his head at Fran. His partner returned the gesture, then directed a question to the room at large. "Did Autumn have conflicts with anyone or do you know whether anyone would want to hurt her?"

Sister Lou's attention flew to Rita. Would the

victim's business partner mention Montgomery Crane's interest in the resort?

"No, I can't imagine anyone wanting to hurt Autumn, much less kill her." Rita looked horrified.

Sister Lou swung her gaze to Kelsey. Would the victim's assistant tell the deputies about January Potts's vicious verbal attack?

"Neither can I, really. Autumn was a really wonderful boss." Kelsey looked distressed.

Sister Lou blinked her surprise. What had just happened? Were Rita and Kelsey so certain that the encounters Autumn had with her cousin and Montgomery Crane had no bearing on her murder? Then why couldn't Sister Lou shake the feeling that the other women were hiding something?

Fran turned to Sister Lou. "What about you, Sister? Can you think of anyone who'd want to hurt Ms. Tassler?"

Sister Lou exchanged a look with the other two witnesses. There was a reason Rita and Kelsey weren't speaking up. For now, neither would she. "I'm afraid I didn't know Autumn well."

That admission will come back to bite me.

Chapter 9

"There's been another murder." Shari rushed into Diego's office at the *Telegraph* after lunch Monday. She was shocked and saddened by the news. She also was determined to do an even better job with the coverage of this tragedy than she'd done with the previous one just a month ago.

Diego had been eating lunch while working at his desk. He put down his sandwich, hit a couple of keys, then turned his executive chair to face Shari. Concern darkened his eyes. "Who's the victim?"

Shari's fingers dug into the top of one of his gray guest chairs. "Autumn Tassler. She owned the Briar Coast Cabin Resort on the northeast side of town."

"I've heard of it. It opened about three years ago." His frown deepened. "She was murdered? What happened?"

"Sister Lou said—"

"Sister Lou found this murder victim as well?"

Shari knew how it must seem. "Her nephew, Chris, told me she had a meeting with Tassler this morning. She's pretty shaken up." And, from the sound of his voice, so was Chris. He probably was having flashbacks to the last time his aunt had found a dead body. It had been a tragedy for his aunt and scary for Chris.

Shari had left a message for Sister Lou on her office voice mail, expressing her concern. She also asked Sister Lou to call when she felt up to it. She didn't know when that would be, but Shari's primary concern was her friend's well-being.

Sister Lou hadn't told Chris much about what had happened, only that she and Autumn's business partner had found the body. The administrative assistant had called the deputies. Unfortunately, Deputy Fran Cole and Deputy Ted Tate had been dispatched to the resort. They'd processed the crime scenes—Autumn's office and her private cabin—and questioned Sister Lou and several of the resort employees, including the partner and administrative assistant.

"I'd be pretty shaken up, too, if I kept finding dead bodies." Diego had loosened his emerald green tie over his crisp cream shirt. Otherwise, he looked as pressed and polished as though he'd just walked out of his house. "There have been three murders in Briar Coast in the last eight years and Sister Lou has discovered two of the three bodies."

"That's not fair." Shari's defense of Sister Lou was reflexive. "The first murder occurred before Sister Lou'd even moved to Briar Coast, and she solved the second one."

"You're right."

Diego's calm acquiescence to the points she'd made went a long way toward soothing Shari's ruffled feathers.

She crossed her arms over her thick violet knit sweater. "I want to cover this story."

"Of course. You did a good job covering the last murder." Diego sat back on his gray cloth chair. Shari wasn't fooled. His pose seemed casual but his gaze was intent. "Are the same deputies working this case?"

"Yes, Cole and Tate."

Diego winced. "Are they still freezing you out because of the last investigation?"

"They're starting to warm up to me." Shari spoke with more confidence than she felt. "I left a voice mail message for both deputies before I came to your office. Hopefully, one of them will return my call."

"I hope so, too. We have to include comments from the sheriff's office in any article we write about this investigation."

Shari stiffened. "Will you pull the story from me if I can't get quotes from them?"

He leveled a look at her. "Don't let it come to that."

"I could report that the deputies refused to comment for the article."

Diego's head was shaking before she finished her thought. "We can't use 'refused to comment.' It's not just about a quote. We need them to provide us with substantive information, progress on the case, anything that will help our community remain vigilant and safe. Maybe one of our readers has information that could solve the murder."

Shari shoved her fists into the front pockets of her rose-colored slacks. "Those deputies can hold a grudge."

Her article detailing the outcome of the last murder—and Sister Lou's role in solving the case—had made the front page of *The Briar Coast Telegraph* at the end of September. There was a direct correlation between the timing of her story and the silent treatment she continued to receive from Fran and Ted.

At least they were taking her calls now after weeks of pouting, but the conversations were one-sided. Shari did most of the talking while the deputies provided one-word answers and grunts.

The thought of dealing with the ticked-off deputies caused Shari's homemade ham-and-cheese sandwich to sit like a rock in her gut. "I can't make the deputies talk to me."

"Yes, you can. If your usual confrontational tactics don't work, try something unusual—being nice."

Shari scowled at her editor's attempt at humor. "This story's on the clock. I don't have that much time."

"We're rebuilding our reputation as a serious and thorough source of local news for our community." Diego spread his hands. "We can't publish crime stories without input from the crime fighters. It'll damage our credibility."

"I'll make it work." Shari strode out of Diego's office.

Everything was finally starting to go her way. She couldn't let Fran's and Ted's hurt feelings impede her covering this story. She had to find a way to reconcile with them. It wasn't just about this story. Her entire career depended on it.

"Autumn's dead?" Sister Marianna's thin lips parted in surprise. "How?"

"That's terrible." Sister Barbara's eyes darkened with concern. "What happened?"

As soon as she'd returned to work, Sister Lou had asked Sister Marianna to meet with her in Sister Barbara's office. She'd wanted to deliver the sad news to both women at the same time.

Sister Lou looked from Sister Marianna beside her to Sister Barbara. The prioress was behind her oak desk, which was a larger version of Sister Lou's desk. "The deputies believe someone choked Autumn in her office probably late yesterday evening. The cause and time of her death will be confirmed with her autopsy."

"Oh, I'm so sorry to hear about this." Sister Barbara adjusted her silver-rimmed glasses. "I'm certain her business partner and employees are badly shaken by her murder."

"They're shocked and upset." Sister Lou's hands were still shaking. She was more disturbed by the morning's events than she'd thought. She clasped her hands together on her lap to stop the tremors from spreading.

"Who are the deputies assigned to the investigation?" Sister Marianna sounded as though she knew the answer to her question.

Sister Lou imagined her answer would confirm her project partner's suspicions. "Deputies Fran Cole and Ted Tate."

Sister Barbara frowned. "Aren't they the same deputies who investigated Maurice Jordan's murder?"

"Yes, they are." Sister Lou didn't mask her unease.

Sister Marianna sniffed. "I certainly hope they'll do a better job with this investigation than they did with the last."

Sister Lou cleared her throat. "I'm sure the deputies will bring the murderer to justice shortly. I left after they questioned me. But they were still gathering information from Autumn's employees. Other deputies were going over her office and cabin."

"They interrogated you?" Sister Marianna's reaction was sharp. "What did they ask?"

"They were very basic questions." Sister Lou tried to sound reassuring. "Why was I meeting with Autumn? When last had I seen her? Was I aware of any problems she was having?"

"Why would they ask you about her problems?" Sister Marianna exhaled an irritated breath. "How could you know something like that? We're her clients, not her confessors."

Sister Lou stared through the picture window that spanned the opposite wall as she considered Sister Marianna's questions. How could she have insight into Autumn's personal life? Yet she knew Autumn's cousin had threatened to kill her. She also was aware of the tension between Autumn and Rita. What she couldn't explain was why neither Kelsey nor Rita had offered those insights, or why she was so certain they were withholding other information.

Sister Lou pulled her gaze from the view of deep green grass and ancient oaks outside Sister Barbara's window. "Those are probably their standard questions."

"Then that explains why they have a hard time solving cases." Sister Marianna's tone was as dry as dust. "I remember how *rude* they were when they interrogated us about Dr. Jordan's murder."

When Sister Marianna made up her mind, she couldn't be swayed from her opinion, and in her opinion, the deputies were inept. Sister Lou wouldn't waste time trying to convince Sister Marianna otherwise. She'd have better luck changing the course of an aircraft carrier.

She turned to Sister Barbara. "I don't mean to seem insensitive, but in light of this tragedy, we should consider whether we'll need to postpone the retreat."

"Yes, you're quite right." Sister Marianna inclined her head. "I'll contact Autumn's partner in the morning."

"In the meantime, I'll send an e-mail to the community asking for prayers for Autumn Tassler and her loved ones." Sister Barbara made a note on the yellow writing tablet beside her phone. The top sheet was a running to-do list. She'd crossed off tasks she'd completed, but the list seemed never-ending.

"That's a wonderful idea. Thank you, Barb." Sister Lou stood, turning to Sister Marianna. "I'll wait for you to let me know if we're going to reschedule the retreat or move forward with it."

The meeting over, Sister Lou turned to leave the office.

"Lou." Sister Barbara's voice stopped her. "Are you all right?"

Sister Lou forced a smile. "I will be." *Once the memories of Maurice's murder scene and now Autumn's recede.* Hopefully, that would be soon.

"I thought you said you were going to rest." Chris strode into Sister Lou's office Monday afternoon.

Sister Lou looked up from the document she was reviewing. "No, *you* said I was going to rest. I said I had work to do."

Although I don't seem to be getting much done.

She'd spent the past almost ten minutes staring at the first page of the report she'd printed.

Sister Lou checked her crimson wristwatch. *It's only noon?* The entire ordeal at the Briar Coast Cabin Resort had taken less than two hours but had felt like an entire day.

The window to her left framed a beautiful fall day. Early-afternoon sunlight stretched across her L-shaped oak wood desk. The smaller window behind her added to the natural light filling her office. Outside, the sky was a warm, rich blue. Fluffy, round, paper white clouds floated above the horizon. The scene added to the tragedy of Autumn's murder. Sister Lou said another quick prayer for the deceased resort owner's peaceful transition.

"Aunt Lou, you're not a machine." Chris hooked his black jacket to the back of one of the guest chairs in front of Sister Lou's desk, then settled onto its thick cushion. His cream cotton shirt was the perfect backdrop for his brown-and-cream-striped necktie. "You had a traumatic morning. You should give yourself some time to unwind and clear your mind before you jump back into work."

"Sweetie, I appreciate your concern, but this isn't the first time I've found a dead body." It didn't get easier, though. The loss of life and especially the rage behind both murderous acts were chilling.

"I know." His voice and expression were grim. "I also know you're still coming to terms with Maurice's murder. That probably added to the trauma of finding Autumn Tassler's body."

An image of Autumn's lifeless body slouched on her executive chair flashed across Sister Lou's mind. She flinched. "Yes, it did." Sister Lou lowered the printouts she'd been holding, amazed at the creases her fingers had formed along the edges.

"Why don't you tell Sister Barbara that you're going to take the afternoon off?"

"I'd much rather work, Chris. I don't want to spend the rest of the day wandering my rooms reliving the events of this morning—or the events surrounding Mo's murder."

Chris rubbed a hand across his eyes. "I hate that you're caught up in another murder."

"This isn't like the last time. I'm saddened that

someone killed Autumn. It was an evil deed and it shouldn't happen to anyone. But I'm not personally connected to her as I was with Mo."

Chris looked skeptical but he let the matter drop. "Did you speak with Sister Marianna?"

Sister Lou nodded. "And with Barb. They're going to make the decision whether to postpone the retreat."

"All right." Chris stood, collecting his jacket from the back of the chair. "I wanted to check on you. I hadn't really expected you to be resting. Are you up to having lunch?"

"No, thank you. I might grab something later."

"Don't skip lunch," Chris chastised as he shrugged into his jacket.

"I wish you wouldn't worry."

He came around her desk and bent to kiss her cheek. "I worry because I love you. Call if you need anything. I'm just across the parking lot."

Sister Lou smiled. His office was a little farther away than that. She stood to hug him. "I will. I promise. And thank you." After one last tight squeeze, she stepped back.

She watched her nephew leave her office. They were all that was left of their family. That was another reason these terrible tragedies resonated with them.

Sister Lou settled back onto her chair. Still, this case was different from Maurice's murder. For one thing, she wouldn't have to deal with Deputy Fran Cole or Deputy Ted Tate. She took a moment to thank God for mercies great and small.

Chapter 10

"Are you sure you're up to talking about it again, Sister Lou?" Shari sat on one of the chairs opposite Sister Lou's desk Monday after lunch.

She wanted to write a thorough article on the latest Briar Coast murder. Sister Lou was a valuable source because she was one of the three people who'd found the body and she knew the victim. But Shari wasn't eager to bring back sad memories for her friend.

"It'll help to discuss it objectively." Sister Lou seemed to steady herself. She straightened her shoulders under her warm blue blouse and rested her hands on the desk in front of her. Her Hermionean cross was pinned to the right side of her collar. "When I spoke with Chris earlier, he was wonderful as always, but I couldn't speak freely because he worries so much about me."

Shari crossed her right leg over her left, smoothing her rose-colored slacks over her right thigh. Just the mention of Chris could distract her. She forced herself to concentrate. "I can understand how he must feel. You're not my aunt, but I worry about you, too."

Sister Lou's onyx eyes, so like her nephew's, flared in surprise. "Thank you, Shari. I care about you, too. Very much."

"Thank you." Shari looked down at the reporter's notebook on her lap. Another warm blush rose into her cheeks. That happened a lot around Sister Lou. She still wasn't comfortable discussing her feelings. But her friendship with Sister Lou and Chris had brought her a long way toward making it seem more natural. "Can you walk me through this morning's events in as much detail as you're comfortable including?"

Sister Lou started at the beginning, with her scheduled morning meeting with Autumn to review the retreat presentation schedule.

"Marianna also asked me to collect the scarf she'd forgotten the last time we'd met with Autumn." Sister Lou broke off to express her frustration. "Marianna has a tendency to take off her scarves during meetings, then leave them behind. It's like a nervous habit, not that she'd admit to having any."

"Why are the two of you working together on the retreat?" Shari looked up from her notes. She adjusted the cream blazer she'd coupled with her rose slacks. "The two of you are like the Odd Couple. You're so calm and she's so uptight."

Sister Lou's full lips twitched as she fought back an inappropriate grin. "I think that was Barb's point.

She told me she hoped my diplomacy would rub off on Marianna. It's not working."

Shari recalled that Sister Barbara Yates was the congregation's prioress. "I guess even in the congregation, when your boss says you have to work with someone, you're kind of stuck."

Sister Lou put on her best poker face. "That sounds about right."

"You've mentioned this retreat before." Shari lowered her notebook to her lap. "I still don't understand what it's about."

"The Advent season is the four weeks leading up to Christmas. During this time, we prepare our hearts and minds to celebrate the anniversary of Jesus Christ's birth."

One of Shari's foster parents had dragged her to Mass every Sunday. She'd been about eleven years old. The messages hadn't stuck because she hadn't wanted to be there and she hadn't cared. Now she did. "How does a retreat help you prepare for Christmas?"

"We focus on a discussion theme for the season. This year's theme is service. 'Whatsoever you do for the least of my brothers and sisters, so you do unto me.'"

She still wasn't making the connection. "How does that fit in with the shopping and the gifts?"

Sister Lou's lips twitched again. "Christmas isn't about gifts. It's about remembering the lessons that Jesus taught us: loving your neighbors, helping those in need, treating others as you'd like to be treated."

"Ah-ha. So that's what people mean when they say, 'Jesus is the reason for the season.'"

"That's right."

"And 'Keep Christ in Christmas.'"

"Exactly."

The approval and warmth in Sister Lou's gaze was much more encouraging of Shari's religious instruction than her foster jailer's angry rants and scathing scolds had been. She was tempted to ask a few more questions about the meaning of the season, and what evergreen trees had to do with Bethlehem—or Nazareth or wherever Jesus had been born—but she was on deadline. Perhaps another time.

"Did anything stand out to you, either in the crime scene or during the statements the deputies took?" Shari had been impressed by Sister Lou's perceptions and insights when they'd worked together to solve Dr. Maurice Jordan's murder. Had her powers of observation detected anything in particular that morning?

Sister Lou's dark eyes took on a faraway look. "I can't shake the sense that something was odd about the way we found Autumn."

"Like what?"

Her friend seemed to hesitate. "She was sitting on her chair."

Shari waited for more. When Sister Lou remained silent, she prompted her. "What was so odd about that?"

"Why wasn't she on the floor?" Sister Lou's voice was faint as though she was talking to herself. "If someone was attacking you, wouldn't you back away—or at least stand up? Why would you let them get close enough to choke you?"

"Maybe the killer picked her up and put her on the chair?"

"Autumn didn't look as though she'd been placed on the chair. She was seated as though she'd been sitting on it when the killer attacked her. And the room was tidy. It didn't look as though there'd been a struggle."

"So you don't think Autumn felt threatened at first, which means her attacker probably wasn't a stranger."

"That was the impression I had."

Shari made a note of that. "Did her partner or any of her employees have theories about who might have killed her?"

"No one mentioned anything." There was an odd note in Sister Lou's voice.

Shari searched her friend's troubled features. "What's bothering you?"

Sister Lou hesitated. "During one of my meetings with Autumn, her cousin barged into the office. They had a heated argument, then her cousin threatened to kill her. Kelsey, Autumn's assistant, is aware of this, but she didn't mention it to the deputies."

Shari's right hand flew across the sheet of paper. "Why didn't you mention it?"

"I didn't feel comfortable bringing it up since Kelsey hadn't."

It may sound like an odd defense, but Shari understood. The other two women—Kelsey and Rita—had known Autumn longer and better than Sister Lou had. If they didn't think the altercation between

Autumn and her cousin was worth mentioning, why would Sister Lou?

Shari finished noting the information. "Can you think of anything else?"

"Just one thing: Autumn's home had been ransacked, presumably by the person who killed her. What was the murderer looking for, and had he or she found it?"

"Good question." Another note, then Shari hesitated. "Chris told me Deputies Cole and Tate were the ones who'd interviewed you." She tried for a casual tone. "How did they seem?"

Sister Lou gave her a wry look. "If you're wondering whether they're still upset about my involvement in Mo's murder investigation, yes, they are."

Shari sighed. "Which means they're still upset with me, too."

"Probably. I'm afraid you'll have a hard time getting them to cooperate with you."

"No surprise there." Shari scowled at her notepad. "If it wasn't for you, they would've arrested the wrong person. Should we have let that happen?"

"Look at it from their perspective. If you were in law enforcement, would you want your case to be solved by a reporter, a college executive, and a sister?"

"That sounds like the beginning of a bad joke." Shari shrugged restlessly. "How about saying the murder had been solved by the victim's friends?"

Sister Lou spread her hands. "I'm on your side."

"I know." Shari rubbed her forehead. Hard. "Diego

wants me to get quotes from Cole and Tate. What do I do if they don't return my calls?"

"Keep after them, Shari. You'll find a way to make them talk."

"What if they don't?"

"You'll figure something out. I have faith in you."

"That makes one of us." Shari expelled a heavy breath. "No, I'm going to take a page from your book and investigate Autumn Tassler's murder myself."

"Won't that further damage your relationship with the deputies?"

"At least I'll be able to give my readers information."

"Your editor wants updates from law enforcement."

"But they're giving me the silent treatment."

"I'm afraid your plan will end up irritating the deputies *and* your editor."

Shari gave Sister Lou a baleful look. "So my choices are: irritate the deputies by pressuring them for a quote, irritate my editor by not quoting the deputies, or irritate my editor and the deputies by working the case myself."

"That sums it up."

She had three choices and none of them was optimal. "That's really irritating."

"Did you know your reporter was going to print this story?" Tuesday morning, Sister Marianna charged into Sister Lou's office. She stopped in front of her desk and shook a copy of *The Briar Coast Telegraph* in the air. It wasn't even eight o'clock.

All that shaking back and forth made Sister Lou motion sick. She switched her gaze from the newspaper to Sister Marianna's face and dug deep for a bright smile. "Good morning, Marianna. Did you sleep well?"

The angry flush in Sister Marianna's thin cheeks deepened. "I am *not* in the mood to be toyed with, Louise. Did you—"

"I'm not toying with you, Marianna. I'm trying to defuse this situation before it needlessly spirals out of control." Sister Lou inclined her head toward her guest chairs. "Why don't you stop waving the paper and have a seat? Make yourself comfortable."

"I don't want to *sit*. I don't want to be *comfortable*. I want you to answer my question."

If only she knew how much of a struggle it is for me to control my temper right now.

Sister Lou filled her lungs with the fragrance of the white tea potpourri that scented her office. She held Sister Marianna's gaze and controlled her tone. "Please take a seat and we'll talk. Otherwise, please leave my office."

Sister Marianna started to argue, but she hesitated. She took a closer look at Sister Lou and reconsidered her actions.

"Really, Louise." She settled onto one of the visitor's chairs. "Did you know Shari Henson was going to write a front-page article about Autumn's murder?"

Sister Lou appreciated the effort Sister Marianna had made to control her tone. *Baby steps.* "For the record, Shari writes the articles. Her editor decides on which page it's going to appear. Details like that matter."

"It doesn't matter whether it was Shari's decision or her editor's to plaster this story all over the front page of the newspaper. What matters is the damage this story will do to our congregation's reputation."

"How do you think it will hurt us?"

"You can't be serious." Sister Marianna's eyes stretched wide in disbelief. "This is the second murder with a connection to our congregation. First, you invited a very controversial figure to be the featured speaker at our Saint Hermione Feast Day celebration. He was found murdered the morning of the presentation."

"Yes, Marianna. I was there."

"I know. In fact, you also were the one who found Autumn's body."

"Are you blaming me for the congregation's connection to the Briar Coast Cabin Resort?" Why not? If Sister Marianna put her mind to it, she could find a way to link Sister Lou to the existence of original sin.

"Of course I'm not blaming you." Sister Marianna took a testy tone. "I realize I'm the one who awarded our retreat contract to the resort. But you must be aware that people will realize that our congregation is the common denominator in these two murders, which happened less than three months apart. How do you think that will make us look?"

Sister Lou sat back on her executive chair as she considered her uninvited guest. Sister Marianna wore a pale yellow blouse. The blue, gold, and white Hermionean cross was pinned to the lapel of her stiff ice gray jacket. She'd already tugged loose her yellow and white scarf. Sister Lou frowned as she recalled the black, gray, and red scarf she was supposed to have retrieved for Sister Marianna. After the shock of finding Autumn's body, she'd forgotten all about it. Apparently, so had Sister Marianna. She'd never asked about it.

She made a mental note to remind Sister Marianna about her scarf later. "Why don't you tell me how you think our connection to these homicides will make us look?"

Sister Marianna lowered her thin eyebrows. "People will think we're somehow involved with them."

"Do you think the Briar Coast community will imagine that a member of our congregation is a killer?"

"Don't say it like that." Sister Marianna's frown darkened. "You know very well that people will jump to such conclusions."

"Then we should remind people of who actually did kill Maurice, and assure them that no one connected to the congregation had anything to do with Autumn's murder."

"We wouldn't have been put in this position if your friend the reporter hadn't seen fit to plaster her story all over the front page of the *Telegraph*." Again Sister Marianna wielded the newspaper like a weapon.

Sister Lou decided against repeating that the only thing Shari was guilty of was producing a well-written article on a subject that was important enough to the community to be included on the front page.

Sister Lou leaned into her desk and folded her hands on its surface. "I'm sorry the article causes you distress. However, it imparts information on an important event that occurred in our community. It's also a sad event. We owe it to Autumn to acknowledge her death. The *Telegraph* has a responsibility to keep the community informed of what's happened so that our neighbors can be aware of possible threats to their safety."

Sister Marianna stood. "Your friend should have kept us out of the article. There wasn't any reason to include us."

Sister Lou maintained eye contact with the angry woman on the other side of her desk. "I don't regret providing an interview for Shari's article. I felt it was my civic responsibility to help her write a thorough and accurate report."

"Really?" Sister Marianna linked her fingers together in front of her waist, still managing to hold on to the newspaper. "I hope you're able to explain that to our associates and partners who no longer want to be involved with the congregation because of our continued bad press. And what will you say to those donors who no longer want to support our ministries because of our connection to two of the three murders that have occurred in the past eight years?"

Sister Marianna didn't wait for Sister Lou's response. She stormed out of the office much the same way she'd stormed in. It was then that Sister Lou realized she hadn't reminded Sister Marianna about her scarf.

Was it possible that the scarf had turned up when the deputies processed the crime scene? Sister Lou froze. That would really give the congregation an awkward connection to the murder.

Chapter 11

"Nice byline, Scoop." Chris again scanned the article that appeared above the fold on the front page of Tuesday morning's *Telegraph*. He gripped the beige receiver of his office telephone as he waited for Shari's reply.

"Thanks, Slick." A smile warmed her voice as it traveled down the phone line.

Chris's lips curved in response. He'd been amused the first time Shari had called him "Slick." They'd only just met but she'd taken an immediate attitude with him. Over time, he'd begun to suspect she used the moniker as a term of endearment.

He held a mental image of her as they spoke on the telephone: thick raven hair that tumbled in unruly waves to her narrow shoulders; cinnamon-kissed heart-shaped face with deceptively angelic features; wide cocoa eyes that glittered with a reckless light. What was she wearing? Probably a pantsuit or skirt suit in a bold, confident color and ridiculously high stilettos that matched her clothes.

"How does it feel to be a front-page fixture?" Chris reread the headline: *Cabin Resort Owner Found Dead.* Beneath that, the byline read, *Sharelle Henson.* It was a solid story with detailed statements from Autumn Tassler's business partner, Rita Morris; her administrative assistant, Kelsey Bennett; and resort client Sister Louise LaSalle of the Congregation of the Sisters of St. Hermione of Ephesus. In somewhat terse quotes, Deputy Fran Cole and Deputy Ted Tate explained that they'd been called to the scene late Monday morning and were just beginning their investigation.

"I'm not a front-page fixture. Yet." Her chuckle was an interesting blend of swagger and self-deprecation. "But that's a goal. I've wanted to be an investigative reporter for so long, but I was afraid I didn't have what it takes."

The personal insight she'd shared with him was so rare. Chris seized the opportunity to widen the view. "When did you know you wanted to be an investigative reporter?"

"Twelve. I think." She was more cautious now, as though she was measuring how much of herself she wanted to share. When the tally was in, it wasn't much at all.

"You were so young when you decided to be a voice for those who couldn't speak for themselves."

Shari's reply came after a beat of surprised silence. "You remember what I said."

"I was listening."

Another brief hesitation. "Ah, no wonder you're such a successful fund-raiser. You listen to people and remember what they say. Pretty good trick, Slick."

"A compliment from you. I don't think my heart can handle the shock." Although the defensiveness behind her words was palpable.

"Don't worry. I won't make a habit of it."

He didn't doubt it. "My remembering what you told me doesn't have anything to do with my fund-raising skills. I remember because I care about you."

The silence was longer this time. In the background, he heard a cacophony of voices and the angry trill of ringing phones.

Had he pushed too far? Chris could feel her pulling away even through the phone line that connected them.

"I should get back to work . . ." Her response trailed off as she mumbled her ad-libbed line.

He wasn't ready to say good-bye. "Why were you afraid you didn't have what it takes to be an investigative reporter? What did you think you were lacking?"

"I don't know." Shari's voice had cooled. "I need to get back to work."

Chris tried to imagine her office cubicle. What did it look like? What would it tell him about her? Did she have photos of people she knew and places she'd been to displayed on her desk? Were cuttingly funny quotes pinned to her cubicle walls?

How could he coax an invitation to her office?

"Let me pick you up for lunch. We can celebrate

your latest front-page story." He glanced down at the headline again. "Well, not celebrate. This is sad news, but I'd like to congratulate you on your article."

"I don't know if—"

"We can grab something from the café." Who could resist the Briar Coast Café? Chris sensed Shari debating with herself. At least she hadn't hung up.

He glanced at his bronze quartz wristwatch. It was almost a quarter past eight o'clock. Would she give him a chance, give them a chance? He held his breath while he waited for her verdict.

"Okay. I'll meet you at noon at the café."

He smiled his relief. "No, I'll pick you up at the *Telegraph*." He really wanted to see her work space.

"All right. Noon. I'll be waiting."

They ended their conversation with well wishes for the morning, then Chris hung up.

His smile faded as he replayed their brief conversation. What had happened to cause her to put up so many walls?

If Sister Lou had the answer, she wasn't sharing it with him. He respected that, of course, but he still wanted to know why Shari had erected such impenetrable barriers—and what he could do or say to prove that, if she let him in, he wouldn't betray her trust.

Shari recradled her phone after ending her conversation with Chris. "I hope I'm not making a mistake."

"Sharelle Henson?" The voice at her back startled Shari.

She spun her desk chair toward the voice. Briar Coast Mayor Heather Stanley stood less than an arm's length from her. Seriously, any closer, and their lips would touch. The mayor could at least wait until they'd been properly introduced. Shari's gaze was drawn to the newspaper gripped in the fist the mayor held at her side.

Shari lifted her eyes to examine the mayor's delicate porcelain features, large violet eyes, wide pale pink lips, and shiny chestnut hair.

"You're Sharelle Henson." The mayor's violet dress made her eyes appear even more intense. Or maybe it was the anger that tightened her attractive features.

"And you're Mayor Heather Stanley. Nice pores." The mayor smelled nice, too, like some kind of powdery perfume.

"What?" Heather reacted as though she thought Shari had lost her mind.

"Could I have some breathing room?" Shari shifted to ease the strain on her neck. "I'm not used to seeing you so up close and extremely personal."

Heather stepped back, giving Shari a furious frown while still managing to look perfect. "I want to talk to you about your article."

Shari gestured toward the single guest seat beside the conversation table in the corner of her cubicle. "I'd welcome the extra space. Make yourself at home."

She was momentarily distracted by Heather's three-inch cream stilettos. "Nice shoes."

"Thank you." Heather's acknowledgment was grudging. She adjusted her stance but ignored Shari's invitation to sit. Shari didn't blame her. The chair wasn't that comfortable. "Writing an article on the resort owner's death didn't show good judgment on your part."

Had she heard the other woman correctly? "The resort owner's name was Autumn Tassler, and she didn't just die. Someone killed her. He—or she—choked Autumn to death."

Heather nodded. "Yes, I know, and I'm sorry for it. But this tragedy is no reason to cause a panic by running an article about it on the front page."

"This information is too important to bury inside. I agree with Diego's decision to put it on page one."

"I'll talk with him about his judgment as well. Believe me."

Shari was sure the mayor would try. "Good luck with that."

Arrogance flashed across Heather's delicate features. And something else, anticipation of the challenge, maybe. "I'm not worried about Diego."

"If not on the front page, where would you suggest we put it? Not that we care."

Heather's arched eyebrow was her only reaction to Shari's editorializing. "That story has no place in this publication at all."

"We're a *newspaper*, not Briar Coast's public relations brochure. We have a responsibility to provide our readers with the information they need to stay informed and, above all, safe."

Heather threw up her arms. "How can people feel safe when you're telling them that someone is running around town strangling their neighbors?"

"That's not what the article told them. Did you even read it?"

"Of course I did. Why else would I be here?" Heather crossed her arms. A chunky sterling silver necklace complemented her outfit. It matched the studs in her ears and the bracelet on her left wrist. "Briar Coast is a safe community. Your article is damaging our reputation."

"Why, because it exposes that your claim of a crime-free town is false advertising?" Shari struggled to understand the mayor's position. It might be an unwinnable war.

"It's *not* false advertising." Heather looked as though Shari had slapped her in the face. Her voice dropped another twenty degrees. "It's who we are and I'm going to make sure it stays that way." She turned to leave.

"Mayor Stanley."

Heather looked back over her shoulder. "Yes?"

"I'm also working on a story about the town's predicted budget shortfall. Do you have a comment?" Shari imagined she could see smoke billowing from Heather's ears.

"Yes, I do." Heather faced her fully. "Briar Coast does not have a budget crisis. You can quote me on that."

Without another word, Heather spun on her enviable heels and strode from Shari's cubicle. Based on the direction in which she'd turned, Shari was pretty sure the mayor was on her way to confront Diego. Unstoppable force, meet unmovable object.

She should sell tickets to that event and advertise it as a fund-raiser for the town.

Worry darkened Sister Barbara's hazel green eyes behind her silver-rimmed glasses. Sister Lou had a foreboding of the reason the prioress had asked to see her this Tuesday morning. It wasn't good.

She remembered Sister Marianna's question: *What will you say to those donors who no longer want to support our ministries because of our connection to two of the three murders that have occurred in the past eight years?*

Apparently, Sister Marianna had more intuition than Sister Lou had given her credit for.

"Thank you for coming, Lou." Sister Barbara's cloudy countenance was in sharp contrast to her sunny yellow blouse. Her chocolate blazer hung on the back of her black executive chair.

"Of course, Barb." Sister Lou settled onto one of the chairs in front of Sister Barbara's desk. "Have you and Marianna decided whether to postpone the retreat?"

"No, we haven't, but that's not why I wanted to talk with you."

I hadn't thought so. "What can I do for you?" Sister Lou waited for the prioress to speak her mind.

"We received calls from three donors this morning." Sister Barbara seemed weary. "They read the article in today's *Telegraph* about Autumn Tassler's murder and they're concerned. This is the town's second murder in three months, and the congregation has a connection to both."

Sister Lou struggled to quash a stirring of impatience. "Why does that cause them concern? We're not committing the murders. In fact, we were cleared of any suspicion in Maurice's murder, and we're not involved in Autumn's."

"They realize we weren't *involved* in those sad events." The fluorescent lights above Sister Barbara's office played over her cap of graying hair. "But they're concerned that we're *associated* with them."

Sister Lou's impatience tugged again. She disagreed with any position that put the congregation in a bad light for not remaining silent and invisible in critical times. "We're part of this community. If we can help inform the public, especially about issues as important as public safety, we have an obligation to do so."

"I agree with you, Lou." Sister Barbara's tone was reassuring. "But we're developing a bit of an image problem."

"It does seem that way." Sister Lou heard the disgruntlement in her voice. She drew in the soothing scents of cinnamon and peppermint that permeated the prioress's office. "What would you recommend that we do?"

"We need to turn this negative association into a positive one, and for that I'll need your help."

Sister Lou frowned. "What can I do?"

Sister Barbara watched Sister Lou closely. "What you did the last time. Solve this case."

Sister Lou's frown deepened in confusion. "The

sheriff's office already has assigned deputies to investigate Autumn's murder."

"Those deputies investigated Maurice's murder, too. You remember how that went."

I doubt I'll ever forget. "They still haven't forgiven Chris, Shari, and me for involving ourselves in their work."

Sister Barbara leaned back on her chair. "Instead of complaining, they should thank you. Without you, the real murderer would still be out there."

"I'm sure things will go better this time."

"I'm afraid that I don't share your confidence, Lou."

"Barb, if we involve ourselves in another of the deputies' cases, we could do irreparable harm to the congregation's relationship with the sheriff's office." She looked askance at the prioress. "Is it worth the risk?"

"Yes." Sister Barbara's response was unexpected. "Lou, our reputation must be restored and sooner rather than later. The deputies move too slowly. A lot of vulnerable people depend on the services we offer, which means we can't afford to lose donors."

The truth in Sister Barbara's words was a heavy burden, but still, Sister Lou hesitated. "I felt I needed to help find Mo's killer. It was my fault that he was in Briar Coast. Also, the congregation was on the top of the deputies' list of suspects."

"You may not have known Autumn well, but she was a member of the Briar Coast community."

"Are you trying to make me feel guilty?" Before getting to know Shari and admiring her directness,

Sister Lou may not have called out the prioress. But Shari's forthright manner was rubbing off on her.

Sister Barbara returned her direct stare. "Is it working?"

Sister Lou's gaze drifted to the view outside the picture window behind Sister Barbara. The sunlight was brilliant on the vivid fall foliage. The scene looked like a painting that she could step into.

"I'm not only concerned about the congregation's relationship with the sheriff's office." Sister Lou returned her attention to Sister Barbara. "I promised Chris that I wouldn't get involved in any more homicide cases."

Sister Barbara nodded her understanding. "I don't want to put you in danger. Perhaps you could just ask a few questions? While you were looking into Maurice's murder, you noticed things that the deputies had missed. Maybe that will happen again."

Such as why Kelsey didn't mention Autumn's cousin's threat or why Rita didn't bring up the businessman who wants to buy the resort. Those questions had been nagging at her since the deputies had interviewed them twenty-four hours ago.

"I'll call Rita and Kelsey and see if they've thought of anything else." Surely, such an innocent question wouldn't ruffle too many feathers in the sheriff's office.

"Thank you, Lou."

"I'll let you know if I learn anything useful." Sister Lou stood to leave.

She intended to keep her word to her nephew to stop her amateur sleuthing, but did a few innocuous questions constitute breaking her promise?

Chapter 12

"Three of our longtime donors called me today. They're . . . unhappy." Chris sat on the other side of Sister Valerie Shaw's desk late Tuesday afternoon. There was enough of a chill in the college president's office for Chris to keep his classic-fit navy sport coat on.

He didn't relish bringing bad news to his boss, but the sooner he pulled off the proverbial adhesive bandage, the sooner the institution could deal with the pain. The first concerned donor had called before he'd met Shari for lunch, but Chris's internal alarm hadn't been tripped until he'd returned to his office and listened to the voicemail messages of two additional anxious supporters. That's when he'd asked for this meeting with Sister Valerie.

"Did their concerns have anything to do with the congregation being mentioned in today's *Telegraph* article on Briar Coast's latest murder?" Sister Valerie adjusted her tortoiseshell-rimmed glasses on her round face. Her normally cheerful brown eyes were troubled.

"Did you know that donors would call because of the story?" In retrospect, he should have expected those calls.

"No, but I should have. That's my oversight. I guessed the reason for their calls because two donors contacted me, also."

Chris's eyes widened with surprise. "Why didn't you tell me?"

"I didn't have a chance until now." Sister Valerie spread her hands. The gesture drew Chris's attention to the blue, gold, and white Hermionean cross affixed to her warm rose blouse.

Donors called the advancement office when they were uneasy about a matter. Calling the college president indicated a much greater disquiet.

Five donors. Chris massaged the tightening muscles at the back of his neck. Those were just the people who'd called Sister Valerie and him. What about the ones who didn't take the time to call, the ones who would stop supporting the institution without warning? "We need a response to address their concerns."

"I agree." Sister Valerie's gaze moved to the commencement photos affixed to one of her office walls. "Our plans for our students are too important to risk our relationships with our supporters."

Chris's mind raced ahead, determining which contributors to contact, dividing them among his advancement team, and drafting the talking points for the call. "We also have to consider the relationships we're building with new donors."

"Especially now when we have such an ambitious fund-raising goal."

Chris heard the distraction in Sister Valerie's voice. It was more than stress. "What else is on your mind?"

"I'm not certain a prepared response will be enough to allay our community's concerns." Sister Valerie broke the brief silence. "We need to do something extra before we have a mass exodus."

"What are your ideas?" He sensed she had at least one.

The considering look in Sister Valerie's brown eyes didn't bode well. "You, the reporter Sharelle Henson, and Lou had success with your last murder investigation."

Chris felt the first stirrings of foreboding. "It was the sheriff's office's investigation, not ours." According to his aunt and Shari, Fran and Ted were still angry.

"But it was the three of you who cleared the congregation of any suspicion. You also solved the case."

"Neither the college nor the congregation are suspects this time."

"The college is connected to the congregation. The congregation was mentioned in the paper. To our donors, that connects both the congregation and the college to this murder, the second one in Briar Coast in three months."

It was a convoluted connection and far-fetched at best, but Sister Valerie had a point. People jumped to conclusions. It was human nature. Chris said, "Shari had to interview my aunt. She's one of the people who found Autumn Tassler's body."

Sister Valerie gave Chris a curious smile. "I'm not criticizing Ms. Henson, just making an observation."

Chris shifted on his chair. The urge to defend Shari had caught even him by surprise. "What does my aunt's involvement in Dr. Jordan's murder investigation have to do with this situation?" As soon as the words left his mouth, Chris realized the answer to his own question.

"Could you talk with Lou about investigating this case, too?"

The muscles in Chris's neck and shoulders tightened with his instinct to protect the ones he loved. "Sister Valerie, I don't want to involve my aunt in another homicide investigation. It's too dangerous."

"I don't want to put Lou in danger, of course." Sister Valerie inclined her head. "Perhaps the three of you could just ask a couple of people a few questions. My hope is that you'll find something that will put some distance between this sad situation and the congregation."

That's how it had started last time, with a few questions. Then his aunt had been threatened. Chris didn't want to go through that again.

He came to his feet. "First, let's see how our donors respond to our outreach efforts."

Sister Valerie looked up at him. "Please keep me updated on the results."

"Of course." Chris left Sister Valerie's office, but other troubling thoughts left with him. If the president of the college was worried enough about its connection to Autumn Tassler's murder to consider asking his aunt to investigate, how had the congregation reacted?

* * *

Sister Lou's phone rang as she settled behind her desk at the congregational office. She'd just returned from a late lunch with Sister Carmen. Sister Barbara's name and telephone extension popped onto her caller identification screen. "Hi, Barb."

"Lou." The prioress's greeting was warm but guarded. "Could you possibly join me in my office now? Deputies Cole and Tate are here. They stopped by to ask you, Marianna, and me a few questions about Autumn Tassler, and the congregation's connection to her and her business. I realize that this request comes without any prior notice."

Sister Lou could envision the scolding look Sister Barbara gave the law enforcement officers as she made her final statement. That image would have brought a smile to her face if the memory of the congregation's previous unpleasant encounter with the deputies wasn't so vivid. Instead, her pulse raced and her heart pounded at the knowledge of the clash to come.

During their last murder investigation, Fran and Ted had spent weeks interrogating each of the congregation's sixty-three sisters before accepting what the sisters had been saying all along: they had nothing to do with Maurice's murder.

Is history repeating itself? "I'm on my way."

"Thank you, Lou." Sister Barbara rang off.

Sister Lou sent a quick prayer for guidance and fortitude before exiting her office.

Her footsteps were silent on the thick, warm rose

carpeting as she strode down the wide hallway to the prioress's office. Fluorescent lighting highlighted the pastel artwork framed on the pale gold walls. Hums of conversations and whispers of laughter drifted from the workstations and through the open doors of the breakroom and other offices along the way.

Furtive glances leaped away before connecting with hers. Had news of the deputies' meeting with the prioress and Sister Marianna cycled through the office already?

Sister Lou knocked on Sister Barbara's open office door. She nodded toward the deputies, Sister Barbara, and Sister Marianna as she closed the door behind her. Fran, Ted, and Sister Marianna had taken the three guest chairs, with Ted in the center and Fran's chair beside the wall. Both deputies were in uniform, but whereas Fran looked freshly pressed, Ted looked like he'd slept in his clothes.

"Thank you for coming, Lou." Sister Barbara made it sound as though they were preparing for afternoon tea instead of a homicide investigation. She patted the arm of the chair beside her. "Paula loaned us a chair for this meeting. I hope you don't mind sitting beside me."

Sister Paula Walton was a member of the leadership team whose office was one door down from the prioress's.

"I don't mind at all." The look she exchanged with Sister Barbara confirmed that the prioress also was remembering their earlier conversation about the murder investigation.

Sister Lou settled onto the proffered chair. Fran inclined her head in greeting. Tendrils of her blond hair had broken free of the big, messy bun at the nape of her neck. Ted's habitual frown marred the features of his wide face. His pale gray gaze challenged her.

Sister Marianna's pointed chin was set at a don't-cross-me angle. Her thin lips were pursed in disapproval. Sister Lou empathized with the other woman. What did the deputies want from the congregation this time? That was the sixty-four-million-dollar question.

Sister Barbara turned to the law enforcement officers. "How can we help you, Deputies?"

"You can start by telling us what business you had with the Briar Coast Cabin Resort." When he addressed the prioress, Ted's tone was marginally more respectful than usual.

Sister Lou narrowed her eyes in puzzlement. They'd had this conversation Monday. "As I explained yesterday, Deputy Tate, the congregation has contracted with the resort to host our annual Advent retreat."

Sister Marianna took up the explanation. "The Congregation of the Sisters of Saint Hermione of Ephesus conducts an annual weeklong Advent retreat to help us prepare our hearts and minds for the celebration of the anniversary of Jesus Christ's birth."

Ted stared at Sister Marianna. His eyes were wide, his lips parted. "I'm getting flashbacks to Catholic school."

"It doesn't appear that the training did any good." Irritation crackled in Sister Marianna's gray eyes. "You would have benefited from a few more years."

Sister Barbara redirected the conversation. "What is your interest in our contract with the resort, Deputy Tate?"

Ted pulled his chastened gaze from Sister Marianna. "It's part of our investigation into the murder of the resort's owner. We want details on the congregation's connection to her."

Warning sirens sounded in Sister Lou's inner ear. *How much of the deputies' interest is based on the congregation's contract with Autumn and how much is payback for my investigating Mo's murder independently from them?*

"Deputies, with respect, I explained all of this to you Monday. Are you reluctant to believe me because of our past misunderstanding?"

Fran's green gaze was cool. "With respect, Sister, it wasn't a 'misunderstanding.' And I resent the implication that we'd let our personal differences affect our professionalism."

Ted jerked his head. "Yeah, that's right."

Sister Lou hadn't misread the deputies. Their resentment emanated from them. "Are you questioning all of the resort's clients—or just those who are members of our congregation?"

"Only the ones who've argued with Autumn Tassler." Fran leaned forward to claim Sister Marianna's attention. The other woman was seated on Ted's other side. "What was the argument about, Sister?"

Sister Marianna crossed her arms over her chest. "Which one?"

Sister Lou flinched. *Oh, Marianna, why would you respond that way?* Couldn't she see how serious this situation was? Sister Lou wanted to leap from her chair and shake Sister Marianna. Instead, she laid her hands flat on her lap and drew comfort from the scent of the cinnamon-and-peppermint potpourri that filled Sister Barbara's office.

Ted eyed Sister Marianna with surprise. "Why don't you walk us through all of them?"

"There were only two." Sister Marianna sniffed with disdain. "Both were about the same thing. *I'm* the client. *She's* the vendor. Or she was. I know what I want but she kept trying to push me in a different direction."

Fran tilted her head. "Did the fact that you weren't getting what you wanted from Ms. Tassler make you angry?"

Concerned with the direction of the questioning, Sister Lou jumped in. "Marianna wouldn't kill Autumn because Autumn recommended mac and cheese when Marianna wanted asparagus and carrots. She wouldn't kill someone over food. To suggest otherwise is absurd."

"I don't know." Fran considered Sister Marianna. "Ms. Tassler's employees said Sister Marianna sounded very angry."

"It was a simple disagreement, nothing more, nothing less," Sister Lou insisted.

"How do you know?" Ted challenged her.

Sister Lou gave Ted a cool smile. "You and I are having a spirited disagreement right now, Deputy Tate. If my lifeless body were found tomorrow morning, would anyone accuse you of killing me?"

"Louise!" Sister Marianna sounded shocked.

Fran sat forward and again addressed Sister Marianna. "So how did you resolve the spirited disagreement, Sister?"

Sister Marianna waved a dismissive hand. "We found a compromise."

"Of course." Ted's lips curved in a mocking smile. "How else would a nun settle an argument?"

"A sister." Sister Marianna sighed with impatience. "And it wasn't my idea."

Ted barked a laugh. "So it was Sister Lou to the rescue. Again."

Fran switched her attention to Sister Lou. "Where were you between six and seven Monday morning, Sister?"

Sister Lou winced at the cold chill of déjà vu. The congregation was under suspicion in a murder investigation. Again. "Is that the time that Autumn was killed?"

The deputies exchanged looks before Fran responded. "Yes, it is."

The killer was an early riser just like Autumn— and Sister Lou, Sister Carmen, and Sister Marianna. Unfortunately, the time didn't rule out Sister Marianna as a suspect the way Sister Lou had hoped it would. "I was jogging around the college's campus."

Surprise crossed Ted's features before he masked his reaction. "Can anyone vouch for you?"

Sister Lou swallowed a frustrated sigh. "Sister Carmen Vega. I was jogging with her."

"What about you, Sister?" Ted's pen was poised for Sister Marianna's reply.

Sister Marianna sent a guarded look to Sister Lou before answering. "I'm afraid I overslept that morning."

Sister Lou struggled to conceal her surprise. She would lay odds that Sister Marianna had never overslept a day in her life. To the other sister, such slovenly behavior would probably be categorized as a cardinal sin.

Why are you lying, Marianna?

Ted stood. "That's it for now. We'll be back if we have any other questions."

"I have a question for you, Deputy Tate." Sister Lou stopped the deputies with her words. "It's my understanding from the resort's employees that Autumn had disagreements and even arguments with several other people as recently as last week. Are those people also suspects?"

It was apparent the deputies had no idea what she was talking about, but neither did they want to admit to it. Why hadn't Kelsey or Rita told the deputies about Montgomery Crane's interest in the resort or January Potts's conviction that Autumn was having an affair with her husband?

Ted exchanged a startled look with Fran. "We don't discuss ongoing investigations."

That makes perfect sense since it's hard to discuss something you have no knowledge of. Sister Lou hid her irritation.

Always the role model for grace and hospitality, Sister Barbara rose. Sister Lou and Sister Marianna stood with her.

Sister Barbara offered each deputy her hand. "We're happy to provide whatever information we can. For now, do you see any reason that we can't continue our plans for our retreat?"

Fran shook her head. "No, but we'll let you know if anything changes."

"Thank you." Sister Barbara inclined her head.

The deputies left, but Sister Lou's sense of dread remained.

"Lou." Sister Barbara turned to her. "We're going to need your help."

By conducting another homicide investigation, Sister Lou could further damage the congregation's relationship with the sheriff's office. However, not getting involved in the case also could hurt the congregation.

Sister Lou said a silent prayer. *I'm open to other options.*

Chapter 13

Paul and Peg Prentiss must be early risers. When Chris arrived at their ranch-style home, they encouraged him to sit on their plump tan cloth armchair in the foyer and served him a hot cinnamon roll and an even hotter mug of cocoa. Both were made from scratch and it was barely nine o'clock Wednesday morning.

The older couple were the College of St. Hermione of Ephesus's most long-term and committed donors. They also bore a strong resemblance to Chris's mental image of Mr. and Mrs. Santa Claus: silver hair, rosy cheeks, and round, cherubic faces.

"We were so pleased when the college promoted you to vice president for advancement, Chris. Weren't we, Paul?" Peg bestowed a sweet smile on her husband. She pressed her left side against Paul as they practically cuddled on the tan love seat.

"Yeah. Thrilled." Paul made a grumpy Kris Kringle. He'd never enjoyed small talk. In contrast, his wife of nearly sixty years could get through an entire evening on it.

Chris swallowed another bite of the moist, sweet cinnamon roll. "Thank you. That means a lot coming from dedicated supporters like you."

Peg sipped her cocoa. "It's so nice to see you again."

Paul grunted, dragging his thick fingers through his mane of silver hair. "He's here because he doesn't want us to jump ship after that article in Tuesday's *Telegraph*."

"The cinnamon rolls are nice, too." Chris winked at Peg.

She giggled her pleasure. "Thank you, dear."

"But you're one-third right, Paul." Chris met the other man's piercing blue gaze. "In addition to enjoying our visits and Peg's homemade pastries, I'm here to allay any concerns you might have about the college."

"For the record, I baked the rolls." A hint of humor eased Paul's stern features. "Peg made the cocoa."

"I stand corrected." Another cautionary tale against judging people based on appearances. Paul looked more inclined to wrestle bears than bake pastries.

"You're a straight shooter, Chris." Paul drained his cocoa and set the empty cup on the decorative table between them. He wiped his heavy silver mustache with the napkin Peg passed to him. "That's one of the things I like about you. So I'll give it to you straight as well. The college is gonna have to separate from the congregation if it wants to retain donors like us."

Was Paul serious? Chris glanced toward Peg, who responded to his unspoken question with a smile. He turned back to Paul. "Neither the college nor the congregation has had *anything* to do with *any* of the murders that have occurred in Briar Coast. Ever."

"That doesn't matter." Paul looked incongruous on the fluffy love seat. "They've been connected with both. And we're not the only donors who're concerned."

Chris frowned. "There's no reason to punish the students for other people's misperceptions."

Paul's intense scrutiny took Chris's measure. "Real or imagined, we're not gonna be associated with organizations that are connected to criminal activities. You'll find a lot of us feel this way."

The insult stung. "I'm sorry for that, Paul. We were founded by the Congregation of the Sisters of Saint Hermione of Ephesus." He made the declaration with pride in the history behind the words. "The sisters gave us our roots, our identity, and our mission. We're not going to disavow them."

Silence stretched between Chris and Paul as they held each other's gaze. Finally, Paul spoke. "Neither of us is giving ground."

Chris stood. "I'm sorry for that. I hope we stay in touch."

Paul stood with him. "What would be the point?"

The older man's words closed the door on Chris's appeal, but the smile that twinkled in Peg's green eyes kept a window open. She gave him hope that someday, sometime down the road, this donor relationship could be healed. Chris shook Paul's and Peg's hands, then walked with the couple to their front door.

Paul claimed that other donors shared his view. How many others would present him with this ultimatum? The congregation was the college's compass. The school couldn't turn its back on its roots. Chris refused to allow that to happen.

He unlocked his bronze Toyota Camry and settled behind his car's steering wheel. He closed his eyes for a silent moment. *I'm open to other options.*

The prioress needed Sister Marianna out of the way.

Since the deputies had stretched credulity by implying that Sister Marianna was a person of interest in Autumn's murder, Sister Barbara thought it best to separate Sister Marianna from planning the congregation's annual Advent retreat. Instead, she asked Sister Lou, who had planned the event several times before, to continue the project on her own.

I'm glad Barb didn't ask me to sit in on that meeting. Sister Lou shivered at the thought.

She parked her orange compact sedan in the Briar Coast Cabin Resort's lot shortly before nine a.m. Wednesday. Sister Lou collected her manila project folder from her passenger seat before climbing from her car. Her steps were hesitant as she crossed the few yards to the main cabin. She tightened her grip on her folder before mounting the three oak steps to the cabin's wraparound porch. Two short days ago, she, Rita, and Kelsey had found Autumn dead in her office. Sister Lou took a moment to prepare herself for her return to the crime scene.

Two men stood close together at the reception area. They leaned against the counter, whispering with Kelsey, Autumn's administrative assistant. Both men appeared to be in their early to mid-fifties. The trio abruptly stopped speaking as Sister Lou approached.

"Sister." Kelsey's voice was several octaves higher than usual. Was it nerves? "Good morning. It's nice to see you again."

"Good morning, Kelsey." Sister Lou inclined her head at the two men beside her before turning back to the administrative assistant. "I have an appointment with Rita."

"Are you Sister Louise LaSalle from the congregation?" The gentleman standing closest to her looked like a spokesmodel. His double-breasted blue pinstripe suit went well with his artificial tan and perfect golden hair. His black Italian shoes looked expensive.

"You have me at a disadvantage." Sister Lou switched her folder to her left hand and offered the stranger her right. She managed a polite smile despite her brittle nerves.

He shook her hand. "I'm Gary Hargreaves, director of finance. It's a pleasure to finally meet you."

"It's nice to meet you." Sister Lou offered her

hand to the quiet gentleman beside Gary. "And may I ask who you are?"

"Urban Rodgers." His handshake was firm and brief, just like his introduction. His tall, muscular form was clothed in black jeans and a black jersey. His youthful dark skin belied his salt-and-pepper, close-cropped hair.

Standing together, Gary and Urban were complete opposites. Gary's polished appearance and manner made Urban's black jersey and dark jeans appear even more rough and casual.

A brief, involuntary image of first Gary's then Urban's large hands wrapped around Autumn's neck shuffled across Sister Lou's mind. She suppressed another shudder.

Sister Lou turned back to Kelsey. "Is Rita available?"

"Sister Louise, what do the deputies have against your congregation?" Gary's question caught Sister Lou by surprise.

Kelsey gasped. "Gary, how could you be so rude?"

Sister Lou's hand clenched the strap of her dark blue shoulder bag. "What makes you ask that?" As though she couldn't guess.

"They asked a lot of questions about you." Gary scanned her features.

What was he looking for?

Urban nodded. "They wanted to find a motive for the congregation."

"*I* didn't have that impression." Kelsey lifted her hands. The nails of her long, thin fingers were neatly trimmed and accented with silver polish. The color contrasted nicely with her ice-blue sweater.

Gary leaned his side against the registration desk. His green eyes were intent on Sister Lou's face. "What did you do to get on the deputies' bad side?"

"I don't know what's in the deputies' hearts." *Although I can guess: bitter disappointment and destructive revenge fantasies.*

The sisters hadn't done anything wrong, but Sister Lou was convinced that the deputies' obsession with their grudge was the reason they considered Sister Marianna a person of interest.

Gary jerked his chin toward Urban and Kelsey. "The deputies asked us so many questions about you. They were really interested in you and your retreat. They acted like they'd hit the lottery when Kelsey told them about Sister Marianna's arguments with Autumn."

Kelsey glanced toward the door. "Is Sister Marianna joining you today?"

"No, she isn't." Sister Lou didn't want to explain the reason she now was working solo on the retreat planning. "Marianna forgot her scarf in Autumn's office last Friday. Did you happen to notice it or did Autumn mention it to you?"

Kelsey shook her head. "No, I haven't seen it and Autumn never mentioned it."

The director of finance interrupted. "The deputies bagged and tagged everything when they examined the crime scene. If her scarf was in Autumn's office, she'll probably never see it again."

Good heavens! Sister Lou grew cold. Had the

deputies filed Sister Marianna's scarf with evidence from the murder investigation?

Sister Lou walked the short distance down the walnut wood–paneled hallway to Rita's office. She knocked on the half-opened door and waited for Rita's attention.

"Sister Lou, come in." The resort partner remained behind her desk. "Could you close the door, please? Thank you for adjusting your schedule for me."

Rita waved a hand over the mini-mounds of paper stacked before her, directing Sister Lou to one of the three guest chairs in front of the desk. They were identical to the ones in Autumn's office.

"You're welcome." Sister Lou tucked the skirt of her cool green suit under her as she sat. She handed Rita the manila folder she carried. "I have the room preferences for the sisters and the preliminary presentation agendas. Do you have any questions on the audiovisual requirements?"

Like Autumn's office, Rita's had a rustic cabin feel—same walnut wood, same abstract throw rugs. On the other side of her office, she'd arranged armchairs, a coffee table, and a caravan desk. But the surroundings felt different. Autumn's space was a business office. She'd had file cabinets, a tall bookcase stuffed with binders and reference manuals, an in-box stacked with internal and external mail, a dry-erase board, and a bulletin board. It also shared personal touches, such as the wood-framed paintings, and the cedar and pinecone scent. Rita's office didn't have any of that. Her space was comfortable but impersonal.

Sometime during her hectic morning, Rita had pulled her blond hair into a lopsided knot on top of her head. She brushed a tendril behind her ear in a flustered gesture. "I haven't had time to familiarize myself with your event."

Sister Lou could imagine how grief-stricken and preoccupied Autumn's partner had been for the past two days. "The congregation's very sorry for Autumn's death. She's in our prayers. We're also praying for you and your employees, and of course Autumn's friends and family."

"Thanks." The word was perfunctory. Rita waved a negligent hand. Her well-manicured nails were polished a deep plum. Sister Lou had a quick image of those nails around Autumn's throat. "I promise to get up to speed with everything quickly."

"Thank you. We respect that you and your employees are grieving, but we'd like to keep the retreat on schedule." She wanted to be respectful of those in mourning, but an invisible clock was ticking. Today was November eighth. The weeklong retreat was scheduled to start on December third, which was the first Advent Sunday. They had less than four weeks.

"Fortunately, you, Autumn, and Sister Marianna have already done the hard part." Rita's lavender jersey appeared as a gem against her faux leather executive chair. "I want to stick to the schedule, too, especially since your retreat will be my last event here."

Sister Lou was startled. "Are you selling the resort?"

"I've wanted to sell it for a while now. It was

Autumn who wanted to hold on to it, even though we're barely making any money." Rita pinned Sister Lou with her tense brown gaze. "You probably think I just gave you a motive for killing Autumn."

"It's not for me to say." However, the information did make Rita a more compelling suspect than Sister Marianna.

Rita gave Sister Lou a skeptical look. "Well, for the record, I didn't kill her." She stood to prowl the room, pausing to touch the back of her armchair, then stopping to gaze beyond the windows. "Yes, I wanted to sell the resort and she wanted to hold on to it. These cabins—I think they were her whole life. She was obsessed with this place. People said she was the first to arrive and the last to leave. For God's sake, you saw where she lived, on this very property."

People said she was the first to arrive and the last to leave. Was Rita never around to witness for herself the hours Autumn kept at the office?

"What about you?" Sister Lou studied Rita's wanderings around her office. She seemed tense and restless. "How do you feel about the resort?"

"It was supposed to be fun." Rita spun away from the window and returned to her desk. Her arms flailed as she vented her frustration. "Autumn made it all about work. Personnel management. Marketing campaigns. Profit and loss. Human resources. What in the h . . . world is onboarding? It would've been different if we were making tons of money."

"Is the resort struggling?"

"It could be doing better, but is it any wonder that it isn't?" Rita threw an arm toward her closed office door. "I'm sure you saw the breakfast club at the reception desk. They've been there, chatting all morning. When does any actual *work* get done?"

Sister Lou was puzzled. "Perhaps, if you're bothered by it, you should say something to them."

Rita snorted. "Autumn takes—took—care of things like that."

"All of that is up to you now." Sister Lou reevaluated Rita's office in the context of her confidences. She'd left the business part of running the resort to Autumn. She'd wanted only the fun parts. Her environment reflected that. It more closely resembled a foyer than a business office.

"I never realized how much I'd miss her." Rita was silent for a beat. "I love to travel and so do my friends. That's why I thought this place in this parkland would be an easy sell."

"It's a beautiful location."

"Yes, it is. Now someone else can make money from it." Rita sighed as she rose to her feet. She extended her hand to Sister Lou. "I'll be in touch later this week about your event."

Sister Lou stood to shake Rita's hand. "I look forward to your updates. In the meantime, good luck with your plans for the resort."

Sister Lou's mind spun with thoughts and impressions as she left Rita's office. Selling the resort was a compelling motive for murder. Though Sister Lou couldn't imagine Rita choking Autumn with her bare hands. It would have ruined her manicure—although manicures could be repaired . . .

She checked her crimson wristwatch. There was plenty of time to make it to the early Mass.

Was that Deputy Ted Tate's gruff voice she heard coming from the direction of the registration desk? Sister Lou cautiously approached the lobby. She stiffened. Yes, that was Ted's voice. Undoubtedly he was with Fran. She braced herself for another frustrating round with the officers.

Chapter 14

Sister Lou stopped when she entered the resort's lobby. Standing near the registration counter several feet away, the sheriff's deputies also froze. This must be how a doe felt once it had been sighted by hunters. The shot was coming, but she didn't know from which direction or how soon.

"Sister Lou." Ted's greeting seemed reluctant. "We were just talking about you."

"Oh?" Sister Lou glanced at the chef, the accountant, and Autumn's assistant. Rita wouldn't be pleased that they were still socializing. Perhaps this was part of their grieving process. "Is there something I can do to help you, Deputies?"

The identically dressed law enforcement officers each gripped their brown felt campaign hats in their right hands. Fran's lightweight brown jacket was zipped over her slender torso. Ted's jacket hung open, revealing his loose-fitting tan shirt and crooked brown tie.

Ted ignored her question. "What're you doing here?"

Sister Lou looked from Fran to Ted. She caught the hint of cedar and pine needles that permeated the resort. "I had a meeting with Rita Morris about the congregation's retreat. I believe you cleared us to continue the preparations."

"Yeah." Ted seemed impatient.

"Are you checking up on me?" Sister Lou adjusted the strap of her navy blue purse on her left shoulder.

Ted's bark of laughter was short and surprised. "We're conducting an investigation—"

"Do you have to be on-site to plan the retreat?" Fran's green eyes held more curiosity than suspicion. "You can't do it with phone calls and e-mails?"

Sister Lou sensed their audience—Kelsey, Gary, and Urban—hanging on their every word almost as though they were waiting for a dramatic moment. "Rita is new to the project. I thought it would be best to meet in person. We're weeks away from the retreat and still have a lot of details to finalize. Reviewing the project face-to-face helps prevent confusion and miscommunication."

Ted arched an eyebrow. "Are you sure you aren't here for Sister Marianna's scarf?"

This was the proverbial shoe everyone was waiting to hear drop.

Sister Lou glanced at Gary Hargreaves, the finance director; Urban Rodgers, the chef; and Kelsey Bennett, the administrative assistant. Their wide-eyed expressions of innocence gave them away.

Yes, it would have been more convenient if they hadn't drawn the deputies' attention to Sister Marianna's missing scarf, but Sister Lou didn't have anything to hide. After all, Sister Marianna had left her scarf in Autumn's office Friday, which was five days ago. If she'd felt some urgency to get the scarf back, she wouldn't have waited two additional days. She was, however, beginning to feel like the Briar Coast Cabin Resort staff's low-budget entertainment. All they needed were a large popcorn and a high-sugar drink.

Kelsey wrung her hands. Her blue eyes were enormous with uncertainty. "I thought that, if the deputies had come across Sister Marianna's scarf during their search, then maybe they could give it back."

That isn't the way it works. "Thank you, Kelsey. Yes, since I was here, I did ask about the scarf. Did you find it?"

"No." Fran smoothed back loose tendrils of curly blond hair that had escaped the bun at the nape of her neck. "When did Sister Marianna . . . lose . . . it?"

Sister Lou detected skepticism in the deputy's tone. "Deputy Cole, what are you implying?"

"Tell me how this plays with you, Sister." Ted crossed his arms. "Sister Marianna came back Monday morning. She and Autumn Tassler got into yet another argument. By our count, this would've been the third. In the heat of the moment, she used her scarf to kill Tassler, then, realizing she'd left her scarf behind, she asked you to get it back for her."

"That's not rational, Deputy Tate." Sister Lou tilted her head as she considered the deputy's charge.

"If Marianna was already holding the scarf, why wouldn't she put it in her pocket? Why would she leave it at the crime scene?"

Ted's gaze wavered slightly. "To throw us off her scent."

Sister Lou started shaking her head before Ted finished speaking. "That doesn't make sense, either. Leaving her scarf at the crime scene would only draw attention to her."

"She was pretty angry with Autumn. She accused her of meddling in the retreat." Arrogance stamped Gary's soft features. His bright green eyes avoided contact with Sister Lou.

"That's right. According to witnesses, they argued several times." Ted settled his hands on his hips, drawing attention to the looser fit of his spruce green gabardine pants. "Those arguments give her motive."

"No, Deputy Tate." Sister Lou folded her hands in front of her. "Those arguments give *you* an excuse to keep a member of the congregation on your suspect list."

Fran scowled. "In addition to a motive, Sister Marianna also had means in the form of the scarf and opportunity, if she arrived at the resort early enough."

Sister Lou faced Fran. "You're assuming Marianna would take someone's life because of a disagreement over green beans versus macaroni and cheese. She wouldn't."

Fran looked stubborn. "When Sister Marianna asked you to get her scarf, did she come to you personally or did she call you?"

"She sent me an e-mail." Sister Lou felt cornered by the deputies' questioning.

"So you didn't actually see her Monday morning." Fran crossed her arms. "Then how can you be sure that she was in her office and not here?"

Sister Lou looked from Fran to Ted, Gary, Urban, and Kelsey. They all looked back at her with expectant expressions.

She held Fran's bottle green gaze. "I have absolute faith in Marianna's innocence."

Now she needed to find a way to prove it to these doubting Thomases.

Sister Lou was renewed after listening to Father Ryan O'Flynn's homily during the eleven a.m. Mass Wednesday in the motherhouse chapel. This morning's exchange with the two sheriff's deputies in front of the audience of Briar Coast Cabin Resort employees faded to the background. She'd gained instead a sense of clarity and calm.

She was a sister with a plan.

Sister Lou navigated the stream of Hermionean sisters and associates on their way to lunch in the motherhouse dining room and returned to the congregational offices. She tossed a greeting to the sister on duty at the office's front desk as she strode through the reception area and down the rose-carpeted hallway.

She stopped in the threshold of Sister Marianna's office. "We need to talk."

Sister Marianna didn't look up from the notes she

was making on a sheet of paper. "It will have to wait, Louise. I'm on my way to lunch."

Sister Marianna's obsessive-compulsive behavior was on full display in her office. There wasn't a sheet of paper out of place, and there was no dust on the furnishings or lint on the carpet.

In a front corner of the room, a brick red blazer hung from a hook on the pale gray steel and plastic coatrack. The blue, gold, and white Hermionean cross was pinned to the left lapel.

Framed watercolor prints of Jesus, the apostles, and St. Hermione were displayed in a neat row across the far wall. On the wall beside her, Sister Marianna displayed her educational degrees—bachelor's, master's, and doctorate—and certificates of commendation. The office was rigidly professional and painfully sterile. It even smelled clean, like a dentist's office. The overall effect was disquieting.

"This can't wait." Sister Lou crossed the threshold and shut the door behind her.

That captured Sister Marianna's attention. She looked up, her gaze shifting from Sister Lou to the closed door and back. She lowered her pen and straightened her back. "Very well. What is it that simply cannot wait?"

"Deputy Cole and Deputy Tate consider you a suspect in Autumn's murder." Sister Lou settled onto one of the chairs in front of Sister Marianna.

"Me?" Sister Marianna's features balanced surprise and amusement. "Good heavens. Why on earth would they suspect me?"

"Several of Autumn's staff told them about the

arguments the two of you had. The deputies consider your disagreements a motive for murder."

"I'm certain I'm not the only person to have argued with that taxing woman. Forgive me for speaking ill of the dead, but she was a challenge." Sister Marianna spread her arms. Her crisp white blouse complemented her short, snow-white hair. "Autumn Tassler was an argumentative woman, God rest her soul."

That isn't the only characteristic Marianna and Autumn share.

Sister Marianna wasn't wrong. Autumn had had confrontations with other people not long before her murder. At this point in time, however, Sister Lou was concerned only with the disagreements the resort owner had had with Sister Marianna. "They're using the arguments and your missing scarf as reasons to investigate you."

Sister Marianna's eyebrows came together. "What does my scarf have to do with anything?"

"They believe the scarf may have been the murder weapon."

Sister Marianna seemed further confused by Sister Lou's explanation. "Autumn was strangled with a scarf?"

"The deputies are looking into that possibility."

"They can look all they'd like." Sister Marianna shrugged. "They won't connect my scarf to Autumn's murder because I didn't kill her."

"You sent me an e-mail Monday morning, asking me to get your scarf from Autumn." Sister Lou considered her project partner critically. "Where were you when you sent it?"

Sister Marianna's winter gray eyes flared with surprise. "Do *you* think I had something to do with Autumn's murder, Louise?"

"Of course not." She was irritated that Sister Marianna had asked that question. "No one who knows you would believe for a moment that you were involved, but the deputies don't know you. We need tangible proof that you couldn't have done this."

"How do you prove a negative?" Sister Marianna drummed her fingers on her desk. For her, it was a surprising display of a lack of self-control.

Sister Lou let her gaze wander to the picture window behind Sister Marianna as she clung to her after-Mass calm. The view provided a different perspective of the congregation's grounds from the window in her own office. It framed the entrance to the congregational offices and the aging oak trees, which lined the winding asphalt driveway that rose toward the visitors' parking lot.

She drew her gaze away from the fall scene outside and back to her colleague. "Where were you Monday morning, Marianna?"

Again Sister Marianna appeared unwilling—or unable—to answer. "As I have already explained, Louise, I overslept that morning and was running behind schedule."

That answer didn't satisfy Sister Lou, nor would it alleviate the deputies' suspicions. "That's not like you. What aren't you telling me?"

Sister Marianna crossed her arms and scowled. "I appreciate your concern, Louise, but I'm innocent. I don't have to explain myself to you or to the deputies."

"You're right. You don't have to explain yourself to me, but you're going to need an alibi for the deputies." She stood to leave. "Please don't underestimate them, Marianna. I know from recent experience that they're formidable adversaries."

"You worry too much." Sister Marianna waved a dismissive hand.

And you may not worry enough. "I'll leave the matter to you. I'm sorry to have delayed your lunch."

Sister Lou turned to leave. She'd always admired Sister Marianna's confidence, but this time, it could cause her more harm than either of them could imagine.

Sister Lou spotted the wandering calico cat as she jogged beside Sister Carmen Thursday morning. This time, the cat was slouched against a lamppost several feet closer to the motherhouse than the last one. Where had she been the past couple of days? Sister Lou hadn't seen her at the dorms and she hadn't been casing the parking lot.

This morning, the cat didn't seem particularly happy to see them. In fact, she seemed bored. Sister Lou inclined her head toward the cat. She rewarded Sister Lou with her patented chin lift before she turned away.

Sister Lou chuckled as she continued her jog. She loved their predawn jogs. It was so quiet at this time of the day. Peaceful. Perfect thinking conditions.

They followed their makeshift five-mile jogging trail: two laps around the motherhouse and the congregational offices, then on to the campus of the College of St. Hermione of Ephesus. Their congregation had founded the college as an all-women's academic institution in 1871. It had become coeducational in 1965.

They jogged through the college's administrative parking lot and up an incline to the residence halls. They would complete three laps around the campus's oval before turning onto the path that led to the center of town. At the path's two-mile marker, they'd turned back to the college to jog the same steps in reverse before returning to the motherhouse. Some people might find that course monotonous, but for them, it was efficient and kept them close to home.

The early-November air was cool. A few fallen leaves crunched beneath their athletic shoes. Having been born and raised in Los Angeles, it had taken more than a few seasons for Sister Lou to get used to the weather in the frozen tundra of upstate New York.

Will I ever get used to Marianna's stubbornness?

"Marianna won't listen to reason." Sister Lou kept pace beside her jogging partner, Sister Carmen, early Thursday morning.

Sister Carmen grunted. "When have you known Marianna to listen to reason that wasn't her own?"

That was a good point. "The deputies are determined to make her their prime suspect."

"Because of the scarf? But they don't have it." Sister Carmen looked sporty and seasonal in her pumpkin orange wicking long-sleeved jersey, neon green Windbreaker, and cocoa running pants.

"And we don't know whether it's the murder weapon." Sister Lou looked ahead toward the next slight incline, which led to the college's residence halls. "Marianna doesn't understand how determined these deputies become when they think they've identified a suspect."

"But you do."

"I remember it well." *Unfortunately.* Sister Lou leaned into the incline and shortened her stride to take the hill.

"That's another reason you should get involved with this case." Sister Carmen's words almost broke Sister Lou's jogging rhythm as they crested the incline together.

She'd told Sister Carmen of the prioress's request that she look into the case because of the concerns several donors had expressed over the congregation's connection to another murder.

"Carm, I'm not a member of law enforcement. I'm not qualified to do investigations." Sister Lou led the way around the loop that embraced the college's three residence halls.

"You faked it pretty well with Maurice's case." Sister Carmen swiped the sweat from her eyes with her fingertips. "You solved it before the deputies did."

"Mo and I had been friends for more than forty years." She still caught her breath when she thought of the way Maurice had been murdered. "I knew him, his industry, his community, and his family. I don't know anything about Autumn."

"You can find out about her." Sister Carmen's tone was encouraging. "Maybe Chris could help. He knows everyone."

Chris. My dear overprotective nephew, who was almost overwhelmed by anxiety when I decided to investigate Mo's murder. What would he say if I took on this case? "I made a promise to him that I wouldn't investigate any more murders."

"I don't want you to be in danger, either." Sister Carmen paused as though she was struggling not only with her breathing but with her words. "Maybe you can just ask a few questions. Find out who would want to kill her."

Sister Lou was torn. She wished that she could help clear the congregation and Sister Marianna, but she'd made a promise to Chris. When she was trying to find Maurice's killer, Chris had worried about her night and day. She also wasn't keen to further test the deputies' civility by stepping on their toes with another investigation.

And suppose I'm not able to solve Autumn's case?

She and Sister Carmen were silent as they jogged onto the oval at the heart of the campus. It was framed by the college's academic buildings and stately trees. Vibrant leaves sprinkled its well-manicured lawns and pedestrian pathways.

At the edge of the oval behind the academic buildings was a student center with a fully equipped exercise room. It was a nice facility, but Sister Lou preferred running outdoors. Even though she was from sunny Southern California, it would have to be pretty cold for her to run on an indoor treadmill. The experience was mind-numbing.

Sister Lou waved at the familiar faces that joined them as she and Sister Carmen completed their first round of the oval. A handful of students, staff, and faculty had braved the predawn darkness and chill November wind for their fitness routine.

"If the deputies focus their attention on Marianna, she'll need your help, Lou. She won't be prepared." Sister Carmen's dire prediction added to Sister Lou's tension.

"She doesn't want my help." Sister Lou tracked the group of seven or eight young women who jogged in a tight formation around the oval. Were they members of the track team?

"She's going to want it after the deputies question her."

But will it be too late by then?

Chapter 15

Chris thanked Sonya Russell-Fine as she offered him a white porcelain mug of Kenyan coffee. Steam from the mug carried the aromas of passion fruit, frankincense, grapefruit, and roasted cacao.

"We belong to the coffee-of-the-month club." Sonya's leaf green eyes gleamed with anticipation as she settled back onto the starfish-patterned, seafoam cloth sofa. The petite woman seemed lost among the swollen cushions and star-shaped throw pillows.

Chris was meeting with Sonya and her husband, Donald Fine, in their parlor late Thursday morning. The visit was part of his advancement team's emergency stewardship campaign. All of the advancement officers were meeting with donors. They needed to convince supporters of the College of St. Hermione of Ephesus to continue their financial gifts. The Fines were potential donors he was hoping would become loyal donors. Had recent events placed that goal even farther from reach?

Several loyal and generous contributors had voiced concern over the college's founding congregation's connection to the Briar Coast Cabin Resort and, by extension, Autumn Tassler's murder. He needed to reassure the growing number of uneasy patrons. This was his third emergency meeting. The first two could have gone better.

Chris sipped the black coffee with caution. He was pleasantly surprised. It was naturally sweet and savory with a hint of cocoa. "This is very good."

"I love it." Sonya wrinkled her tip-tilted nose and shook her slender shoulders beneath the jacket of her raspberry pantsuit. She took another swallow. "Donald's not convinced."

Chris smiled. How many cups had she had before their ten o'clock meeting?

"It may be an acquired taste." Donald sat close beside his wife on the bright sofa. He looked comfortably wealthy in a tan business suit. His black shirt was unbuttoned at his neck. He was drinking from a normal-sized sea blue ceramic cup instead of the jumbo mugs with images of flying seagulls that Chris and Sonya cradled.

The couple was rumored to be still madly devoted to each other after more than forty years of marriage. That might explain why Donald had acquiesced to the parlor's seafaring theme. The motif was present on the matching sofa and love seat, as well as the armchair on which Chris sat. It also was carried out in the framed drawings of beaches, boats, lighthouses, and seagulls displayed on the four walls. The illustrations were done in colored pencils, watercolors, and oils. This led Chris to believe that Sonya had chosen the parlor's décor.

"Nonsense, you're not even trying to tolerate the coffee." Sonya slapped her husband's knee before turning to Chris. "But you aren't here just for the divine coffee and our even more divine company, are you, Chris?"

It wasn't just the caffeine talking. Sonya Russell-Fine was known to be sharp and direct.

Chris smiled. He could be direct, too. "A few members of the community are concerned because one of the sisters was quoted for an article about the Briar Coast Cabin Resort owner's murder."

Donald sent him a level look. "The sister quoted in the article is your aunt, isn't she?"

"Yes, she is." Had Donald heard the pride in his voice?

"Well, I understand your donors' concerns." Donald's brown eyes grew troubled. He dragged a large, thin hand through his silver and chestnut hair. "I'm worried, too. Briar Coast was a sleepy little town. That's one of the reasons we love it here. Now there have been two brutal murders in three months and both times the congregation has been involved."

That was the topic of discussion behind most closed doors across town. During his first emergency stewardship visit, the Prentisses had insisted on the college separating from the congregation. That wasn't going to happen. With his second visit, Chris had done his best to deflect the criticism and remind the donors of the excellent programs and services the college provided for its students. It was too early to tell whether that presentation had worked. He started to launch into his defense with this couple, but Sonya spoke first.

"Pull yourself together, Donald. You're becoming hysterical." She patted her husband's knee again. "And the congregation wasn't *involved* in either of those ghastly events. How ridiculous. They were tangentially connected." She turned to Chris. "More coffee?"

"No, thank you." Chris sipped the sweet, dark brew, buying himself time to process Sonya's defense of the congregation. "The recent murders have brought grief and concern to Briar Coast. The losses are very personal for the sisters because of the congregation's association with both victims."

"That can't be a coincidence." Donald shifted to face Chris more directly. He rested his right arm along the back of the sofa behind his wife.

Sonya snorted a laugh as she reached for the coffee carafe to refresh her mug. The shining auburn tresses of her professionally styled chin-length bob swung forward. "Have you been watching the *Father Dowling Mysteries* reruns again, dear? They make you so suspicious."

Donald lowered his eyes to the thick sandstone carpeting. His cheeks flushed. "No, they don't."

Sonya gave him an indulgent smile. "Then what are you implying, Donald? That the sisters somehow channeled a higher power to smite their guest speaker and the resort owner?"

Donald appeared frustrated. "I'm just saying there's more going on behind the scenes."

Chris watched in some dismay as his hostess filled her massive coffee mug to the top. Again. This couldn't be her second serving. It had to be her third. Or her fourth. He wasn't even halfway through his first. Should he intervene?

Sonya took a deep drink of the hot, strong java. "Yes, darling, it's called community involvement. When you roll up your sleeves to get things done for your neighbors, you expose yourself to different people, different experiences. Sometimes they're good, sometimes they're bad. In this case, sometimes they're murder."

Donald shook his head. "I just don't understand it."

"Well, darling, that's because you haven't volunteered a day in your life." Sonya squeezed her husband's knee. "Trust me when I tell you there's nothing nefarious going on at the congregation. We don't need to take up arms against the sisters."

"Thank you, Sonya." His hostess had just done his work for him. "The prioress will be grateful when I tell her how eloquently you've defended the congregation."

Sonya's radiant smile was at least partially caffeine induced. "Please let Sister Barbara know that she can continue to count on my support."

Donald frowned. "How much money have you been giving them?"

"It's my money to give, Donald. He forgets that he isn't the only financial genius in the family." Sonya cocked her head as she continued to cradle her coffee mug. "What's new at the college?"

Chris launched into his teaser announcement about the college's proposal to freeze tuition. But in the corner of his mind, his fears for the congregation multiplied. What impact were the community's suspicions having on the donations the congregation depended on for the services and programs it provided?

"Sister Lou. I've been wondering how long it would take you to show up." Deputy Ted Tate slouched back on the black faux leather chair behind his desk in the Briar Coast County Sheriff's Office.

Sister Lou had been surprised that she could still enter the office's bullpen unescorted. She'd half suspected Ted would have placed her name on the top of a list of people who were barred from admittance. The room's silver marble flooring and cheerful yellow walls conveyed a friendly environment, but at least two of its residents were speaking a very different language.

She stopped beside Ted's desk late Thursday morning, disconcerted to find it in even greater disarray than the last time she'd seen it. There were layers upon layers of papers and folders, some branded with coffee rings from his cracked and stained mug. His bronze nameplate was partially buried under the paper explosion. His messy workstation was thrown into stark contrast with his partner's well-organized, uncluttered desk, which butted up against his.

Sister Lou turned her attention to Deputy Sheriff Fran Cole's desk and her bronze nameplate—a match to Ted's—which stood on the dust-free edge of her desk. Fran was bent over her keyboard, hard at work on . . . something. Sister Lou felt the chill from the other woman's snub.

Sister Lou projected a serious, determined demeanor. "Good morning, Deputies. Have you found Sister Marianna's scarf?"

Fran hit a couple of keys on her desktop computer's keyboard before spinning her black swivel chair to face Sister Lou. "Have you?"

Translation: No, the sheriff's office hasn't recovered the suspected murder weapon.

Sister Lou ignored the bait. "Do you still think her scarf was the murder weapon?"

Ted leaned forward on his chair. He'd definitely lost weight. "Do you have reason to believe it's not?"

Sister Lou turned to Ted. "Is it your intention to answer every question I ask with your own question?"

Ted taunted her with a grin. "What do you think?"

The bullpen seemed rather relaxed for a department in the middle of a murder investigation. Several deputies were chatting on their desk phones. Others had congregated around the coffee station. The open box of pastries explained the scent of fresh cinnamon rolls that floated on the air.

Uninvited, Sister Lou settled onto the visitor's chair closest to Ted's desk and continued to figuratively beat her head against their virtual stone wall. "I have at least one reason to believe Autumn wasn't choked with Sister Marianna's scarf."

Ted rocked his chair back and forth as he studied Sister Lou. "Wanna share?"

Sister Lou looked away from him. His swaying was making her motion sick. "Sister Marianna didn't kill Autumn."

"How do you know that?" Fran's blond curls struggled to remain allied with the bun at the nape of her long, slender neck.

Sister Lou tilted her head. "The better question is whether it's too early to settle on a suspect, especially since the best you can do is a couple of disagreements and a missing scarf."

"It's a start and a theory." Fran's gaze was stubborn.

Sister Lou could be stubborn as well. She glanced again at Ted. "Have you considered that, even if Sister Marianna's scarf turns out to be the murder weapon, she may not have been the one who used it?"

"We knew you'd pull that one out sooner or later," Ted crowed in his most obnoxious voice yet. "We're going to have it DNA tested."

The scarf has to be found first. "May I ask who else you've interviewed?" Sister Lou treaded carefully, aware of the tension that burdened her relationship with the deputies.

It wasn't careful enough.

"No, you may not." Ted snapped his outrage. "Who the hell . . . heck—do you think you are?"

Fran's response was more moderate. "Sister, we're under no obligation to even tell you the stuff we've already told you."

Ted continued his bluster. "Yeah. You're lucky we've told you what we did."

"I know that I am. Thank you." Sister Lou tried a conciliatory tone. "Have you spoken with Autumn's cousin, January Potts?"

Ted scowled. "Why?"

Sister Lou hesitated. "During one of my meetings with Autumn, her cousin stormed into her office. She was furious. Before she finally left, she threatened to kill Autumn."

"When?"

"Why?"

Fran and Ted responded simultaneously. Sister Lou answered Ted's question first. "About two weeks ago. Kelsey overheard the argument as well."

"What was the argument about?" Fran asked.

Sister Lou was uncomfortable sharing such personal information, but this was a murder investigation and an innocent woman was under suspicion. "Ms. Potts accused Autumn of having an affair with her husband."

Ted gave Sister Lou a suspicious look. "Why didn't Kelsey tell us this?"

"I have no idea." Sister Lou spread her hands. "You'll have to ask her."

Ted didn't move. "How far would you go to get your friend off the hook?"

Sister Lou stood. The kernel of temper was a little harder to restrain this time. "While you're questioning my integrity, perhaps you could ask January Potts why she wanted Autumn dead. I trust you're capable of multitasking."

She turned to leave. Déjà vu. She was bringing the deputies important information about their case.

However, just as with Maurice's murder, they were either too proud, too stubborn, or too dense to give her information credence.

Is it the information—or me?

Sister Lou's phone rang a few minutes after five o'clock Thursday afternoon. Still focused on the document she was drafting, she picked up the phone. "Sister Lou LaSalle."

"January Potts has an airtight alibi." Ted was crowing again.

Sister Lou saved her computer file and shifted her full attention to the call. "What is it?"

"She was helping her husband get ready for work Monday morning. You know, getting his clothes together, making his breakfast, packing his lunch, all the little wifely chores."

Wifely chores? "Those sound more like acts of caring and affection, wouldn't you agree?" *Or perhaps we should all have wives.*

Ted grunted. "Anyway, the time of death was between six and seven in the morning. Her husband left for work around seven-thirty."

Sister Lou turned to contemplate the scene framed by the window at the side of her office. The image was dazzling with vibrant autumn hues—red, orange, gold—set against the rolling green lawn and evergreen bushes. Fallen leaves tumbled on the breeze that swept across the grounds and wove between the tall, old oak trees that circled the perimeter.

"Her alibi is her husband?" *Who she suspects had an*

affair with her cousin. Am I the only one who's dubious about that alibi?

"That's right." Ted responded in a gloating tone.

Sister Lou imagined the rather cheery bullpen in the sheriff's office: the table of coffee and treats toward the back of the room, the sunshine yellow walls, and silver marbled floors. In the center of it all, Ted sat behind a tornado of papers. The sounds of ringing telephones and various office equipment were muted in the background, but the periodic tapping of his computer keyboard suggested Sister Lou didn't have Ted's full attention.

"Did her husband corroborate her alibi?"

Ted's silence seemed lengthy. Had he hung up on her or was he consulting with Fran? "We haven't spoken with the husband."

Sister Lou's spinning thoughts jerked to a halt. *Is anyone running this investigation?* "When will you be speaking with Mr. Potts?"

"Are you trying to take over *our* investigation? Again?" Ted was in full cantankerous mode.

"I'm simply trying to understand the progress that you're making." *Or not making.*

"You don't have to understand it."

Sister Lou took a breath. Diplomacy was becoming harder to maintain. Her inner voice struggled to come out. "You want to narrow your efforts to Sister Marianna and exclude everyone else. That's unwise."

"Everyone else has corroborating alibis."

For Sister Marianna's sake, all Sister Lou had to do was maintain her control longer than the deputy.

That's all. As luck would have it, Ted's patience was unraveling. She could hear it in his voice.

Sister Lou gave him a little push. "Have you interviewed everyone and verified all of their alibis? If so, you've been incredibly busy indeed, Deputy Tate." If she listened closely, she could hear Ted grinding his teeth.

"What's Sister Marianna's alibi?"

I wish I knew. "Sister Marianna is incapable of murder."

"In the right—or wrong—situation, anyone is capable of murder, Sister."

"Not Sister Marianna." She was sorry for whatever experiences had given Ted his harsh perspective, but her resolve remained firm.

"Well, I'm afraid I just don't have your faith, Sister." Ted's chuckle was humorless. "I hope you continue to see stars and unicorns for the rest of your life." He disconnected their call.

Sister Lou's hand lingered on the beige receiver after cradling her phone. The congregation's position with the sheriff's office in this latest murder investigation was becoming dire. Sister Lou let her hand slip from the phone as she sat back on her chair. She had to do something about this situation before it spun any further out of control. She prayed that Chris would understand—and forgive her.

Chapter 16

"I need your help." Sister Lou sat on the overstuffed sky blue armchair in her sitting room later Thursday evening. A vibrant jewel-toned throw pillow was tucked at her back. She faced her nephew, Chris, and their friend Shari. Earlier, the trio had shared dinner in the motherhouse dining room.

"Anything." Chris spoke from his usual position on the matching sky blue sofa. An afghan in a bold abstract pattern lay across its top. He'd loosened his navy-and-gray-striped tie the second he'd entered her apartment and hung his suit jacket in her closet. But his gunmetal gray slacks and ice-blue dress shirt still looked crisp and fresh.

"Absolutely." Shari had met them straight from work. The reporter still wore her slim-fitting green pants and kiwi green sweater. She'd curled up on Sister Lou's matching love seat. Her emerald green three-inch stilettos were on the floor beside it.

The armchair, sofa, and love seat stood on a

scarlet-and-gold-patterned area rug, surrounding a honey wood coffee table.

"You don't know what I'm going to ask of you." Their enthusiasm humbled Sister Lou. She met Chris's eyes. "You may not like it."

Shari shrugged. "You wouldn't ask us to do something illegal or immoral, so I'm willing to chance it. What'd you need?"

Sister Lou braced herself for Chris's reaction. She hated to put him in this position. "I need your help to investigate Autumn Tassler's murder."

Chris's onyx eyes widened with surprise, then narrowed with concern. "Aunt Lou, I thought we agreed that you wouldn't do this anymore."

Shari's expression also clouded with worry. "We don't want anything to happen to you. We were fortunate the first time. I don't think we should push our luck."

Chris sent Shari a grateful look before returning his attention to Sister Lou. "We understood how important it was for you to find Maurice's murderer. He was your friend, but you didn't know Ms. Tassler that well."

Chris and Shari were concerned for her safety, and she appreciated that. If the situation were reversed she'd feel the same. But the situation wasn't reversed and she had to at least try to get to the truth.

Sister Lou smoothed the skirt of her beige suit. Its matching jacket was in her closet. "I do have a connection to this investigation. The deputies have accused a friend of the murder."

"What?" Shari straightened on the love seat, uncurling her legs and lowering her stockinged feet to the red and gold area rug.

"Who?" Chris's eyebrows furrowed.

"Marianna." Sister Lou's voice reflected the disquiet she felt. "They've heard that Autumn and Marianna had a few disagreements and believe that gives her a motive for murder."

"That's ridiculous." Chris seemed disgusted. "Where do the deputies get these ideas?"

Sister Lou wondered the same thing. "I wish I knew. Marianna has a temper and she's never shied from confrontation—"

"No, she hasn't." Apparently, Chris's recollection of his one unpleasant exchange with Sister Marianna was still a vivid memory.

Sister Lou continued, "However, those arguments aren't motives for murder."

"What did they disagree about?" Shari asked.

"They had different ideas about the menu." The explanation sounded more ridiculous every time Sister Lou said it. "Marianna didn't welcome Autumn's input."

Shari blinked. "That's it? That's what they're using as motive for Sister Marianna murdering Autumn Tassler?"

"Yes." Sister Lou hesitated, reluctant to bring up the other strikes against Sister Marianna. "Also, Marianna doesn't have an alibi for the time of Autumn's murder, which was between six and seven o'clock that morning."

"I wouldn't, either," Shari pointed out. "I live alone."

"Shari's right." Chris rested his right ankle on his left knee. "That could be a problem, but it still doesn't seem like enough to consider her a suspect."

Sister Lou shifted her gaze between Chris and Shari. "Does your interest mean you're willing to help me?"

Shari exchanged a look with Chris. "Yes, but at the first sign of danger, we end the investigation. Agreed?"

"Agreed," Chris responded.

"Of course," Sister Lou concurred.

Shari continued, "I'm going to report on the case for the *Telegraph* just as we did with Maurice's investigation."

"That would be helpful, Shari. Thank you." Sister Lou hadn't considered that angle. "It could correct the public's image of the congregation and the college if we show that the congregation's only role in this tragedy is our pursuit of justice for the victim."

Chris gave Shari another approving look, which wasn't lost on Sister Lou. "Several donors are concerned about the connection between Autumn's murder and the college and congregation. Maybe your articles will help reassure them and any others who are having second thoughts about supporting us."

Shari nodded but her eyes were clouded with concern. "Just as long as you both realize that my reporting will be impartial. I'm going to report whatever we find—good, bad, or indifferent."

"We wouldn't expect anything else." Chris's gaze lingered on Shari.

Sister Lou pretended not to notice her nephew's growing infatuation with the reporter. "We know that you have too much integrity to compromise your stories."

Shari's cheeks flushed and she lowered her eyes. It was apparent that the reporter couldn't see what others saw in her: strength, intelligence, kindness. Hopefully, in time she'd realize that and so much more.

Sister Lou turned her attention to the paintings that hung on the warm yellow walls of her cozy little sitting room. The soothing religious scenes and landscape images helped clear her mind. "How should we approach this investigation?"

Shari raised her gaze to Sister Lou's. "I'll check out the *Telegraph*'s archives and learn everything I can about Autumn Tassler and her resort."

"Thank you, dear. That would be wonderful." Sister Lou was already gaining confidence in their mission.

Chris cocked his head. "Have you identified other possible suspects?"

Sister Lou placed her hands on the arms of her chair. The overstuffed cushions were soft to her touch. "I told the deputies that Autumn's cousin, January Potts, accused Autumn of having an affair with her husband and threatened to kill her. She's at the top of my list."

Shari blinked. "No doubt."

Chris's eyes were wide with disbelief. "Why isn't she on the top of the deputies' list?"

"Deputy Tate said she has an alibi, her husband." Sister Lou spread her hands. "She claims she was helping him get ready for work and making his breakfast at the time Autumn was being murdered."

Shari turned to Chris. "If you were married and your wife accused you of having an affair, would you eat the breakfast she made for you?"

Chris gave Shari a cautious look. "Remind me to stay on your good side."

"I'm serious." Shari raised her hands. "Her alibi is suspicious."

Sister Lou had the same suspicions. "Unless he doesn't know she suspects him of having an affair. Let's find out."

Shari rubbed her hands together. "It's exciting to have the team back together."

Sister Lou shared Shari's enthusiasm. "I appreciate your help. We're stronger together."

"Yes, we are." Chris echoed their sentiment, but Sister Lou heard the hesitancy in his voice and knew he was still worried.

Sister Lou understood his unease. *Are we in over our heads?*

"We should train for next year's marathon." Sister Carmen's proposal startled Sister Lou from her thoughts during their early Friday morning jog.

"What brought this on?" Sister Lou gaped at her exercise partner.

"I've been thinking about it for a while." Sister Carmen's short raven curls bounced around her round face as she kept pace with Sister Lou. "I've estimated that we've been jogging thirty miles a week for the past seven years. How much more would we have to run to train for a marathon?"

Sister Lou jogged up the winding driveway that led from the motherhouse toward the visitor parking lot that separated the congregation from the College of St. Hermione of Ephesus.

It sounded so reasonable when Sister Carmen explained it that way. But . . . "Running a marathon is a huge achievement. It's not something we can take lightly."

Sister Carmen snorted. "Seven years of dedicated running isn't taking anything lightly."

"When's the marathon?" Sister Lou felt the walls of inevitability closing in on her.

"The end of May."

Sister Lou was loath to squash the hope she heard in Sister Carmen's voice. "I'll think about it."

"Don't take too long. Registration goes up five dollars each month."

Sister Lou was tempted to decline now and save the money. "I'll keep that in mind."

"In the meantime, you keep speeding up. What's wrong?"

Tension was returning to Sister Lou's shoulders. The confidence that had been building yesterday evening as she'd brought the amateur sleuth team back together had evaporated when her radio alarm clock went off this morning. "I don't know what I'm doing."

"You're running five miles, and I'm running them with you." Sister Carmen's flippant response tempted Sister Lou to turn around and go back to bed.

"Carm." Sister Lou used her warning voice.

"Sorry, I couldn't resist." Sister Carmen tossed her a cheeky grin. "What're you talking about?"

Sister Lou looked ahead to the parking lot that separated the congregation's property from the college's campus. Mission-style wrought-iron lampposts lit their improvised jogging course in the predawn shadows. Sister Carmen's neon orange wicking jersey also kept the darkness at bay. She practically glowed. In comparison, Sister Lou's gray jersey was lost in the shadows.

"Chris and Shari have agreed to help me investigate Autumn Tassler's death—"

"That's fantastic news!" Sister Carmen's coffee brown eyes sparkled in the dim light. "How did you get Chris to agree?"

"As soon as he learned that the deputies were focusing on Marianna, he agreed to help." Sister Lou drew in a deep breath, filling her lungs with cool morning air and familiar fall scents—moist earth and faded leaves.

Sister Carmen sobered. "The threat to Marianna makes it personal to all of us."

"It also makes it more urgent." Sister Lou felt the strain.

"You're right. There's a lot at stake."

Sister Lou gave a mental groan. "Marianna's reputation, the congregation's reputation, and donors for the congregation as well as the college. What made me think I could do this?"

"Do you have a choice?" Sister Carmen's voice was somber.

They jogged in silence for a time, their pace perfectly synchronized after seven years of exercising together. The path was silent except for the periodic crunching of fall leaves under their running shoes. They climbed the incline on their way to the college's residence halls, leaning in and shortening their strides.

"Is it true that some of the college's donors want the college to separate from the congregation?" Sister Carmen managed the question as they crested the short hill.

"It's true." The idea still hurt Sister Lou's heart. Did those donors realize what they were asking? The congregation had founded the college and was still very much involved in its well-being.

As they circled the residence halls, Sister Lou glanced up and scanned the windows. Most of them were dark as students remained safe and warm in their beds. Not surprising; it wasn't yet six o'clock. But a few rooms were lit. Either those students left desk lamps on or there was a small group of early risers, hitting the books.

"We have to clear Marianna's name. Soon." Sister Carmen's declaration cut short Sister Lou's musings.

"I agree, but it will take me forever to learn about Autumn before I even start investigating." From her peripheral vision, Sister Lou caught Sister Carmen's quick glance.

"Then get to know her while you work the case."

Sister Carmen's use of the law enforcement slang reminded Sister Lou that her friend enjoyed police procedural TV shows. "Besides, it's not just what you know. Your strength is what you observe. That's how you solved Maurice's murder."

"I hadn't considered that my strength." *Am I like Shari in that I'm not aware of how people view me?* "I don't want to disappoint anyone."

Sister Carmen snorted again. "You're not disappointing us. We just want you to try. The only person you'd possibly disappoint would be yourself."

There was that.

Never let them see you sweat.

First thing Friday morning, Shari stood on the threshold of the bullpen in the sheriff's office. She inconspicuously inhaled a deep, steadying breath. She could almost taste the warm pastries and fresh coffee. How could a sheriff's office smell like a bakery? She'd bet cash money that no other law enforcement office in the country smelled like this one.

She spotted Deputy Fran Cole and her partner, the ever-grumpy Deputy Ted Tate, at their respective desks toward the center of the room.

Shari swaggered up to them. Her sky blue stilettos tapped a cocky tattoo against the silver marble flooring. "Morning, Deputies. How's the case going? Any leads?"

Ted spun on his desk chair to face Shari. He gave her a wide-eyed look of mock surprise. "*You're* asking *us* for a lead on a murder investigation? But we thought you, Sister Lou, and Chris LaSalle were the crack detectives."

"Wow, you guys are really thin-skinned, aren't you?" Shari glanced at Fran, who seemed absorbed with something on her desktop computer. She turned again to Ted. "So is that a no, you don't have any leads?"

"None that we're going to share with you." Ted gave her a look that was even more belligerent than his normal expression.

Shari bit back an irritated sigh. "The first forty-eight hours of a murder investigation are the most critical. It's been four days."

"Thanks for the update," Fran responded without looking away from her computer monitor.

Shari gave the taciturn Ted a hard look. "Have you lost weight?"

Ted straightened on his chair and sent a self-conscious look toward his partner. "A little."

"Well, good for you. Must be torture resisting those pastries."

Ted gave her a noncommittal grunt.

Shari turned away to scan the bullpen. The sunny yellow walls and white trim were uncharacteristically cheerful for a law enforcement bullpen. The low level of activity that hummed around the room wasn't surprising. Briar Coast wasn't exactly a hotbed of criminal activity. Speeding, vandalism, and jaywalking usually topped the police blotters that ran in the *Telegraph*. The two murders during her time here were tragic outliers.

As everyone in town liked to remind their neighbors, Briar Coast had had only three murders in the past eight years, with the last two occurring in the past three months.

Shari returned her attention to the uncooperative deputies. "Do you have any suspects other than Sister Marianna Tuller?"

Fran looked away from her computer file long enough to send her a baleful look. "You've been talking with Sister Lou."

Shari considered the tall, slender deputy, from the disorderly blond hair struggling to stay together at the base of her neck to her tan sheriff's shirt. "Why do the two of you always fixate on the congregation? Bad memories of Catholic school?"

Fran returned to her computer monitor.

"Why are you here?" Ted rescued the deep red McIntosh apple from beneath a pile of papers and folders on his table. He tossed it back and forth between his hands.

Shari gestured toward the fruit. "Is that what's keeping you away from the pastries? Kind of a poor substitute, huh?"

Ted glowered at her and returned the apple to his desk. "What d'you want?"

Shari waved her reporter's notebook. "I'm covering the investigation for the *Telegraph*. Do you have anything for me?"

Fran looked up again. Her green eyes scrutinized Shari. "You, Sister Lou, and Chris are investigating this case as well, aren't you?"

"Don't you people have enough to do?" Ted was disgusted.

Shari sighed. "I've got an article to file for my paper." And if she didn't get a quote from at least one of the deputies, Diego would make her wish she'd never heard of the *Telegraph*.

"You write stories." Fran's tone was less than complimentary. "Sister Lou saves souls. Chris raises money. *We're* the ones who investigate murders."

Shari spread her arms. "Then tell me about your investigation so I can write my story."

Ted grunted. "Why should we?"

"I'd expect that response from a seven-year-old." Shari rolled her eyes. "Prove to me that you're too evolved to hold childish grudges."

"We don't have anything to prove." Fran's attention was still on her monitor as though Shari's presence in the bullpen didn't register with her anymore.

"Fine." Shari threw her hands up. "But this town needs to feel safe. They need to know their law enforcement is doing everything they can to find whoever murdered Autumn Tassler."

"And we are." Fran's tone was sharp.

"Like what?" Shari responded in kind. "What are you doing to find the killer hiding in plain sight in this community?"

Ted turned on her. "You can't come in here, demanding answers."

Shari stepped closer to his desk and leaned in. "I want answers. My readers deserve information. Are you going to give me an update or not?"

Ted held her gaze with his cold gray eyes. "No comment."

Shari straightened and looked toward Fran. No response there, either. She inclined her head. "All right. I'll let my readers know that the Briar Coast County sheriff's deputies assigned to the case have confirmed that they haven't made any progress."

She turned to march out of the bullpen. She didn't have to wonder about Diego's reaction to her update. She knew it wouldn't be pretty.

Chapter 17

Two o'clock on a Friday afternoon was an off-hour for the Briar Coast Café. The eatery was crowded, but less so than Chris was used to seeing it.

He sat with Sister Lou and Shari at a blond wood table near a window toward the front of the café. Chris took a deep drink of the dark roast coffee, black, no sugar, that filled his white porcelain mug. His aunt was drinking unsweetened chai tea, but Shari also had chosen coffee. He'd watched in horror as she'd added sugar, French vanilla–flavored cream, and cinnamon to her hazelnut coffee. The brew danced a fine line between coffee and candy.

He lowered his mug and his gaze shifted to the thick unfrosted brownie on the delicate white porcelain plate in front of him. He cut a piece with his fork. Its fresh-from-the-oven scent exploded toward him. It became part of the enticing fragrance of warm pastry, cinnamon, chocolate, confectioners' sugar, and butter that swam around the café. The treat was rich and sweet to his taste buds. Its texture was soft and moist in his mouth.

Beneath those bakery scents, Chris detected the aromas that lingered from the lunchtime crowd: fresh vegetables, soups, and well-seasoned meats.

"I know it hasn't been twenty-four hours yet, but have you learned anything that could give us a starting point?" Sister Lou's brownie had both chocolate chips and walnuts.

Shari pulled a notebook from her oversized olive green handbag. Before opening the notebook, she swallowed a bite of her chocolate chip and walnut brownie with sour cream frosting. Looking at it made Chris's teeth hurt. She hastily swallowed. "I did an Internet search of Autumn Tassler and the resort. She opened her place three years ago."

Chris drank a mouthful of his hot, strong coffee. The mug was warm in his palms. "I remember. The *Telegraph* ran an announcement about the opening, but the article focused more on the resort. It didn't have much information on Autumn."

"That's why I widened my search beyond the *Telegraph*'s archives." Shari licked frosting from the corner of her mouth. "Autumn Tassler was an interesting person."

"In what way?" Sister Lou sat forward.

Chris could see and feel his aunt's interest. She wore a pale pink blouse with her brown pantsuit. He'd noticed that she'd started adding brighter colors to her outfits. Was that Shari's influence?

Shari looked up from her notebook. "Autumn married Roy Fortney when she was twenty-six. He decided to go back to school for his master's in finance degree and she worked two jobs to support them and help him with his tuition."

"That's a lot of responsibility." Chris had a feeling this wasn't a happy story.

"I know. Unfortunately, her sacrifices weren't appreciated." Shari's chocolate brown eyes promised retribution for all unappreciated wives. "After Autumn supported his education and helped him build a successful company, Roy filed for divorce and married a much younger woman."

Sister Lou shook her head in disgust. "Such a shame."

"I'm sure he thought that every time he wrote her alimony check." Shari's dry tone brought a smile to Chris's face.

Sister Lou smiled as well. "How did she come to start her resort?"

Shari sipped her candied coffee. "It seems to have taken her five years to get her act together. Her monthly alimony was pretty significant."

"She deserved it." Chris finished his first mug of coffee. He wanted another but Shari's report was too compelling for him to excuse himself to return to the coffee station.

Shari continued, "She used her alimony to get her MBA and open her resort. Her ex-husband was still paying her alimony, which she apparently reinvested in her resort."

Chris's attention perked up even more. He scanned the room to make sure no one in the café was eavesdropping. "That gives her ex-husband motive. Maybe he didn't want to continue the alimony payments."

"It also gives his new wife a motive." Sister Lou sipped thoughtfully from her mug of tea. "She probably didn't like the fact that her husband was still paying alimony to his ex-wife."

Chris inclined his head. "Good work, Shari."

"That was an excellent report." Sister Lou smiled. "Thank you. There's something we need to follow up on, though."

"What's that?" Chris finished off his brownie.

Sister Lou cradled her mug between her small palms. "Rita Morris, Autumn's business partner, said the resort was making very little money. That was one of the reasons she wanted to sell it. But if the resort is booked solid with events from all over this region and Autumn is reinvesting in it, why is it losing money?"

Shari frowned. "Do you think someone's cooking the books?"

"It's possible." Sister Lou finished her brownie, then washed it down with the rest of her unsweetened chai tea. "Autumn didn't want to sell the resort, though."

Shari's winged eyebrows took flight. "Do you think that gives Rita a motive for murder? She wanted to sell but Autumn didn't?"

"It's possible." Sister Lou spread her hands. "I sensed tension between them. But if we're looking at Rita for the sale, we should also look at Crane Enterprises, the company that wanted to buy the resort."

Chris considered the view through the window beside him as he processed the information they'd already collected on the case. His car sat beside Shari's in the parking lot behind the café. Beyond the lot, the tree-lined streets hosted mostly small businesses that already were decorated for Christmas weeks before Thanksgiving. Some of the stores had started posting their Christmas decorations right after Halloween. Was he the only one who found that commercial ploy obnoxious?

He turned back to his aunt and Shari. "We've been here less than an hour, and in that time, we've identified five possible suspects: Autumn's ex-husband, his new wife, her business partner, someone with access to the resort's accounts, and the company that offered to buy the resort. Are the deputies looking into these people as well?"

Shari finished her heavily doctored coffee. "I spoke with them this morning. They didn't give me any information but I had the sense they were only looking at Sister Marianna."

"We also need to speak with the employees." Sister Lou leaned into the table and folded her arms on its surface.

"I thought they had alibis." Chris frowned. "Several of them arrived together."

Sister Lou pursed her lips in thought. "Autumn was murdered between six and seven in the morning. The killer could have left her office unseen and then entered the main resort cabin with a coworker, giving himself—or herself—an alibi."

Shari blew a breath. "Wow, our list of suspects just got a lot longer."

Sister Lou frowned. "And, as usual, time isn't on our side."

* * *

She couldn't concentrate. Late Friday afternoon, Sister Lou gave up all pretense of productivity. She saved the electronic document she'd told herself she was drafting and pushed away from her desk. Restless, she wandered across the room. The thick rose carpeting was soft beneath her sensible black pumps.

Through her office's rear window, Sister Lou studied the nearly naked maple trees that stood beside the winding driveway. Along the rolling lawn, dying and detached autumn leaves tumbled and tossed in the faint breeze. A deep breath released the knotted muscles in her neck and shoulders. The white tea scent from the tiny basket of potpourri that stood on a corner of her desk soothed her.

It had been more than an hour since she'd returned from meeting with Chris and Shari at the Briar Coast Café. Parts of their conversation still played on a loop in her mind.

Wow, our list of suspects just got a lot longer.

And, as usual, time isn't on our side.

Her shoulder muscles tensed again. She lifted her gaze to the cloud-covered gray sky. "I don't know what to do. So many people are depending on me, but I feel inadequate to this task. I need Your guidance. Help me to understand what I'm meant to do."

The knock on her half-open door surprised her. She looked at her crimson wristwatch. It was a few minutes past four in the afternoon.

"Come in." She turned toward the door.

Sister Marianna walked in. Sister Lou went cold

at the expression on the other woman's face. The aggressive force of nature she'd come to know and try to love was absent. She didn't recognize the uncertain, confused, and frightened person who'd entered her office.

"Marianna, what is it?"

"Louise, I need your help."

Chapter 18

Sister Lou gestured to the cushioned seats in front of her desk. She watched in growing apprehension as Sister Marianna walked toward them on unsteady legs, then collapsed onto the closest one.

"What's happened, Marianna?" Sister Lou resumed her seat behind her desk.

Sister Marianna drew a shaky breath. "The sheriff's deputies came here—to my office—to interrogate me." Her gray eyes were wide with disbelief. Her voice strained with incredulity. "*Me.*"

Dread left a metallic taste in Sister Lou's mouth. "What did they ask you?"

"They wanted to know about my scarf, what it was made of, the design, the length, and when was the last time I'd used it." Her eyes seemed to plead with Sister Lou. "Louise, they swabbed the inside of my mouth."

They have Marianna's DNA!

Sister Lou's mind wiped blank. She pressed against her chair's padded back. The deputies were putting all of their efforts on Sister Marianna. *Why won't they even consider any of the leads I've offered them?* "Start from the beginning and tell me everything the deputies said to you."

Sister Marianna made a visible effort to pull herself together. Against the material of her navy skirt suit, her already pale skin appeared almost translucent. Her deep breaths caused her shoulders and chest to rise, then abruptly drop.

"All right. They arrived shortly after three o'clock." Sister Marianna folded her hands together on her lap. The skin above her knuckles showed white. "I escorted them back to my office from the reception area and they immediately went on the attack. I find it impossible to believe that Deputy Tate was educated in a Catholic institution. He is an especially odious man."

Finally, something on which we can agree.

Sister Marianna continued, "They asked me where I was Monday morning at the time that Autumn was murdered. Then they told me they were continuing their search for the murder weapon. That's when they pulled out a very large cotton applicator and demanded a sample of my DNA. The entire process was demeaning, demoralizing, and invasive."

Continuing their search. Why had the deputies gone back to the scene of the crime?

"But they haven't *found* a scarf?" Sister Lou was grasping at straws but even small details mattered.

"No, they have not. I also told them that I knew that they were very well aware of the fact that I'd misplaced mine."

"What was their response?"

"They said that they were confident they'd find it. Once they did, they'd send it to their forensics lab for testing. They said they wanted me to be aware of that. Why? Why would I need to be aware of that?" Sister Marianna's voice rose in near hysteria.

"Marianna, stay with me. I need you to continue to concentrate." Sister Lou considered everything Sister Marianna had just told her as she rolled her pen between her right thumb and index finger.

Why are they still so focused on Marianna and her scarf?

"Louise, they were so feral." Sister Marianna interrupted the heavy silence.

Sister Lou's mind worked to find the missing pieces of this dire puzzle. "Someone's framing you, Marianna."

"What?"

Sister Lou waited for her hearing to return. "The deputies want to believe our congregation is somehow involved in this tragedy and someone is feeding their conspiracy."

"But how do I prove my innocence when someone is deliberately trying to make me look guilty?" The fear was stark on Sister Marianna's face and in her voice.

Who could blame her?

Sister Lou stood to pace the room. "Chris, Shari, and I have started investigating Autumn's murder."

"You didn't tell me that." Cautious relief crept into Sister Marianna's words.

Sister Lou turned to pace back toward her desk. She stopped an arm's length from Sister Marianna's chair. "Where were you the morning Autumn was murdered?"

The other woman's expression closed. "I told you. I was running late. I overslept."

Sister Lou shook her head. "You never oversleep. If you want us to help clear your name, you have to confide in us. We can't prove your innocence if you keep us in the dark."

Sister Marianna returned Sister Lou's stubborn stare. Finally, she leaned back on her seat, crossing her arms and legs. "Very well. If you must know, I was sulking."

The image of Sister Marianna sulking wasn't any more believable than her excuse of oversleeping. "Why?"

Sister Marianna threw up her hands. "Because Barbara assigned you to assist me with the retreat, and you seemed to be taking over the event planning. It was my project. I asked Paula and Angela to meet with me to give me their insight. That was about seven-thirty Monday morning."

Sister Lou was taken aback. She returned to her desk, searching her mind for a suitable response and coming up with . . . nothing. "I'm sorry that Barb's decision caused you pain, Marianna. I'm sorry for my part in that. But, unfortunately, your feelings haven't given you an alibi, though. The deputies will claim that, although the timing would have been tight, you could have killed Autumn at six o'clock and returned in enough time to meet Paula and Angie by seven-thirty."

Sister Marianna shifted forward on her seat. "I want to help with the investigation."

Oh, now that would be unwise. "That won't be necessary, thank you. Chris, Shari, and I can handle it."

"Ridiculous." Sister Marianna tossed her hand in a cutting gesture, a clear indication that she'd regained her self-assurance. Sister Lou felt equal parts of relief and regret. "This investigation is to clear *my* name. I should *definitely* be involved."

"Actually, Marianna, this investigation is about finding Autumn's killer. That's the only way we can repair the congregation's reputation."

Steely determination glinted in Sister Marianna's gray eyes. "What's our next step?"

Sister Lou swallowed a sigh. To paraphrase *Star Trek: The Next Generation*, resisting Sister Marianna was futile.

How am I going to explain this to Chris and Shari?

Shari closed the passenger-side door of Sister Lou's orange compact car late Saturday afternoon and waited as Sister Lou emerged from behind the steering wheel. Sister Lou had driven the two of them to January Potts's house Saturday morning. The ride had been an adventure.

"We must have made it here in record time." Shari was still reeling from Sister Lou's driving and her announcement that Sister Marianna had invited herself to join their amateur sleuth team. "How exactly does Sister Marianna want to help us?"

Sister Lou adjusted the strap of her navy blue purse on her right shoulder as she walked down the tree-lined block toward the Potts's residence. "She wants to participate in our interviews, help with research, and attend our status meetings."

"Oh wow." Dazed, Shari fell into step beside her friend. Together, they navigated the minefield of running, screaming, laughing children. It was still early in the day. Shari wondered about the quantity of sugar the children had already consumed.

Sister Lou just smiled. Shari considered her friend's serene expression. On the surface, Sister Lou seemed at peace with this unexpected event. Shari hadn't realized the other woman was such an accomplished actress.

"Does Chris know Sister Marianna's going to be helping us? I got the impression they don't get along."

"I told him this morning. They'll be fine." Her mysterious smile suggested otherwise. "Here we are."

Shari set aside her doubts and prepared for the upcoming interview.

The Potts residence stood on the corner of the block. It was a big Craftsman-style stone home with dark brown wood trim and a low-pitched brown roof. Shari followed Sister Lou up the stairs to the wide, stone front porch and waited while she rang the doorbell.

Minutes later a tall woman with dark blue eyes and

a cap of light brown hair opened the door. Irritability marred her thin features. "May I help you?"

Her navy blue slacks and soft white long-sleeved jersey looked expensive, too expensive for puttering around the house. Was she on her way out?

Sister Lou gave the other woman a friendly smile. "Mrs. Potts, I'm Sister Lou LaSalle, and this is my friend Sharelle Henson. I was one of your cousin's clients."

January Potts barely glanced at Shari. She gave Sister Lou a dismissive look. "I had nothing to do with my cousin's business. You'd be better off speaking with her partner, Rita Morris. I'm sure you can reach her through the resort."

"We've actually met." Impressively, Sister Lou's smile remained in place. "You may not recall, but I remember you. I was the client in Autumn's office when you came to discuss a rather personal matter with her."

January's face flooded with embarrassed color. Shari wished she'd witnessed the confrontation that caused the other woman such discomfort. She almost felt sorry for her. Almost.

"Oh yes. I remember now." January's voice cooled even as her face heated. Neat trick.

Sister Lou nodded toward Shari. "We wanted to express our condolences on your loss."

January considered them for a brief, silent moment before stepping back. Her movements were almost insultingly stiff. "Come in."

Shari followed Sister Lou across the threshold.

The house's open floor plan was more space than Shari had ever seen in one person's home—or even in a furniture store. She adjusted the strap of her oversized olive green handbag farther up her shoulder as she followed their unwilling hostess into her foyer. January's white canvas shoes were silent against the honey wood flooring. Shari froze on the edge of the spacious foyer.

The room looked as though someone had spilled bubble bath all over it with vicious abandon. Everything was a nauseating shade of pink. Thick rouge drapes framed sheer blush curtains that allowed natural light to flood the square room. Salmon throw pillows nestled on the rose sofa and matching armchairs. Shari was reluctant to sit.

Sister Lou didn't appear distracted by the abundance of pink. She took off her brown wool winter coat and rested it on the arm of the sofa. Shari debated sitting on her emerald coat before reconsidering. She tentatively lowered herself beside Sister Lou and folded the garment across her thighs. By letting them keep their coats, January avoided giving the mistaken impression that they were welcome in her home.

Sister Lou set her handbag on her lap. The dark blue material complemented her pale green sweater, one of her new more colorful pieces of clothing. "We felt compelled to pay our respects to you on the death of your cousin. Based on your recent exchange, though, it doesn't appear that the two of you were close."

"We used to be." The expression in January's dark

blue eyes was an odd combination of defiance and embarrassment. On the overstuffed pink armchair, she looked like she'd settled onto a bottle of Pepto-Bismol.

"What changed?" To her knowledge, Shari didn't have any living relatives, but she couldn't imagine being so distant in response to their death.

January's smile was cool, her eyes colder. "Didn't your friend tell you? Autumn slept with my husband."

Sister Lou shifted on the thick, frilly rose sofa to better face January. "Autumn and I talked after you left. She denied your accusation."

"Of course she would." January sneered as though she thought Sister Lou was as dumb as a stone. Shari disliked the woman even more. "Quite frankly, I'd lost respect for her."

"That's unfortunate. May I ask what happened?" Sister Lou sounded genuinely concerned. Shari made a mental note to ask how she managed that.

She concentrated on evaluating their suspect and her environment as meticulously as she was certain Sister Lou was doing right now. The sister had mad powers of observation. What did she really think of the pink theme? What was her assessment of the framed displays of dried roses and flowers that covered the pale pink walls? What did they symbolize? Was January a gardener? Or perhaps those roses and flowers were from bouquets her husband had given her during happier times in their apparently disintegrating marriage.

January exhaled an impatient breath. "Autumn's

husband left her for a younger woman about five years ago. I learned that, ever since her divorce was finalized, she'd had a string of one-night stands—all with married men. It was as though she was trying to be the other woman her husband had left her for. That's just pathetic."

"I see." Sister Lou's tone told Shari she didn't "see" anything.

Shari would have to wait to ask her friend what she was actually thinking. For now, she'd just follow her lead. "It's too bad that your cousin slept with your husband. That's a big betrayal, but it takes two to tango. I'm surprised you haven't left him."

January looked taken aback by Shari's directness. "I threw him out two weeks ago."

Shari pounced on the information. "Two weeks? But your husband was your alibi for the morning Autumn was murdered."

"*Alibi?*" January gave a humorless laugh. "Why would *I* need an alibi? I didn't murder my cousin."

"You threatened to kill her." Sister Lou offered the reminder.

Shari tilted her head. "If you weren't making breakfast for your husband Monday morning, what *is* your alibi for your cousin's time of death?"

"Did you come to my home to accuse me of murder?" January sat straighter on her armchair. Her gaze moved between Sister Lou and Shari. "Those were words spoken in anger. They weren't to be taken seriously. I did *not* kill Autumn."

"Who would want to kill your cousin, Mrs. Potts?" Sister Lou asked.

"She really had you snowed, didn't she?" January sneered at them as though she thought Shari and Sister Lou were gullible marks. "Autumn wasn't some kind of saint, you know. Plenty of people had reasons to want her dead."

Shari spread her hands. "We're all ears."

January looked startled. "Maybe one of her lovers."

Shari frowned. "You mean, like your husband?"

Sister Lou spoke over January's outraged gasp. "When did you discover that Autumn was having an affair with your husband?"

January's dark eyes flared as though the question brought back the memory of her discovery. "Three weeks ago. About."

"Right before you confronted Autumn." Sister Lou seemed to already know the answer. She was after a confirmation only.

"That's right." January nodded once. The movement was jerky, as though her temper was rising. "I went to face her the next day—after I threw out my adulterous husband. I didn't waste any time putting an end to their lying and cheating."

Shari glanced impatiently between Sister Lou and January. "Who would want to kill your cousin? Give us a name."

"What do you care?" January scowled. "Are you some kind of private investigator or something?"

"Something." Shari liked that comparison. She

pulled her notepad from her olive green purse. "I'm a newspaper reporter."

January gasped. Her eyes stretched wide, horror replacing anger. "I didn't agree to an interview."

"Consider this background information. I'll protect you as one of my sources." Shari offered a negligent wave. "Who do you think wanted your cousin dead?"

"She's quite trustworthy." Sister Lou encouraged January when the other woman hesitated. A flush of pride filled Shari's cheeks at the sister's praise.

January shrugged, settling back onto her puffy pink chair. "Well, her ex for one. Roy."

Shari wrote down the victim's ex-husband's name. "Roy Tassler?"

"No." January shook her head again. "Roy Fortney. Tassler was Autumn's maiden name. She went back to it after the divorce. Roy resented paying alimony."

"Excuse me if I don't cry for him." Shari took more notes. "But he did cheat on Autumn while she was paying all of his bills. Then he left her for the other woman. Can you think of anyone else who'd want to harm your cousin?"

"Roy's new wife, Isabella, of course." January looked like the cat who'd eaten the canary. "Now that I consider it, if Roy didn't like making the alimony payments, Isabella was ten times more resentful. She said Autumn was bleeding Roy dry. And I heard she had a screaming match with Autumn in her office at the resort."

Shari looked at Sister Lou. "There was a lot of that going on."

Sister Lou shared a surprised look with Shari before turning back to January. "Who told you this?"

January shrugged a shoulder. "It's a small town, Sister. How do you think we know the deputies suspect Sister Marianna Tuller of my cousin's murder?"

Chapter 19

"Diego's going to ruin your career." The warning came from behind Shari in the *Telegraph*'s office first thing Tuesday morning. Such ugly words from such an attractive voice. Shari was torn between amusement and dismay.

She turned to see Briar Coast's glamorous mayor standing behind her. The tall, slender brunette's scarlet winter coat screamed, *Power!* The black buttons were still fastened and the belt was cinched tightly at her narrow waist. Shari's gaze dropped to the day's copy of *The Briar Coast Telegraph*, which Heather Stanley gripped in the slim black gloves she hadn't yet removed. It perhaps held the key to the mayor's presence in Shari's humble cubicle.

Shari stood, raising her gaze to Heather's violet eyes. It was unreal how attractive the woman was. "Mayor Stanley, how nice to start my day with you."

Was it the wry note in Shari's voice that brought the glint of admiration to the mayor's eyes or was Shari making too much of it?

"I suppose all good crime reporters have an edge to them." Heather's makeup was expertly applied. Did she do it herself or did she have a makeup artist on retainer?

"I'm not a crime reporter. I'm an investigative reporter." Shari folded her hands at her hips in fake modesty. "I cover all kinds of news."

"That's right." Heather gave her a tight smile. "The *Telegraph* doesn't have a crime reporter—because Briar Coast has very little crime."

Shari nodded toward the newspaper in Heather's hands. "Except for two murders in the last three months."

Heather considered Shari for a quiet moment. "You have a lot of talent. You're a great writer, and I can tell from your articles that you know the right questions to ask for your readers."

"Beware of strangers bearing gifts," Shari quipped. "You'll understand that I'm suspicious of your praise after our previous encounters."

Faint amusement swept over Heather's features. "You're wasted in our quiet little town."

"Okay. I'll play along." Shari pushed her rolling chair under her desk and leaned against its back.

"I'm being sincere." Heather nodded. Her perfectly coiffed mane of chestnut hair bounced, then settled back into place. Amazing. "Shari, clearly you're the kind of person who needs a lot of action. You need to be where that action is so that you can be part of the mix, have the pulse of the community.

I have connections that I'm happy to use to help further your career."

Her words stole Shari's breath. "Does Diego know you're trying to lure away his reporters?"

"Not all of them, just you." Heather's expression was inscrutable. "It's a friendly gesture, one professional woman to another. If we don't watch out for each other, who will? I don't see any reason to ask Diego's *permission*. Do you?"

"Nicely played, Mayor. I like the way you turned the tables on me." Shari flashed a grin. "You and Diego have known each other a long time, haven't you?"

Heather lifted a finely arched eyebrow. Was there anything about her that wasn't perfect? "Diego and I have worked together in the past, but let's not change the subject."

"Yes, let's." Shari straightened from her chair. "Is your past with Diego the reason you're all over us like a cheap suit to stop covering hard news?"

"I'm prepared to use my connections to help you, if you're interested."

"Nice dodge." Shari flashed another grin. "Mayor Stanley, I've worked in a lot of big cities. I haven't enjoyed any of them as much as I've enjoyed Briar Coast. Thank you for your generous offer to help me pack up and leave town, but I'm happy here in *our* quiet, little community."

Heather stuffed her hands in her pockets. A sigh lifted her slender shoulders under her power coat. "My offer stands, if you change your mind."

"I won't change my mind about leaving Briar Coast,

but let me know if you change yours about the *Telegraph* covering hard news."

"I'm confident that I won't change my position, either. Your coverage of these murders is unnecessary. All it accomplishes is building fear in our community. Our residents don't need that. This is a safe place."

"You sound just like our former editor in chief, Perry Whatatool—"

"O'Toole."

"You'd both rather bury your heads in the sand and pretend that nobody dies in Briar Coast. They either live forever or disappear without explanation."

"What's the point of scaring your readers?" Heather seemed genuinely concerned.

"I prefer to think of it as *informing* them." Shari channeled her inner Sister Lou and held on to her patience. "Suppose one of those informed readers knows something that helps solve the case? Or if even one learns something that helps keep them even safer? Would that really be so bad?"

Heather tilted her head. Her chestnut locks cascaded over her shoulder. "Suppose several of these informed readers leave Briar Coast because they no longer feel safe here? Wait, I can answer that. I'll have fewer residents and you'll have fewer readers."

With that parting and pointed salvo, the mayor turned and disappeared.

"Why did that reporter do *another* article on Autumn's murder?" Sister Marianna stormed into

Sister Lou's congregational office first thing Tuesday morning.

Sister Lou paused in the act of responding to an e-mail as Sister Marianna confronted her, brandishing a copy of *The Briar Coast Telegraph* like a weapon.

Sister Lou folded her hands together on her desk and smiled into her associate's frigid gray eyes. She could feel Sister Marianna vibrating on the other side of her desk. "Good morning, Marianna. It's a beautiful day, isn't it?"

And indeed the day was beautiful for mid November. Chubby white clouds floated against a vivid blue sky. The crisp air had been invigorating, carrying the sweet scents of earth and autumn leaves as she'd walked from the motherhouse to her office.

Sister Marianna lowered her hands to her sides in a series of jerky motions. She appeared rigid in her navy skirt, red blazer, crisp white blouse, and red, blue, and black–patterned silk scarf. Her blue, gold, and white Hermionean cross was pinned to her blazer's right lapel. "I don't have time for pleasantries, Louise."

"Neither do I." Sister Lou's hand directed Sister Marianna's attention to her full in-box. "I have quite a bit of work to get through before this afternoon."

Are we really going to waste time arguing the merits of a newspaper article over which neither of us has control? It would appear so.

Sister Marianna ignored Sister Lou's concerns. "The *Telegraph* article keeps Autumn's murder—and our connection to it—in the forefront of everyone's mind."

"I disagree." Sister Lou settled back on her executive chair. "Shari did an admirable job with the article. She described Autumn personally and professionally, allowing readers to celebrate her life. She also detailed her contributions to the community."

The reporter must have worked all weekend, doing research and interviewing Autumn's employees and business associates. The article gave the impression that Autumn didn't have any friends, though, which supported the image of a workaholic.

"Our donors are unhappy with our association with yet another murder in this town." Sister Marianna strode farther into Sister Lou's office. She sat on the closest visitor's chair. "And the college's donors want the college to separate from the congregation."

Sister Lou felt a spark of temper. "It's in Shari's article that Autumn regularly donated to the congregation's ministries, including the college. Why would we want to hurt one of our most loyal supporters?"

"No one cares about that, Louise. This article only fans the debate over the college and congregation separating."

Sister Lou gestured toward Sister Marianna's newspaper. "The article quotes our prioress and the college president. I'm sure that Barb and Val's public display of unity has set aside any idea of the two institutions separating."

"Just because *we're* not discussing the separation doesn't mean it's not still on the minds of our donors and the donors of the college." Sister Marianna leaned back against her seat, still fuming. "You have to tell her to stop writing any more articles on this incident."

The declaration startled Sister Lou. "That's not the way it works, Marianna. It's not *our* newspaper. We don't control its content."

"Well, you could at least speak with her about it."

"I won't do that, either."

Sister Marianna sighed and wisely switched subjects. "When are we going to start interviewing suspects? We're running out of time."

Sister Lou had prepared herself for that question. "Shari and I spoke with Autumn's cousin, January Potts, on Saturday. She gave us some background on Autumn's ex-husband and his new wife. She also admitted that she'd provided a false alibi for the morning of Autumn's murder."

Sister Marianna's eyes widened. "You questioned a suspect on Saturday? I should have been there."

"Marianna, you can't be present when we speak with people about Autumn's murder. You're too close to this case." This reasoning worked on every police drama Sister Lou had ever seen, and she watched quite a few.

Unfortunately, the television-scripted line was powerless over Sister Marianna. "That's *exactly* the reason I should have been there. I have the most at stake in this situation. Do not leave me behind on any future interviews."

Sister Lou pictured herself having to monitor Shari's bluntness and Sister Marianna's temper during one of those meetings. The image almost rendered her catatonic.

She held Sister Marianna's stormy gray gaze and prepared to bluff. "Marianna, you asked me to help you clear your name. I'll handle this investigation my way or I won't do it at all."

Sister Marianna gaped at her, but Sister Lou's gaze remained steady.

"Fine, but I'll expect a full report on each and every interview you conduct." Sister Marianna rose from the visitor's chair. "We'll review your meeting with Autumn's cousin after work today."

I wish I could say that I'm looking forward to it.

Chapter 20

"Next time, give me more on the murder." Late Tuesday morning, Diego presented his verdict on Shari's follow-up article on the investigation into Autumn Tassler's murder. His critique was more generous than Shari had expected, but she knew she wasn't out of the woods yet.

"Sister Lou and I spoke with Autumn's cousin, January Potts." She sat forward on the gray chair across from her editor in chief. "She admitted that she'd lied when she gave her husband as her alibi for the time of Autumn's murder."

Diego's narrow-eyed stare was the only indication of his interest. It was his biggest "tell." His warm lavender shirt enhanced the effect of his coffee brown eyes. The colors her editor in chief included in his wardrobe continued to surprise her. They were an indication of the strong confidence the man had in himself.

"What was the deputies' reaction?" Diego's question caught Shari off guard.

"We haven't told them. We want to speak with Sherrod Potts first."

Diego arched a thick black eyebrow. "Why?"

It wasn't easy to remain still under that penetrating stare. "The deputies had their chance to verify January Potts's alibi. They'd rather focus on payback against me and Sister Lou. This time, we want to do the legwork on our leads before we share them."

"Makes sense."

"I know." Shari allowed her gaze to wander around her boss's office. He'd taken organization to a whole new level. It was just after ten a.m. Diego already had reviewed today's editions of their two closest rival newspapers. He'd distributed select articles to the section editors for follow-up. His in-box was empty and his out-box was full. Judging by his productivity—and his loosened gray tie—he must have gotten a very early start on his day.

"You have to mend fences with the deputies." It was couched in reasonable tones, but Diego's statement was still an order, not a request.

Shari crossed her legs. She tapped her right brown stiletto, which matched her tweed slacks, in an irritated rhythm against the air. "I want to do my best job for you, Diego. I really do. But I don't think I can work with Deputy Cole or Deputy Tate." Just thinking of Ted triggered her gag reflex.

Diego smiled as though she'd amused him. "Could you try?"

"I did try." Shari scowled in remembered aggravation. "I spoke with them before Sister Lou and I met with January Potts, but they weren't willing to share any updates with me."

Diego leaned forward on his executive chair, folding his large hands on his table. "You put a lot of hard work into the human interest article on Autumn Tassler. It's a solid piece and an important story."

"Thanks." Shari waited for the other shoe to drop.

"But at the end of the day, this is a murder investigation. You can't cover a murder investigation without on-the-record quotes from murder investigators."

Shari felt a spurt of irritation. "You're right, but they're the ones holding a totally childish grudge, which is ridiculous. If Sister Lou hadn't solved the last case, they would've charged the wrong person with her friend's murder. I mean, come on. Sister Lou, Chris, and I ran circles around the deputies last time."

"Thinking about it that way isn't productive. We need to be seen working *with* the deputies, not against them. It speaks to our credibility."

Shari tugged her right earring. The sapphire jewel was cool between her fingers. "What am I supposed to do if they won't talk to me?"

"You're a resourceful reporter. You'll figure something out." He gave her an encouraging smile.

Shari resisted her urge to roll her eyes. "I'm still going to work with Sister Lou on her investigation. Like I told you, she's already gotten some good information that we're going to follow up on."

Diego inclined his head. The fluorescent overhead light gleamed on the thick waves of his black hair and highlighted the few silver strands buried among them. "Share whatever you find with the deputies. That might convince them to open up to you."

"Maybe, maybe not." Shari stood, smoothing her bright yellow sweater. "Sister Lou keeps the deputies in the loop. Fat lot of good it did her last time, though."

"Hopefully, this time will be different." Diego's eyes twinkled with humor.

Shari frowned at him. "Are you laughing at me?"

"Never."

She didn't believe him. She crossed her arms and leaned against the back of the visitor's chair. "I had another visit from the mayor first thing this morning. She wanted to discuss the Autumn Tassler article."

A curtain settled over Diego's coffee brown gaze. "I know. She stopped by my office, too."

Shari's gaze swept his meticulously organized desk again. "You managed to get a lot done this morning despite her interruption."

"She didn't stay long."

"So, what's with the two of you?"

"What do you mean?" He did his sphinx impersonation.

"Do you two have a history?"

"Why do you ask?"

Shari sighed. "Do you know how irritating it is to have a question answered with a question?"

Diego spread his arms. "I'm looking for clarification."

"The minute you sat on that chair, you assigned me to investigate the town council's activities and the mayor's agenda. How did you know I would find something?"

"A hunch."

"If I hold you upside down, will a straight answer fall out of your pockets?"

"There's no need for violence." Diego gave her a chastising look.

This time, Shari bit back her exasperation instead of expressing it. *Perhaps Sister Lou's diplomacy is rubbing off on me.* "Does Heather Stanley have a habit of attracting conflicts?"

Diego ran his hand over his hair. "I wouldn't call it a 'habit.'"

Shari sensed his frustration. She straightened from the visitor's chair. "If this isn't the first time she's been in a situation like this, I wouldn't call it an accident."

"Are you Sharelle Henson?" The curt female voice with the British accent assaulted Shari's back from her cubicle entrance later that morning.

Shari completed the sentence she was typing into her computer before saving the file and rising from her desk. She took the four steps to the threshold and tapped the nameplate affixed to her exterior cubicle wall. It read SHARELLE HENSON, REPORTER.

"I guess so." Shari propped her shoulder against the doorway and crossed her arms. She had to tip her head back to meet the stranger's eyes. "Who're you?"

The uninvited visitor was almost shaking with anger. Her blue eyes snapped with temper even as she stepped back to put more distance between them. "Bella Fortney. Roy Fortney's wife." Her British accent clipped her words—or maybe it was her temper.

"Bella? As in the Twilight Saga?" Shari hadn't read the young adult romantic fantasy novels—what was so sexy about a dead guy munching your neck and sucking your blood?—but she'd heard of the popular series.

"It's short for Isabella," her visitor snapped.

Shari had recognized the name *Fortney*. It was the surname of Autumn Tassler's ex-husband, the prince who'd left her for a younger woman. And here was the younger woman. She was taller than Shari, perhaps six feet. Had she been a model? Her features were beautiful, practically perfect despite the ugly angry flush. Her light brown hair was parted in the center and fell in straight tresses down her back.

Beneath her black fur coat—was it mink?—she wore a scarlet dress. Black leather boots disappeared beneath the dress's ankle-length hem. The diamonds in her ears and around her neck looked real, as did her silver Gucci clutch. Even her perfume smelled expensive.

"I'd use Isabella." Shari gestured toward her guest chair, inviting the woman to sit. "What can I do for you?"

Isabella stomped farther into Shari's cubicle, her fur coat billowing around her, and threw herself on the proffered seat. She gripped her copy of the day's

Telegraph in her fist and shook it at Shari. "You can write a retraction for this libelous article!"

Shari's spine stiffened. Libel was a serious accusation, even when it was screeched by someone who appeared on the verge of a breakdown. And whose upper-crust British accent tuned in and out at will.

"Well, now that everyone in the surrounding counties knows you're unhappy with the article, can you explain why?" Since it was almost noon, hopefully most of her coworkers were at lunch and missed the banshee's charge.

"Where should I start?" She crushed the newspaper and threw it to the floor. Definitely over-the-top. "You wrote that Autumn worked two jobs to put my husband through business college, then he divorced her."

"That's not true?" Shari had pulled that information from multiple sources, including court documents pertaining to Autumn's divorce and interviews she'd granted other publications.

"Yes, but . . . it didn't happen that quickly." Isabella stuttered.

Shari wanted to roll her eyes. It took a Herculean effort not to. "How many years have you and Autumn Tassler's ex-husband been married?"

Isabella's nostrils flared. "*My* husband and I have been married for almost six years."

"Autumn's divorce was final five years ago." Shari tilted her head. "So I guess the question is what's your definition of *quickly*?"

Isabella's blue eyes shot daggers. "There wasn't a

connection between Roy's getting his degree and the divorce."

"Says who?"

"Roy!"

"Uh-huh." Shari leaned forward. "So the two of you weren't seeing each other while he was still married? He never mentioned wanting to wait until *after* he graduated to tell his wife about you?"

Isabella's gaze wavered.

"I thought so." Shari sat back. "Is there anything inaccurate in the article?"

Isabella considered the crumpled newspaper on the ground. "I suppose not." Her tone was grudging. "But you've caused my husband and me a great deal of embarrassment by airing our personal affairs in this rag."

Shari again stiffened. "If you don't want your personal affairs aired, you shouldn't have had one with a married man whose wife was working two jobs to support him. Or is that the reason you wanted her dead?"

Isabella reared back on her seat with shock. "My husband has many lawyers on retainer. I can have any one of them sue you."

It was getting harder not to roll her eyes. "That's a weird response, Isabella, although it's not a denial." Shari channeled her inner Sister Lou as she studied the other woman. The fur. The jewelry. The shoes. Money meant a lot to her. "What did you and Autumn argue about?"

Isabella gasped. "How do you know we argued?"

"It's a small town." The response had worked for January Potts.

"That woman was bleeding us dry with her ridiculous demands."

"Her ridiculous, *court-ordered* alimony demands?" Shari shook her head as though in pity. "That sounds like a motive for murder."

Isabella popped out of her chair. She turned her most fearsome glare yet on Shari. "If you publish anything of the kind, my husband and I will sue you and this paper into ruin."

Shari rose to her feet although she was still at a significant height disadvantage. "Is that a confession?"

"It's a promise!" Isabella screeched, making a dramatic exit from the cubicle.

Shari considered the empty threshold. Despite being given multiple opportunities, Isabella hadn't once denied her involvement in Autumn's murder. "What was that about?"

Shari turned back to her desk, muttering to herself, "And what's up with her accent? If she's British, I'm the queen of England."

"For an innocent human-interest article, you've had quite a few attacks for it." Chris made the comment after Shari had filled him in on her busy morning.

They were enjoying a late lunch at the Briar Coast Café. It was almost one o'clock on Tuesday afternoon but the establishment was still packed. They'd been lucky to get the last open table toward the front of the café even though they were hit with a blast of cold air each time the door to the popular eatery opened.

The café was fragrant with the scents of soups, savory meats, and sweet pastries. The scents wafted out through the ventilation. The aromas were perfect marketing for the dining establishment and explained why the café was always crowded with carry-out and dining-in customers.

Chris studied his companion. Her thick hair framed her heart-shaped face and partially obscured her silver dangling earrings. Her vivid lemon yellow sweater more than made up for the gray mid-November day.

She'd made her encounters with the mayor and Autumn's ex-husband's new wife into dramatic and amusing anecdotes. But those confrontations must have been brutal. Nevertheless, she'd stood her ground and defended herself well. Chris scowled when he recalled that the mayor had offered to help Shari get a position with a bigger newspaper. It almost made him regret voting for her.

Shari gave him an exasperated look as she swallowed a spoonful of New England clam chowder. "I don't get it. I know the mayor doesn't want voters to know people get murdered in Briar Coast, but we can't pretend it didn't happen."

"Of course not."

"And Isabella Fortney doesn't want people to know she'd slept with her husband while he'd been married to someone else, but Autumn already told that to every newspaper that ever interviewed her."

"'Hell hath no fury like a woman scorned.'" Chris bit into his roast beef and Swiss on whole grain sandwich.

"I admire that about Autumn." Shari gave him a cheeky grin. "She didn't fade into history after her divorce. She made the cheating scumbag pay, then dragged his dirty laundry across the media."

Shari's reaction was in keeping with what Chris was learning about her. She was a fighter, a survivor. Fearless. "I could see you doing something like that, getting your pound of flesh. Have you ever taken revenge on an old boyfriend?"

Shari paused with her glass of iced tea halfway to her parted lips. "What makes you think *I* wasn't the one who did the dumping?"

Chris considered her reckless cocoa eyes, bow-shaped mouth, and mass of wavy raven hair. "I can see you leaving a string of broken hearts behind as you crisscrossed the country."

She arched a winged eyebrow as she sipped her drink. "Now you're mocking me."

"No, I'm not." Even the thought of her leaving Briar Coast could hurt his heart. Chris stopped thinking about it.

"You've probably broken more than your fair share of hearts yourself." She lowered her glass and captured his eyes. "You're smart, well established, and attractive. I bet the young women at the college can't volunteer fast enough to help with your phone-a-thon fund-raisers."

"I'm not in charge of the phone-a-thons."

"Ah, well, I'm sure they find that disappointing.

More broken hearts." Shari gave him a saucy look as she returned to her soup.

She was doing it again. Every time he tried to get to know her better, she turned the conversation to him. Why? What was in her past that she wanted to keep buried there?

Chris finished his sandwich and brought his roast chicken and vegetable soup closer. The spices that flavored the dish made his mouth water even before his first spoonful. "When you broke up with these boyfriends, did you let them down gently or were there a lot of tears and pleading?"

Shari chuckled. "Are you breaking up with me? I hadn't realized we were dating."

"I'm just curious." Chris met her amused gaze, giving the impression of boundless patience as he waited impatiently for her response.

Shari tilted her head as she considered him. "If you divorced your wife and married your mistress, would you resent having to pay alimony?"

He frowned. "Why are you asking me that?"

"In her interviews, Autumn admitted that she was livid that Roy had cheated on her, then divorced her to marry his mistress."

"She had every right to be angry."

"Of course." Shari leaned into the table in her excitement. "But he never fought the terms of the alimony, which are very favorable to her."

"Are you saying that you don't think her ex killed her?"

"I don't." Shari shook her head. "But I do think Roy's willingness to pay the alimony made Isabella crazy. She loves his money and didn't like him sharing it."

"That moves Isabella higher on our list of suspects."

"Isabella never denied killing Autumn. I think we should ask Roy about his wife's attitude toward his ex." Shari gestured toward him with her half-empty glass. "Let's run this by Sister Lou."

"I think she'll agree with you." Chris also thought Shari's evasiveness about her past was masterful.

He wasn't willing to give up on his quest to get to know the secretive reporter better. There were other avenues his investigation could take, including questioning his aunt. She and Shari were close. What the reporter resisted sharing with him, perhaps she'd already confided in his aunt.

Chapter 21

Sister Lou pulled into a parking space in the front lot of the Sleep Ease Inn Hotel Wednesday evening. The budget accommodations were located on the opposite side of Briar Coast from the congregational offices. The hotel held sad memories for Sister Lou. This is where her friend Dr. Maurice Jordan had been murdered.

It's also where Autumn's cousin, January Potts, had banished her husband, Sherrod, to until he made amends. Only she seemed to know what those amends entailed, though.

"Will you be all right?" Shari's question drew Sister Lou from her grief. "I could get Chris to interview Sherrod Potts with me another day, if you'd rather."

"I'll be fine, and Mr. Potts is expecting us." Sister Lou climbed from her orange compact sedan, feigning a confidence she was far from feeling.

Shari joined her as she crossed the parking lot to the hotel's front entrance. She paused in the hotel lobby, reacquainting herself with its ivory and orange carpeting, walls, and furniture. She hadn't been back to the establishment since Maurice's murder had been solved.

The hotel's restaurant was on her left across the spacious lobby. As she recalled, its dimly lit interior took her back to the 1970s with its polished maple wood and red velvet décor. It also was the last place Sister Lou had seen Maurice alive.

"Sister Louise LaSalle." The hissing sound came from a distance in front of her.

Sister Lou followed the noise to the bony man hurrying toward her from the registration desk across the lobby. He smoothed his thinning red hair and adjusted his dark suit as he scurried her way.

"How are you this evening, Alvin?" Sister Lou folded her hands in front of her hips.

Alvin Lyle was the hotel's general manager. Their relationship had gotten off to a complicated start when Sister Lou had called the sheriff's office after finding Maurice's body in his hotel room.

"I *was* just fine." His nasal voice was never far from a whine. "Are you looking for more bodies?"

Shari looked at the fussy man in surprise. "Does your hotel attract a lot of corpses?"

Sister Lou covered her laughter with a cough. "You've met my friend Sharelle Henson. She's a reporter with *The Briar Coast Telegraph*." As Sister Lou recalled, Shari and Alvin's first meeting hadn't gone very well.

"Yes, I remember." Alvin considered Shari through suspicious little brown eyes. "What is she doing here?"

Shari was more amused than offended. "She's here to speak with someone, but she's not going to tell you who because she doesn't think it's any of your business."

Alvin tried but failed to look down his nose at Shari. Unfortunately for him, her three-inch stilettos lifted her at least one inch above him. Instead, he aimed his glare at Sister Lou before spinning on his heels and stalking back to the registration desk.

"That's one fragile ego." Shari observed Alvin's theatrics.

Sister Lou started toward the elevators. "Some people are desperate to prove their worth while others are more secure in theirs."

"That's deep."

They boarded the elevator with a young family who seemed to be guests of the hotel. The space was a little tight until the harried parents herded their boisterous brood off a couple of floors before Shari and Sister Lou's destination.

At the sixth floor, Sister Lou led Shari off the elevator and glanced around. The shadowy hallway was dim, musty, and eerily empty. The hotel showed its age in the faded striped wallpaper and worn ivory and orange carpeting.

"Well, this is creepy." Shari lowered her voice. "Are you sure we didn't detour onto some horror movie set?"

"If we have, I'm pretty sure this is the scene where the audience yells, *Don't get off the elevator.*" Sister Lou followed the instructions of a sign mounted to the wall that directed them to turn left to find Sherrod Potts's room.

It was at the end of the hall. Sister Lou knocked on the door, then waited for his answer. Although the last time she'd knocked on one of these hotel doors, she hadn't gotten the answer she'd expected.

Sherrod Potts shook their hands, then stepped back to let them into his hotel room. His piercing bottle green gaze seemed to sum up Sister Lou and Shari in short order. "It's good of you to stop by to express your condolences about Autumn."

Shari had shared with Sister Lou pages and pages of information on Sherrod that she'd gathered from the Internet, including his picture. It didn't do the man justice. He was tall, perhaps Chris's height at a few inches over six feet, with a swimmer's lean, broad-shouldered build. His chestnut hair was on the verge of needing a barber's visit. Even in casual clothing—dark blue slacks, sage green knit sweater, and shiny black shoes—he exuded the aura of authority and wealth associated with captains of industry.

Sherrod directed them to the armchairs in front of the window across the room. "Can I offer you some coffee? I'm afraid that's the only refreshment I have."

Shari accepted his offer, but Sister Lou declined. She was already getting a residual caffeine buzz from the scent of coffee permeating their surroundings.

The room was more spacious than the one that had been assigned to Maurice. Still, it was quite a step down from the comfort of the Craftsman-style home he shared with his wife.

The standard hotel room chill didn't seem to bother Sherrod or Shari, but Sister Lou kept her coat on as she settled onto the chair closest to the writing desk. She followed Sherrod's movements as he prepared the single-serving hotel coffee machine for Shari. As the coffee brewed, he lowered himself to the desk chair. Behind him, his laptop was open on his desk. The monitor had gone dark.

Sister Lou settled her navy blue purse on her lap and rested her hands on top of the soft vinyl. "Autumn was helping my congregation plan our annual Advent retreat."

"So I understood from Ms. Henson's article in the *Telegraph*." Sherrod inclined his head toward Shari. "It was a good piece."

"Thank you." She seemed surprised by his praise. Shari had shrugged out of her emerald green wool winter coat and folded it on the back of her chair. Her massive olive bag was beside her feet. "You can call me Shari."

"Sherrod. The *Telegraph* has come a long way in a short period of time. I enjoy reading it again."

Sister Lou smiled at Shari before addressing Sherrod again. "We were surprised when January told us you'd temporarily separated, especially since she said the morning Autumn was murdered, she was cooking breakfast for you."

Sherrod stiffened as though Sister Lou's question had blindsided him. Then his features relaxed as his green eyes sparkled with good humor. "I should've realized there was more to your request to meet than offering your condolences. You're at it again, aren't you?"

Sister Lou glanced at Shari. She was tempted to plead ignorance, but Shari shrugged her winged eyebrows in silent communication. *The gig is up.*

Sister Lou met Sherrod's direct gaze with uncharacteristic boldness. "I apologize for the subterfuge, Sherrod, but my congregation is once again under suspicion for a crime that none of us would ever commit. I'm only defending our reputation."

Sherrod sighed. "I'm used to subterfuge, Sister Lou. In the corporate world, it's standard operating procedure, both externally and internally. What I'm not used to is being set up."

"What?" Sister Lou and Shari echoed each other. In Shari's voice, Sister Lou heard the shock she felt.

Sherrod stretched his arms to encompass his surroundings. Bitter irony tinged his words. "The reason I'm squatting here instead of living in my own home, which I bought and paid for, and sleeping in my own bed, is that someone sent my wife an anonymous letter, stating that I was having an affair with her cousin. And my loving wife chose to believe a faceless, gutless accuser rather than her husband of almost twenty years."

Shari's jaw dropped. She looked at Sister Lou. "I didn't see that coming."

"Neither had I." Sherrod rose, serving Shari the disposable cup of fresh coffee and the hotel packet containing a stirrer, sugar, sweetener, and cream. She seemed disappointed by the meager offerings.

Sister Lou smelled Shari's coffee, but nothing else, not cologne, aftershave, not even dinner. His room was obsessively clean. His only personal effects in plain view were his laptop, briefcase, and cell phone. The closet and bathroom doors were closed. These were the signs of a man in denial. He hadn't accepted that he was living in a hotel instead of his home.

Sister Lou turned away from the dresser and back to Sherrod, who'd remained standing in the cramped space. "Do you have any idea who would tell your wife that you were having an affair?"

"Especially with her cousin." Shari shook her head as she stirred cream and sweetener into her coffee. "That would really jam you up."

"I've been racking my brain, trying to figure that out." Sherrod rotated his neck and shoulders like a swimmer preparing for a meet.

Sister Lou recalled details from her and Shari's meeting with January. "Do you remember when your wife received that anonymous letter?"

"I'll never forget. It was October twenty-sixth." Sherrod paced away from Sister Lou and Shari. "About two and a half weeks ago, not that I'm count-ing the days."

Three weeks? That made the letter the source of January's misinformation about Autumn and Sherrod.

"That day, January asked you to leave." Sister Lou worked out the timeline in her head. "The next day, she confronted Autumn."

Sherrod snorted. "She didn't ask me to leave. She literally tossed me out—or at least my belongings."

Sister Lou shifted to keep Sherrod in sight as he prowled his hotel room. "I was in Autumn's office when your wife threatened to kill her if she didn't stay away from you."

Sherrod stilled, turning back to her. "Jan's not a killer." He kneaded the back of his neck. "She's hot-headed and impulsive, but she's all talk, no action."

"Really?" Shari looked around the hotel room with exaggerated motions. "From where I'm sitting, she *acted* to push you out of your own house."

Sister Lou changed the subject. "If you're certain she's innocent, why would you lie to provide her with an alibi? You're not going to tell the deputies the truth, are you?"

"Not unless they ask. I'm sorry, Sister Lou, but I'm stupid enough to still be in love with her." Sherrod's self-deprecating smile held boyish charm. He returned to his chair.

Shari frowned at him. "Why would someone send your wife an anonymous letter accusing you of having an affair with her cousin?"

Sherrod leaned forward, folding his hands between his knees. "I have no idea."

"I have one." Sister Lou turned on her seat again. "The person who sent your wife that letter wanted to frame her for Autumn's murder just as they want to frame Sister Marianna."

Shari stared at her, wide-eyed. "Are you saying the killer sent January Potts that anonymous letter?"

Sister Lou breathed deeply. "Yes, I am."

Chapter 22

"Why are you fixated on my life before Briar Coast?" Shari gave Chris a mildly curious look Thursday afternoon as they shared another late lunch at the Briar Coast Café.

Chris lowered his gaze to his ham and cheddar on whole grain sandwich. "I'm not fixated."

Shari gave him a dubious look, her fork poised above her salad. "This is the second time this week you've invited me to lunch, and both times you've grilled me about my past."

"I don't grill, either." Chris bit into his sandwich. The spicy mustard, well-seasoned ham, real cheddar cheese, and freshly baked bread exploded on his taste buds. The café must hire magicians as chefs.

Chris could have sworn Shari didn't like vegetables, but her selection today of a spring mix salad—albeit with a healthy dose of honey mustard dressing—contradicted that idea. Just when he thought he was beginning to know her. Never a dull moment. It was both frustrating and exciting. He washed down his sandwich with a gulp of iced tea.

"What would you call it?" Shari poked her fork into her salad bowl, collecting romaine lettuce, carrots, cucumbers, peppers, cheese, and dressing.

"Getting to know you better. We're friends, aren't we?"

"Of course we're friends." Shari rewarded him with a pensive frown. "But why does the past matter? You know who I am now."

What was it about her past that was so upsetting?

Chris's gaze drifted away from Shari while he contemplated that question. Outside, it was gray and gloomy. They were still a week out from Thanksgiving, nevertheless several of the businesses around the café were displaying Christmas decorations and promoting holiday sales.

A group of male and female students from the College of St. Hermione of Ephesus sat at a table toward the back of the café. Chris recognized most of them. Soon enough, semester finals would be knocking on their classroom doors. For today, ebullient laughter bounced from their table and good-natured smiles brightened their faces.

At a nearby table, five slightly older patrons—three men and two women—spoke in low, tense tones as they huddled together. Based on the scowls that clouded their expressions, Chris presumed they were coworkers, grousing about their morning. He recognized a couple of them as well. Their expressions didn't bode well for the town administrative office they worked for.

He looked again at Shari and found her cocoa gaze waiting for his response. Her patience was uncharacteristic and, therefore, suspect. "Your past helped shape the person you are today. I care about you. I don't just want to know who you are now. I want to understand who you were, and I'm interested in who you want to be."

Shari sipped her tall glass of lemonade as she seemed to contemplate his request. "How has your past shaped you?"

She was doing it again, deflecting a question about herself by turning it to him. Chris was willing to play along—to a point. "Losing my parents at the same time thirteen years ago has made me over-protective toward the people I care about. That's one way that something from my past has helped shape my present."

Shari's smile seemed forced. "And, knowing you, your future."

"At least give me credit for working on it." Chris offered an embarrassed smile. "What about you?"

Shari sat back on her chair. "I can tell you about my present. I like to think about my future, but I really can't think of one thing to say about my past."

"Something in your past made you reluctant to confide in other people. What was it?"

"Maybe you should be the investigative reporter." Her laughter was strained. "You're nothing if not persistent."

"That's the fund-raiser in me."

"I think I was born this way." Shari shrugged.

"Some people would say you're being secretive

because you have trust issues." Chris searched for insight in her body language, but Shari was good. She appeared relaxed as she sat across the table from him. Her arms were loose in her lap. Her eyes were direct. Her expression was interested, but not by a twitch or a wrinkle did she give her thoughts away.

She conveyed good humor with the glimmer in her eyes and the curve of her lips. "Why can't it mean that I just don't have anything to share?"

If he didn't know better, he'd think she was in the witness protection program. "Point taken. We'll leave our pasts behind and just concentrate on who we are now."

"I find that much more interesting."

Something in her voice hinted that she didn't believe him. And she was right. He wasn't willing to surrender. This was a strategic retreat. There were other ways to learn about her past. Shari Henson wasn't the only one who could surf the Net.

"The deputies warned me you'd try to interview me." Rita Morris looked harried as she rifled through manila file folders in her desk drawer late Thursday afternoon. Her ready smile was not in evidence. "It's been ten days, and except for our business meeting, I haven't seen you. The deputies thought you would've been back by now. They keep asking if I've seen you and if you've called. So annoying."

Sister Lou sensed Shari's growing agitation as they stood together just inside the room. The reporter was doing a miraculous job of containing her tension, but Sister Lou jumped in to fill the silence just in case. "Sharelle Henson and I want the same things the deputies are after: justice for your friend and to safeguard Briar Coast from further tragedies."

Shari interrupted. "So instead of keeping tabs on us, they should focus on finding Autumn's killer."

"I agree with you on that one." Rita glanced at Shari briefly before returning her attention to the folders in her desk drawer. "But what I don't understand is why a newspaper reporter and a nun are investigating my business partner's murder."

Sister Lou studied Rita's tense features and agitated body language. "I'm not a nun. I'm a sister. Nuns are cloistered." Sister Lou considered Rita's distraction as she corrected the other woman. "Shari and I have a very good reason for looking into Autumn's murder."

The smell of panic overlaid the resort partner's office. It was in even greater disarray today than the last time she'd been here. The beautiful furnishings were buried under manila folders, purchase orders, unopened mail, and catalogs. Piles of newspapers, magazines, and other periodicals grew along the flooring. The office no longer bore any resemblance to the showroom it had once been.

Rita shook her head. "I'm sorry, Sister, but the deputies told me not to talk to you, and I don't have the time, even if I wanted to."

Sister Lou tightened her grip on her shoulder

bag. "The deputies have an innocent woman under suspicion."

Rita's surprised eyes shot up to catch Sister Lou's gaze. "And you're trying to cast suspicion onto someone else? The deputies thought you would. They said you were looking at January, Autumn's cousin."

Sister Lou strode across Rita's office and raised a stack of travel magazines from one of the two chairs in front of her desk. "May I?"

"Sure." Rita looked confused.

Sister Lou placed the magazines on the floor, then nodded to Shari. She shed her brown wool winter coat, hanging it over the back of the chair, then took her seat, setting her navy purse on her lap.

Shari removed several event planning association periodicals from the other guest chair. She tossed her winter coat over her chair and placed her handbag beside her feet before sitting. "Did you know January lied about her alibi?"

Rita stopped digging through the piles on her desk and met Shari's eyes. "Do you think she killed Autumn?"

Sister Lou gave Shari an almost imperceptible shake of her head. Their goal was to find information that would clear Sister Marianna, not to implicate someone else.

She raised her hand to encompass the disheveled office. "If you don't mind my saying, you seem a little overwhelmed."

"I *am* overwhelmed." Rita drew a manila folder

from her drawer and slammed it on top of the paper pile before her. She flipped through several of the printouts that fluttered inside the folder. "How am I supposed to keep up with these purchase orders and contracts and mail, much less these stupid magazines Autumn subscribed to?"

"Now we know why Autumn worked such long days." Sister Lou considered Rita. Panic flared in the resort partner's light brown eyes.

Rita gave her a resentful glare. "I could work twenty-four hours a day for a year and not be able to keep up." She pushed herself from her chair and paced her office. "I had no idea she did all of this stuff."

That explains Rita's attitude toward Autumn and the resort.

Shari frowned at Rita's back. "Who did you think did everything?"

"I didn't realize she had so much to do." Rita paced back and forth in front of the six-foot-tall maple wood bookcase. She dragged both hands through her shoulder-length, pale blond hair. Judging by her tousled tresses, this wasn't the first time she'd done that today. "If it wasn't for Kelsey, I wouldn't know where anything was. Apparently, Autumn told her everything."

Shari frowned. "Didn't Autumn ever ask you for help?"

Rita shrugged. "A few times and then she stopped. Whenever she asked, I'd just remind her that it was her idea that she took care of the business side and I'd take care of making the customer connections.

I was still stinging over the implication that she didn't think I was savvy enough to handle the business part. All she thought I was good for was socializing. But I guess she was right."

Shari arched an eyebrow as though in agreement. "What are you going to do, look for a new partner?"

"No way. I have to sell the resort." Rita returned to her desk and settled onto her seat. "Autumn must have enjoyed being insanely busy. That's not me. Life is for living. No one could do all of this and have a life."

"Then you don't think Autumn was seeing anyone romantically?" Sister Lou asked.

"Autumn didn't share girl talk." Rita scowled at her cluttered desk. "I just figured she must not have had any to share."

Sister Lou frowned, recalling January's accusation that Autumn had had a string of lovers. "Are you familiar with the rumor that Autumn was promiscuous?"

"Autumn? Promiscuous?" Rita's laughter seemed to surprise even her. "I doubt that very highly." She swept an arm above her desk. "Autumn didn't talk much about her personal life, but I can tell you unequivocally that this is an antiaphrodisiac. I haven't felt horny all week." Her face flamed. "Sorry, Sister."

Shari looked puzzled. "Then who would start a rumor that she was sleeping around?"

Rita gave her a skeptical look. "Someone with a very creative imagination."

* * *

Sister Lou noticed Kelsey alone at the registration desk as she and Shari were leaving the resort. The administrative assistant seemed busy. Her blond corkscrew curls swung as she looked back and forth from the sheet of paper beside her to the computer into which she was transferring data.

Autumn told her everything.

Sister Lou touched the reporter's hand to get her attention before approaching the administrative assistant. "Kelsey, may we speak with you?"

"I suppose." The administrative assistant looked back and forth between Sister Lou and Shari, causing her curls to pop and snap around her head.

Those curls, her girlish clothing, and indecisive speech gave the other woman a youthful impression. But a closer inspection of her round features found fine lines bracketing her mouth and flaring from the corners of her wide blue eyes. Those creases and the experience in her watchful gaze placed Kelsey in her mid to late forties, at least.

Sister Lou glanced around the lobby. "Would you be able to sit with us? We'll only keep you a few moments."

Kelsey shrugged. "I guess." She came around the registration desk. Her gait bounced as she walked on her toes in her black patent leather wedge shoes. "Let's sit here. That way I can really still keep an eye on the desk."

Sister Lou followed Kelsey to a group of three scarlet-padded chairs on the edge of the resort's main lounge area. She waited until everyone was seated. "I'm sorry that I haven't expressed my condolences to you on Autumn's death. I know that she cared about you."

Kelsey nodded, flinging her curls against her forehead. "She really was just a great boss. The best I've ever had."

"I'm so sorry." Shari's voice was low with caring and concern. Like Sister Lou, the reporter sat with her winter coat folded on her lap. Her gold sweater glowed against the scarlet box chair.

Sister Lou watched Kelsey closely. "I've been wondering why you didn't mention Autumn's encounter with January Potts to the deputies."

Kelsey's eyes widened as she looked from Shari back to Sister Lou. "I really thought you were going to. You were in Autumn's office."

"You're right. I should have." Sister Lou could see the other woman's point of view. She hadn't initially mentioned the encounter to the deputies because she thought Kelsey knew the two women better, but that shouldn't matter. "Did Autumn's cousin often visit her at work?"

"I really wouldn't say often." Kelsey's curls were becoming a distraction. Sister Lou had to work to stay focused on their exchange.

Shari studied Kelsey with a fascinated expression. The reporter winced when her gaze dropped to Kelsey's shoes. "Was the argument Sister Lou witnessed the first time January had come to the resort?"

The fine lines across Kelsey's brow deepened as

she considered Shari's question. "No, I don't really think so. She may have come once or twice before. Why? Is it really important?

"Probably not." Sister Lou sighed. Her frustration mounted as she tried to find clarity over the motivation behind Autumn's murder.

Her gaze wandered the resort's lobby. A few guests were coming in and out of the main cabin and crossing between rooms. It was a warm, welcoming space. Sister Lou could see its potential for great success. She was sorry that Autumn wouldn't realize that dream. What would happen to the resort now?

She turned her attention to Kelsey again. "Rita said Autumn told you everything."

"Did she say that really?" The pink flush filling Kelsey's cheeks enhanced her Kewpie doll appearance. "Well, I really don't know about that."

"Did Autumn mention anything to you about her relationship with her cousin? Do you know if she was having trouble with anyone else?"

"No." Kelsey's eyes widened as though in distress. "Although, she did have an argument with her ex-husband's new wife a couple of days before she was killed. I don't really know what that was about."

Sister Lou suspected that Kelsey was aware of the topic of the other women's argument. The nagging feeling returned that there was something else Kelsey knew but wasn't ready to discuss. What could Sister Lou do or say to persuade the other woman to be more forthcoming? "Autumn deserves justice,

Kelsey. That's all we're after and the reason we're asking you these questions."

Kelsey nodded. "That's all I really want, too. Justice for Autumn."

Then why did Sister Lou have the impression there was someone else the other woman was trying to protect?

Chapter 23

"Why are you keeping secrets?" Shari crossed her legs, smoothing the material of her cobalt blue pants as she sat on the other side of Diego's desk in his office early Friday morning.

"What secrets?" Diego looked fresh and alert in a baby blue shirt paired with a crimson tie. His large, white ceramic coffee mug was within easy reach of his right hand.

"I'm convinced that you and Mayor Stanley have baggage."

"I've told you that we don't."

Shari took a sip of coffee from her own mug, the one Diego had given her when she'd returned to the newspaper in October. "Then why did you assign me to spy on her?"

"I didn't."

"That's how it feels."

Diego continued as though she hadn't interrupted him. "I asked you to monitor the mayor's and town council's offices for suspicious activities"

"And I found something, just as you expected me to."

"I know." Diego lowered his eyelids as though he was trying to mask his frustration.

Shari didn't feel a need to mask hers. "Then confront Mayor Stanley. Tell her you think the town council president is trying to undermine her authority."

"She wouldn't believe me."

"Why not—if, as you say, the two of you don't have a history?" Shari was certain she'd caught him in his deceit. If she weren't so irritated, she'd be gloating.

Diego gave her a cautious look. "When I was a reporter in El Paso, I uncovered government corruption in the local agency she worked for. She was meant to take the fall but, luckily, the investigation found that her boss had set her up."

"Did your article name her as a suspect?" A reporter's nightmare: getting the story wrong and hurting innocent people in the process.

"Initially." Diego's regret still lingered in his sigh. "In subsequent articles, I stated that her boss was charged with the crime, but by then, the damage had been done."

"So you do have a history, and it's a negative one."

Diego sipped his coffee. It was an obvious stalling tactic. "We've crossed paths before and, no, it didn't end well. But that's in the past and better left there."

Shari blinked. That's what she'd been telling Chris about herself, but perhaps the college administrator had a point. She could see how Diego's past still affected him. He seemed remorseful. Had he had feelings back in the day for their stunning mayor? Had his coverage of her agency prevented him from pursuing those feelings?

She'd probably never know the answers to those questions, but she wanted to know one thing. "Did you follow Mayor Stanley to Briar Coast?"

"Yes." His tone closed the door on that line of inquiry.

Shari respected his privacy—for today. "So far, I haven't found anything else that raises a red flag. The council's and mayor's agendas match up for the most part. Their budget projections are similar."

"Similar but not the same." Diego's eyes held hers, but his thoughts seemed miles away. "There are different interpretations of their agendas and different calculations on some of the town's budget line items."

"It's politics." Shari had read, seen, and heard it all. "Both offices dislike each other intensely. No surprise. The council members are all ultraconservatives and make the mayor seem like a flaming liberal."

"There's something more than the town council president's political challenge going on and it's staring us in the face. We just can't see it yet." Diego took a deep drink of his coffee. His large hand masked the Toronto Raptors logo emblazoned on the mug. He settled farther back onto his chair. "I've got a gut feeling about this, and my gut hasn't failed me in almost thirty years in the news business."

"What does that make you, fifty-two?"

"Fifty-one."

"At least now I know what you did to tick off a government official."

A ghost of a smile hovered around Diego's firm lips. He wasn't going to let her bait him into telling her more about his past with the mayor. "Something else we have in common. You have an entire sheriff's department giving you the silent treatment. Have you been able to mend those fences?"

This must be how Chris felt when he was trying to get answers from her and she changed the subject. It was annoying, but that didn't mean she'd stop doing it. "I'm working on it. Sister Lou and I are going to meet with them. We're hoping they'll agree to an information exchange."

"Good." Diego hesitated. "If you'd been assigned that story in El Paso, you wouldn't have made the same mistake I did."

"Then why did you?"

He frowned. "I didn't listen to my gut. I listened to my editor when he told me to report the information the officials gave me. I should have done my own investigation."

Shari wanted to remove the brooding expression from Diego's classic features. "As you said, it's in the past."

"The past shapes us. It can make us stronger or it can rule us."

There was a message for her in those words. It made her uncomfortable. Shari rose. "I'll let you know how the meeting with the deputies turns out."

Diego arched a dark, blunt eyebrow. "We should

run an update on the story soon. We don't want to put this on the back burner. Someone in our community was murdered. It should be everyone's priority to find out what happened."

Shari turned to leave, calling over her shoulder, "Instead, it seems like someone is doing his or her best to hide the truth about what happened—and why."

"I'm not supposed to speak to you." Urban Rodgers, the Briar Coast Cabin Resort's head chef, called out to Sister Lou and Shari as they waited for him in the main lobby late Friday morning.

Once again, Urban was dressed all in black: T-shirt, jeans, and sneakers. His close-cropped salt-and-pepper hair was uncovered. Evidently, the chef rejected the traditional white pants, smock, and toque.

In her peripheral vision, Sister Lou caught Kelsey's wide-eyed reaction from behind the registration desk. When she'd offered to page Urban, he must not have given any indication that he intended to shoot down Sister Lou's hope of getting helpful information from him about their deceased employer—and from the length of the hallway.

"Let me guess." Shari adjusted her handbag on her shoulder. Her winter coat was unbuttoned, revealing her robin's-egg blue knit sweater and navy slacks. "The deputies warned you about us."

"Right." Urban stopped, scowling at them from about an arm's length away.

Shari exchanged a side look with Sister Lou. "This

seems to be the deputies' new standard operating procedure."

Sister Lou sighed her agreement before addressing their reluctant source. All the while, she was aware of Kelsey's observation. "Mr. Rodgers, if you could just give us a few minutes of your time—"

"I won't give you a scapegoat for Autumn's murder." He leaned forward as though trying to intimidate her. Sister Lou didn't move.

The chef was a mountain of a man, perhaps three hundred pounds and six feet six inches tall. His torso could double as a brick wall. The muscles straining the sleeves of his black jersey could stop a speeding locomotive. His black jeans were loose on his tree-trunk legs.

Urban's broad, dark brown face was scarred as though someone had realized they'd need more than harsh language to get past him. The deep knife cut extended down the side of his face from the corner of his grim left eye to the edge of his clenched square jaw. Sister Lou shivered, imagining the pain from the encounter. The resulting mark added a sense of danger to angular features that would have been attractive if they weren't so dour. He was probably in his late fifties or early sixties, but his scowl made him seem older.

In the face of such blatant hostility, how should she proceed? Walking away wasn't an option. There was too much at stake. She asked God for guidance and found the answer in Urban's eyes. Their black depths held more than anger. There was a wealth of grief and pain as well. He'd cared for Autumn, perhaps more than he was willing to accept.

His emotion moved Sister Lou. She reached out, placing her hand on his upper arm. It was like concrete beneath her fingertips. She met his glare, letting him see the hurt she still felt from losing Maurice. "I know what it's like to have someone you care about taken from you so brutally. You think that, if only you'd come in earlier that morning, you could have saved her. You'll never know. But you do know that you can help her now by finding the person who killed her—the right person. I assure you, Mr. Rodgers, we're working toward the same goal: justice for Autumn."

The monumental chef was silent for several long seconds. His gaze went between Sister Lou and Shari. Sister Lou sensed him debating whether he could trust them.

Finally, he straightened. "Urban."

Sister Lou extended her hand to him. "I'm Sister Lou, and this is Sharelle Henson of *The Briar Coast Telegraph*."

Urban's hesitation was brief before he shook their hands. "A reporter?" He looked to Shari. "You're doing a story on Autumn's murder?"

"I've already written one. I'm working on a follow-up." Shari released Urban's hand. She followed him and Sister Lou to the sofas and chairs arranged in the far left section of the lobby, out of sight of casual attention.

Urban waited until Sister Lou and Shari sat on the

pine green sofa before positioning himself on the nearby matching armchair. "I don't read the paper."

Shari stiffened beside Sister Lou. "You should. If you had, you would've known that Sister Lou solved the last murder in Briar Coast last month."

"Yeah?" Urban settled his sphinxlike stare on Sister Lou.

Sister Lou returned his gaze. "How long have you known Autumn?"

"Ten months." Urban didn't elaborate.

"How long have you worked for her?" Shari sounded as though she'd guessed the answer.

Urban switched his attention to the reporter. "Ten months."

Sister Lou empathized with the exasperation she recognized on Shari's expressive features. She called again on God to grace them both with patience. They couldn't give in to their frustration. Urban reminded her of some of the high school and college students she'd taught before leaving academia to work in the congregational offices. They masked their emotions beneath layers of attitude. Many, many layers.

Sister Lou tried again. "Do you know whether Autumn was having any problems with anyone?"

"Yes. Sister Marianna." Urban's thoughts weren't revealed by even a flicker of his expression.

Was he being honest or was he trying to goad them? Sister Lou's gaze swept the lobby area again. Its open floor plan was beautifully decorated in natural walnut wood and fluffy pine green furnishings.

The large picture windows allowed sunlight to flood in. The scenic paintings on display around the room looked like original artwork. Several guests enjoyed the spacious accommodations, but many more were on the resort grounds enjoying the final days of fall.

Sister Lou swept her arm to draw Urban's attention to their surroundings. "Her business was struggling. Her ex-husband's new wife was harassing her. Her cousin threatened to kill her, but you sincerely believe that the greatest conflict your friend faced was a menu dispute for our congregation's retreat?"

His wavering gaze was Urban's first sign of uncertainty. His voice softened. "Autumn mentioned that she needed Rita to do more, but Rita wanted to sell the resort. Said it wasn't fun anymore. Autumn wasn't complaining. She was just tired and frustrated. She worked all the time, but she loved this place. She'd never have sold it."

Sister Lou had a memory of Autumn being irritated that her partner had brought an older gentleman to the resort. Was he the potential buyer? "To whom did Rita want to sell the resort?"

Urban frowned as though trying to recall the name. "Montgomery Crane of Crane Enterprises. Wealth."

"I recognize that name." Shari sounded excited. "The guy's filthy rich. He owns resorts all over the country that cater to specific types of vacations: skiing, hunting, camping, fitness, amusement parks, you name it."

But would he kill for a resort? Would Rita?

Sister Lou considered the chef. "Did Autumn know you loved her?"

Urban looked amused. "I care—cared—about her, but not like that. There aren't a lot of restaurants that want a big black man with a scarred face as their head chef. Autumn was a good person. She gave me a chance. Didn't ask a lot of questions about my past."

Shari tipped her chin toward Urban's face. "So who gave you that scar?"

His smile was meant to intimidate. "A reporter. I got the scar, but she didn't get the story."

Shari looked smug. "Now I know you're pulling my leg. She would've gotten the story."

Urban's laughter was rusty. He stood to leave. "Maybe the deputies are wrong about you. You seem like good people, but you may be too late to help your friend."

"What do you mean?" Shari stood, too, and buttoned her coat.

Urban glanced toward the registration desk. Kelsey jumped as though she'd received an electric shock, then disappeared from the desk, bouncing on her toes.

He turned back to Sister Lou, who waited beside Shari. "Your friend left her scarf in Autumn's office, right? The deputies found it."

A cold chill raced through Sister Lou.

Chapter 24

"You found a scarf in Autumn's office?" Sister Lou confronted Deputy Fran Cole at her desk in the Briar Coast County Sheriff's Office late Friday morning.

She sensed Shari's tension behind her. It reflected her own. They'd come to the sheriff's office straight from their conversation with Urban Rodgers at the resort. They were convinced that someone was setting up Sister Marianna for Autumn Tassler's murder. They needed answers. That's the reason they bypassed Deputy Ted Tate's desk. Uncooperative was in his DNA. Trying to get information from him about this critical matter would lead to an inescapable slide into insanity.

Fran looked up from her computer. Several unruly blond curls had sprung free of the bun at the nape of her neck. Her bottle green gaze was steady. "Yes, we found a black-and-gray-patterned silk scarf in Autumn Tassler's office."

Sister Lou couldn't penetrate Fran's enigmatic

expression. Her grip tightened on the strap of her shoulder bag.

Shari moved to Sister Lou's side. "When did you find it?"

"What's it to you?" Ted barked from his desk. Sister Lou ignored him.

Fran's attention shifted to the reporter. Her expression didn't change. "Yesterday."

Shari crossed her arms over her chest. She'd again unbuttoned her winter coat. "Ten days after the murder. Doesn't that seem a little strange to you?"

"What are you trying to say?" Ted's pale gray eyes were blazing.

He circled his desk to join them in front of Fran's. His tan shirt and spruce green gabardine pants were even baggier than they'd appeared last time.

Shari turned to face him. Her hair floated around her shoulders. "You searched Autumn's office November sixth right after her body was discovered. No scarf. Almost two weeks later, you happen to search her office again and—ta-da!—scarf." She turned back to Fran. "I want in on the magic trick."

Sister Lou understood Shari's sarcasm but the deputies didn't appear to appreciate it. Their little quartet also seemed to be attracting attention. The deputies seated at other desks as well as the ones at the coffee station, surrounding the inevitable box of pastries, kept glancing their way. Despite the office's cheerful décor and the tantalizing aroma of fresh coffee and cheese Danishes, Sister Lou knew she and Shari weren't in friendly territory.

"Are you accusing us of planting evidence?" Ted crowded Shari. His voice was unnecessarily loud.

"Did you?" Shari angled her pointed chin.

"Of course we're not accusing you of such a thing!" Sister Lou shouted over Shari's response in a vain attempt to drown her out. She put her hand on the confrontational reporter's shoulder, then turned to Fran.

"What prompted you to take a closer look at the crime scene?" Sister Lou could read Fran's expression now. Her green eyes were hard with temper. She was probably thinking of charges to level against Shari and Sister Lou.

Fran rose. Unlike Ted's now-baggy sheriff's uniform, Fran's looked tailor-made for her tall, slender figure as though she'd come from a wardrobe fitting at a movie studio. "Rita Morris wanted to remove the crime scene tape from Tassler's office. It was making guests uncomfortable and depressing the staff."

That made sense. An image of Rita overwhelmed by her paperwork popped into Sister Lou's mind. She let her arm fall away from Shari's shoulder. "Did Rita call you personally?"

Fran leaned back against her desk. "No, her assistant did."

Shari shifted beside Sister Lou. "Where's the scarf now?"

Ted grunted behind her. "That's none of your business."

Fran folded her arms over her tan shirt, accompanied by a plain black tie. "It's at a forensics lab in Buffalo."

Shari gave Ted her back and turned to Fran. "When will you be getting the results?"

Fran shrugged a shoulder. "About a week. Depending on the findings, we hope to make an arrest at that time."

Ted stepped around Sister Lou and Shari to get closer to Fran. "Why are you giving them all of our information?"

Fran's gaze shifted to her partner. "What difference does it make, Ted? If Sister Marianna's guilty, she's guilty. There's nothing they can do."

Ted lowered his voice. "We've lost the element of surprise."

Fran returned her attention to Sister Lou and Shari. She appeared satisfied, almost gloating. "Oh, I think they already knew where this would end."

Shari planted her hands on her hips above her navy blue slacks. "You're the ones who're directionally challenged if you think this will end on the congregation's doorstep."

Sister Lou found comfort in Shari's unwavering support. "There are people with much stronger motives than a disagreement over food. How much time have you spent looking into *them?*"

"Guilty parties always look to shift the blame, Sister." Ted's smile was mocking. "But I've heard the truth will set you free."

Sister Lou inclined her head. "Indeed it will, Deputy. Indeed it will."

* * *

"We need to talk." Sister Lou caught Sister Marianna at her congregational office just as the other woman was leaving for lunch early Friday afternoon.

Sister Marianna wore a blue, green, and yellow–patterned silk scarf with her navy blazer, white blouse, and gray slacks. Like her, Sister Marianna wore her blue, gold, and white Hermionean cross on her blazer's right lapel. Her scarf was already starting to slip from its position around her collar.

"Good heavens, Louise." Sister Marianna returned to her desk and gestured for Sister Lou to take one of the guest chairs in front of her desk. "You nearly ran me over in my own doorway. Do you have cause for such theatrical behavior?"

Besides the fact that you're under suspicion for murder?

How to start? Sister Lou had discussed that question with Shari as they drove back to the *Telegraph*. Then she'd discussed it with God on her way back to the congregational offices.

The direct approach was best. "Marianna, yesterday the deputies found your scarf in Autumn Tassler's office. They sent it to a forensics lab in Buffalo."

Sister Marianna looked puzzled. "That's quite impossible, Louise."

Sister Lou shook her head, baffled. "Why is that impossible?"

Sister Marianna rose from the executive chair behind her desk. She marched to the pale gray steel and plastic coatrack, which stood in a front corner of her office. Her low-heeled black pumps were silent on the rose carpeting.

She reached into one of the pockets of her black wool winter coat and pulled out a black-gray-and-red-patterned scarf. "I found my scarf in my coat pocket earlier this week."

A gasp of relief stole Sister Lou's breath. Her eyes widened in surprise. *Thanks be to God.*

She stood and crossed to Sister Marianna, drawing close to consider the silk accessory dangling from the other woman's right hand. "It's been in your pocket this entire time?"

"Apparently. And if you'd allowed me to attend your meeting with the sheriff's deputies as I've repeatedly asked you, I could have told them and cleared up this confusion."

"Why didn't you tell *me*?"

Sister Marianna shrugged. "I didn't remember putting it in my coat pocket. I've been using the underground passageway to get from the motherhouse to my office, so I haven't needed this coat since you assumed the retreat planning." Sister Marianna let Sister Lou hear her displeasure.

Curious. Had it occurred to Sister Marianna that if she'd controlled her temper, not only would she still be in charge of the retreat but she also wouldn't be a suspect in a murder?

Sister Lou kept that observation to herself. Sharing it would be a waste of breath. She gathered the scarf from Sister Marianna's hand and examined its black-, gray-, and red-dot pattern more closely. "It's not until you really look at it that you see it's handmade and that it doesn't have a manufacturer's tag."

We found a black-and-gray patterned silk scarf . . .
That's what Fran had said. No mention of the red
dye. Was that an oversight—or a clue?

Sister Marianna seemed lost. "Yes, well, as you can
see, I have my scarf. I don't know from where the
other scarf came."

Sister Lou lifted her eyes to Sister Marianna.
"From the killer."

Shari's phone rang as she was settling in for a late
lunch at her desk Friday afternoon. "*Telegraph.* Sharelle
Henson."

"Hi, Sharelle. This is Becca Floyd. I'm the managing editor of *Buffalo Today.* I wanted to compliment
your excellent reporting on the last two Briar Coast
murder investigations."

Why was the managing editor of Buffalo's largest
daily newspaper—essentially the *Telegraph*'s main
competitor—calling her?

"Thank you." Shari sounded more tentative than
she'd intended.

Her competitor's managing editor continued.
"Your coverage does a wonderful job of providing
the facts of the case as well as humanizing the victim
so that the reader has more than a name and a few
stats. You present the whole person."

"I appreciate your saying that." Was Becca Floyd
trying to kill time between deadlines? Why was she
calling?

Shari looked over her shoulder. As the *Telegraph*'s

office drew closer to its news deadline, the tension pressing down on the reporters, copy editors, and editors increased. Keyboard clicks were faster. Shouts across the newsroom were louder. Telephone interviews were more desperate.

"You must spend hours on research for your articles." Becca continued her jovial tone as though they were good friends.

"I enjoy it. And it's worth it." Shari looked at her cooling plastic storage bowl of homemade chicken soup. The scents of the vegetables and seasonings wafted up to her, prompting her stomach to growl in protest of the delay. "The victims were human beings. They deserve to be remembered and discussed in the context of more than a murder case."

"Very well said." Becca's tone was approving. "We've always monitored the *Telegraph* as a matter of course, but now we're excited to read it. I wanted you to know that."

"Thank you. I appreciate your call." This conversation was just too surreal. Even after she rang off with her competitor's managing editor, Shari sat staring at her telephone receiver as her lunch grew cold.

What had that phone call been about?

A knock outside her cubicle interrupted her thoughts. She turned to see Diego walking to her small conversation table and settling onto her guest chair.

He caught and held her gaze. "Shari, please tell me that you didn't accuse the sheriff's deputies of planting evidence to frame Sister Marianna Tuller for Autumn Tassler's murder."

Shock zinged through her like an electric current. "I never said that."

Diego seemed to exhale. "I know you can push boundaries, but I couldn't believe you'd do anything like that."

It was some comfort that her editor believed in her. "Who told you that I did?"

"The sheriff told me Deputies Cole and Tate said you went to the sheriff's office this morning and accused them of planting Sister Marianna's scarf at the crime scene."

"That's not exactly what happened." Shari's cheeks heated as she recalled the exchange. She maintained eye contact with her boss almost defiantly. "Ted asked me if I was accusing them of planting the scarf and I simply asked if they were."

Diego briefly closed his eyes. "There's no 'simply' in this situation with those deputies."

Shari recognized the truth of his words, albeit too late. She turned her back on her chicken vegetable soup and folded her arms. She crossed her right leg over her left and tapped it against the air. "I'm never going to be friends with Tate and Cole."

"What if you worked on not being mortal enemies?" Diego balanced his forearms on his thighs and leaned forward. "Come on. We're a newspaper. We need to have reliable working relationships with the community services we cover, and that includes the sheriff's office, Tate, and Cole."

"I'm working on it."

"Really?" Diego searched Shari's expression as though reassuring himself.

"Yes, really."

"Great." Diego sat back on his chair. "What can you tell me about the significance of the deputies finding Sister Marianna's scarf?"

"Not much." Shari stilled her leg. "The deputies want us to believe that the first time around, they missed it. Then ten days later, they get the idea to search Autumn's office a second time—out of the blue—and, voilà, they find the missing scarf."

"Ten days later? That sounds a little suspicious."

Shari spread her arms wide. "That's all *I* said and they got all defensive."

"It was probably *how* you said it." Diego's slight smile irritated Shari.

"Why am I always in the wrong?"

"That's what I was wondering. Do the deputies think Autumn Tassler was strangled with a scarf?"

Shari let Diego's first comment slide. "They don't know. They sent it to a forensics lab in Buffalo."

"What does Sister Lou think?"

Shari's sigh lifted her shoulders and cleared her lungs. "That we're running out of time."

Chapter 25

"Amber traffic lights mean 'caution,' not 'punch the gas,' by the way." Shari offered the clarification as Sister Lou powered her orange compact sedan through an intersection.

Sister Lou pulled into a lot in the town's main business area to park her little car. "I wasn't driving that fast." She climbed from her driver's seat, then pressed the button on her car key to lock her vehicle.

She took a moment to assess the two-story stone building on the other side of the road. The fairy-tale structure housed Crane Enterprises. She looked both ways before jaywalking across the street.

"I disagree." Shari hustled to catch up with her. "Have you ever gotten a speeding ticket?"

"I've had my share." *And several other people's shares.* Upon reflection, Sister Lou didn't see any need to mention that her license had been suspended for a month over the summer.

"Between your jaywalking and your speeding, I'm beginning to think you're a rebel in disguise."

"I'm not a rebel, I just want to get where I need to go."

"You don't always have to do the driving. I can drive sometimes."

Sister Lou paused in front of Crane Enterprises. "The *Telegraph*'s in the center of town. Since we usually have to pass it to get where we're going, it's more convenient if I drive. But if my driving makes you uneasy, I understand. You can drive."

Shari gave her an exasperated look. "Your driving doesn't make me uneasy. It's just fast. *Really, really* fast."

"I'm sorry. I'll slow down." She always meant to—until she got behind the steering wheel and her inner racecar driver emerged. Sister Lou returned to her contemplation of Crane Enterprises' headquarters.

"This isn't what I was expecting." Shari looked at the building and its surrounding area. "Why do you think Montgomery Crane put his company in Briar Coast instead of Buffalo or even New York City, where he's from?"

While the comfortable little gray stone cottage blended in with the other storybook storefronts and offices in the immediate area, it didn't fit the image of a growing corporate enterprise. Its rounded walls and square-paned windows gave it more than a touch of whimsy. Hansel and Gretel should come dashing through the mahogany front door any moment, their cheeks covered in chocolate frosting.

"Mr. Crane must be a practical man. It's cheaper to lease office space in Briar Coast." Sister Lou pushed her hands deeper into the pockets of her winter coat against the chill mid-November air. Snow was coming. After living in upstate New York for more than seven years, she could almost smell it.

Rows of boxwood evergreen shrubs on either side of the paved walkway escorted them to the front door, although the promise of heat was more than enough invitation. Despite the tree-lined sidewalk, the tidy lawn didn't entertain a single fallen leaf. Was that decreed by a meticulous gardener or an obsessive client?

Sister Lou pushed opened the front door to Crane Enterprises—and bit back an utterance of surprise.

Beside her, Shari gasped. "Who knew?"

The cool glass-and-silver-metal interior was in complete contrast to the company's fairy-tale exterior. Fluorescent lighting gleamed against the silver-and-white-tiled flooring. Four cardinal red–cushioned, box-style chairs stood along the far left paper white wall, delivering a shock of color to the silver and white lobby. The glass wall to the right afforded a view inside employees' offices.

A glass-and-metal circular receptionist station stood sentry before a winding white-tile-and-metal staircase at the other end of the floor. It was staffed by a handsome young blond who grinned at them from behind his workstation.

"We get that all the time." His accent identified him as a New England transplant.

"I feel like Alice Through the Looking Glass."

Shari continued to look around. "This room belongs in an interior design magazine."

Sister Lou returned the receptionist's smile. His nameplate identified him as Joel Wolf. "I'm Sister Lou LaSalle and this is Sharelle Henson. We have an appointment to see Montgomery Crane, please."

"Please make yourselves comfortable." Joel's brown eyes sparkled up at Sister Lou and Shari from his artificially tanned face. "I'll let Mr. Crane know you're here."

Sister Lou settled onto a seat beside Shari. Moments later, a tall and handsome older gentleman jogged down the stairs toward them. Sister Lou recognized Montgomery Crane.

He extended a large, dark hand. "It's good to see you again, Sister Lou." Montgomery's baritone voice rumbled with warmth. He shook her hand with a smile before switching his attention to Shari.

Sister Lou stood in response to his greeting. "This is my friend, Sharelle Henson, of the *Telegraph*. Thank you for meeting with us."

Montgomery turned back toward the staircase, nodding to Joel. He led them upstairs to his office. "I don't have to tell you that murder is a heinous, evil act, and not just because it breaks one of the Ten Commandments."

"We agree." Sister Lou climbed the winding steps behind Montgomery. The empty spaces between each step allowed her a view of the main floor. Small design elements like that one made the office seem even bigger and more open.

He stepped aside to allow Sister Lou and Shari to

precede him into his office. Here as well, the space was larger than the exterior led one to believe. His clutter-free modular blond wood desk and well-organized bookcase reflected a rigid sense of discipline. It reminded Sister Lou of Sister Marianna. Company photos hung on the office's bright white walls. They captured grand openings and other milestones, many chronicled in the media.

"May I take your coats?" Montgomery added their coats to the black metal coatrack in a corner behind his desk. He gestured to his red guest chairs, then settled onto his red faux leather executive seat. "How can I help you?

Montgomery had coupled his crisp white shirt with a red power tie. His gunmetal gray slacks were a perfect match for the suit jacket that hung from his coatrack. Beneath his veneer of corporate polish, Sister Lou sensed that Montgomery was all Bronx, New York. Decades ago, she'd taught at a Catholic high school in the borough. She heard the neighborhood in his voice and saw it in the way he moved as though he'd roll over anyone who blocked his path.

Sister Lou balanced her navy bag on her lap. "We understand from Rita Morris that you've made several offers for the Briar Coast Cabin Resort."

Montgomery's scrutiny shifted from Sister Lou to Shari and back. The dusting of gray in his otherwise dark, close-cropped hair belied his still-smooth features. "Because of that, you think I killed Autumn."

Obviously, he hadn't founded Crane Enterprises by being stupid nor had he expanded it by beating around the bush.

Shari matched his directness with a bluntness of her own. "Where were you the morning of November sixth?"

"I've read your articles on the murder investigation. They're good." Montgomery's dark gaze weighed Shari. "The deputies are okay with you interrogating people?"

"No." Shari cocked her head. "Is that a problem?"

Sister Lou held her breath while Montgomery seemed to contemplate the reporter's reply. She admired Shari's bravado even as she worried that the reporter would get them tossed out onto the street.

Montgomery's almond-shaped dark brown eyes twinkled. His lips twitched. He leaned back on his chair. "I was on a flight back from New York. Would you like to see my boarding pass?"

Shari shook her head. "No, I believe you."

"I'm flattered." Montgomery glanced at Sister Lou. "Anything else?"

Sister Lou relaxed, grateful for their host's indulgence. "In your opinion, how were things between Rita and Autumn?"

"Tense." Montgomery shifted his broad shoulders. "It was more than just their disagreement over whether to sell, but I don't know what."

"You have your suspicions, though." Sister Lou could tell by the look in his eyes.

Montgomery sighed. "About three weeks ago, Autumn asked me for advice. She was worried about her business. She was growing clients, growing events, but not making any real money. She thought someone was stealing from her."

Shari pounced. "Who?"

Montgomery leaned into his desk. "Either Rita or one of her employees. That's when she told me she hadn't done background checks on anyone she'd hired, not even the guy balancing her books. I advised her to do the checks, even retroactively."

Sister Lou frowned. "Did you tell the sheriff's deputies about Autumn's suspicions?"

Montgomery shook his head. "I don't know if she found anything."

"Did you recommend a background screening service?" Sister Lou's mind was racing with ways to follow up on this potential lead.

"Yes." Montgomery pulled a manila file folder from his desk drawer and handed it to Sister Lou. "Here's the list of Autumn's employees and the name of a company that does a full screening: drugs, criminal records, finances, everything."

"That's intrusive." Shari voiced her disapproval.

Montgomery arched an eyebrow. "This is business. I don't take unnecessary risks when my money's involved."

Sister Lou opened the folder. "How did you get this list?"

Montgomery looked troubled. "Autumn asked me to make the initial contact with the company. She thought someone was hacking her computer. She didn't want to tip anyone off before she contracted with the company."

Sister Lou rose. She held the folder securely in her right hand. "Thank you for your time and for this information."

Shari stood with her. "You've been very helpful."

Montgomery returned their coats. "I liked Autumn. She was tough and genuine. I hope her killer is found. Quickly."

Sister Lou shook his hand. "So do we."

The key to solving the case might be in her hands. Literally. Sister Lou tightened her grip on the folder.

"Do you think the company Montgomery Crane recommended to Autumn could lead us to the killer?" Chris sounded cautiously optimistic.

Sister Lou shared her nephew's hope for good news. "It's possible."

They sat together in the College of St. Hermione of Ephesus's President's Dining Room Monday afternoon, two weeks after Autumn's murder.

They were waiting to host two of the institution's most prominent donors for lunch, Roy and Isabella Fortney, Autumn Tassler's ex-husband and his new wife.

The room was designed for entertaining prominent donors and other important guests. Its blond wood paneling was elegant and bright, making the room seem spacious and welcoming. The mahogany rectangular dining table was a smidge long for four people. Their solution had been to arrange the place settings together toward the head of the table, making conversation much cozier. Sister Lou settled more comfortably on the soft blue cloth and mahogany wood dining chair. The room was a little chilly.

Chris checked his watch. Their guests were running a bit behind. "Thanks again for making time for this lunch, Aunt Lou. It's important to have a member of the congregation's leadership team here.

"I agree. We need to present a united front."

Just as Sister Lou spoke, Sister Valerie's administrative assistant led the Fortneys into the dining room. Sister Lou smoothed her beige dress as she rose with Chris to greet them.

"Thank you both for coming." Chris stepped forward to offer Roy Fortney his hand. Her nephew looked very polished in his slate gray, pinstripe suit.

Roy shook first Chris's hand, then Sister Lou's. "I apologize for keeping you waiting. Isabella wasn't well this morning."

"Morning sickness." Isabella gave her husband a pointed look as she accepted Sister Lou's hand. Her British accent had lengthened her vowels. Sister Lou smiled. Shari had told her Isabella had been born and raised in Ann Arbor, Michigan.

"Congratulations on this blessing. When are you due?" Sister Lou noticed Isabella's hand lay limp in her own. *Is that the lingering effects of her morning sickness?*

"Thank you. He's due in June." Isabella withdrew her hand from Sister Lou's. She turned her back to Roy, allowing him to remove her fur coat. Was it mink? The shimmery silver sweater dress beneath outlined her still-slender figure.

Sister Lou glanced toward Isabella's stomach. She

was only two months along. "Do you already know the baby's gender?"

"I haven't been tested, but I know it's a boy." Isabella crossed to the table and waited for Roy to pull out her chair.

Sister Lou smiled at Chris as he held her seat for her.

The door to the kitchen opened as Chris and Roy settled onto their chairs. The aroma of savory meats and seasoned vegetables floated into the dining area. The student workers had arrived to serve the first course, their garden salads.

Sister Lou recognized the young man and young woman assigned to the event. She exchanged warm greetings with them before they hurried back to the kitchen. Their luncheon conversation was casual, ranging from Isabella's pregnancy, sports, Isabella's pregnancy, next year's election, and back to Isabella's pregnancy.

As they came to the end of their main course of pecan sesame chicken and spinach, Chris broached the reason he'd asked the Fortneys to lunch. "I understand you're concerned the college's reputation will be hurt by the congregation's connection to the two recent murder investigations."

"I'm not." Roy jerked his head toward his wife. The accountant wore a brick red turtleneck sweater and smoke gray slacks. "Bella is."

Isabella's lips tightened with disapproval. "*You* should be concerned as well." Her appropriated British accent whispered on her words. She turned to appeal to Sister Lou. "*You* can understand why we don't want to be associated with an organization that's connected to such crimes. I mean, it's murder. Murder is a sin."

Sister Lou imagined Isabella mentally patting herself on the back for making that point. She glanced toward Roy. Murder wasn't the only thou-shalt-not among the Ten Commandments, but she'd leave that judgment to God.

Beside her, Chris tensed, but his voice remained level. "The sisters haven't committed murder."

"You can't prove that." Isabella flipped strands of her long, light brown hair behind her shoulders. "Under the circumstances, Roy and I agree that we can't associate with the college as long as the college associates with the sisters."

"*We* didn't agree to that. *You* did." Roy kept his attention on his meal, ignoring Isabella's glare.

"The congregation founded the college." Chris frowned. "We're not going to sever ties with it."

Isabella shrugged. "Then we will not support you."

"That's your right, of course." Sister Lou leaned against her chair. The soft blue cushion over the wood backing provided firm but comfortable support. "We'd never ask you to compromise your principles."

Isabella's smile was knowing. "I'd think you'd be more deferential, considering this whole luncheon is meant to convince us to keep giving you money."

"You misunderstand our mission." Sister Lou's lips twitched with genuine humor. "We practice Christ's teachings. He prayed with the rich and poor, the diseased and healthy, those welcomed in society and those who were reviled. Even as the Pharisees and scribes persecuted him, he never bowed to them. If you support our ministries, we would welcome your donations. But we'll never compromise our mission."

Isabella's face flushed red. Her accent slipped. "I support Christ's teachings."

"I'm glad." Sister Lou sliced into the succulent chicken.

Isabella looked to her husband, who continued with his meal, before turning back to Sister Lou. "With a baby on the way, I was concerned about Roy's donations to the church and the college. He was already paying a huge alimony to his bloodsucking ex-wife. But now that she's dead, we don't have to worry about that anymore."

Isabella's callous comment left Sister Lou speechless on several levels.

Roy rushed into the sudden silence. His smile seemed strained. "What Bella means is that she's aware of my commitment to the congregation and the college, and that commitment has nothing to do with this great meal. Thanks. We'd better get going, though. There's a lot to do to prepare for the baby."

Sister Lou observed the couple's hurried movements. *What's the rush? Is Roy afraid his young wife will make another incriminating statement?*

Chris helped Sister Lou from her chair as Roy assisted Isabella. They congratulated the expectant couple again as they strode with them to the building's exit. Roy set a brisk pace.

Sister Lou turned to Chris. "Isabella's comment

about Autumn makes me think that not every suspect is on that employee background checklist."

Chris helped her with her coat. "We'll need to add Isabella's name."

Sister Lou's brow furrowed. "And how many others?"

Chapter 26

"Have you identified the murderer yet?" Sister Marianna's clipped tone betrayed her impatience, but Sister Lou recognized her associate's underlying unease.

Sister Marianna had joined Sister Lou, Shari, and Chris in Sister Lou's apartment in the motherhouse after dinner Monday evening. They were discussing the status of their investigation into Autumn Tassler's murder. Sister Lou had invited Sister Marianna because she'd taken on the project primarily to clear the other woman's name. She'd also invited her because Sister Marianna had insisted on attending their meetings since Sister Lou had barred her from their case interviews.

Sister Marianna sat on the opposite end of the sofa from Chris, across from the matching love seat that Shari had claimed. Sister Marianna's posture was even more rigid than usual as she sat on the comfortably overstuffed furniture. Her thin knuckles showed white as she gripped her mug of hot chai tea.

The room was fragrant with the aroma of the tea Sister Lou had served and the cinnamon-and-apple potpourri she kept fresh on a corner table.

She settled back on her overstuffed armchair. The jewel-toned throw pillow at her back helped prop her up. "We haven't narrowed down the suspects yet."

"But we have a list of employees Autumn was running background checks on. It could give us a motive." Shari seemed to have acquired a taste for the chai tea. Perhaps the three packets of sugar substitute helped.

The reporter usually slipped off her shoes and curled up on the love seat, but not tonight. Instead, she sat primly on one of the cushions. Her silver stilettos were still on her feet. Was her more professional comportment a reaction to Sister Marianna's presence?

Sister Lou bit back a smile. *Marianna has that effect on people.*

"Autumn Tassler was running a resort. That employee list must be huge." Sister Marianna sounded horrified. Her snow-white hair was a sharp contrast against the bold abstract pattern of the afghan folded across the back of the sofa.

"It's not as lengthy as you'd think." Sister Lou studied the scarlet and gold area rug beneath the honey wood coffee table. "Autumn contracted with outside vendors for most of the services: security, housekeeping, landscaping, marketing, and human resources. The only departments she had on-site were accounting, catering, and administration, and those were very small staffs."

"How do you know that?" Sister Marianna looked dubious.

"She told me." Sister Lou sipped her tea. "The deputies can get the results of the background information."

"We can't give the list to the deputies." Shari's cocoa eyes widened with dismay. "We'll never see it again."

Chris loosened his sapphire tie. The jacket of his slate gray suit hung in the closet. "The employees' background checks are confidential. We aren't in a position to get that information."

"I can try." Shari turned to Chris. "I've used the Internet to find information on our suspects before."

"I agree with Shari." Sister Marianna's declaration was surprising, considering her resentment of the reporter. "The deputies won't share with us what they learn about the resort employees' backgrounds."

Sister Lou raised her hand to get everyone's attention. Surprisingly, it worked. "We'll *share* the information with the deputies. We can make a copy of the list. But we have to keep in mind that it doesn't include all of our potential suspects."

Sister Marianna's jaw dropped. "Excuse me?"

Shari spoke at the same time. "What do you mean?"

Sister Lou contemplated the paintings that hung on the warm yellow wall across the room. The religious scenes and landscape images always helped clear her mind. "Someone wants to make us think that Autumn's murder was a crime of passion, but I believe that person had been planning to kill her for at least two weeks."

"Honestly, Louise, how could you possibly know that?" Sister Marianna waved her hands with impatience.

Shari's expression brightened with realization. "Because January Potts received the anonymous letter accusing her husband of having an affair with Autumn, about two and a half weeks before Autumn was killed."

"That's right." Sister Lou gave her an approving smile. "But Sherrod Potts and Autumn weren't having an affair."

Sister Marianna scoffed. "So he says."

Sister Lou leaned forward to refill her mug. Steam from the chai tea wafted toward her face. "Rita confirmed that Autumn didn't have a social life, but someone wanted to give January a motive for murder."

"They also wanted Sister Marianna to have a motive," Chris added.

Shari cradled her mug between her hands. "The fact that Rita wanted to get out of the resort business and Autumn turned down a very lucrative offer gives Rita a motive."

Chris drained his tea. "That's not a manufactured motive, though. That one's real."

Sister Lou considered her mug of tea. "So is Isabella Fortney's motive, which is Autumn's alimony checks. Isabella's pregnancy adds an urgency to their situation."

"Isabella told us she wanted Roy to stop paying

alimony." Chris frowned as though remembering their earlier meeting. "She wants to save money for their baby."

Sister Marianna held her mug while Sister Lou refilled it with tea. "We've just discussed four people who are much more viable suspects than I am, January and Sherrod Potts, Rita Morris and Isabella Fortney. Why aren't the deputies harassing *them* instead of *me?*"

"Who knows?" Shari crossed her right leg over her left, swinging it back and forth. "We told them January lied about her alibi. They didn't even look into it."

Sister Lou exchanged a look with Shari. "I believe they're still holding a grudge against Shari and me. It's time that we made amends."

"Are we going to train for the marathon?"

Sister Carmen's question brought a smile to Sister Lou as she jogged beside her friend early Tuesday morning. "I haven't ruled it out."

Sister Carmen was persistent—in a good way. Sister Lou wished she had even a tablespoon of the other woman's enthusiastic can-do attitude. Instead, she often was pursued by demons of doubt.

In the predawn hours, Sister Carmen's citrus orange Windbreaker and phosphorus green running pants glowed. Sister Lou's teal blue Windbreaker and black exercise pants made her look like a shadow beside her jogging partner.

"Good." Sister Carmen's raven curls bounced

with excitement. "We can register today, then get serious with our training early in the New Year."

In less than twenty seconds, she'd gone from not ruling it out to submitting her registration and mapping a training schedule. *Great! On to the next challenge.*

"Then I guess I'm all in." Sister Lou filled her lungs with the crisp morning air and the scents of earth and autumn leaves.

Sister Carmen's coffee brown eyes sparkled in the light from the mission-style wrought-iron lamp-posts. The lamps lined their improvised jogging path from the congregation offices and mother-house to the College of St. Hermione of Ephesus. To extend their training miles for the marathon, they'd need to take the pedestrian trail all the way into the town's center. It was a daunting plan, but it brought her friend such joy.

"Great." Sister Carmen returned her attention to their course and the parking lot that separated the congregation from the college. There was an extra spring in her step. "This could become our annual event."

"Let's not get ahead of ourselves, Carm." Sister Lou wondered where the calico cat was this morning. She was disappointed that the cat wasn't there to greet them.

Sister Carmen broke their brief silence. "Are there still donors who want the college and congregation to separate?"

Sister Lou wanted to be as encouraging as possible for her friend in the face of such a depressing situation. "The unity that our leadership and the college's leadership have shown has reassured those who can be reassured. The one or two who still have concerns understand that our institutions will forever be connected."

"Their request was outrageous." Sister Carmen's words were rough with anger.

"I completely agree."

They jogged together in silence for many minutes. Sister Lou allowed her physical exertion to exercise her temper. Sister Carmen undoubtedly was doing the same. Her ire stirred each time she thought of the donors who expected the college to separate from its founding congregation. *What were they thinking?*

Sister Lou shortened her stride and leaned into the incline that brought them to the students' residence halls.

Lights glowed in most of the dorm room windows. Students were probably studying and working on end-of-semester projects. Finals were just two short weeks away. It wasn't quite six o'clock. Had those students stayed up late or gotten up early? Sister Lou said a quick prayer for their success as she drew closer to the buildings.

When Sister Carmen spoke again, her voice was much calmer. "What've you learned so far from your investigation of Autumn Tassler's murder?"

What hubris makes me think I have the ability to solve the murder of another human being?

After more than two weeks, she still couldn't answer that question. But she couldn't give up now. She exhaled a sigh of frustration. "I feel even more out of my depth with this case than I'd felt with Maurice's."

"Why do you feel that way?"

"You suggested I learn about Autumn during our investigation."

"That's what they do on TV."

Sister Lou decided against pointing out that they weren't in a television program. "Depending on whom I speak with, I get a very different image of Autumn."

"That's interesting. Give me an example." Sister Carmen gave her a wide-eyed look as they started their first lap around the college's oval in the heart of its campus. Their running shoes were almost silent against the footpaths. The oval was deserted now, but in a few minutes other joggers and power walkers—the college's students, staff, and faculty— would join them as they circled its well-manicured lawn, stately trees, and historical buildings.

Sister Lou selected an incident to share with her friend. "For example, Autumn's cousin, January Potts, thinks Autumn was promiscuous. She's certain Autumn was having an affair with her husband."

"What?" Sister Carmen stumbled over her feet.

Sister Lou caught her friend's elbow to steady her. "Autumn's partner, Rita Morris, and all of her staff insist that Autumn worked all the time, so when would she have been able to engage in serial affairs?"

"Good point." Sister Carmen was steadier on her feet.

Sister Lou released her friend's arm. "Then there's

Autumn's ex-husband's new wife, who resents that Roy Fortney had to pay alimony."

"Ah, the jealous *new wife*, which is a twist on the jealous *ex-wife*." Sister Carmen laughed at her own joke.

"Isabella claims the alimony checks are keeping the resort open." Sister Lou glanced at the college's library at the quarter-lap point of the oval. Its lights were on earlier than usual, offering students extended study hours.

"That gives January and Isabella motives." Sister Carmen seemed engrossed in Sister Lou's updates. "I told you your strength was in your observation skills."

"I'm still missing something. We have far too many suspects." Sister Lou smiled to acknowledge the familiar faces among the growing crowd of morning exercisers.

"I'm sure the list of other suspects makes Marianna feel better."

Sister Lou acknowledged the truth of those words. "The deputies will feel worse when we talk with them."

"You're right." Sister Carmen glanced at her. "Can I come?"

Chapter 27

A movement in her doorway broke Sister Lou's concentration as she sat behind her desk at the congregational offices later that morning.

"May I interrupt you, Lou?" Sister Barbara Yates waited just outside her office for permission to enter.

Even if she weren't the congregation's prioress, Sister Lou would have dropped what she was doing to speak with Sister Barbara.

"Of course." She saved the electronic file she'd been reviewing and turned away from her computer monitor. "What's on your mind, Barb?"

Sister Barbara smoothed her dark gray slacks before taking the far right guest chair in front of Sister Lou's desk. Her Hermionean cross was affixed to her rose blazer, which she wore with a white blouse. A smoke-gray-and-pink-patterned scarf—another original creation from Sister Katharine and her committee—completed her outfit.

The prioress winked at Sister Lou as she settled onto the guest chair. "I wanted to thank you for everything you've done, from helping to reassure donors to taking over the retreat."

"I'm happy to do whatever I can to help." Sister Lou noted that Sister Barbara's body language appeared relaxed but behind her silver-rimmed glasses, her normally twinkling hazel green eyes were clouded.

"I understand from Marianna that you've narrowed down the suspects for Autumn Tassler's murder."

Sister Lou drew her mug of tea to her. The scent of the chai wafted up to her. The smooth white porcelain was warm against her palms. She understood Sister Marianna's desire to reassure the prioress, but it was always best to deal with the facts. Few things were worse than false hope.

"Perhaps Marianna misunderstood." Sister Lou held Sister Barbara's gaze. "We have a list of potential suspects. The deputies probably have a similar list. We want to review the names with them today."

Hopefully, the deputies would be more welcoming in person this afternoon than they'd sounded on the phone when Sister Lou had called this morning to arrange the meeting.

"Marianna sounded so hopeful." Sister Barbara's gaze strayed to the back of the office.

Sister Lou was confident the other woman's focus was on something other than the artwork on the walls or the view of the front landscaping through the rear window. Beyond her office, telephones rang, printers whirred, and laughter and conversations carried down the hall.

"The list is proof that we have reason to be hopeful."

Sister Lou tried to project a confidence that was still shaky. "There are a lot of people with much stronger motives than Marianna."

Sister Barbara brought her attention back to Sister Lou. "Will Marianna accompany you to the sheriff's office?"

The thought of Sister Marianna and her powder-keg temper participating in what was bound to be a contentious meeting with Fran and Ted was enough to strike fear in Sister Lou's heart.

"Shari Henson's joining me. I'll update Marianna when I return."

"That's probably for the best." Sister Barbara nodded her understanding of Sister Lou's unspoken concern.

Sister Lou sank back onto her chair in relief. "I understand how important this meeting is for the congregation. I pray that we return with good news."

"So do I." Sister Barbara's sigh seemed to rise from deep inside. "The Advent retreat starts December third. That's twelve days from today, less than two weeks. I hope that this cloud clears from the congregation before then so that we can prepare to welcome the Savior's birth with joyful hearts."

"That's what we all want."

"I know." Sister Barbara winked again as she stood. "Thank you again, Lou. I know you've had a lot on your plate for the past several months. You've handled everything so beautifully."

Sister Barbara's caring and appreciation were two of the reasons the congregation valued her leadership.

Sister Lou stood to take Sister Barbara's hand. "Of course, Barb."

Sister Lou didn't want to raise Sister Barbara's hopes, but she believed the information she and Shari planned to review with the deputies would be sufficient to clear Sister Marianna with most reasonable people. Unfortunately, the deputies had proven themselves to be completely unreasonable.

She watched Sister Barbara leave her office and disappear down the hallway. Only then did Sister Lou reclaim her seat. Clearing Sister Marianna's name was the priority, but Sister Lou feared that if they didn't find the killer, a cloud would remain over the congregation. There were Briar Coast residents who were concerned that the congregation was connected with both of the town's recent murders. The only thing that could stop the whispers would be to prove that coincidences were real.

But how?

The familiar scents of warm pastries and fresh coffee assailed Sister Lou as she entered the bullpen of the Briar Coast County Sheriff's Office late Tuesday afternoon. Beside her, Shari's black stilettos snapped tauntingly against the silver-marbled flooring. Sister Lou came to a stop toward the center of the room, where Ted's and Fran's desks stood back-to-back. Both sheriff's deputies looked up at her approach. Their expressions were less than welcoming.

Fran made an effort to sound pleasant. "You said you had some kind of a list for us, Sister."

Sister Lou pulled the copy of the employee background check list from her purse. The original remained in her nightstand. She walked past Ted's disorganized desk and offered the single sheet of paper to Fran. "As I explained when I called this morning, Autumn was concerned that someone was embezzling from her resort. She'd hired a security company to run background checks on all of her employees."

"How d'you know this?" Ted's words were thick with skepticism.

Shari turned to Ted with a cool smile. "Montgomery Crane, founder and CEO of Crane Enterprises, told us Autumn had asked him for advice. He gave us the information. Do you want to add him to your suspects list?"

Ted crossed his arms over his chest, covered in his now loose-fitting tan uniform shirt. "Why? You run out of room on yours?"

Shari's editor wanted her to repair her relationship with the sheriff's office. This exchange probably wasn't helping.

Sister Lou worked to redirect everyone's attention. "It's possible that one of her employees learned that Autumn was checking into his or her background and decided to stop her."

The ice in Fran's bottle green eyes started to thaw. She exchanged a look with Ted before scanning the sheet of paper. "Is this a list of all of her employees? There aren't very many for such a big resort."

"Autumn mainly contracted with outside vendors for resort services." Sister Lou adjusted her purse on her right shoulder.

"All right." Ted's manner was dismissive as he pulled his chair farther under his desk. "We'll look into it."

Sister Lou's temper stirred. "When?"

"Are you going to *look into it* like you *looked into* January Potts's alibi?" Shari settled her hands on her hips. "That alibi turned out to be false. Have you followed up with her?"

Fran turned her anger to Shari. Several strands of her blond hair had worked free of the bun at the nape of her neck. They floated around her thin, alabaster features. "Are you telling us how to do our jobs?"

Shari didn't back down. "We're trying to help you."

Sister Lou put her hand on Shari's right shoulder. The reporter's scarlet wool sweater was soft under her palm. "Shari's right. We have a vested interest in finding Autumn's killer and removing the cloud that's been cast over the congregation. Beyond that, we all have a responsibility to work for the safety of our neighbors."

"You think you two can do our jobs better than we can?" Ted dragged his beefy right hand over his round, clean-shaven head. "We're trained law enforcement officers. You're a nun and a glorified stenographer."

Shari's muscles tightened beneath Sister Lou's

hand. "And we still solved the last murder before you did."

Sister Lou squeezed Shari's shoulder in warning. She understood her friend was upset, but rising to the deputy's bait wouldn't advance their cause. Sarcasm and anger: those were Ted's default characteristics. All around them, telephones rang and printers rumbled. Conversations between deputies carried across the room. In the estimated five minutes since they'd arrived, the box of freshly baked doughnuts had been visited at least a dozen times. It was an indication of Ted's willpower that, even surrounded by warm, rich pastries on a daily basis, he'd still been able to lose weight. Had Fran noticed?

Sister Lou settled onto the guest chair beside Fran's desk. "You want answers, just as we do."

"We didn't have to share the list with you." Shari still wasn't backing down.

Fran pinned the reporter with a look. "Are you withholding information?"

Shari arched an eyebrow. "Are you?"

Time to change the subject. "The scarf you found in Autumn's office doesn't belong to Sister Marianna."

Fran dragged her attention from Shari to frown at Sister Lou. "How do you know it's not hers?"

Ted snorted. "Because they don't want it to be."

Sister Lou hurried to answer before Shari again felt compelled to reply. "Sister Marianna found her scarf."

"Convenient." Ted slouched lower onto his chair.

Fran nodded her agreement. "We told you that

we found the scarf at the crime scene. Then Sister Marianna miraculously finds her scarf."

"'Tis the season for miracles." Ted's voice dripped with skepticism.

And goodwill to all, but you continually forget that part. "Was Sister Marianna's DNA on the scarf you found?"

"No, and neither was Autumn Tassler's." Fran sighed. "But if the scarf isn't Sister Marianna's, whose is it?"

"That's obvious." Sister Lou looked from Fran to Ted, then back. "The killer's."

Ted rolled his eyes. "Here we go again."

"Can you believe those deputies?" Shari was still fuming over their clash with the sheriff's deputies as she and Sister Lou entered the main building of the Briar Coast Cabin Resort.

Sister Lou stopped just inside the main lobby and turned to her young friend. "Deputies Cole and Tate can be challenging—"

"That's an understatement."

"But, Shari, your editor's right. You've got to find a way to work with them."

"He's asking for the impossible." She folded her arms above the scarlet wool sweater she wore.

"I have faith in you." Sister Lou relaxed when she won a smile from Shari. She turned toward the registration desk. "Good afternoon, Kelsey. Is Gary Hargreaves available, please?"

Kelsey's big, dark blue eyes were curious. Her

corkscrew pale blond curls nearly shivered with excitement.

"Is this about finding Autumn's killer?" She dropped her voice to a stage whisper. "Everyone's been acting really weird."

That wasn't surprising, considering that fifteen days ago, their employer had been murdered on the resort grounds. Their place of employment had become a crime scene. "In what way?"

"Well, Gary's started locking his office every time he leaves it. Really. Even to go to the john." Kelsey picked up her telephone receiver and pressed a few buttons. "Hi, Gary. Sister Lou and Shari Henson are here to see you." She paused, frowning in concentration. "Well, Gary, you're really going to have to tell her that yourself." She disconnected the call, then rolled her eyes. "He's on his way."

Sister Lou thanked Kelsey, then led Shari a few steps away from the front desk to wait for the accountant. It didn't take long for Gary to appear, hurrying down the long main hallway toward them.

"I was told not to talk to you." He wagged a finger toward Sister Lou as she stood beside Shari.

Shari slid a look toward Sister Lou. "This is becoming a regular refrain."

While Urban Rodgers had greeted them four days ago looking as though he'd spent the morning backpacking with survivalists, Gary Hargreaves looked like he'd spent his lunch break in a salon. He seemed to be in his late forties or early fifties. His thick, wavy, golden blond hair was professionally styled. His artificially tanned skin made his green eyes glow. The dark blue suit was tailor-made for his tall, lean form. He hadn't purchased those black leather shoes from a discount store. They tapped against the polished walnut wood flooring until he halted less than an arm's length from Sister Lou and Shari.

Sister Lou's eyes dropped to Gary's hands at his side. They were well groomed, but not perfect. They glittered. She leaned forward and spoke softly, aware that Kelsey was watching them like a Broadway play. "Mr. Hargreaves, polish is so hard to remove. I recommend fake nails."

Gary's eyes widened with shock. His cheeks flushed with embarrassment. "Come with me." He spun on his heels and hustled back down the hallway without waiting to see if they followed.

"How did you do that?" Shari spoke in hushed tones.

Sister Lou whispered back. "It was a calculated risk that he wouldn't want his coworkers to know his grooming included shiny pink nail polish."

Gary had set a brisk pace for their trip deep into the resort's administrative area. He scratched at his nails as he moved. The door to Rita's office was closed as they strode past. *Is Autumn's partner hard at work or away from the resort?*

The accountant stopped in front of another closed door much farther down the hall. Sister Lou and Shari waited as he unlocked his office.

"Take a seat." His invitation was less than gracious. "For the record, I wear nail polish for my role in a community theater performance of *Priscilla, Queen of the Desert*."

"I didn't mean to pry, Mr. Hargreaves. I was trying to be helpful." Sister Lou shrugged out of her coat. The office was a little chilly, but not cold enough to keep her coat on. She hung it on the back of one of the two matching chairs in front of his desk. Shari did the same with her coat.

Gary unbuttoned his suit coat before sitting behind his desk. "We need to make this quick. I'm very busy, and I was warned against speaking with you."

Shari crossed her right leg over her left. "What did the deputies say would happen if you spoke with us?"

Gary frowned. "You'd make outrageous claims to try to clear your friend."

Sister Lou did a visual scan of the accountant's impeccable office. It was almost too well organized. Behind him, his computer monitor was locked. He must have taken the precaution to safeguard highly sensitive financial documents. Kelsey had mentioned that he'd only recently started locking his office. *Is Autumn's death the reason for his added security or has something else changed?*

The accountant's work space showcased a wide variety of mementos he appeared to have collected on various international trips: a framed, stylized cloth map of the Caribbean island of Aruba; black-and-white photographs of himself in front of famous Parisian landmarks; a dark wood, hand-painted carving of an elephant. Perhaps from Thailand? In the course of her ministry work with the congregation,

Sister Lou had traveled abroad extensively. She suspected Gary didn't get the same group discounts.

"We're grateful for your time, Mr. Hargreaves." Sister Lou heard soft music in the background. The chords had an international flavor.

"Call me Gary." The invitation was grudging.

Sister Lou smiled. "Gary, as I explained to the deputies, we're on the same side. Do you know whether Autumn had any concerns about the resort? Had she been distracted or preoccupied before her death?"

Gary shook his head. "Autumn didn't form relationships with the staff. She wasn't cold. She just didn't encourage confidences and she didn't share any, either."

Although Rita made the comment that Autumn told Kelsey everything.

"How long have you worked for her?" Shari glanced around the office.

Did she see what I saw? Sister Lou turned her attention back to Gary.

He sat straighter and lifted his chin. "I'm the longest tenured of any of her employees. I started here before the resort officially opened."

"That's impressive." Sister Lou understood the source of his pride. She swept her hand to indicate the images on his walls and the crafts on his desk. "I see you've also made the most of your vacations."

Gary grinned. "Yes, I enjoy traveling."

"Do you work with one of the resort's travel agency partners to plan them?" Sister Lou kept a casual demeanor.

"Yes, I use Briar Coast Travel." Gary seemed to relax. "They're local. Are you planning a trip?"

"I might be." Sister Lou stood, offering the accountant her hand. "Thank you again for your time, Gary. I hope Autumn's killer is found soon."

Grief shadowed the accountant's features. "So do I."

Sister Lou quietly led Shari from his office. Would he lock the door behind them or was that only when he left the room?

Kelsey bobbled toward them as they entered the lobby area. "Did he tell you why he's being so weird?" She posited the question in a stage whisper.

Shari gave the administrative assistant a curious look. "We didn't ask him."

Sister Lou tried to temper Shari's response. "Everyone handles grief differently. He'll be back to his old self in time."

"I hope so," Kelsey groused as she turned to bounce back to the registration counter. Her mannerisms were so youthful, but there was experience on her face.

Sister Lou exited the main cabin and climbed in behind the wheel of her orange compact. She waited as her friend strapped in. "Could you contact Briar Coast Travel to learn as much as you can about Gary's trips? How much have they cost? How often does he go? How long does he stay?"

Shari glanced at her. "Do you think *Gary* is the embezzler?"

"Those trips weren't inexpensive." She put the car in gear and pulled out of the parking lot.

"So tell me, how did you know that mentioning

his grooming habits would get us an invitation to his office?"

"How many men do you know who'd want to discuss their salon visits in the middle of their employer's lobby?"

"Good point. I'll look into Gary's travel, but I can't see him killing someone. I doubt he'd want to risk his mani-pedi."

Chapter 28

"Ah, Louise, I'm glad you're here. We need to talk." Sister Marianna came around her desk and ushered Sister Lou into her office late Tuesday afternoon.

Sister Lou lowered the hand she'd raised to knock. She watched in confusion as Sister Marianna welcomed her into her office. That was unusual. Her look of displeasure wasn't.

Sister Lou smoothed her cream pantsuit before lowering herself with some caution to the padded visitor's chair. "It seems we both need to speak with the other. You first, Marianna. What's on your mind?"

Sister Marianna returned to her faux mahogany wood desk. She pinned Sister Lou with a direct stare. "Frankly, Louise, it pains me to have to say this, but you're making a mess of this investigation."

She'd wondered how long it would take Sister Marianna to launch her attack. Waiting eleven days showed an admirable amount of restraint for her.

Sister Lou relaxed back on her armchair and said a quick prayer for patience and understanding. "In what way?"

"It's been *eleven* days." Sister Marianna tossed up her arms, causing her pale blue blouse to crease. "You still don't know who killed Autumn Tassler."

Neither did Sister Marianna nor the deputies, but Sister Lou refrained from pointing fingers. "Before we can identify the killer, we need to understand the motive."

"How hard could that be? Someone wanted her dead." Sister Marianna spread her arms. Her vocal register was arcing toward an impressive octave.

"Why?"

"Why what?"

"Why did someone want her dead?"

"How should I know?"

Sister Lou remembered her prayer for patience. "You've just proven my point. If we don't understand why someone wanted to kill her, we won't be able to identify who committed the crime."

Sister Marianna sighed. "What motive have you come up with?"

There were signs of tension and distraction around Sister Marianna's office. Her work space wasn't as rigidly organized as Sister Lou had come to expect. Mail and other papers filled her usually empty in-box. A manila file folder lay as though forgotten on her blond wood conversation table. Her pale gold blazer was folded on the back of her seat instead of hanging on her coatrack. The strain was getting to the other woman. Understandably.

"As we discussed the other night, we have multiple motives, depending on the suspect." Sister Lou collected her thoughts. "There's jealousy, which would fit her cousin. But as for her business partner, her ex-husband, his wife, her business rival, and possibly an employee, money appears to be the more popular cause."

"Those are two motives and more than thirty people." Sister Marianna gave her a wide-eyed stare.

"We only have thirty suspects. Autumn employed twenty-five people. In addition to her employees, we have five outside suspects."

"You're not including me on your list?" Sister Marianna sat back on her seat.

"You're not guilty, Marianna."

"I know that." Sister Marianna made a visible effort to pull herself together. "What are your plans to eliminate your suspects?"

"Autumn's business rival and her ex-husband have moved to the bottom of my list." Sister Lou cocked her head. "You mentioned that you have concerns regarding the way I'm handling the investigation. What would you recommend I do?"

"You need to be more forceful, Louise." Sister Marianna leaned into her desk. Her eyes snapped with impatience. "These suspects need to prove their innocence."

Sister Lou's eyebrows flew up her forehead. Sister Marianna's forceful approach was one of the reasons she preferred to leave the other woman behind when she met with potential suspects. Considering the struggle Sister Lou had this morning keeping Shari's temper in place, she could only imagine the juggling act she'd have undertaken if Sister Marianna had tagged along. The difference between the two women was that Sister Lou could help Shari keep her temper in place. Sister Marianna was a loose cannon. Period.

"Marianna, these people don't *have* to speak with me. Perhaps the deputies could take a stronger approach, but I have to be diplomatic."

"Then you have to get regular updates from the deputies."

Strange how times had changed. When Sister Lou was investigating her friend's murder, Sister Marianna was adamant that the deputies should handle the investigation and the congregation should not get involved. Now that she was a suspect in a murder investigation, Marianna wanted Sister Lou to ruffle the deputies' feathers. She'd take a pass on that, thanks anyway.

"Marianna, you've been cleared of suspicion for Autumn's murder."

Sister Marianna's lips parted in surprise. "Why didn't you tell me that when you first arrived?"

"You wanted to discuss my handling of the case first."

Sister Marianna's shoulders sagged with relief. "And you're certain that I'm no longer a suspect?"

"Yes, we're positive." Sister Lou smiled at her associate's reaction. "Shari and I met with the deputies this afternoon. The lab didn't find traces of either your DNA or Autumn's DNA on the scarf. The deputies conceded that it wasn't your scarf that they'd found at the crime scene nor was it the murder weapon."

Sister Marianna grinned. "Well, then, our job is done. The congregation's been cleared. Barbara and Valerie will be thrilled to hear it."

Sister Lou held up a hand to slow Sister Marianna's celebration. "I'm afraid we're not completely clear yet. Until the real murderer is found, we'll continue to have a cloud of suspicion over us."

"Oh, Louise, you're making too much of this." Sister Marianna waved a dismissive hand.

"I hope you're right, Marianna." But Sister Lou wasn't willing to take the risk.

"Your guy has an interesting background." Shari disregarded the traditional greeting when Sister Lou answered her desk phone early Wednesday morning.

Perhaps that contributed to Sister Lou's confusion. "My guy?"

"Gary Hargreaves, Autumn Tassler's ne'er-do-well accountant."

"What makes him my guy?"

"Play along with me."

"All right." She was still confused. "What have you learned?"

A couple of keyboard strokes carried over the phone line. From her evaluation of the background sounds, Sister Lou determined Shari had made this call from her cubicle at the *Telegraph*. She must have gotten an early start, too. It was the day before Thanksgiving, and Sister Lou had a long to-do list if she was going to take the day off.

"Buckle up. This is good." Shari seemed to enjoy

the presentation almost as much as the investigation itself. Either that or her friend had had too much caffeine—and it wasn't yet eight o'clock. "One Gary Theron Hargreaves. Born July thirteenth in the year of our Lord 1965 in Trenton, New Jersey. Age fifty-two. He arrived in Briar Coast September 2013, or at least that's when he started renting his condo."

"Did he move here for a job?"

"Good guess, but no." Shari projected her best game-show voice. "Autumn hired him January 2014, one month before she opened the resort. By the way, guess what day she launched her Briar Coast Cabin Resort enterprise?"

Sister Lou searched her memory and came up blank. "When did she open it?"

"Valentine's Day. Irony much?" Shari laughed. "Starting a resort with your alimony checks, then opening it on Valentine's Day. The more I learn about this woman, the more I like her."

"Autumn seemed to have a flair."

"I'll say." Shari paused before continuing. "Before setting up in Briar Coast, our pal Gary moved around. A lot: East Coast, West Coast, South, Mountain States. He's never stayed in one place for long. Makes you wonder if he was running from something, doesn't it?"

"Not necessarily." Sister Lou turned her desk chair away from her computer to contemplate the cold, late-fall scene outside her office window—and the little she knew about Shari. "I've learned that a person's abrupt departures could mean they're running toward something rather than away. They may not have realized it yet."

Shari hummed noncommittally. "Let's put a pin in that for now. Gary was running from something. He'd been arrested for embezzlement at least twice before. Other times, he may not have been arrested, but he was caught."

Sister Lou closed her eyes in mild disappointment. The signs were there. Autumn may have seen them, too. Still she held on to hope. "Are there any indications that Gary was trying to do better?"

"I'm afraid not." Shari's voice was subdued as though the reporter sensed Sister Lou's disappointment. "I called Briar Coast Travel as you suggested. You were right. He does take several expensive, international trips each year. His next one is a weeklong winter cruise to the Mediterranean."

Sister Lou frowned at the audacity. "Is he traveling on a discounted or packaged special?"

"No. His travel agent said this time, he's going first class." Shari made a disgusted sound. "You'd think someone who'd been arrested for embezzlement not once but twice would stop pushing his luck."

"It must be a sickness."

"Must be." There was a shrug in Shari's voice.

"Is he carrying any debt?"

"Some, but not much." The phone line picked up the sound of rustling. *Shari must be checking through papers on her desk.* "In addition to his trips, Gary has a membership to Fit Up Health Space. We both know that's an exclusive gym. He also has a standing weekly appointment to a beauty salon, and he's a member of some shoe-of-the-month club. Even with my shoe fetish, I think that's nuts."

"It does seem excessive." Sister Lou inhaled deeply, drawing in the soothing scents of her white tea potpourri. "Based on all you've just reported, it seems Gary was the one stealing from the resort's accounts."

"He had access to them," Shari continued as though using her fingers to count off the points. Sister Lou imagined the reporter cradling the receiver between her shoulder and chin as she proceeded. "The motive would be his spending habits. He had plenty of opportunity. He's the resort's accountant."

"You've summed all of that up very nicely."

"I suppose you want to give this information to the deputies?" Shari sounded like she was being forced to go to the dentist—or worse.

"No, not yet."

"Why not? Is something wrong?"

"Gary may very well have been the embezzler, but can you envision him killing Autumn?"

There was a brief pause on the line. "Now that you mention it, no. I can't see him ruining his weekly manicure."

"Neither can I." Sister Lou's lips curved in appreciation of Shari's observation. "I think we're once again getting another question for every one we answer."

"Do you want to talk with Gary before we go to the deputies?"

"I think that would be for the best." Sister Lou spun her chair back to face her desk. "I also want to know why he's locking his office door."

* * *

"You two again?" Gary spoke in a stage whisper as he hurried past resort guests. He stopped his customary arm's length from Shari and Sister Lou, who waited for him in the main lobby of the Briar Coast Cabin Resort later Wednesday morning. "I've told you everything I know and probably more than I should have."

Kelsey stood behind the front desk, shaking her head and rolling her eyes at Gary's near-hysteria. She turned and disappeared, bouncing into one of the two offices behind the registration desk.

Sister Lou wouldn't be able to embarrass him into meeting privately with them again, but she'd learned a thing or two from her fearless friend. "Shari and I have a question or two about your international trips. Would you like to discuss them here or in your office?"

A chill breeze struggled in from beneath the resort's front door. The scents of strong coffee, breakfast meats, and fresh pastries floated out to greet her, though not nearly as tempting as the aromas of the Briar Coast Café's offerings.

In her peripheral vision she noticed guests walking in the direction of the dining hall for an early lunch and those coming from a late breakfast. They were older couples and extended families who'd checked into the resort for the long Thanksgiving weekend. The air hummed with the sounds of their excited chatter and bursts of laughter. She remembered when she'd been a part of an extended family. Now it was up to her and Chris to keep their family traditions and memories alive—and to start new ones.

"Fine." With that single grudging syllable, Gary again led them to his office.

Sister Lou followed him and Shari. A little farther than halfway down the main hall, they stopped in front of Gary's office. Why had he locked his office door before coming to meet them in the lobby?

He held the door as they entered, then closed it before confronting them. "What do you want to know about my vacation?"

"Wouldn't that be *vacations* in the plural?" Shari emphasized the *s* at the end of the word. She faced Gary, crossing her arms. Her winter coat hung open over her citrus orange sweater and chocolate corduroy pants. Muted colors for the outspoken reporter.

"We're not just interested in your international trips." Sister Lou shrugged out of her coat and folded it over her joined arms. It was stuffy in Gary's office. "You have a membership to an exclusive health club and a shoe-of-the-month club."

Gary's features battled between shock and outrage. "Are you spying on me?"

"Yes." Shari swept her right arm to encompass his office and everything in it. "How are you able to afford this lifestyle? You can't possibly make that much for a small, struggling resort."

"The resort isn't struggling." Gary marched past them to stand behind his desk.

Shari circled to keep their target in her sight. "You should know. You're the accountant."

"That's right." Gary's words were clipped with irritation. "And I'm telling you the resort isn't struggling. By all accounts, our profits should have been more significant."

Gary sounded so sincere. Either he believed what he said or he was a skillful liar. Sister Lou stepped to his desk and sat uninvited on one of his guest chairs. Shari followed suit, peeling off her coat.

Sister Lou rested her coat and purse on her lap. "Did you know Autumn was doing background checks on all of her full-time employees?"

"Of course I did." Gary lowered himself onto his wheeled executive chair. "We had to complete the paperwork giving the third-party vendor permission to collect the information. People were angry about it."

"How angry?" Shari asked.

Gary shrugged. "Rita was angry enough to confront her over it."

Shari gaped. "She ran a background check on her partner?"

Gary scoffed. "Rita isn't an equal partner. She only invested forty percent, and she contributes even less than that."

"Who else?" Sister Lou prodded.

Gary didn't hesitate. "The security manager quit because of it. So did the grounds manager."

Sister Lou heard warning bells. "Were either of the managers angry enough to cause trouble for Autumn?"

"I don't think so." Gary's tone was thoughtful. "They both found other jobs pretty fast."

"I don't understand." Shari crossed her long legs

in her corduroy slacks. "Why would she do background checks on everyone unless she thought one of you was stealing from her?"

"Someone *was* stealing from her." Gary threw himself against the back of his chair with palpable frustration. "And apparently that same person was manipulating my month-end reports to hide the situation from Autumn."

Shari turned to Sister Lou. "The hacker Montgomery Crane mentioned."

"You spoke with him?" Gary looked surprised and impressed. "I told Autumn I thought the hacker was someone at the company that manages our employee benefits."

Shari gave him a considering look. "Did you serve the benefits vendor on a platter because you were afraid she'd find out about you?"

Gary folded his arms as though he were closing himself off from them. "Since you've been snooping around in my past, you probably know I've been arrested for embezzlement."

"*Twice*," Shari clarified.

"Autumn knew." Gary's features tightened. "I'd told her before she hired me. She said with the small amount she was able to pay, she was lucky to have found me. But I was the lucky one. She saved my life."

His testimony inspired Sister Lou. "Everyone deserves a second chance—or a third. But how do you afford your trips and club memberships on your salary?"

Gary's mutinous expression eased. "I handle the finances for Fit Up Health Space in exchange for my membership. I also work with several small local businesses, including the travel agency. I've changed, Sister."

"How?" Shari shoehorned all of her suspicions into one word.

Gary paused. "I didn't want to screw up the chance that Autumn was giving me. I thought it could be my last, so I did some soul-searching and realized my past was about the adrenaline rush."

"Not the money?" Shari arched a winged eyebrow.

"And the money." Gary inclined his head in acknowledgment. "So I took on extra work to earn the extra money, and found hobbies—acting, travel, and exercise—for the rush."

"What about your shoe-of-the-month club?" Shari asked.

Gary's expression was defensive. "Everyone has a weakness. What's yours?"

"Coffee." Shari didn't even hesitate.

"I'm happy for you, Gary. It took strength to turn your life around." Sister Lou started to rise, then paused, nodding toward his door behind her. "We've heard that you've recently started locking your door when you're not in your office. May we ask why?"

"I'm protecting myself." Gary glowered. "If someone killed Autumn because of the background checks, who's to say they won't come after me next because I manage the accounts?"

Shari's eyebrows knitted. "You think locking your door will protect you?"

Gary shrugged. "At least this way, they won't be able to sneak up on me."

"The killer didn't sneak up on Autumn." Sister Lou looked around Gary's office as she pictured Autumn's crime scene. "Autumn didn't expect this person to become violent with her. She let her guard down. The killer's someone she trusted."

Chapter 29

"Are you sure I don't have to bring anything to the congregation's Thanksgiving dinner tomorrow?" Shari finished her turkey on whole grain sandwich and pulled her bowl of turkey and rice soup closer.

Chris heard the nerves in Shari's voice as they shared lunch at the Briar Coast Café Wednesday. The closer they got to the informal get-together, the more apprehensive the reporter became. At this rate, she'd become a collection of nerves by Thanksgiving Day. He'd have to wheel her into the motherhouse dining room.

"For the fourth time, I'm positive." He lowered his soup spoon. "This isn't my first Thanksgiving with them. If it would make you feel better, you could bring a dessert. Sister Carmen would love you for it."

"I don't want to bring something and look like a nerd." Shari glared at her soup. "But I don't want to show up empty-handed and look like a freeloader, either."

Chris changed the subject. "You said your interview with Aunt Lou and the resort's accountant was productive."

Immediately, Shari's frown disappeared. "Your aunt may have missed her calling. It's amazing watching her put clues together."

"Although I worry about her safety, sometimes I think she's right where God intended her to be." Chris swallowed another spoonful of soup. "I'm sure the deputies would disagree."

Shari sipped her lemonade. "They're lucky to have her help."

Chris heard the resentment in her voice. "What do you have against the deputies? Or is it all law enforcement?"

"I don't have anything against law enforcement specifically." A mischievous light danced in Shari's dark eyes. "I have issues with authority figures in general: deputies, editors, vice presidents for advancement."

Chris smiled in appreciation of her teasing. "And why are you antiestablishment?"

"Isn't everyone?" Shari feigned surprise.

Chris regarded the restless reporter for several beats in silence. Her heart-shaped face was tilted at a challenging angle. Her reckless cocoa eyes were direct. Despite her confrontational pose, it was obvious that she was avoiding . . . something. "Why do you always do that?"

"Do what?"

Chris frowned in concern. "That's textbook avoidance: change the subject, then pretend not to know what the other person's talking about when he challenges you on it."

"I *don't* know what you're talking about." She sipped her soup. Funny how doing that allowed her to evade eye contact.

"Whenever Aunt Lou or I ask you a personal question, you avoid answering by turning the question back to us."

"Maybe you shouldn't ask so many personal questions."

Chris shifted aside his food tray and folded his arms on their small dining table. He dropped his voice. "You're a hard person to get to know."

"There's a fine line between *getting to know* someone and *prying*."

"There's something about you that makes me want to pry."

"I recommend fresh air and a healthier diet."

"I don't think that'll work."

"More sleep."

"Not that, either."

"Then how about a little soul-searching?" Shari finished her soup and sat back on her chair, increasing the distance that separated them.

"Do you think confession will be good for my soul?"

"Do you have something to confess?"

"Just that I want to get to know you."

Shari sent her gaze around the crowded café before returning her attention to Chris. "We've been through this before. I don't see a point in rehashing the past."

"The past made us who we are today. I doubt that you've done anything so terrible that you can't discuss it."

"*I* haven't done anything."

If he'd been trying to get a rise from her, it had worked. If he hadn't, it had backfired. "You can trust me, Shari."

"Right now, I'm trusting you to drop this."

Chris hesitated. "If that's what you want."

Sister Lou wasn't comfortable sharing Shari's confidences. He respected that. If Shari couldn't or wouldn't trust him enough to confide in him, there were other ways of collecting information. But he'd rather find out from her.

The thick, warm rose carpeting in the congregational office's hallway muted Sister Lou's footsteps Wednesday afternoon. She was on her way to the main lobby, where Briar Coast Mayor Heather Stanley had shown up unexpectedly, requesting to meet with her.

Fluorescent lighting bounced off the pale gold walls as Sister Lou passed the conference rooms, administrative assistants' desks, offices, and break room. She caught snippets of conversations and laughter through the open doors and workstations along the way. They trailed her down the hall—along with a vague sense of unease. What did the mayor want? Would her encounter with the town official be as contentious as Shari's had been?

Sister Lou stopped in the lobby. She exchanged a smile with Sister Jane at receptionist's desk before approaching the mayor.

Heather Stanley immediately set aside her smartphone and rose as Sister Lou crossed to her. She was a striking figure in a wool opal skirt suit with matching pumps. She carried her crimson winter coat. Her thick chestnut hair was swept behind her shoulders. Her perfect porcelain skin was flushed, presumably from the chill breeze outside.

Sister Lou offered the younger woman her right hand. "Good afternoon, Mayor Stanley."

Heather's hand was cool, at odds with her friendly smile. "Good afternoon, Sister LaSalle. Thank you for allowing me to interrupt your day."

"Please call me Sister Lou. How can I help you?" Sister Lou allowed her hand to drop to her side. She channeled her inner Shari to project an air of bravado.

Heather surveyed the lobby. "Is there someplace where we could speak privately?"

"Yes, of course." Sister Lou hoped she didn't sound as reluctant as she felt.

She led the mayor into the first empty conference room she came to. This was the room in which she'd revealed to the deputies the person who'd killed Maurice. It had been more than two months since she'd been inside. If it weren't for the mayor, she wouldn't have returned today.

Sister Lou allowed the mayor to precede her into the room and trailed her to the table.

She took a moment to get her bearings. A large, honey wood, rectangular table, surrounded by ten powder blue–cushioned honey wood chairs, dominated the narrow space. A caravan desk stood at the rear. The room was chilly enough to keep its occupants alert. Sunlight flooded the interior from the large picture windows. A hint of white-tea potpourri lingered in the air.

She turned to the mayor. "Please make yourself comfortable. Can I get you anything?"

"No, thank you. I'm fine." Heather circled the table and took the seat on the end. "I'm sorry to interrupt your lunch break. This is very important, otherwise I wouldn't have come unannounced."

Sister Lou sat across the table from her. "Not at all, Mayor. How can I help you?"

"You can stop investigating Autumn Tassler's murder." The mayor attempted to pin Sister Lou with her arresting violet eyes.

Sister Lou wouldn't be pinned. "May I ask the reason for your request?"

"You've been interrogating prominent members of the community." Heather sat back on her chair. She crossed her right leg over her left and folded her hands on her lap. "They couldn't possibly know anything about Ms. Tassler's murder."

Because they're prominent? "The people I've been speaking with have provided information that's useful to the investigation."

"Then pass that information on to the deputies. This case has nothing to do with you."

"I disagree." Sister Lou folded her hands on the table. "When the deputies began their investigation, they again put our congregation under suspicion. We had to prove our innocence. So, yes, this case has a lot to do with us."

Heather spread her arms. "I'm sure you can appreciate that the deputies have to follow every lead. They're doing a very difficult job. But it's my understanding that Sister Marianna isn't a suspect anymore."

The mayor's grasp of the murder investigation wasn't surprising. The sheriff probably updated her daily.

Seated across the table, the mayor appeared self-assured, confident in her authority. But on closer examination, Heather's body language was tight. Stress radiated from her raised shoulders. The knuckles in her clasped hands were pale. Neither Sister Lou nor the mayor wanted to be here.

Sister Lou searched the other woman's wide eyes. "Is your campaign contributor one of the murder suspects?"

Heather's lips parted. Her large eyes widened. She pushed herself up from her seat and started toward the door. "I think I've made myself more than clear. Your involving yourself in this case is only complicating matters. Your talents lay with your community work, Sister. Leave the murder investigations to the professionals."

Sister Lou rose as well to escort her from the congregational office. "At the risk of sounding immodest, I believe my track record is proof that I *can* solve murders."

The mayor glanced at her as they entered the main lobby. "Murder investigations are dangerous, Sister. You probably don't want to push your luck."

Sister Lou gave the public official a beatific smile. "I don't count on luck, Mayor Stanley. I put my trust in God. It's *His* guidance that I rely on."

The mayor seemed at a loss for words. She offered Sister Lou her hand and wished her a good day. Sister Lou watched Heather leave the building and walk to her car in the front parking lot. Which one of her supporters had asked the mayor to meet with Sister Lou? Was it the same person who'd sent the anonymous letter to January Potts?

Diplomacy *is not a dirty word.*

"I'm going to write the article with or without your cooperation." Shari had clenched her left fist around her office telephone's black receiver so tightly it might have to be surgically removed. She drew a deep, calming breath and channeled her inner Sister Lou for this phone call with Deputy Ted Tate.

She'd chosen Ted for her guerilla interview tactic because Fran was the more reasonable of the two deputies, although not by much. Ted definitely had the shorter fuse. She hoped she hadn't miscalculated.

"Then go ahead and write it without me." Ted's words were soaked with spite.

He knew Shari needed a quote from the sheriff's office for her follow-up article on Autumn's murder investigation. A few words from him or Fran would add credibility to her story. That's probably the reason neither of the deputies had returned the multiple voice mail messages she'd left for them. Their silence had pushed her article to the cusp of her deadline.

The clock on her computer monitor read seventeen minutes after two o'clock in the afternoon. She had a little more than forty minutes to file her copy if she wanted it to appear in the Thanksgiving edition of the *Telegraph* tomorrow morning.

"And here I thought we'd become friends, Ted." Shari relaxed her grip on the telephone receiver one finger at a time. "I thought we'd turned the page on our relationship when we gave you the list of resort employees and told you about the background checks."

Ted grunted. "You couldn't have done anything with that list on your own. You don't have the authority."

"True." She decided against telling him about the information she'd scraped together on Gary Hargreaves, their self-proclaimed reformed accountant. "But you and Fran wouldn't have known about the background checks without us. What've you found out?"

"Are you asking for a quote or information?"

"Both, of course." Shari lifted her half-empty mug of coffee and drank deeply. She'd have to push a little harder. "You know how this works, Ted. We give you something, then you give us something. That's the give-and-take of our relationship."

Growing up in foster care, Shari had trained herself to tune out background noises. That talent was handy in a newsroom. The closer they came to the day's deadline, the louder and more frenetic the newsroom activities became.

And the more desperate she became to wrap up her copy.

"Our relationship?" Ted barked a laugh. "We don't have a relationship."

"It's at a rocky stage right now, but that's because you won't admit that we've helped with your investigations before and we can do it again." It was maddening that the deputy was able to remain calm while Shari was having a series of anger fantasies. She unconsciously tightened her grip on her receiver again as her irritation rose.

"Law enforcement is *our* job. I don't know what *you* do." Ted sounded like he was chewing nails. *Finally.*

"Look, I know your feelings were hurt when I wrote that it was Sister Lou who solved Dr. Jordan's murder, but I have to report the truth." Shari could almost hear the vein burst in the deputy's temple.

"You, Sister Lou, and Chris LaSalle could've gotten yourselves killed. Do you realize that?" Ted's words came quickly, like rapid, sustained gunfire. "You could've gotten other people killed. This isn't some mystery theater, dinner party, whodunit crap. This is real life."

"We're aware of that. We—"

"Your snooping around in an active investigation compromises evidence, endangers others, and generally screws up our case."

Shari's pen was poised above her notepad, ready to transcribe any information Ted let slip—and hopefully, a printable quote. "And yet, we didn't do any of those things. Maybe one of the reasons you don't want to talk with us is that you're afraid we'll solve this case first, too."

"You're wrong." The knocking in the background sounded like Ted pounding his desk. "We're throwing all of our resources at this case, working long hours, chasing down information. We know how important this case is and we're not going to rest until it's solved."

Score!

That was the quote she'd been waiting for. Dreaming of. "Thank you, Ted. You've been very helpful." Shari disconnected the call. Now she could file her story.

The back-and-forth with the deputy had been brutal, but it had been worth it.

What would Ted and Fran say when they read her article tomorrow morning? Whatever their reaction, it probably wouldn't be printable.

Chapter 30

"Louise, why did the mayor come to see you today?" Sister Marianna's question preceded her into Sister Lou's office late Wednesday afternoon. She settled onto the guest chair directly in front of her.

Sister Lou made a show of lowering her pencil and setting aside the report she'd been revising. She'd expected this visit much earlier. Sister Marianna had either been busy or she was slipping.

Sister Lou gave her guest a gracious smile. "Good afternoon, Marianna. Did you have a pleasant lunch?"

"Yes, yes." Sister Marianna was as cranky as ever. "Now, tell me about the mayor's visit. It's not a good sign that a public official has come to see you out of the blue."

Sister Lou's smile held fast. "I'm looking forward to tomorrow's Thanksgiving festivities, aren't you?"

Sister Marianna gritted her teeth. "Certainly, I am. Now, about the mayor's visit, Louise . . . ?"

Her mission accomplished, Sister Lou grew serious.

"Your instincts are correct. Mayor Stanley wants us to drop our investigation into Autumn's murder."

"Well, she's right, of course. We've cleared the congregation of any and all suspicion. I can now focus on my responsibilities to the congregation and you should do the same. Surely, the deputies can handle the cleanup."

Sister Marianna wore a warm brown skirt suit. Today's handmade, one-of-a-kind scarf was a cheerful citrus orange pattern. In a way, it was a relief having the old Sister Marianna back. Sister Lou had missed the other woman's assertiveness, condescension, and officiousness while she'd been under the deputies' scrutiny. She hadn't missed their regular confrontations, though.

Sister Lou shifted to sit at an angle on her executive chair. She toyed with her pencil as she contemplated the watercolor rendering of St. Hermione of Ephesus that hung on the opposite wall of her office. "Aren't you curious as to why the mayor wants us to stop investigating Autumn's murder?"

"Not at all." Sister Marianna's lack of curiosity was amusing.

"I am." She faced the other woman with a smile. "Someone went to the mayor to ask her to tell us to stop asking questions about a murder. Don't you want to know who, when, or why?"

"Really, Louise." Sister Marianna's impatient sigh bordered on dramatic. "Is it so surprising that the deputies would complain about you to the mayor? You know things between you and the sheriff's office have been tense ever since you stepped on their toes with your amateur sleuthing into Dr. Jordan's death."

If my previous investigation was so amateurish, why did you ask for my help when the deputies made you a suspect? "The deputies weren't the ones who asked the mayor to intervene."

"Then who did?" Sister Marianna's smooth brow creased with confusion. Her recently discovered inquisitiveness was somewhat satisfying.

Sister Lou glanced at the half-full mug of chai tea beside her forearm. It had helped to settle her stomach after she'd rushed through lunch to get back to her projects. "The mayor wouldn't say, but she led me to believe it was a wealthy political supporter."

Sister Marianna threw up her arms. "That's even more reason for you to stop traipsing all over Briar Coast, interrogating people. You don't want to aggravate the mayor's supporters. They could be our supporters, too."

"Someone was murdered, Marianna. Someone we knew. I'd think that would be important, as well."

"Of course it's important, but the deputies can handle it. It's their job. It's time you focused on yours."

Sister Lou ignored the shot of temper through her veins. She sipped her cooling chai tea. "The deputies may not consider you a suspect any longer, but the congregation's still the subject of gossip and speculation. There are people who don't think it's a coincidence that we've had a connection to the town's last two murders."

Sister Marianna spread her hands. "We can't help what other people believe."

"Actually, we can, by finding the real killer. We owe that to Autumn and to ourselves."

Sister Marianna's sigh was long and deep. "Do you know what I think, Louise?"

"I'm sure you'll tell me, Marianna."

"I think you investigate these cases because doing so makes you feel special. I think you enjoy being the center of attention."

Do you also think I enjoy putting myself and the people I love in harm's way? "That's not the reason I agreed when Barb asked me to clear the congregation's reputation, nor is it the reason I said yes when you came to me for help."

Sister Marianna stiffened. "I appreciate your intervention, but why did you do it if not for the attention?"

"There are easier, safer ways of attracting attention, Marianna." Sister Lou's lips curved in a small smile. "I chose to look into Autumn's murder to protect the congregation and to find justice for someone I respected."

"The congregation is no longer in danger and you didn't even know Autumn Tassler that well."

Sister Lou considered Sister Marianna's words. They made sense. Why, then, were questions still plaguing her? "If the congregation's out of danger, why did someone try to frame you and why did someone ask the mayor to warn me off the case?"

* * *

"What is this *crap?*" Ted snarled from behind Shari as she sat in her cubicle, absorbed in her work first thing Thanksgiving morning.

She must have jumped a foot off her padded gray desk chair. She spun her chair to confront the deputy, her pugilistic personality coming to the forefront.

"What is your *problem?*" Shari stood.

She'd been so involved in her work, she hadn't noticed the ringing phones, the clacking keyboards, or the shouted conversations all around her. So much noise and it was only eight o'clock in the morning.

Her glare swung from Ted to Fran, who stood beside him, then back to Ted. Both deputies were in full uniform, thick brown winter jackets, tan shirts, black ties, spruce green gabardine pants. They each carried their brown felt campaign hats tucked under their right arms. Emergency services and daily newspaper personnel had something in common: neither took federal holidays off. It was Thanksgiving and they were all on the job.

"What is this?" Ted waved the Thursday edition of the *Telegraph* at her like a bat. She thought she could smell the smoke billowing from his ears.

Shari's eyes dropped to the newspaper. She didn't have to see her article to know it was at the center of today's storm. Its headline read: *Deputies Throw Resources at Stalled Murder Case.*

Apparently, the bill had come due. "You mean the update on the Tassler murder case."

"Why did you say that we're stalled?" Fran jabbed her index finger at the paper.

The deputies were vibrating with tension. Shari could feel it from where she stood almost a yard away. "Do you have any leads?"

Fran scowled at her. "We don't have to share our evidence with you."

Shari folded her arms over her chest. "I disagree and so would the community you serve. We have a right to know."

"Where did you get that quote?" Ted swung the newspaper again.

Shari knew the quote he was referring to. There was only one in her article: *We're throwing all of our resources at this case, working long hours, chasing down information. We know how important this case is and we're not going to rest until it's solved.*

She raised her eyebrows. "You gave me the quote during our telephone interview. It's good."

"I didn't give you permission to use it." Ted sounded outraged.

Shari shook her head. "You knew I was interviewing you. If you didn't want to be quoted, you should've said, 'No comment.'"

Ted's gray eyes widened with realization. "You deliberately goaded me into responding to you."

"Did I?" Guerilla interview tactics. Shari hoped she'd pulled off the innocent act. Her attention dropped to the paper in Ted's fist. "I think I made you look pretty good."

"*You* made *me* look good?" Ted's mouth moved but it took a moment for the words to come. "Who do you think you are, Dan Rather?"

"More like Gwen Ifill." She gave Ted a cheeky grin.

Fran practically sneered. "Not even close."

So the deputy was familiar with the late, great Peabody Award–winning journalist and television news anchor. That was surprising. Fran didn't strike Shari as a fan of public broadcasting. "Look, the public needs to know there's a murderer in Briar Coast. My job is to arm them with information to help them protect themselves. Who knows, they might even be able to provide you with useful information, like Sister Lou and I have."

Fran inclined her head toward the paper. "You also let them know that Sister Lou and her congregation are in the clear."

"They needed to know that, too." Shari shrugged.

"You think you're clever?" Ted's lips tightened with anger. "You're not going to get another word out of us about this case or any future ones. From now on, it's *No comment* all the way."

Shari watched the deputies march out of her cubicle. That probably hadn't gone as well as it could have. She stared at the *Telegraph* lying on her desk. Ted's quote was good. Diego had been pleased with it, which had made her feel redeemed in his eyes.

But what am I going to do the next time?

"You should apologize to the deputies." Chris's unjust ruling triggered all of Shari's defenses.

They were continuing the conversation they'd begun in Chris's car late Thursday afternoon. Insisting they should ride together, he'd picked up Shari from her apartment and driven them to the motherhouse for the congregation's Thanksgiving buffet dinner.

The festivities were held in the same room in which the congregation had hosted the celebration for the new and returning members of its leadership team. As soon as she'd entered the spacious hall, the mouthwatering aromas of the Thanksgiving meal had assailed her: savory meats, seasoned vegetables, warm breads, and sweet pastries.

"Why should I apologize? I haven't done anything wrong." Shari frowned as she moved through the main serving line in the recreation hall. Why was she bothering to add green bean casserole to her plate of turkey and stuffing if Chris was just going to ruin her appetite?

The room was bursting in vibrant fall colors—red, gold, orange, and brown—in the tablecloths, napkins, and recyclable paper plates and cups. The hall was filled with the friends and family members of the sisters who'd chosen to celebrate the holiday at the motherhouse rather than travel out of state or even across town for the weekend.

"I know how uncooperative the deputies are." Chris accepted the casserole serving spoon from Shari and added the side dish to his plate. "But Diego's right. Their comments add credibility to your story."

Urgh! Chris had a point even if she didn't want to hear it. Shari turned to scowl at him but was temporarily distracted by how handsome he looked in his burnt umber sweater, navy slacks, and canvas shoes. He'd had the day off. He had tomorrow, Friday, off, too. The perks of working for a college.

Shari, however, had worked a full day and hadn't had time to change before dinner. She was still in her garnet sweater, turquoise pants, and matching stilettos.

"I've tried to work with them." Did Chris hear the defensive note in her voice? "We told them about January Potts's false alibi. They haven't followed up with her. We gave them the list of employees for the background check and the vendor's name. They haven't told us what they've learned from it."

Shari added still-warm whole-grain dinner rolls to her plate and Chris's plate before leading him to the beverage table. Their options included fruit punch, lemonade, iced tea, and a choice of sodas, beers, and wines. Shari waited to see what Chris chose.

"The run-in you had with them this morning probably drained all of that goodwill." Chris selected a bottle of beer.

With an inner sigh of relief, Shari took a bottle as well. "And that's my fault? I should apologize? Even if I did, they probably wouldn't accept it." She moved on to the dessert table, looking for her sugar solace.

"It's a first step toward reconciling with them."

The pastries and baked goods spread across the small dessert table rendered Shari speechless: apple pie, pumpkin pie, chocolate cake, coconut cake, and various puddings, cookies, and brownies.

Shari selected two chocolate-frosted brownies with walnuts. The thick, rich treat seemed to know her name. These sisters knew how to lay out a buffet. She took one of the brownies and put the other on Chris's tray.

He gave her a puzzled smile. "Isn't pumpkin pie more appropriate?"

"Chocolate is appropriate in every situation." She noticed that he didn't change the selection. "Anyway, the deputies should be reaching out to *us*. We're the ones who've provided critical information toward solving the case. They need us more than we need them."

"And that, Padawan, is why you fail."

Shari smiled at his paraphrased reference to the *Star Wars* saga. "What do you mean?"

Chris maneuvered around furniture and people as he escorted Shari to a table for four where Sister Lou sat conversing with Sister Carmen. "That attitude isn't going to help with your investigative reporting."

Shari sighed. "How do you suggest I build these bridges with the deputies, then?"

"For starters, consider limiting your outer voice." Chris's tone was dry and he continued his weaving path across the room. "Your assertiveness is one of your most attractive traits, but it also puts people on the defensive."

"You find my assertiveness attractive?" Shari was caught off guard by his comment and forgot to be offended.

He looked at her over his shoulder. "I'm in the minority."

She scowled. "Right. So refrain from speaking the truth."

"That's not what I said. You need to choose when to compete and when to cooperate. Right now, the deputies aren't our enemies. Whoever killed Autumn is."

Shari caught Sister Lou's eye as they approached the older woman's table. "Then I should channel my inner Sister Lou?"

"That would be a good start." Chris took a seat beside Sister Carmen, leaving the chair beside Sister Lou for Shari.

Sister Carmen said the grace over the meal. Shari had become more comfortable with the prayer, bowing her head as Sister Carmen gave God thanks for another year of friendship, health, and prosperity.

Once the grace was complete, Sister Carmen smiled at Shari. "Good work on the article."

"Thank you." Shari returned Sister Carmen's smile. "The deputies didn't like it. They said they'll never speak to me again."

"Oh dear." Sister Carmen looked troubled. "What are you going to do?"

Shari flicked a look toward Chris. "I'm going to meet with the deputies tomorrow to start building that bridge Chris recommended."

"That's a good idea." Sister Lou's tone was pensive. "We have less than two weeks until the congregation's Advent retreat, but we haven't made any progress on finding Autumn's murderer. I think the investigation would go faster if we could persuade the deputies to partner with us."

Sister Carmen sipped her beer. "What makes you think that?"

Sister Lou looked at her friend. "They have access to evidence and materials that could help unlock information on Autumn's murder."

Shari turned to Chris abruptly. "You're a good friend. I wanted to say that before the moment passed."

The look of surprise on his strong, angular features made the admission worthwhile. "Thank you. What makes you say that?"

She should have known he wouldn't take the comment at face value. "You didn't tell me what I wanted to hear. You told me what I needed to hear. This isn't just about getting along with people. It's about my career."

"We'll go with you." Sister Lou patted her forearm where it lay on the table beside her walnut brownie. "There's strength in numbers."

Shari had hoped they'd say that. "The deputies will probably appreciate the protection."

Chapter 31

Shari couldn't concentrate. At work Friday morning, she sat at her desk blindly staring at the same page of the four-page town council meeting memorandum for at least ten minutes. Questions bounced around her mind like a tennis ball. How would the sheriff's deputies respond to her, Chris, and Sister Lou later that afternoon? Could she convince the deputies to work with her despite their angry exchange yesterday morning?

Her desk phone rang, pulling her out of her thoughts. Her caller identification revealed a *Buffalo Today* newspaper phone number. Curious. "*Telegraph.* Sharelle Henson."

"Sharelle, it's Becca Floyd, managing editor of *Buffalo Today.*" The familiar voice was jovial and energetic. "Did you have a good Thanksgiving?"

"Yes, I did. Did you?" Shari was still amazed at how wonderful it felt to have real friends with whom to celebrate the holidays.

"Your reporting keeps getting better and better."

Becca sounded excited. "Your Thanksgiving article on the Tassler murder case update was your best article yet."

"Thank you." She wouldn't be human if she wasn't flattered. She wouldn't be Sharelle Henson if she wasn't suspicious. Would the *Buffalo Today* managing editor call her every time she enjoyed one of her articles? Should she be offended if Becca didn't call?

"That quote you got from the deputy was great, really strong." Becca's compliment seemed over the top.

"He didn't think so." Shari's tone was dry. She checked the time on her computer monitor. It was just a few minutes after nine a.m.

"Really?" Becca's voice jumped a couple of octaves in surprise. "What's wrong with him?"

"I ask myself that every time I talk with him."

The managing editor laughed as though she'd never heard a funnier joke. Shari's curiosity grew. She glanced at her empty coffee cup and wished she'd gotten a refill before answering her telephone.

"You have to be pretty tough to work the police beat." Becca paused. Shari sensed she was measuring her next words. "Are you tough, Sharelle?"

Shari frowned at the telephone receiver in her hand, then placed it back against her ear. "That's an odd question. Why are you asking?"

"I like your style, Sharelle. You're forthright." Becca's chuckle was startled. "The reason I'm asking is that our newspaper has an opening for a tough investigative reporter. We're very interested in talking with you about this position."

Had she heard correctly? Shari sat back on her padded, gray desk chair. "You want to interview me for a job with your newspaper?"

"That's right." Becca sounded amused. "You have a great sense of the news and how to approach it to make your readers understand why the story matters to them. Also, your writing has raised the bar for the other reporters at the *Telegraph*."

It was Shari's turn to laugh in surprise. "I'm not responsible for the new writing style here. Our new editor in chief did that. He's improved the staff's morale and given everyone a sense of purpose."

Becca broke the short silence. "You sound as though you really admire him."

"We all do. We respect him and he respects us."

"That's impressive." Becca sounded distracted. Was she taking notes? "In any event, we'd like to bring you in for an interview for our investigative reporter opening."

Becca seemed confident that Shari would accept her invitation for an interview. Shari considered the *Telegraph*'s offices, modest and aged. The walls were dented and dingy. The carpeting was swollen with the stench of newsprint. *Buffalo Today*'s office was probably much more modern, comfortable, and fresh.

But the *Telegraph* was home.

Shari responded without regret. "Thank you for your invitation. I'm flattered, of course, but I'm happy with the *Telegraph*."

"You are?" Becca's surprise was almost funny. Shari sensed the other woman composing herself. "I don't mean to be indelicate, but I think a job with our organization pays better."

Shari burst into laughter. "I'm sure it does."

"Then why are you turning down an opportunity to interview with us?"

"It's about more than money. As I said, I like my boss. He believes in me and encourages me. I've never had that before. And I like this town. I haven't been here that long, but it's growing on me."

"You can still live in Briar Coast and commute to Buffalo. We're not that far away."

"Far enough, but that's not the point. I don't want to just live here. I want to be a part of the community. Working for the *Telegraph* is the best way for me to do that."

Becca's sigh signaled her deep disappointment. "I hope your paper and Briar Coast realize how lucky they are."

"I doubt that they do." Shari attempted a little levity to get through the awkward moment. Nothing like this had ever happened to her before. It was pretty cool, if a little uncomfortable.

"Promise me that if you ever do decide to leave the *Telegraph*, you'll call me first."

"I promise, but you'll probably be waiting for a very long time." Shari paused. "I'd like a promise from you, too."

"What's that?"

Shari cleared her throat. "I won't ask you not to offer my editor, Diego, a job, but could you let me know first? I'd be devastated if he left the *Telegraph*."

"Actually, we wanted to offer Diego a job. Just like you, he didn't even accept an interview."

Shari looked over her shoulder in the direction of Diego's office. "Isn't that interesting?"

Even though Fran and Ted had agreed to this meeting, Sister Lou sensed they weren't willing to cooperate with her, Chris, or especially Shari. Their silence was deafening. She and Chris were doing most of the talking as they sat in a small conference room in the Briar Coast County Sheriff's Office after lunch Friday afternoon.

"We'd like to assist you with the investigation into Autumn Tassler's murder." Sister Lou tried a different tack in an effort to get a response—any response— from the deputies.

There was a chill in the room. Sister Lou didn't know whether it was a lack of heat or the deputies' attitude. The conference room was hidden in the back of the bullpen. Still, the scents of fresh coffee and warm pastries had followed them past the doors. Sister Lou could use a cup of coffee right about now, although she'd prefer chai tea.

Ted grunted. "It's been almost three weeks. *Now* you're thinking about working with us? Why?"

"Why not?" Shari shrugged. "Don't you think you could use some help?"

"What's that mean?" Fran pounced on Shari's question.

Chris leaned forward, drawing the deputy's attention away from Shari and toward him. "It's in all of our interests to solve Ms. Tassler's murder as soon as possible. A group effort will help us achieve that goal."

"This case is complicated." Sister Lou voiced her perspective. "It's a lot more difficult than Maurice's murder because there are so many conflicting opinions about who Autumn was and how well her resort was performing."

Ted didn't appear mollified. "Is it too much for Sister Super Sleuth?"

"And what do you have to show?" Shari's cocoa eyes were scalding as she glared at the deputies on the other side of the small, rectangular, maple wood conference table.

"Shari—" Chris's low voice held a note of caution.

Sister Lou caught his eye and gave him an almost imperceptible shake of her head. At times you needed to be diplomatic. At other times, you had to come out swinging. Their diplomacy wasn't working. Maybe they should let Shari swing away. Chris yielded the floor.

Shari's voice was tight as she continued. "We brought you information on January Potts's false alibi and the fact that someone planted a fake scarf to implicate Sister Marianna. We also gave you the list of Autumn's employees and the name of the company doing the background check. It's time you gave us *something*."

Ted's face flushed. He stuttered with outrage. "*We* have to give *you* something?"

Shari held his wide-eyed stare. "Did I stutter?"

"The chef has a record." Fran's level response seemed to settle the room. Well, everyone except Ted.

Ted turned to her like a shot. "What're you doing?"

"She has a point." Fran settled back on her padded conference chair and gave Shari, Sister Lou, and Chris a hard look. "They've given us useful information. Besides, Shari's proven that there's nothing we can do to prevent her from writing about the case. We might as well cooperate."

Ted's expression darkened. "I'd rather not."

Fran gave him a sarcastic look. "At least if we work with them, we'll be able to control the message."

Shari interrupted. "I'm not going to let you control—"

"Shari." Sister Lou placed a gentle hand on top of Shari's where it rested on the table between them. No point in pushing their luck.

"Urban Rodgers was arrested for assault." Fran sat forward, folding her hands on the surface of the conference table. "Gary Hargreaves, the accountant, has been arrested twice for embezzlement."

Shari looked scornful. "We knew about Rodgers and Hargreaves."

Sister Lou glanced at the framed color photos displayed on the conference room's walls. They captured moments in time with the deputies volunteering in the community: Toys for Tots drives, staffing food and game stands during town fund-raising events, packaging meals for families in need. These were events in which the sisters also had participated, proof that on more than one occasion, the congregation and the sheriff's office had found common ground. It was their interest in and love for the community they both served.

"Then I guess you don't need us." Ted's response was thick with sarcasm.

Sister Lou drew her attention from the photographs on the walls. "Our point is that we need each other."

"What about Autumn's other employees?" Chris looked between Ted and Fran. "There were twenty-five names on the list."

"The vendor's got a few left to look at. The rep said he gave Autumn the report, but our guys never found the file." Ted grunted. "According to the rep, most of the employees came back clean. Rodgers and Hargreaves were the only ones that popped."

Fran nodded. "That's why they're on the top of our list. Rodgers has a temper, and we're examining Hargreaves's bank records for withdrawal and deposit patterns that match those of the resort's account."

Sister Lou detected the excitement in the other woman's voice. The deputy enjoyed tugging on clues and following leads. Was that the reason she got into law enforcement?

Sister Lou addressed Fran. "Neither of those gentlemen murdered Autumn."

Ted rolled his eyes. "Did God tell you that?"

Sister Lou wondered whether she should tell Ted that his hostility was losing its impact. "Autumn knew about their criminal records and hired them anyway. They're grateful to her."

Ted barked a fake laugh. "Thanks for your opinion,

Sister, but we'll keep them on *our* list of suspects. Who're *you* looking at?"

"We're interested in Isabella Fortney." Chris propped an elbow on the table. His dark gray suit jacket hung on the back of his maple wood and slate gray–cushioned chair. "Isabella wanted Roy to stop paying alimony."

"We haven't ruled out Rita Morris and January Potts, either." Shari's voice held more than a hint of reluctance. "Did you confront January about her false alibi?"

Fran shrugged. "She's sticking to her story."

Ted sprawled back on his chair, visibly more comfortable with the conversation. "If you're still looking at the Potts wife, you might as well keep the husband on the list, too."

"Keep him on your own list." Shari gestured toward Ted with her pen. "Sister Lou doesn't think he was having an affair with Autumn, so he doesn't have a motive."

Ted gave Sister Lou a dismissive look. "She's a marriage expert, too, now?"

Shari glared at the deputy. "Her opinion's good enough for us."

Chris nodded his agreement, causing the deputies to give Sister Lou a closer look.

Sister Lou struggled not to smile at the baffled expressions on their faces. "Who else is on your list of suspects?"

Ted exchanged a look with Fran before responding. "We're taking a longer look at Montgomery Crane, unless you disagree, of course."

Sister Lou ignored the deputy's sarcasm. "Why would Mr. Crane give Autumn business advice if he was willing to kill her for the resort?"

Apparently at a loss, Ted looked to Fran, but her attention was on Sister Lou. "What's on your mind, Sister?"

Sister Lou was impressed by the other woman's perception. "Between us, we have so many suspects: Urban Rodgers, Gary Hargreaves, Sherrod and January Potts, Rita Morris, Montgomery Crane, and Roy and Isabella Fortney."

Chris sighed. "And we have strong motives for all of them."

Ted dragged his thick hand over his bald pate. "Maybe more than one person was involved."

"Autumn was strangled. Isn't that method too personal for more than one killer?" Shari seemed to delight in contradicting Ted every chance she got.

Fran drummed her fingers on the table. "We don't have anything that makes one suspect more suspicious than the others."

Sister Lou balanced her elbows on the table and linked her fingers together. "Then we need to take a harder look at the victim. To which motive was Autumn most vulnerable?"

Chapter 32

"Which of your wealthy donors wants us to back off of the Tassler investigation?" Diego's deep voice carried outside of his office in the *Telegraph*'s building late Friday afternoon.

Shari froze mere steps from his door. Who was he talking to? Without shame she strained to listen and was rewarded with the mayor's voice.

"How many times are you going to rerun the same three paragraphs in your articles about the Autumn Tassler murder investigation?" Heather's rhetorical question made Shari bristle.

What the—?

"My reporters don't rehash the news, Heather." Diego sounded almost as irritated as Shari felt. "It's beneath you to insinuate that. Your time would be better spent asking what your donors don't want your constituents to know about the investigation."

Good question! Shari leaned closer to the wall to hear Heather's response.

"I'm not anyone's puppet, Diego, and it's beneath

you to insinuate that I am." As a response, Heather's words were infinitely disappointing. "Tell your Woodward and Bernstein wannabe to investigate something else."

Shari's eyes stretched wide. *Woodward and Bernstein wannabe?*

Angry strides swept her into the room before she realized her own intent. She confronted the mayor, who was wearing a very powerful sapphire blue midcalf-length skirt suit with matching pumps, tastefully accessorized with a simple pearl necklace and matching earrings. "Why don't you tell me yourself?"

Heather's perfectly plucked winged eyebrows knitted. "This is a private conversation."

"How private could it be?" Shari waved a hand toward the threshold. "The door's open."

"She has a point." Diego sounded amused. "Besides, we're talking about her work. She has a right to hear what we're saying."

Shari flashed her boss a grateful look before returning her challenging gaze to the mayor. She wasn't used to getting support from a supervisor. In the past, her editors had been almost indecent in their haste to throw her under the bus, even when the error was one they'd made during their overzealous editing of her articles.

"Sister Lou said you'd also asked her to stop investigating Autumn's murder." Shari gave the other woman a considering look. "How did the Fortneys word their request for your intervention?

Did they explain why they want Sister Lou to stop asking questions?"

"What makes you think it was the Fortneys?" Heather crossed her arms. Her expression gave nothing away.

Shari caught the slight shift in the mayor's reaction. Sherrod Potts? Really? She'd expected better of him. "Don't you want to know who killed one of your constituents and why? Because I certainly want to know who killed one of my neighbors."

A flash of irritation streaked through Heather's violet eyes. "That's what we pay our deputies to find out."

Diego shifted on his seat. "Mayor Stanley, while your interest in our work is noted and appreciated, you don't run this paper. I do, and I don't take editorial direction from your office. I run a newspaper, not your public relations firm."

Heather switched her deadly stare to Diego. "Actually, Mr. DeVarona, your publishers run this paper. Perhaps I should give *them* a call."

"Please, use my phone." Diego gave her a taunting smile.

Shari enjoyed her front-row seat to this epic battle of wills. She shifted her attention between Heather and Diego. Which titan would blink first?

Heather gave Shari a cursory look before returning her attention to Diego. "I know you've had your bloodhound interrogating my staff. What do you think she's going to find?"

"Bloodhound? What's with the insults? You're not the only one who's had a bad day, you know."

Heather's attention was locked on Diego. Shari doubted the other woman had even heard her. She also didn't think Diego was going to reply to the mayor's question. When he remained silent, Heather expelled an aggravated breath.

"This isn't El Paso." She spun on her expensive heels and marched through the door, leaving behind a whiff of her barely there perfume. Her footsteps faded down the hallway.

Shari took a moment to process the brief exchange before facing her boss. The air was heavy with residual tension. She could almost taste the secrets. "Her parting comment about El Paso was a reference to your shared past, wasn't it?"

Diego's sigh was the closest he'd ever come to revealing his feelings about what just transpired. Even to Shari's untrained ears, it revealed a lot. "It's complicated. In El Paso, Heather had trusted the wrong people. That's how her boss had been able to implicate her in their agency's scandal. Her poor judgment damaged her political career and hurt the town."

Shari hadn't found this level of detail during her Internet search into the mayor's background. "Then, it wasn't just your article that damaged her career. The mayor bears some responsibility, too."

"My article didn't help."

"That's guilt talking." Shari waved a dismissive hand. "Anyway, it's been thirteen years. Don't you think she's older and wiser now?"

"We'll see."

"Are you asking me to dig through her administration for her sake or for Briar Coast?"

"Both."

Shari headed toward the door. "Then, if we save the mayor from herself, we'll save the town. Easy enough."

"So, my past. How do people even start a conversation like this?" Shari's tone was an interesting mix of defiant and defensive.

Chris sat across the table from her in the Briar Coast Café late Saturday morning. She'd invited him for coffee and pastries—and presumably conversation. He was almost done with the former and still waiting for the latter.

Weekend traffic at the café was even heavier than it was during the week. The line at the counter extended out the door, but most people were taking their orders to go. This explained how he and Shari were able to get a table.

Chris returned his attention to his coffee companion. Her mass of raven curls was gathered in a ponytail as though she'd been in a rush to leave her apartment this morning. The style drew his attention to her features: high cheekbones, pointed chin, full lips, and especially her reckless cocoa eyes.

She looked so different today in her lemon yellow knit sweater and powder blue jeans. Her beat-up, bright orange sneakers were the real surprise. They took about three inches off her height. He hadn't realized how petite she was.

Chris was similarly dressed in a purple cable-knit sweater, faded dark blue jeans, and black hiker's boots. He sipped his dark roast coffee, black, no sugar. Its sharp bite helped distract him from his guilt. "I'm sorry that I've been pressuring you to tell me about your past. I never should've done that."

"Are you backing out now?" Her tone was playful, but her gaze unsure.

"No, I still want to know more about you—when you're ready to tell me."

Shari lowered her gaze to her half-full ceramic mug of hazelnut coffee. She'd added cream, two sugar substitutes, and cinnamon to the drink. "No, you were right. I want us to be friends, you, me, and Sister Lou. I just don't know how. This is new to me."

Chris studied the top of her head. In her twenty-six years, she'd never had one close friend? Was that by choice? In his mind's eye, he pictured Shari as a lonely little girl, feigning a tough exterior to hide her fear and uncertainty. His heart hurt for her. He wanted to go back in time to reassure her that everything was going to be okay. She wouldn't be alone forever.

On impulse, he reached across the table and cupped his hand over the thick, bright sweater covering her slender forearm. "Tell me something you're comfortable sharing."

"That's the thing. There aren't a lot of those." She took a deep breath, then met his eyes. "I didn't grow up in one of those Hallmark card households. I lived with foster families."

Families. Plural. "How many?"

She laughed without humor. "Six foster homes in fourteen years, since the age of three. The last one tried to charge me rent above and beyond the money the state paid her, so I left."

"You've been on your own since the age of seventeen?" She was right; her childhood had been very different from his. He'd grown up in privilege compared to her experiences. Thanks to his parents and his aunt, he'd known that he had more to be thankful for than a lot of children, but knowing it and living it were two very different things.

Shari shrugged off his surprise. "I was almost eighteen."

"What did you do?" He sensed her growing discomfort. "You don't have to answer if you don't want to."

"No, it's okay. I've never had anyone this interested before." She slipped him a smile. "I managed. Then one of my high school teachers got this brilliant idea that I could get a scholarship to a local college. She was right. After that, I applied for every scholarship and grant I could find. I moved into an apartment, got a job, and worked my way through school."

She was his new hero—along with his aunt and parents, of course. Shari was tough because she'd needed to be. Without it, she wouldn't have survived. But watching her interact with his aunt and the other sisters, Chris realized she'd been looking for a safe place to show her softer side. He hoped she realized she could stop searching. She'd found that place with them in Briar Coast.

He looked at his empty cup of coffee. He could use a refill. And a cookie. "What made you change your mind about sharing your past with me?" Was it something he'd done? Something Sister Lou had said? Or had it just been time?

Shari sipped her coffee pensively. "I had a feeling Diego and the mayor had known each other before Briar Coast. After I bugged him about it for the umpteenth time, he gave me half of the story. Then yesterday, the mayor confronted him about a couple of stories I'm working on."

"Autumn's murder?"

Shari nodded. "And behind-the-scenes research on her administration. Before she left, she told him this wasn't El Paso. That's when he gave me the rest of the story of his past with our mayor. It bothered me that he'd kept that from me even after I'd asked him. I realized that must be how you felt about my keeping my past from you."

"I'm glad you shared this with me, but I apologize again for pressuring you. It wasn't fair of me."

Shari was shaking her head even as Chris spoke. "No, you were right. And I'm glad that I told you about my childhood, too. It felt . . . good."

Chris smiled. Her admission touched his heart, but he was certain she had a lot more about her past to share. "I just have one more question for you."

"What's that?" There was more curiosity than wariness in her eyes this time. Great strides.

"Do you want a cookie?"

* * *

"We're going to have to get some shorter races in to help us prepare for the marathon in the spring." Sister Carmen panted the observation as she jogged beside Sister Lou early Sunday morning.

The mission-style black lampposts combined with Sister Carmen's fuchsia Windbreaker and electric green jogging pants to hold back the darkness during their five-mile run. Only their aerobic exercise and layered clothes could keep the late-November cold at bay.

"Sounds good." Sister Lou was only half listening.

"Let's hear it." Sister Carmen exhaled.

"What?"

"Whatever's bothering you."

In the shadows, Sister Lou could sense her jogging companion rolling her eyes.

"How do you always know when something's on my mind?" Sister Lou concentrated on her breathing, slow and steady. Fall was aging in the air. Winter was getting closer. She could smell the cold.

"We've been jogging together six days a week for the past seven years."

Sister Lou caught the note of exasperation in her friend's voice. Her lips curved in chagrin. "Am I speeding up again?"

"Yep."

"Sorry." She made an effort to slow her pace as they jogged past the residence halls. With the students on Thanksgiving break until tonight, most of the dorm-room windows were dark. Fall-semester classes would resume bright and early tomorrow. Perhaps the calico would return as well.

"Don't apologize. Just tell me. What's on your mind?" Sister Carmen didn't sound as breathless this time.

Without the students or the birdsong, the campus was eerily silent and lonely this morning. Their footfalls seemed to echo as they approached the campus oval. They traced the well-manicured lawns that circled the redbrick academic buildings and large mature trees.

Sister Lou wiped the sweat from her upper lip with the back of her right hand and strained to keep a steady pace even as her anxiety rose. "We have only one week before our Advent retreat. Everything's in place for the event, except Autumn's murder is still unsolved."

Sister Carmen wiped her hand over her forehead beneath her warm gold knit cap. "What do you have so far? You know the means."

"The killer strangled Autumn with his hands, but he must have used gloves because he didn't leave prints." Sister Lou brought an image of the crime scene to mind. Autumn was slumped on her chair. Her tongue protruded between her parted lips. Her sightless periwinkle blue eyes were stretched wide.

Sister Carmen raised her hands. Her gloves were a perfect match to her hat. "Not surprising. He probably kept his gloves on."

Sister Lou glanced at her own black winter gloves. "Good point."

"Of course." Sister Carmen frowned as though offended. "And he tried to frame Marianna. That's significant."

"True. It means he knew about the tension between Autumn and Marianna, and maybe even the tension between the deputies and the congregation."

Sister Carmen nodded. "Now, opportunity?"

"Autumn always started work early. A lot of people knew that, and the resort's main office is practically empty at that time of day."

"No chance of witnesses."

"Right." Sister Lou inclined her head.

"Motive?"

"Too many. We could make the motive for money apply to her partner, her ex-husband, his wife, or we could make jealousy the motive for her cousin. There may be others that we don't know about."

"From what you know about the victim, what motive seems most logical?"

Sister Lou considered her longtime friend. She pulled her black knit cap down lower over her ears. "Have you been watching Investigation Discovery TV again?"

"Maybe you should watch it. It could give you some ideas." Sister Carmen kept pace with Sister Lou as they completed their final lap around the oval, then started toward the path to the center of town.

"You've made another good point."

"Of course I did." Sister Carmen gave her a suspicious look. "What d'you mean?"

The sun had started to rise and work its way through the half-naked tree branches.

"I've been thinking of this the wrong way." Sister Lou led them back toward the motherhouse. "I've been asking why someone would kill Autumn."

Sister Carmen's eyebrows knitted as she sought Sister Lou's gaze. "What should you be asking?"

Sister Lou arched an eyebrow as she returned her friend's look. "Why would she let them?"

Chapter 33

"I appreciate your meeting with me on such short notice." Sister Lou looked around her crowded sitting area Sunday afternoon. After the ten a.m. Mass, she'd invited the group together to discuss the revelation she'd had during her morning run.

Deputy Fran Cole and Deputy Ted Tate were sharing her love seat, which was appropriate, considering the looks Ted was giving Fran in her civilian clothes. The slender deputy wore a fitted teal sweater and tight black jeans. Her unruly ash blond hair was loose around her shoulders. Ted wore a royal blue University of Buffalo sweatshirt and jeans made baggy by his weight loss.

Sister Lou had brought in a straight-back pale blue chair from her bedroom for Sister Marianna. Her retreat project partner's casual dress consisted of black slacks and a white sweater.

That left the overstuffed sofa for Shari and Chris. The pair, both wearing jeans and bulky sweaters, seemed cozy together. They must have resolved their temporary disagreement.

"What's brought this about, Sister?" Ted dragged his attention from his law enforcement partner. He seemed to have forgotten the mug of chai tea he held between his palms.

"I think I've narrowed down the suspects for Autumn's murder." Sister Lou's gaze once again swept the room.

"How?" Chris sat forward on the sofa. The movement brought him even closer to Shari.

Sister Lou looked toward Fran and Ted. "When we discovered Autumn after her attack, her office was tidy."

"That's true." Fran gave Sister Lou a considering look. "It didn't look as though there'd been a struggle."

"Exactly." Sister Lou switched her attention to Chris, Shari, and Sister Marianna. "It's as though whoever murdered Autumn walked right up to her; as though Autumn wasn't expecting an attack."

"Or the perp surprised her." Ted shook his head, baffled. "How does that help?"

Sister Lou considered Ted's comment. "I don't think the killer surprised her. I observed Autumn's interaction with several of our suspects. When January Potts, her cousin, came to her office, she stood. It was as though she was preparing for their confrontation. However, she never stood when one of her employees entered her office. And she wasn't as defensive when she spoke with Rita Morris or Montgomery Crane."

"That's true." Sister Marianna sat straight on the

chair. Her feet were neatly crossed at her ankles. "She was antagonistic toward them, but she was very relaxed with her staff."

"So what are you saying?" Ted shrugged. "You think someone on her payroll killed her? That still leaves us with twenty-five names. How does that narrow it down?"

"But not all of them would have thought to frame Sister Marianna for their crime." She gestured toward the person in question, seated directly across the sitting area from her.

"You're right." Shari looked at Sister Marianna. "The killer either knew the deputies had been suspicious of the congregation before, or they knew that Autumn and Sister Marianna had been arguing."

Chris swallowed some of his tea. "That means you've narrowed it down to someone Autumn felt comfortable with and who knew about the tension between Sister Marianna and Autumn."

Sister Lou realized her nephew deliberately repeated Ted's use of the phrase "narrowed it down." As usual, Chris was defensive on her behalf, this time with the deputy. She smothered a smile.

"Who's on your list, Sister?" Fran lowered her tea.

"I think we should focus on her partner, Rita Morris, and her administrative assistant, Kelsey Bennett."

Shari's tone was concerned. "Kelsey seems very devoted to Autumn. Do you really think she could've done this?"

"Kelsey couldn't hurt a fly." Sister Marianna

chuckled. "I also don't think she's smart enough to frame me."

Ted gave Sister Marianna a dubious look. "It doesn't take a Ph.D. to plant a scarf at a crime scene."

Chris exchanged a look with Sister Lou. In the onyx eyes so like her own, she read his shared concern that they were running out of time before the congregation's retreat. Neither voiced that fact, though, because justice would take precedence. If the congregation had to attend the retreat with the cloud of suspicion hanging over them, however unwarranted, then so be it.

"We're only looking at two people." Chris pitched his voice above the others to claim their attention. "What can we do to see whether one of them is our killer?"

Sister Lou held up her left hand. "I have an idea about that."

Ted snorted. "Of course you do."

Sister Lou ignored him and looked to Fran. "The vendor contracted to do the employee background checks for Autumn said he'd given the file to her at the end of his assignment, but you hadn't found it during any of your searches."

"That's right." Fran nodded.

"I think the killer has it." Sister Lou felt a rush of satisfaction. Things were coming together.

"That makes sense." Sister Marianna gave a nod of approval.

"I agree." Chris's tone expressed his excitement.

Sister Lou felt it, too. "We need to plant the idea

with our suspects that the vendor provided us with a duplicate file. If I'm right and the file is the reason Autumn was killed, the killer will try to take it from us."

Fran exchanged a look with Ted before responding to Sister Lou. "That's a very good idea. We'll set that up."

"Great." This had gone even more smoothly than she'd hoped. She shared a smile with the deputies. "What can we do to help?"

"You?" Ted's bushy brown eyebrows met above the bridge of his blunt nose. He looked from Sister Lou, to Shari, to Chris, then to Sister Marianna before settling his dismissive gaze on Sister Lou. "Nothin'."

Shari's lips parted in surprise. "What d'you mean, nothing? Sister Lou just narrowed the list of suspects for you from thirty to two, and came up with a plan to catch the killer. What've *you* done?"

"Thanks for your input, but we'll take it from here." Fran leaned forward to place her empty porcelain mug on the tea service. The tightness around her lips denoted her strained temper. Sister Lou felt the same way.

She inhaled a calming breath, drawing in the fragrance of the cinnamon-and-apple potpourri that sat in a bowl on the corner table in the little sitting area. "We've been involved up to this point. I'm sure you can understand that we'd want to be included when the killer is finally caught."

"Come now, Louise." Sister Marianna's tone was ridiculing. "This isn't your purview."

Sister Lou leveled a look at her associate. The

muscles in the back of her neck clenched. "Then why did you ask for my help?"

Sister Marianna seemed taken aback. An embarrassed flush filled her cheeks. "I—I only meant that your part is done."

"It doesn't feel like it." Shari's words were sharp. "It seems like we're missing something. Like a resolution."

Sister Lou sought her nephew's reaction. He'd remained almost conspicuously quiet throughout the exchange, but she read the concern in his eyes. He didn't want her involved in capturing the killer, but he wasn't going to gang up against her as Sister Marianna and the deputies were doing. He silently let her know his thoughts, then he lowered his gaze.

Sister Lou's frustration spiked. She didn't want to worry her nephew, but neither did she want to walk away from this case without seeing it through to its end.

"Look," Ted said, "we'll talk to Morris and Bennett now. Hopefully, get this set up for tonight. If one of 'em takes the bait, we'll call you once we've got one of them in custody."

Not good enough. "That hardly seems fair, Deputy Tate. We want to be there when the person is actually taken in. A phone call's not the same thing."

"I'm afraid that's all you're getting, Sister." Fran rose from the love seat.

Ted joined her. "Yeah, let us do our job. You wouldn't want us saying Mass for you, would you?"

"Sisters don't celebrate the Mass, Deputy, only priests do that," Sister Lou corrected him.

"Whatever. We'll call you. Hopefully, this will all be over tonight." He turned to escort Fran from the room.

Sister Lou stood and watched Sister Marianna leave with the deputies.

"This could be dangerous." Chris straightened from the sofa and helped Shari to her feet. "I don't want either of you getting hurt."

Sister Lou nodded. "I understand."

"Me, too." Shari picked up the tea service.

Curious, Sister Lou followed the reporter into her kitchenette. Chris stayed behind. Shari rested the service on the kitchen counter, then turned. Sister Lou recognized the defiance in the younger woman's expression. She was certain she had a similar look in her eyes.

Shari cocked a winged eyebrow. "Out back?"

"Six o'clock?"

"I'll drive."

Sister Lou sighed. "Fine."

Chapter 34

The gray outdoor lampposts were spaced equidistant along the edge of the sidewalk and across the Briar Coast County Sheriff's Office's front parking lot. They provided ample light for Sister Lou and Shari's stakeout. From the passenger seat of Shari's sage green, four-door Honda Civic, Sister Lou had an unobstructed view of the front of the sheriff's office. They'd parked directly across the one-lane road from the building.

"You used these binoculars when you attended the football games at your last college?" Shari returned Sister Lou's binoculars to her. "You must have really enjoyed the games."

"I did." Sister Lou held up the binoculars and adjusted them to get a better look at the building's entrance. "They always filled the bleachers. Everyone had a great time."

"We've been here for almost an hour." Shari shifted behind the wheel. "Do you think the deputies set the trap?"

"I'm confident they did." Sister Lou lowered the binoculars. "They want this to be over at least as much as we do."

"Especially since they're already at least three hours into overtime."

Sister Lou glanced at her companion, handing the binoculars back to her. "You've been working long days on this investigation as well."

"We all have."

"True." Sister Lou kept her eyes on the view across the street.

"I've got to get a pair of these." Shari returned the binoculars to Sister Lou.

Christmas lights ringed the lampposts on the streets and in the parking lot. Sister Lou loved Christmas lights. Wide limestone steps led from the asphalt lot to the sheriff's office's walnut wood double doors. Bare trees and evergreen bushes bordered the parking lot. Christmas wreaths hung on the doors and front-facing windows. The well-maintained exterior matched the modern, clean, and well-kept interior of the sheriff's office. It was an indication of a healthy investment in the community's safety.

They'd arrived during the office's second shift, which explained the lack of activity around the building. Cruisers were already on patrol and other deputies had settled in for duty.

Or so it seemed.

A worse-for-wear brown sedan lumbered into the sheriff's office's parking lot. It pulled into a space toward the center of the lot. A young woman emerged from the driver's-side door. She wore a sheriff's deputy uniform. All of her hair appeared to be tucked under her campaign hat, which was pulled low over her head.

A late arrival to the second shift?

Sister Lou lifted her binoculars to her eyes and zoomed in on the recent arrival. There was something about the cadence of her walk that stirred a memory in the forefront of Sister Lou's mind. The deputy had a brisk gait and bounced on her toes. In her mind's eye, Sister Lou pictured pale blond corkscrew curls, large, dark blue eyes, and round features.

"Kelsey Bennett." Sister Lou thrust the binoculars to Shari without looking at the young reporter.

"What?" Shari spoke on a disbelieving breath. She took the binoculars from Sister Lou and pressed them to her face. "How can you tell with her hat pulled over her face?"

"Look at the way she walks. Kelsey bounces on her toes like that." Sister Lou sensed their combined excitement charging the air in the cozy Civic. She watched the figure bounce up the front stairs to the office's entrance.

"Here we go." Shari spoke in a singsong voice as she passed the binoculars back to Sister Lou.

"Let's wait in the parking lot." Sister Lou let herself out of the car.

"It's cold out there." Shari joined her despite her protests.

"Oh, come on." Sister Lou led the way across the street. "I'm the one from sunny Southern California.

You're from the frozen tundra of Chicago. Who should be more susceptible to the cold?"

The parking lot was smaller than it seemed from across the street. Sister Lou stopped beside Kelsey's battle-scarred brown sedan. Her senses were on high alert as the minutes crawled by. No one reemerged from the building and neither of their cellular phones rang. What was happening inside?

Sister Lou checked her wristwatch again. "Shouldn't they have called us by now?"

"I thought I was the only one losing my—" Shari cut herself off as Kelsey reappeared in the building's entrance. "You've got to be kidding. How does a murder suspect walk into a sheriff's office, then walk back out again without handcuffs?"

Sister Lou wanted the answer to that riddle as well. She watched in disbelief as Autumn's killer trotted down the front steps. *She is empty-handed. What happened inside?*

Kelsey bounced down the steps and started toward her car. She was perhaps twelve feet away from Sister Lou when she glanced up—and froze. Sister Lou sensed the second Kelsey recognized them.

"We've been made." Shari's whisper seemed to come from Sister Lou's mind.

Kelsey spun from them and took off running in the opposite direction. In reflex, Sister Lou gave chase.

"What are you doing?" Shari's question flew after her.

I don't know.

She was literally chasing down a murder suspect,

one almost half her age. What made her think she could do this? But since she'd engaged in this folly, she couldn't see her way clear to stopping. Her muscles settled into her jogging stance: leaning forward from her waist, bending her arms, and stepping heel to toe. She lengthened her strides as Kelsey weaved her way across the grounds of the sheriff's office. If she made it to the sidewalk, Sister Lou would lose her. Her arms pumped. Her muscles strained. Her breathing came faster.

She'd been jogging since she was a teenager, half a century ago. But she needed more than physical ability to stop Kelsey. She needed her wits.

Sister Lou tightened her grip on her oversized navy purse. She drew a deep breath—and aimed for the back of Kelsey's knees. Bull's-eye! Her target tumbled like a house of cards.

Sister Lou stood over the fallen suspect. *Now what?*

"Sister, you've got some brass ones." The voice behind her was surprisingly familiar.

Fran gasped. "Ted!" She knelt to cuff Kelsey. "Shari called."

"Sister Lou!" Shari was panting after running the length of the parking lot. She was carrying her stilettos.

Sister Lou caught her breath. She was shaking more from reaction than exertion. "I'm all right."

Shari threw her arms around her in a don't-ever-scare-me-like-that-again embrace. "You're amazing. I'm going to start jogging with you and Sister Carm."

Sister Lou hugged her back. "Carm and I are training for the marathon."

"Oh. Never mind, then." Shari stepped back. "Does Chris jog?"

The calico was waiting for her as Sister Lou hurried out of the motherhouse on her way to meet Chris Monday morning. Her nephew was driving them to the sheriff's office to meet with Fran and Ted. Sister Lou wasn't looking forward to yet another confrontation with the defensive deputies. She'd rather spend the morning with the cat. The calico was lounging again, this time stretching out on the single concrete step at the end of the red brick walkway that led to the motherhouse's front door. She scanned her surroundings like a queen surveying her realm.

Sister Lou paused on the walkway beneath the step and hunkered beside the cat. She extended her right hand toward the calico, seeking permission to pet her. The cat sniffed her fingertips before her pale green eyes met Sister Lou's. She inclined her head in royal approval. Sister Lou lifted her chin in acknowledgement.

"How ya doin', cat?" Her voice was soft and playful. Sister Lou stroked her index and middle fingers in a long, slow line back from the bridge of the calico's little cat nose. The cat closed her eyes as though in bliss. Her fur was so smooth and soft. "I should give you a name," Sister Lou whispered.

The calico's eyes popped open as though in surprise at the idea that Sister Lou would presume to name her.

Sister Lou's lips twitched in amusement. "I apologize. What was I thinking to assume I could take such liberties?" She continued her slow, measured strokes from the calico's brow to the back of her head. The cat's eyes slid closed again as she relaxed. Sister Lou could feel herself relaxing, too. Tension she hadn't realized she was carrying in her back and shoulders eased away. "It's so cold out here. I wish I could invite you to live with me. Then I could take you in from the cold, but pets aren't allowed in the motherhouse. Would you like me to find someone who could take you in?"

The cat's pretty green eyes popped open again. This time, if possible, they stretched wider and expressed even greater shock than before. The calico cat abruptly hopped off the step, startling Sister Lou. Gaining her balance on the brick walkway, she met Sister Lou's gaze over her shoulder. After one final look of disdain, she marched away from the motherhouse. Sister Lou tracked the cat's progress as she headed toward a tree-lined path that was a shortcut to the college's campus.

Message received, cat.

The calico cat valued her freedom far too much to ever become someone's pet. Don't we all?

"We made the decision to keep you out of this sting operation for a reason." Fran moved her scowl from Shari to Chris, then finally settled on Sister Lou. "The situation wasn't safe. This time you were lucky. Hopefully, there won't be a next time."

"I still can't believe you ran down a perp." Ted regarded Sister Lou with renewed respect. His expression was making her uncomfortable. She wanted the grumpy deputy back.

"Neither can I." Chris's tone was tense. Sister Lou sent him another apologetic look.

It was early Monday morning. Sister Lou, Shari, Chris, Fran, and Ted were in the familiar small meeting room in the back of the sheriff's office. The atmosphere in the comfortable room was markedly different this time. The tension of grudging cooperation was gone. In its place was relief, satisfaction, and pride in a job well done.

"How did you know it was Kelsey in the fake deputy's uniform?" Ted asked.

Shari arched an eyebrow. "The costume couldn't have been that fake. It fooled your coworkers."

Fran and Ted had alerted their office to the sting. The entire office had been on the lookout for suspicious strangers. Unfortunately, it hadn't occurred to anyone that Kelsey would try to sneak into the sheriff's office dressed as a deputy. Something must have alerted her, though, because she never made it to the bullpen. Instead, she left the building almost immediately.

Ted scowled at the reporter. "We've already explained that most people hadn't been paying attention to her because they were busy working."

Sister Lou sipped the coffee the deputies had offered them, which highlighted another difference between the two meetings. The deputies hadn't offered refreshments last time. "Has she said anything that would give us insight into why she killed Autumn?"

Fran swallowed a mouthful of coffee. "Not yet, but the investigative services company was able to give us more background on her. Kelsey Bennett isn't her real name. That identity only showed up about two years ago. Her actual name is Angelica Webb."

"Yeah." Ted picked up the tale. "Angelica was serving a twenty-five-year sentence for murder when she broke out of prison."

Shari interrupted the deputy. "She must have realized her cover would be blown when the investigative services company did the employee background checks for Autumn."

"That's right." Sister Lou was amazed. "It's starting to make sense now. Urban and Gary weren't keeping secrets. They'd told Autumn about their criminal backgrounds when they first applied for their jobs with her. She stepped out on faith and hired them anyway."

Chris set his coffee mug on the table. "Kelsey—I mean Angelica—was the only one with something to lose because of the background check. Has she confessed to the murder?"

"She asked for a lawyer. I think she's going to take her chances with a trial." Fran turned to Shari. "I enjoyed your article in this morning's *Telegraph*, wrapping up the investigation."

"Yeah, you did a good job," Ted's praise came grudgingly.

Shari grinned at the deputies. "Thanks. This one was especially gratifying to close."

"I agree." Fran switched her attention to Sister Lou and offered a smile of friendship. "Now you should be able to relax and enjoy your retreat this weekend."

Sister Lou returned her smile. "Absolutely. I'm looking forward to it. And I'm glad we were able to work together on this case."

Fran nodded in agreement. "Thanks for your help. I admit your input was invaluable."

"Yeah." Ted sighed. "And let's hope it never happens again."

Sister Lou exchanged a look with Chris and Shari. She remembered a similar promise they'd made to each other after they'd identified Maurice's killer. "We've tried that before."

Chapter 35

Sister Valerie Shaw sat back on the chair behind her large desk late Monday morning. She looked like the proverbial cat who'd downed the entire bowl of cream. "I'm very pleased to report that all of the donors who'd left us after hearing rumors of the congregation's involvement in poor Autumn Tassler's murder have returned to the flock. That's thanks in large part to today's *Telegraph* article that credited the congregation for helping to catch Ms. Tassler's killer. I also want to thank you, Chris, for all of your exceptional work in reaching out to our donors."

Chris unsuccessfully fought the flush of embarrassment rising up his neck. He was very conscious of Lorna Alexander, vice president for finance, staring at him as she sat on the matching guest chair beside him. "Thank you, Sister Valerie. I'll share your praise with my team."

"Please do." Her brown eyes glittered with excitement behind her tortoiseshell glasses. "Because of you and your team, we have the foundation to pursue our fund-raising campaign to freeze the college's tuition for four years and increase the number and value of our scholarships. I couldn't be happier."

Because she was happy, so was he, although the estimated dollar amount needed to fulfill their ambitious goal was still somewhat daunting.

"Yes, Chris, very impressive work." Lorna was short on sincerity. "All of that while helping to solve a murder. Amazing. How were you able to find the killer?"

Lorna's silver nail polish nearly matched her gray pantsuit. Chris looked into her pitch-black eyes. Was that envy or jealousy lurking in their depths? "As the article explained, it was a group effort with my aunt, Shari Henson, and me working with Deputies Cole and Tate."

Lorna arched a perfectly shaped eyebrow. "But that's not the real story, is it? Rumors are that your aunt is a super detective."

Sister Valerie's interruption saved Chris from having to respond. "Sister Barbara and I already spoke with Sister Lou. But we'd like to thank both of you, and Shari Henson, for all you did to prove the congregation's innocence."

Chris took a deep breath, catching the scent of the hazelnut coffee that was constantly brewing in Sister Valerie's office. "We were glad to help."

Lorna folded her arms and crossed her legs. "I'm surprised that you were able to get those donors back and pull in new ones. Obviously, I was wrong."

Chris nodded his appreciation of her admission. "Hopefully, they'll support our campaign."

Sister Valerie touched the Hermionean cross affixed to the right lapel of her chocolate blazer. "Ah, but Chris had faith in the success of this project, Lorna."

Lorna shrugged. "I'm sorry, Sister, but I've never been one for blind faith."

A gentle smile curved Sister Valerie's lips. She exchanged a look with Chris before addressing her vice president for finance. "Chris's faith isn't blind. That's why he and his team spent so many hours on rebuilding existing donor relationships and building new ones."

His faith was definitely not blind. Experience had taught him that when sisters like Sister Valerie and his aunt put their minds to a project—whether it was raising money to freeze college tuition or solving murders—that project will get done. He could either get on board or get out of the way. Getting on board was much more interesting.

"So you solved the murder." Mayor Heather Stanley stood in the doorway of Shari's cubicle at the *Telegraph*'s office late Monday morning. She displayed the latest edition of the newspaper.

"It was a team effort." Shari tried to read the mayor's expression as she sipped her coffee from her white porcelain mug. Perhaps it was petty of her to taunt the mayor by turning the text screened to the mug toward her: CAN I QUOTE YOU? But it also was kind of funny. A private joke between her and her coffee.

Heather entered Shari's spacious cubicle and settled uninvited onto the faded gray guest chair. "Autumn Tassler's killer turned out to be an escaped murderer. What the hell? That must've added to your adrenaline rush."

Where was the mayor going with this impromptu chat? The muscles in Shari's back stiffened as her defenses went up. "The deputies have gotten a lot of well-deserved kudos from the sheriff for their role in her recapture. He gave them written commendations for their files."

"I know. I left congratulatory messages for both of them this morning. I'll try to reach them in person again later." Heather's power outfit of the day was a belted amethyst A-line dress. The color complemented her violet eyes. The hem ended just beneath her knees. "Based on the deputies' quotes in your article, you seem to be getting along now."

Shari's gaze dipped to the newspaper in Heather's possession before lifting again to the mayor's eyes. "It helped that Sister Lou gave them equal credit in solving the case when we all know she's the one who caught the killer. Literally."

"You think very highly of Sister Lou."

"I do, and we both know I'm not easily impressed." Shari saw the flicker in the mayor's eyes. She was probably wondering if Shari was referring to her. Let her wonder. Shari continued to sip her coffee.

"I'm sure she appreciates your sentiment." Heather

leaned back on the guest chair as if they were two friends having a casual conversation.

Shari wasn't falling for it. "You're not here to fill out a Sister Lou Fan Club membership application. What's on your mind, Mayor?"

"You're damn direct. I like that about you." A slight smile curved Heather's lips and brightened her eyes. "Do you think it was a good idea to include the detail that Autumn Tassler was killed by an escaped murderer?"

"That Angelica Webb had killed before and was an escaped and dangerous criminal are pretty important details." Shari considered the mayor. "Why wouldn't I include them in the story?"

"It's damn inflammatory. That kind of information only scares the hell out of people. All your readers need to know is that the deputies now have the killer in custody."

"Readers deserve to know a lot more than that." Shari set her mug on her desk behind her. "How does it help a community to withhold information from them?"

"It prevents mass hysteria. It's my job to make sure people in the community feel safe."

Shari tilted her head to the side and considered the mayor. "No, your job is to make sure the residents *are* safe, and my job is to give them the information they need to decide whether you're doing your job."

Heather's violet gaze frosted over. "And who the hell gets to decide whether you're doing your job?"

"The fact that you're complaining about me tells

me that I am." Shari felt the waves of frustration pouring off the mayor. They kept her warm.

Heather stood to leave. "There's a fine line between serving the public good and irresponsibly scaring people. One day, you're going to cross that line."

"Today's not that day." Shari held the public official's cold gaze until the mayor turned and marched out of her cubicle.

Shari was well aware of her obligations to the public trust. And she knew how fine the line was between information and sensationalism. But she didn't need the latter to pitch her stories to Diego. Fortunately for her—and the mayor—Diego didn't run stories just for sensationalism, either. Her stories ran on their value to their readership.

She rose from her desk and set off for her editor's office. She might as well let him know about her latest run-in with the mayor. She'd hate for him to get a call from town hall before giving him her side of the story.

Shari stopped in front of Diego's open office door and gave a cursory knock. "The mayor had concerns about the Tassler murder investigation article."

Diego sat back on his chair and gestured toward one of the empty seats in front of his desk. "Let me guess. She disapproved of our including information that Angelica Webb was an escaped murderer."

His crisp cream shirt was set off by a pale pink tie. His bronze suit jacket hung on the coatrack in the corner of his office. It was late morning. The editor's in-box was empty but his out-box was full. The faint, enticing aroma of coffee rose from the pot standing on his file cabinet. Like Chris, Diego drank the brew without cream or sugar. Why bother?

Shari settled onto the chair in front of him. "How'd you guess?" She appreciated Diego's referring to the decision as "our." It showed her editor had her back.

"Heather's predictable. How did you handle it?"

"I told her the public had a right to know." Shari withstood Diego's probing stare.

"Why do I have the feeling that you said more than that?"

Shari blinked. "I don't know. Why do you?"

Diego shook his head with a chuckle. "Because, Shari, you can be predictable, too."

"I think I'm offended."

"That's why you and Heather keep butting heads. You're a lot alike."

"Now I know I'm offended." Shari propped her elbows on the arms of the guest chair and linked her fingers together over her lap. "Why didn't you interview for the job at *Buffalo Today*?"

Diego stiffened. "How do you know about that?"

Shari smiled. "They asked me to interview, too. Why didn't you go?"

"I'm happy where I am. And you?"

"I'm starting to like Briar Coast." That was an understatement. She was falling in love with the town—and its residents. Who would have thought Shari Henson would be cut out for small-town living? Who would have thought she'd have found a place she could call home?

Diego nodded as though they were kindred spirits. "It's not about the money, is it? It's about the stories we can cover here and the work we have left to do."

"And in your case, there's also Mayor Stanley."

Diego smiled as he turned back to his computer. "We have work to do."

Shari took the hint and left—for the moment.

Chapter 36

"Tell me again how my aunt chased down a convicted killer." Chris hadn't had an appetite since last night when he learned the risks his aunt had taken.

"She was *amazing*." Shari waved the fork she was using to eat her blackened chicken salad. Her appetite was unaffected. "She raced after her with long, quick strides."

"But she was running after a serial killer." His mind rebelled at the image of his middle-aged aunt chasing someone who had killed two people, one with her bare hands.

Shari swallowed a mouthful of lettuce. "We didn't know she was a convicted murderer at the time."

"But you knew she'd killed at least one person." His heart pounded in his throat. His pulse thundered in his ears. He struggled to breathe. "You also knew you weren't supposed to be anywhere near the sheriff's office last night."

Shari considered Chris as she chewed her salad. "You're really upset about this."

"Of course I am." He struggled to keep his voice down. Images sped across his mind, preventing him from thinking clearly. "How would you feel if someone you loved raced unarmed after a convicted murderer?"

Shari lowered her fork and met Chris's eyes with solemnity. "Someone I love did race unarmed after Angelica Webb. She's your aunt and you've known her all of your life, but she's my friend. The best friend I've ever had."

Chris swallowed back the emotion blocking his throat. "Then why did you let her do something so reckless?"

Shari braced her arms on the table and leaned closer to her companion. "Your aunt earned a doctorate in philosophy, was a college professor, was elected to her congregation's leadership team—twice."

"I know all of that." Why was Shari giving him his aunt's résumé?

"Does she seem reckless, thoughtless, or dumb?"

"Of course not."

"Then, why are you upset?" Shari leaned back onto her chair. "Yes, she took a risk. I'm not saying I wasn't scared. But knowing your aunt, it was a calculated risk and not a foolish one."

"That depends on your definition of *foolish*," Chris grumbled. Shari's laughter tugged his reluctant lips into a half smile.

He studied the scene outside the window. Christmas

had exploded on the street. Lights, garlands, and ribbons wrapped the lampposts and trees bordering the sidewalk. Wreaths, bows, and stars made storefronts more festive. The clouds dotting the gray sky looked swollen with snow. The first flakes of the season would fall any day now.

Chris switched his gaze to the café. It was a warm oasis in the growing chill of the season. Sisters from the congregation and groups of students, staff, and faculty from the college joined employees of the nearby businesses for the afternoon break.

He returned his attention to Shari. "So my aunt is a warrior?"

Shari chuckled. "You should've seen her."

He shook his head. "I would have had a heart attack."

They continued their meal in silence for several moments before Shari changed the subject. "I've found a new apartment. I'm moving in this week."

Chris paused with his soup spoon halfway to his mouth. "Congratulations. Could you use some help?"

Her eyes widened in surprise. "Yeah, I could. Thanks."

"Sure. I'm glad you decided to stay in Briar Coast."

"So am I." She ate another forkful of chicken and lettuce. "You know, these lunches are beginning to feel like dates."

Chris looked up from his soup bowl again. He heard the forced bravado in her voice. There were teasing lights in her eyes. And just beneath that a vulnerability that made him want to hold her.

He lowered his spoon and held her gaze. "Do you want them to be?"

She angled her chin with characteristic challenge. "Yes, I do."

He smiled. "So do I."

Chapter 37

"Eating at your desk again, Louise?" Sister Marianna interrupted Sister Lou from her final review of one of the Advent retreat presentations.

Sister Lou set her bowl of homemade chicken noodle soup on her desk and looked up at her visitor. She dug a little deeper to find the energy to tease the other woman. "Greetings, Marianna. And how are you this fine afternoon?"

Sister Marianna lowered herself onto one of the guest chairs, smoothing her long gray skirt beneath her. "Must we always go through this, Louise?"

"No matter how busy we get, we must never forget the little courtesies of our customs." Sister Lou struggled against a smile.

Sister Marianna sighed deeply. "I'm well, Louise, and how are you?"

"I'm quite well, thank you, Marianna. Much better now, in fact." The sense of triumph gave her a fresh burst of energy. "What can I do for you?"

Sister Lou regarded her associate. Sister Marianna's

Hermionean cross was fastened to the right lapel of her navy blazer worn over her lightweight salmon sweater.

Sister Marianna settled more comfortably onto her chair. She must have intended to stay for a while. "Did you ever determine who was embezzling money from the resort?"

She was glad they'd solved Autumn's murder, but thinking about the case brought back so much grief. "The deputies tracked the money to a separate account Angelica Webb had opened under her Kelsey Bennett alias. They think the embezzlement was another attempt to shift suspicions for Autumn's murder to someone else."

Sister Marianna shook her head. "That woman has a very sick mind."

Sister Lou couldn't agree more. "She spent so much time and effort planning to murder another living being."

Sister Marianna continued after a brief pause. "I understand the mayor stopped by to speak with you this morning."

Sister Marianna would bristle to be called nosy, but she did have an almost insatiable curiosity when it came to events that occurred in and around the congregational offices.

Sister Lou nodded. "The mayor believes Angelica Webb is behind the fake call from Sherrod Potts's assistant, asking the mayor to intervene with me on his behalf. Ms. Webb probably also sent January Potts the anonymous note claiming Autumn was having an affair with Sherrod."

"It was good of the mayor to tie up those loose ends for you. She's becoming a frequent guest of yours."

"I'm hoping the next time she stops by, she brings a donation for our ministries." Sister Lou's look invited the other woman to share the joke with her.

"That would be welcome indeed." Sister Marianna took the remark seriously.

Sister Lou again lamented Sister Marianna's seeming lack of humor. In the seven years that they'd known each other, she couldn't remember even one frivolous moment involving the other woman. "Is there anything else I can do for you, Marianna?"

"Did the mayor say anything else?" Sister Marianna folded her hands primly on her lap.

"She thanked the congregation for our part in solving Autumn's murder."

Sister Marianna gave her a wry look. "You mean she thanked you."

Sister Lou shook her head. "We did this together, you, Chris, Shari, and I, and even the deputies, as much as they didn't want our involvement. And I couldn't manage without Carm's counsel."

"And we couldn't have managed without your leadership." Sister Marianna stood to leave. "I'm sorry that I was so difficult during this whole experience. You knew what you were doing. I was wrong to question you."

"I wouldn't say that." *Shari might.*

Sister Marianna's tense features eased into a smile. "You're very kind. But you have a gift, Louise. Thank you for using it to help me."

"Of course, Marianna. I'm glad that I was able to help."

Sister Marianna paused in the doorway. "Who knows, if word gets out, you could open a side business as a private investigator, then you could donate your fees to our ministries."

The other woman flashed a grin before disappearing down the hallway.

Sister Lou stared after her in surprise. Sister Marianna had discovered a sense of humor. This was indeed a season of miracles.